A Walk With Giants

Volume II
1957 - 1974

Picture of Mizuho on page 334
first mentioned on page 327
= nt.b.

by T. Daniel McGinley

The Cover

The statue of the Special Forces soldier is on display at Fort Bragg North Carolina. On your left (looking at the statue), from top to bottom and from left to right; Special Forces Patch with Special Forces and Airborne Tab, Combat Medic Badge (2nd Award), Master Jump Wings.

Beret Flashes;

302nd SF Det (Reserve), 77th SF Group Fort Bragg, 12th SF Group (Reserve) 5th SF Group (Vietnam), 1st SF Group Okinawa, 10th SF Group (Fort Devens), 46 SF Company (Thailand), SF Command (Fort Bragg), Special Forces Association, Special Forces Crest.

On your right (looking at the statue), from top to bottom;

Sport Parachuting Patches

Land of Lincoln Sky Divers (Chicago IL)

Chicago Sky Divers, (Chicago IL)

Special Warfare Center, Sky Diving (Ft Bragg NC)

Trojan Sport Parachuting Club (Ft Devens MA)

Carlos E. Leal Sport Parachuting Club Thailand

Printed in the United States of America

Dedication

At this point in my life, I wasn't surprised when I met a person with Giant characteristics. Being raised during the Great Depression and being involved in two wars (World War II and the Korean War), I have met many Giants during my walk down life's road.

The surprise came when I went back in service for the Vietnam War and became involved with Special Forces. It was unbelievable how many Giants gathered to fulfill their mission, "De Oppresso Liber"

Space has limited the number of Giant stories. Not being published in this volume, does not lessen their importance. I owe my very existence to many of the not mentioned herein. Their memories will be with me the rest of my days.

I proudly dedicated this work to all Special Forces Operatives, that I have met and to those I have had the privilege to serve with. The stories contained herein are testimonies of the fact;

"I HAVE WALKED WITH GIANTS"

TABLE OF CONTENTS
Volume Two 1957 - 1974
Special Forces Assignments

Chapter One

Chapter Two

Chapter Three

Chapter Four

Chapter Five

Chapter Six

Chapter Seven

Chapter Eight

Chapter One

Reserve Power

You hear a lot of talk, both pro and con, about Military Reserve Units. Keep in mind this nation owes it's very existence to the Citizen Soldier. Starting with the Colonial Soldiers, who laid down the plow and picked up their musket, through World War II, to include, our Reserve Units today. The Citizen Soldier, stood up to be counted. Any that would say different are talking from ignorance. They would be well advised to study history.

The standing Armed Services, are not capable of going it alone. In every case they call upon the Reserve Forces. When things get really tough, additional Citizen Soldiers are called upon by activating the Selective Service (drafting) System. I have served in three wars. I'm proud of the fact that I served as a reservist, a Citizen Soldier.

In World War II, I was serving in the Illinois Reserve Militia. I was activated to Federal Service with a letter from the Draft Board, "Greeting, your friends and neighbors have selected you." When the war ended I was assigned to the Inactive Army Reserves. In 1950 as a Reservist, I requested activation to the Regular Army to serve in the Korean War. I received a medical discharge in 1951.

On 10 March 1957 I joined the 302nd Special Forces Reserve. Later (1961) the 302nd was renamed the 12th Special Forces Group. I went to Vietnam in 1967, as a reservist from the 12th Special Forces Reserve. The best reserve units, I have served with, were the 302nd and 12th Special Forces. Their story has to be told.

302nd Special Forces

The year was 1956. I was working as a civilian advisor for an Army Reserve Center, 4454 Cermack Road, Cicero, Illinois. The job didn't pay that well, but being around the military filled a void left by my medical discharge from Korea. The Center had three units training at their location, each on a different night. Although I didn't belong to any of them, I had the responsibility of providing logistical support to all three. Two of the units were quite large, they didn't need, nor seem to want much help. In fact the more the civilians side of the house left them alone, the better they liked it. I suspect a little hanky panky was going on, but that didn't bother me.

The smallest unit had about 75 people assigned to them. They had little or no equipment or supplies. An extremely friendly group who seemed to enjoy whatever it was they were doing. You would see part of this group in the Armory several times a week including Saturday and Sunday. No one outside their unit seemed to know what their mission was. I suspected they were one of those "If I tell you, I will have to kill you," units. I liked their attitude and helped them every time I got a chance.

Part of my job description at the Reserve Center was Property-Book Officer. I signed for all the Reserve Center property. I issued property or supplies to whatever unit needed a particular item to accomplish their mission.

The 302nd Special Forces was my favorite unit. I made sure they got whatever they asked for. This took a lot of juggling and scrounging from the Reserve System. Many times I went to the active duty units for specialized items.

The 303nd Special Forces Detachment meet every Thursday night. I was working late one Thursday. I had to catch up on some paper work, in preparation for an Engineer Unit's Annual IG inspection. My concentration was interrupted by Captain Kaufman the 302nd Commander opening the door to my office.

"Mac why don't you join us for a cold beer after we call it a night?"

"Thanks for the invite sir, I have a little work to catch up on. See you in about one hour. This was a most welcomed and surprising invitation. The 302nd was not in the habit of inviting nonmembers to their after meeting get together's.

By the time I got to Murphy's Bar and Grill, most of the 302nd had arrived. Captain Kaufman was the first to see me and extended a warm welcome. I knew most of the members present. Nevertheless, the Captain introduced me to each one. In addition to stating their names, he added their military rank, and what unit they served with on active duty.

"Mac, this is Sergeant Major Philip Kerrigen, Phil served with Merrill's Marauders in WWII." Merrill's Marauders was the title given to Col. Frank D. Merrill's 5307th Composite Unit (Provisional). A 3,000-man force, that staked out a piece of Burmese jungle, and dared the Japanese to challenge them. They did and wound up losing to the Marauders in five major battles and 17 skirmishes. Phil and his unit fought behind the enemy (Japan) lines for almost three years. SGM. Kerrigan, was also served with the 1st Special Service Force. The 1st SSF was a special operations unit in WWII. The Captain continued,

"This is Lt. Joe Golden, our Intelligence Officer. Joe served with the OSS, The Office of Strategic Services in WWII. I can guarantee you that after two beers, Joe will tell us some of the bizarre missions he took part in. To tell the truth Mac, we all look forward to his great stories."

I knew about the OSS. The primary operation of the OSS in Europe was called the Jedburgh mission. It consisted of dropping three-man teams into France, Belgium and Holland. Their mission was to, train partisan resistance movements and conduct guerrilla operations against the Germans. All, in preparation for the D-Day invasion. I was impressed learning about Kerrigen's, and Golden's war time experiences.

After the war, President Harry S. Truman disbanded the OSS. But not before it had left a legacy still felt today. From its intelligence operations came the nucleus of men and techniques that would give birth, to the Central Intelligence Agency, on September 18, 1947. Indeed, the first directors of the CIA were veterans of the OSS. From its guerrilla operations, came the nucleus of men and techniques that would give birth to the Special Forces in June 1952.

"Chief Warrant Officer John J Condieh, is our Administrative Officer. John was with the 187 in Korea, and made two combat jumps. John was wounded on the second jump." I would soon learn, CWO Condieh was a highly talented and reliable Administrative Officer who's talent would influence my future. Next on the introduction list,

"SSG. Oldrich Olchivick is our parachute Rigger. Rick was in a German POW Camp in WWII. He escaped, made it to England, then the USA. He joined the 11th Airborne. Rick was a likable guy with a heavy Czechoslovakian accent. We would become very good friends.

Captain Richard J. Thomas was next to be introduced. Not much was said about Cpt. Thomas except that he worked for the government. Back in the 50's, when you were told, someone worked for the Government, you didn't ask any more questions, if you didn't have a need to know.

The introduction was interrupted by additional members arriving to join the meeting. ISG Art Liskie, a veteran of the Korean War, and the recipient of the Silver Star, was next on the Captain's introduction. Then Sergeant Walter Huminsky. Walter was new with the 302nd, he served with the 82nd Airborne on active duty. SGT. Lowell Bochman popped his head in the door. He couldn't stay, just wanted to say hello. Lowell was the unit's communications NCO, a multi talented individual, truly an asset to the 302nd.

Next to arrive was Captain Jim Stoyer. He was accompanied by two active duty Special Forces Captains. They didn't stay long enough to be introduced. They had a quick huddle with Cpt. Hoffman and left. I found out later one of the Captains, was SGT. Olchivick's brother, Stan. Capt. Hoffman turned to me and said,

"Now Mac tell us a little about yourself." Everyone laughed.

Warrant Officer Condieh broke in and started to read from a report. They knew more about me than I knew about myself. Captain Kaufman explained they had run a security check on me. He further explained, and it was imperative to know more about me before attempting to recruit me to join the 302nd Special Forces. He went on to say they appreciated all that I had done for them. As far as he was concerned, I was a member of the unit. Then the Captain, popped the question.

"Why not make it official McGinley?" For a moment or two I was speechless.

A Walk With Giants 1957 - 1974

Those who know me, will testify that me being speechless, is a rare occurrence. I always have something to say. Silence wasn't then nor now, one of my virtues. I am a quick draw on voicing my opinions. I was honored by being asked to join.

"You bet I would like to join the 302nd. How do I go about it?"

After a very loud, "welcome aboard," from everyone at the table, Mr. Condieh opened a manila folder. My enlistment papers were all filled out.

"Sign here, here and here." Talk about an ambush. They didn't give me a chance to change my mind. Of course I wouldn't have. I was proud of being offered membership. I officially joined the 302nd on 10 April 1958. Suddenly my mind wandered back to Korea and the MSG, which infiltrated our perimeter. I was positive, he belonged to a unit like this.

The pride of belonging grew throughout my association with the 302nd Special Forces. This pride was directly proportional to the unit's dedication to missions and the accomplishments, of their members. This was one dedicated unit, "Giants" everyone. I for one, wouldn't want them against me in battle. My only concern was, could I measure up to their standards?

Jump School

Jump qualified is a must to be a member of Special Forces. I reported to Headquarters and Service Company at Fort Benning Georgia March 1959 for Airborne Training. It was there I  discovered Airborne people do not know how to walk. Everywhere they go, they run. They call it the Paratroop Shuffle. But that's just to fool you. It's running, plain simple running.

It really seemed to me they can't stand inactivity. If they didn't have you running, you were doing PT. They honestly thought they were giving you a break by letting you do 50 pushups or 15 pull-ups.

Making you do 60 sit-ups was their idea of being extra kind. I didn't mind the PT, I had worked out to prepare for this course and considered myself in very good shape. One thing that always gave me trouble no matter how hard I tried, was running.

Pushup, Give me Ten

Having any rank while going through Airborne Training is not a good thing. It makes you stand out in the crowd, I was a corporal. It didn't take long for the Drill Sergeant to give me his undivided attention. We were on one of our many runs on the PT track circling the 34ft jump tower. I had accumulated a lot of saliva and had to get rid of it. Not thinking anyone was watching, I transferred the liquid to the ground.

"What are you doing Corporal? Are you spitting on my PT track? Drop and give me 10." He meant 10 push ups.

As I was doing my pushup, the class continued their run. I had a hard time keeping up before, now I'll never catch them. By the time I finished the 10 push ups, the class was going around the curve at the far end of the track. There was no way I could catch them. I needed a short cut.

Thinking I was clever, I formulated a plan to cut across the track. I crouched down beside the 34-foot Jump tower and waited until the class passed, then I fell in behind them. Slight problem, I was behind the wrong class.

"Is that my Corporal? How did you get in front of us Corporal? Get back where you belong. The Captain is going to think you are faster than we are." The Drill Sergeant didn't give me a chance to answer, he kept asking question and then the familiar,

"Give me 10." I knew that was coming. The class kept running. This time he had them circle me singing Airborne chants.

"Airborne every day all the way, airborne up the hill down the hill, airborne, airborne."

"What are you?" The Drill Sergeant yelled out.

"AIRBORNE all the way AIRBORNE." Was the class response.

When I finished the 10 pushups, we continued the run. Of course the airborne chants continued also. Every day the runs got longer.

I knew something was wrong. All of a sudden, I could breathe easier. Suddenly I wasn't tired, I felt I could run forever. This was the first time I had experienced getting my second wind.

"Class, quick time march." The Drill Sergeant ending the run.

"I'm challenging you Drill Sergeant Walker." The rule at jump school you could challenge the instructors if you thought you could out do them.

"Is that my Corporal? Class, stand at ease. The Corporal wants to see me on the track." All this time, I was running in a small circle.

MSG Harden B Walker was an American of African decent. There was no doubt in my mind, his mission was to make me quit airborne training. He stayed on my case. When the Drill Sergeant joined me, we headed down the oval track. I felt great. To challenge this guy seemed to give me extra energy. Once around the track, then twice. Every time we passed the class they cheered us on. This was not a race. We did the Paratroop Shuffle side by side.

"Corporal Mac, let's call this the last lap." I was glad to hear his words. I didn't know how long I could keep this up.

The first week of training was referred to as ground week. In addition to regular PT, we practiced parachute landing falls (PLF's), aircraft exits from a C-119 mockup. All the training contributed to our overall condition. We not only were getting stronger, we were experiencing an attitude change.

The second week was called Tower Week. Most of the training was related to an actual jump from an aircraft. We continued practicing PLF's but this time it was with equipment and a swing landing trainer that simulated the motion we were to experience on a live jump. I couldn't help wishing I had this training back in the Carnival days. The PT continued. As did the "Give me 10."

34-foot tower

The 34-foot tower was the device that separated the men from the boys. Being Airborne is voluntary, you could quit at any time. The tower convinced many they didn't want to be Airborne. Climbing the three flights of stairs starts the mind working.

"What am I doing here?" Is a question you ask yourself throughout the program. "What do I care what people think, if I quit?" Another popular thought.

When you reach the top that is built to simulate an aircraft including two mock-up doors, you time to quit, has almost run out. You harness is hooked up to a cable by the safety NCO's. You are given one more equipment check then the commands,

"Stand in the door." Then the command, "Go."

Now the 34-foot high tower looks like its about 200 feet from the ground. After the initial shock, the glide down the five hundred foot cable is uneventful. After reaching the mound at the far end of the cable you are assisted by other students to unhook. With your harness still on, you're required to double time back to the tower base, for your grade.

"Unsatisfactory." The instructor yells out. And he will repeat this command until the student has four satisfactory exits. Then and only then are you allowed to take your harness off and take a seat in the bleachers and wait for the rest of the class to finish.

Tearing the Tower Down is a term used to describe exiting the tower 34 times: One jump for every foot of the tower's height. One student out of every class is selected to preform this task. My Corporal stripe assured my selection.

I was exiting the tower for the tenth time. This was the last group. The rest of the class had received their satisfactory grades. Surely I will receive mine on this jump. I should have got the message when I saw that MSG Walker had replaced the other tower grader.

"Unsatisfactory back to the tower." It was at this point I knew I was to tear the tower down. "Unsatisfactory, Unsatisfactory." I lost count I didn't know how many times I had jumped. I knew I was hurting. The mound men started to massage my arms and legs. After every unsatisfactory, the class would cheer me on. The safety NCO's increased their words on encouragement. Those were the only things that made me press on.

"I'm going to tear this tower down. Tear it down, to a point they won't be able to repair it." Were the words that expressed my attitude. You can hurt just so much, then it doesn't matter anymore.

"Satisfactory." I didn't understand the word. I headed for the tower.

"That's all Corporal. You did it, you tore the tower down. Go back for your grade." The Safety NCO's were blocking my way. I went back to the grading platform. MSG Walker was looking everywhere except at me. I just stood there at parade rest. Finally, Walkers eyes looked my way,

"Satisfactory." Then turning to the class, "My little Corporal did a fine job. No big deal, I knew he could do it."

The first device we encountered during week three, Jump Week was the wind machine. A giant fan had the power to inflate the parachute and drag the student rapidly over the hard ground. While laying on your back, two other students held the skirt of the canopy as high as they could. When the wind machine was turned on, it filled the canopy, and the student starts the ride of his life.

Recovery From The Drag

The object was to pull on the right or left riser, then pivot on your back. The inflated canopy would turn the student until they were facing forward. At this point the student vagariously dug their heels into the ground. The same force would pull the student to their feet. Without hesitation the student has to run around the inflated canopy. That same wind machine that a moment ago was dragging them would now collapse the chute.

"Get up. Run around the canopy." Was the command that motivated the student. If for some reason, the instructor wasn't satisfied with the performance. There was always the old standby, "Give me 10."

The next training device was the 250-foot free tower. Majestically this four armed steel structure reached for the heavens. Slowly it would raise four jumpers and stop ten feet from its top. On a given command from the instructor the student continued the journey to the top and then released.

The view was great but the free falling parachute ride was too short. Upon impact with mother earth, the two-week ground training suddenly made sense. A Parachute Landing Fall and the run around the canopy were executed without thinking. Repetitive training works. The class was ready for their first live jump from an aircraft in flight.

More training on aircraft exits, field rolling the parachute after the jump, and jump commands filled our schedule. They held emergency procedures and deployment of the reserve parachute training at the end of the course. (Probably didn't want us to quit). In the event the main parachute didn't open we had to be proficient on how to deploy our reserve. Everyone paid strict attention to this portion of the training.

Suspended Agony they called it. We spent hours hanging in a parachute harness practicing reserve deployment. Then we were taught what to do if we landed in water. Emphasis was put on, getting out of your harness. Tree landing is one I was sorry later I didn't pay more attention to. The safe procedure in the

event we landed in high tension wires. They claimed if you put your hands and arms behind the nylon risers, the insolation factor of the nylon would protect you from lighting up like a Christmas tree. I'll take their word for it. I didn't want to try it.

10

C 119 Jump Plain

Then the big day came. We were bused to the airstrip. The amount and the volume of the conversation lessened as we got closer the waiting aircraft. The C-119 looked a little intimidating.

The I jumped when I was twelve, cockiness, was absent from my mind. That was a big airplane and I was a small jumper.

"Am I out of my mind? What am I doing here?"

I didn't think we were going to make it off the ground. It seemed we used a lot of runway. I might have been a little paranoid. The last time I was in an aircraft, (my short-lived Carnival days) it crashed in a hedgerow. Finally we were airborne. Well we weren't Airborne yet (it takes five jumps) but the C-119 was.

"Attention, we will have a slight delay." A voice announced over the intercom. "We have to wait for the wind to die-down." Recovery from drag procedures suddenly became my dominating thought.

"What am I doing here?" Yes I'm repeating myself. Finally the green light came on. Stand Up. Hook Up." All jumpers hooked their static lines to a cable that runs the length of the aircraft.

"Check your equipment." At this point while someone is checking your equipment, you check the man in front of you.

"Stand in the door." First jumper, throws his static line to the side and places his hands on each side of the door frame. Looking straight forward, knees slightly bent, he waits for the command to exit the aircraft. All other jumpers stand in line behind the first jumper waiting for their turn in the door. It's too late to quit now.

"Go!" Vigorously the jumper leaves the aircraft. Bent at the waist, chin tucked tightly against their chest, hands holding the reserve and feet tight together. You're one fifth the way of being Airborne

Nothing, I mean nothing will ever replace the feeling of your first military jump. Doesn't matter what you have done in the past, what you accomplish in the future, Sky Diving, Wing Walking, Balloonist? Nothing can equal your first Military Jump.

You have done more than just jumped out of an aircraft in flight. You have

GO!

demonstrated your trust in the forces that got you to this place in time. The relentless training, the people who packed your parachute and maintained your equipment, the people who maintained the aircraft, and the talent of the pilot. Most of all, you have proven for all to see, you had what it takes to become a member of the United States Airborne. The word "Quit" will never again be in your vocabulary.

I met a lot of great people at jump school. Happenings and experiences we shared are still embedded in my memory. Commendatory is another element of the Airborne community. It really doesn't matter which branch of service you're in. If you are Airborne, you belong to the tight nit society, a society of Giants.

Marine Recon

1st Marine Recon is one of the Special Operation elements of the Corps. Although they run their own pre jump school, their Airborne Wings have to be awarded by the US Army at Fort Benning Georgia, home of the Airborne. There were six enlisted and one officer Marine in my class. Because I was from a Special Forces unit, we got along fine. In fact we hung around together.

A Corporal (two strips) in the Army out ranks a Marine Sargent with three stripes. For that reason I share a two-man squad room with S/SGT Richard Van Sickle another member of the 302 Special Forces. Two Marines Sergeants although they had, three stripes were not authorized private rooms.

Marines like the Navy are very rank conches. They demand lower rank walk a narrow line. If a ranking Marine gives an order the subordinate jumps. One morning shortly after I arrived at jump school, I answered a knock on my door.

"Corporal McGinley, I'm Sergeant Shelton. Just leave your boots outside your door at night and Owens will see to it they are shined. Owen shines my boots and does a good job."

"No thank you Sergeant Shelton. I do my own boots." This didn't please the Marine. Sergeant. Shelton went on to explain that every time they send young Marines to non Marine facilities for training, they have a discipline problem when they return. He almost pleaded with me to have Owens shine my shoes.

"Sergeant Shelton, I don't wear issue boots. As you can see, I have Corcoran Boots. Corcoran Boots require spit-shining. Younger troops are not going to spit shine, my Corcoran." Unhappy the Marine Sargent walked away.

"That sounded like a good deal Mac. They can shine my boots." S/SGT Van Sickle announce.

I guess the frown on my face made him change his mind. Van rolled over and went to sleep. S/SGT Richard C. Van Sickle was a tall lanky guy that was trying to join the 302nd Special Forces. His enlistment was contingent on him passing Jump School. Several times during the course, just before he fell asleep he would ask,

"Mac, do you think we are going to make it?" Asking the question once or twice OK. But over and over started to get to me.

"Van Sickle, why don't you just quit? Then you won't have to worry yourself to death." As soon as the words were out of my mouth, I was sorry. Van was a good guy. Like all of us, a little nervous. Finally after the first jump his attitude changed.

"Mac we are going to make it."

'Do you really think so Van?" I replied, shaking my head.

"Corporal McGinley report to the orderly room." Now what, Did someone forget to give me 10 pushups?

Captain John Eisenbraun the Company Commander, MSG Walker, and two other instructors and the Marine Lieutenant, were waiting in the CO's office.

"Corporal McGinley reporting as directed Sir." Followed by a salute.

"Have a seat next to the Lieutenant Corporal. I want to congratulate both you gentlemen on your progress. We seldom have two students with exact scores competing for honor graduate." I couldn't believe my ears. "We intentionally put extra pressure on both of you to make one of you back off. You both took it and pressed on. That left us with a problem. There is only one honor graduate slot." It turned out MSG Walker was assigned to pressure me. MSG James McCaskill the Platoon Sergeant was assigned to pressure the LT.

"We came up with a solution gentleman. You will take turns wearing the Blue Honor Graduate Helmet, on the next four jumps. You will alternate between jumps. That will give you two jumps each. By the way, the Honor Graduate leads the stick out of the aircraft. Congratulations again." I left the orderly room with my head in the clouds. I'm sure, the Marine Lieutenant O'Connor, felt the same.

"Where is my Corporal?" The voice was familiar.

"Here Drill Sergeant."

"Put this helmet on and get in front of your stick." (A stick is a group of people leaving the aircraft on the same pass.) We were making our second jump.

The next three jumps were equally as exciting as the first two. When I lead the stick, the Marine Lt would be second out. When he lead the stick, I took the second position. Jump five seemed to be a little more exciting. Maybe it was because this was the jump we would earn our wings. We would be Airborne Qualified, as soon as the last man hit the ground.

14

We were put in formation to be awarded our jump wings. Everyone had a big smile on their face as though we were the only ones in the world that had ever earned the Paratrooper Badge.

"Open ranks march." This was the command to put space between the ranks, making room for the CO and his party to pin the badges on each student. Correction each new Paratrooper.

The Commanding Officer would stop in front of each man and pushe the two sharp prongs on the back of the wings through the left side of the our jackets. MSG Walker handed each jumper two securing clasps. Having each jumper secure his own wings saved a lot of time. After Walker handed me the clasps, he slapped the wings, causing the sharp prongs to penetrate my skin. That is why they call your first set of wings, "Your Blood Wings."

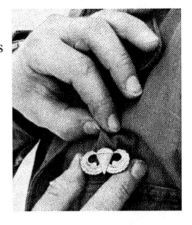

It hurt good. At this point in time Jump School was the best training I had ever had. I was confident there was no better training anywhere.

At the graduation celebration that afternoon we were initiated. We learned what the term Prop-Blasting meant. A steel pot (helmet) was filled with every kind of liquor available. Beer was used to top it off. Then the helmet was passed around for each new Paratrooper to partake of its contents. This by far took more nerve than it took jumping out of an aircraft, feeling a real prop-blast.

I sat at the Marine table. Before long, like all good Marines they started singing the Marine Hymn. They were surprised that I knew the words. I knew verses of the Marine Hymn the Marines didn't know.

My advantage, I was around during World War II. Back then everyone knew the songs of every branch of service. School kids sang them in school. They were song at all public get together s'. It seems to me America had more respect for their service members back then. Most stayed at the prop blast to the end. They were scheduled for transportation the next day. I left the party early my training wasn't over.

Enlisted E-5 and above and all officers had additional training. Air Transportability & Aerial Delivery of Heavy Equipment training would take another week or two depending on good weather. I wasn't an E-5 but like the Marines I was in a Special Operations type unit and had to take the training regardless of rank. Because of this additional time, they caught me.

When I filled out the paperwork for jump school, one of the questions was, "Do you have prior service?" I answered yes. When asked where? I stated World War II. I didn't mention I served in Korea.

My reason was simple. You can't go to jump school with a disability. Because of wounds, I was given a Medical Discharge from Korea. The extra time at Fort Benning provided the extra time for my active duty records to catch up with me. I was called to the commanders office and asked why I falsified my application. I answered with a question.

"If I stated I had a medical discharge Sir, would I have been allowed to attend Jump School?" The CO agreed, probably not. That didn't satisfy them. As far as they were concerned I lied on my application. I don't know what they were planning. When I pointed out, a person with a medical discharge, had just maxed their tough Airborne Course, they had to take another look. Might be a little embarrassing. I finished Air Transportability & Aerial Delivery of Heavy Equipment training. Airborne qualified, Van Sickle and I, headed home to the 302nd Special Forces.

16

77ᵗʰ Special Forces

Like most Reserve units, the 302ⁿᵈ took
annual training with an active duty organization.
Since the 302ⁿᵈ was a subordinate unit of the 77ᵗʰ
Special Forces Group, we took our annual
training at Fort Bragg, North Carlina. The 77ᵗʰ
took their training mission seriously and gave no
quarter. Their attitude was
"If you can't hack it, pack it."
No problem, the small unit from Chicago

77ᵗʰ Special Forces Crest

had a stout heart. They could handle anything dished out to them. At
the end of every active duty training period, the 302ⁿᵈ received superior
evaluation ratings from their active duty, Special Forces, counter parts.

Another important training opportunity, was the utilization of
active duty schools. The 302nd filled all allotted school slots offered
and requested additional ones. You didn't have to be Airborne
qualified to join the 302ⁿᵈ Special Forces. However, you had to
volunteer to take the airborne course within three mounts of joining. In
addition, attend the Special Forces Qualification course at Fort Bragg.
If for any reason you didn't qualify, you would be given the choice of
accepting a non-Special Forces assignment or released from reserve
duty.

Taking full advantage of training opportunities, the 302ⁿᵈ
Special Forces came up with some impressive numbers. One hundred
percent of the unit was airborne qualified. All were Special Forces
qualified and Special Forces trained in their job specialty. Ninety
percent was HALO (High Altitude Low Opening) Qualified. Seventy
percent certified SCUBA qualified by the US Navy. Sixty five percent
were graduates of the Special Forces O&I (Operations & Intel) course
at Fort Bragg, NC. The 302ⁿᵈ filled every O&I slot offered to them.
Percentages are only indicators. The quality of this dedicated unit was
reflected in the caliber of assigned personnel. This truly was a unique
group of Giants.

The mission of Special Forces Units is to plan and conduct
clandestine operations separately or as part of a larger force. Infiltrating
and ex-filtrating specified operational areas, by air, land, or sea.
Conduct operations in remote areas and hostile environments, for
extended periods of time. Always with a minimum of external

directions and support. Develop, organize, equip, train and advise or direct indigenous forces. Train, advise and assist other U.S. and allied forces and agencies. Plan and conduct unilateral SF operations; perform other special operations as directed by higher authority. All Special Forces Training, both active and reserve, is focused on this extensive mission.

Each year the 302nd Special Forces, would conduct this type of unit training with they're, active duty Special Forces counter part (77th Special Forces), at Fort Bragg NC. The training was made as realistic as possible. Real world situations were set up to include an indigenous force. The indigenous force consisted of active duty and reserve SF personnel. To insure quality control, senior active duty Special Forces instructors were assigned each Reserve SF A-Team. The paramount duty of the active duty SF, was that of evaluators. At no time where they allowed to interfere with how the reservists handled any situation. Their role was that of evaluation.

However, if the Reservists were doing well, the active duty SF could throw in additional problems. Additional problems were welcomed by the 302nd. In fact quite often the 302nd, threw in some of their own tricks to catch the active duty off guard. Keep in mind, just to join a Reserve Special Forces unit, you had to be qualified in your job skill. Another factor that played an important role was that every member of the 302 Special Forces had been in combat, either WWII or Korea or both. No draft dodgers in this unit.

My first Fort Bragg evaluation exercise with the 302nd Special Forces was August 1959. We were to act as a Guerrilla unit in the exercise. I traveled to Fort Bragg via my personal vehicle.

Since I didn't arrive with the main body, the active duty Special Forces assigned to the 302nd didn't meet me at the unit's reception.

The unit reception accomplished two things. First, it served as a get acquainted tool, a chance to meet at your counter part. The other a place to assign the mission and learn the rules of engagement.

When I finally caught up with SGM. Kerrigen and Captain Kauffman, the reception was over. I was told that the assigned mission was to link up with a guerrilla force and blow up the enemy's ammo-dump. Didn't seem difficult to me, that is, until I found out the target was to be manned by all active duty Special Forces. Then the idea hit.

"Why not pretend I didn't arrive?" Nobody has seen me. Let's keep it that way.

Both the SGM and Captain thought that was a great idea. It would be to the 302nd advantage, to have an agent undercover so to speak.

"Mac you won't be paid if you don't sign in." Cpt. Kauffman announced.

"No problem Sir." The SGM' answered, "We can handle that."

"Gentleman, I don't give a rat's nose if I get paid or not. If we blow that target, that will be pay enough." As soon as the words were out of my mouth, I was sorry I said them. Of course I care if I get paid. Another example of engaging the mouth before the brain. I told you I was good at that.

A difficult situation if I have ever seen one. The unit's target was on top of a hill. We could be sure the hill would be booby-trapped and have trip-flares all over the place. The rules of engagement stated the target had to be hit between twenty-two hundred and zero two-hundred hours. To make matters worse, the target would be manned by an active duty Special Forces A-Team. They only had to be alert for four hours

"There was no way, to accomplish this mission." SGM. Kerrigen pointed out. Captain Hoffman agreed, "No way short of a miracle." I was getting tired,

"Goodnight gentlemen, see you in the morning." Kerrigen came back with,

"No you won't, we are jumping in Nijmegen Drop Zone at zero-four-thirty hours." Then we will be bussed to Camp Mackall to start the exercise. Pointing to a map, he continued,

"We will be in this area, just past Camp Mackall's landing strip, near this creek." I could see a dirt road close to their area.

"I'll be on this road tomorrow about ten hundred hours. Have someone meet me and guide me to your location. Good night again gentlemen." I departed for my room at the Leo Guest House, next to the NCO Club.

I couldn't sleep all night. Kept thinking of a way to hit, that seemingly impossible target. Then came the dawn. No not the real dawn, the dawn like in "I got an idea." The real dawn came about three hours later.

The active duty A-Team, has to get in and out of the target area. All we have to do is use the same path to blow the target. I knew it would be impossible to get close enough, to clandestinely observe the target in the daylight. Clandestinely no, but open and notorious, would be the way to get the job done. I couldn't wait, to reveal my plan to the 302nd. At this point I didn't have the full plan, but I had faith in my devious mind. I would figure it out.

I took a taxi to a used car rental lot on Bragg Boulevard. There she was a nice rusty Chevy Pick-up Truck. My next stop was a second hand clothing store on Raeford Road. At this point I was bubbling over with joy. I had everything I needed to execute my, not quite finished plan. I am sure they will make me a General  after I pull this stunt off. A short stop at my room to change clothes, then to Camp Mackall to find the 302nd.

Didn't have a problem getting on Camp Mackall, my orders to active duty for training, took care of that. My problem was getting a civilian vehicle on Camp. After a lot of negotiation and a couple of white lies, I was issued a temporary pass. My second problem was finding the 302nd. I passed Camp Mackall's landing strip and DZ twice. The area was large enough to drop a Battalion of Paratroopers, with their equipment, and I missed it twice. My mind was on the plan. A plan that was coming together as I drove. When I found the DZ, the rest was easy. I made a right turn on an old logging road and in about five minutes my guide was flagging me down. My first question to Olchivick was;

"How did you know it was me in this old truck?

A Walk With Giants 1957 - 1974

"By your hairdo, Mac, by your hairdo." (I'll explain that hairdo thing later). I was greeted by almost uncontrollable laughter by my buddies of the 302nd.

"Where in the world did you get those bib-overalls and straw hat?"

"It's part of my plan SGM. An ingenious plan I might add."

"Come over here and I'll show you what we came up with." The team was gathered around a mock-up of our target. The captain was proud of his plan and was eager to explain it to whoever would listen.

"We are going to hit the target from three directions, simultaneously. We can be sure they have trip flares surrounding the target. The chances are slim, but maybe one of the teams will make it. Our only chance here is speed. We just, might pull it off." I had to break in,

" Sir, what if I could show you a way to miss all trip-flair's and booby-traps?" The Captain answered with a question,

"Where did you get those bib-overalls?" Everyone laughed.

"OK guys, you had your fun, I have been up all night with this idea. At least hear me out." I think they realized I was serious and getting a little ticked off

"Go ahead Mac let's hear your plan."

"First of all, no one on the active duty side, has ever seen me. Dressed like this, driving that old truck, I would blend in with the local population."

"What old truck, you have a Buick Convertible." Olchivick jumped in with,

"No SGM, Mack has an old, I mean very old truck." I had to stop. This back and forth conversation, it was sidetracking my story. I didn't understand my plan well enough to handle all the interruptions. I raised the volume of my voice.

" Gentlemen let me have the floor. Hold your comments until the end, please. At the expense of repeating myself, no one knows I am at Fort Bragg. There is a road in front of the target. My plan is to have a truck breakdown in front of the target. With a little luck, someone from the hill, will come down to investigate. I'll observe their path down the hill, make a mental note and report back to you. After dark you can use the revealed path to hit the target. Captain, you can still hit the hill from other directions as a diversion. That's it guys, now your comments."

The Captain was the first to speak,

"That's a great, simple plan but great." What does this guy mean, simple? I was up all night with this plan. Of course I keep my thoughts to myself.

"Let's go for it, was the overall response." I had a bite to eat, filled an ice chest with cold beer (bargaining items) and took off to execute my plan.

As luck would have it, the target was only one mile from the 302nd's bivouac area.close to the road. Approaching the target I noticed steam coming from under the trucks' hood. Lady luck was working this day. The steam would support my truck break down story. I stopped the truck right in front of the target hill. I got out and opened the hood. I no sooner got the hood open when two SF target guards were at my side. I didn't see which way they came from. The plan was not working.

"Can we help you sir?" one SF trooper asked.

"Old Nellie, stops on me now and again. Guess she's getting a mite old. She'll start up in a few minutes. Got to give the old gal a little rest." I wanted to keep talking, didn't know exactly what would come out next, but I wanted to keep talking.

"Do you want me to look at her sir? I'm a very good mechanic." The last thing, in this world I needed, was a good mechanic.

"Thank you lad no, she'll start in a few minutes. I'll just sit here and sip on a cold one, care to join me?" I opened the cooler of iced beer.

"Wow! You got ice cold beer?"

"Yip, beer is so cold you have to wear gloves to keep from freezing your finger's. Are those your buddies up yonder?" I asked pointing to the hill. "How many are there? Might have enough for them too?"

"We got cold beer down here" one of the troopers yelled to his buddies on top of the hill

"Bring it up. We can't leave the target." That was my opening. I picked up the cooler and headed up the hill.

"Not that way, stop! " I took another step in a different direction.

"Hold it sir, hold it, we'll show you the way." I felt great. The plan just might work. Like leading the lambs to the slaughter. I followed my guides up the hill, making mental notes.

Straight to the tall pine, left three paces to a very large bush. Straight again about fifty feet. I continued the mapping process until I reached the top. I was surprised at the simplicity of the path leading in. They didn't use much imagination. Although I had just eaten, I accepted the food offered by my active duty host. I in turn offered my cold beer. I asked a lot of questions which they were almost eager to answer.

"What are you lads' doing here, playing war games?

They explained they were training reservists from Chicago. They went on to explain the reservists were going to hit this location at 0200. How do you know the time they're going to strike? Laughingly, they said they had it all laid out. This amazed me. We didn't have any active duty assigned to us this year. The only active duty near us was the evaluator. If the evaluators got involved in the mission, the mission would be null and void. I was convinced, this guy didn't know what he was talking about. I better be taking off.

"Old Nellie, will start now, that she has had a rest."

Thanked the lads for their chow and started down the hill. A trooper jumped in front of me as a guide. I turned and told my friends that I would be passing by again about 2200 hours. If they wanted, I would have my wife cook up a pot of hot chili and of course, bring them some more cold beer. That would be great was their response. I anticipated my guide's turns all the way down the hill. I was right on the money. I cranked up old Nellie and returned to the 302nd's area.

After explaining the safe approach to the target and the fact I was told they expected the 302nd to hit the target at 0200 hours. Captain Kaufman got very upset. He told me the 302nd received a radio message from headquarters that we were to strike at exactly 0200 hours. The fact the active duty on the target knew the time, rightfully so angered him. It was quite evident someone wasn't playing fair.

I also informed the Captain I told the SF target guards I would be back around 2200 hours and bring them home made chili and more beer. I suggested I keep that appointment. In addition to bringing food and drink we could deliver a three man-hit team. Have them hide in the ditch across from the target. At 23:15, hit that target with all the explosives they could carry. Everyone agreed to the modified plan.

We took up a collection for beer and canned chili. Rick and I went to a country store, about three miles down the road, and did our shopping. When we got back to camp, we opened all the chili cans and dumped the contents in a large cook pot and added other ingredients. Very hot peppers were on the top of the list. Then we added three bottles of tabasco sauce, a bottle of soy sauce, and two bottles of A-1 steak sauce. To top this special mixture off someone added six boxes of Ex-lax.

I approached the target area at exactly 2200 hours. I kept the truck lights off until our three man hit team vacated the vehicle. As I turned the lights on, I yelled out "cold beer and hot chili, come and get it." I was soon joined by two of the target guards.

"We weren't sure you were coming back Sir."

"My word is my bond lad. I mean what I say. You can take that to the bank. You lads carry the beer and chili, I'll tag along behind."

The slight overcast made it difficult to follow. About half way to the target, someone grabbed my arm and put their hand over my mouth. It was the 302nd three-man hit team. They took my place and followed the target guards to the top of the hill. I headed to my waiting truck.

I had my hand on the trucks door handle when the explosion wet off. The sky lit up as the sound rumbled through the trees. Mission accomplished. The only sound remaining was the sound of two teams arguing.

"You weren't supposed to hit until 0200 hours."

"How did you find out what time we were to hit?" Finally the arguing simmered down.

"No use letting this beer get warm or wasting the chili." Rick Olchivick announced with his unmistakable Czechoslovakian.accent.

"Mac, come on up, join us."

No thank you I thought to myself. Rick nor the other two members of the hit-team were present when we added x-lax to the hot chili recipe. They were rigging the explosives for the raid. It seemed to me that this was a good time to depart the area. I left the keys in the

A Walk With Giants 1957 - 1974

truck and departed on foot for the 302nd bivouac area, two miles down the road. The following day all three members of our now famous hit team made several unscheduled trips to our makeshift latrine. To this day, I haven't told them of the x-lax.

We received an excellent rating from the **77th** Special Forces. We threw a farewell party and invited all the evaluators and the opposing A-Team. A couple of the team guarding the target kept asking me where we meet before. The party was almost over before they discovered I was the old farmer with the truck.

It was June but the water was cold at McKeller Pond. After throwing me in, many followed. We had a great time. If you ever party with Special Forces and there is a body of water near, you can bet the party will end up in the water. It doesn't matter if its summer, winter, day, or night. The dress can be formal or casual. The party will end up in the water . . . It's traditional.

We stayed at Bragg three days longer to get parachute jumps in to cover us for jump pay when we got back to Chicago.

Special Forces Qualification Course

Once you meet the initial qualifications, you're still a long way from wearing the Green Beret. You had about six months of training ahead. It was to be a time of physical and mental testing to see if you have what it takes to be a member of Special Forces.

The Collective Training Phase consisted of SF doctrine and organization, unconventional warfare operations, direct action operations, methods of instruction, and airborne and airmobile operations.

Individual skill training includes land navigation, patrolling and the obstacle course. You have to swim wearing boots and fatigues. They tested your endurance on the obstacle course. Many long marches with a loaded rucksack, another endurance test. Trainees are constantly assessed on their ability to work as a team member and accomplish the mission. After passing all these tests, you are selected for the next step, Military Occupation Skill.

During the MOS (Military Occupation Skill) trainees are directed to a Special Forces specialty, which will be based upon individual desires, background and aptitude. I chose SF Medical Sergeant MOS 91B4S (later changed to 18D).

SF Medical Sergeant training includes: advanced medical procedures, which consist of trauma management, surgical, dental and veterinary procedures. The SF medic is also an integral part of civic action programs, which bring medical treatment to native populations. It also includes training indigoes' personnel SF Medical Procedures.

The SF Medical and Laboratory (Dog Lab) portion of my training was taken at the Academy of Health Sciences, Fort San Houston Texas (Special Forces later had their own Dog Lab). It was by far the most difficult training I have ever taken. I have to say in all modesty, many people are alive today because of Special Forces Medical Training.

After MOS (Military Occupation Skill) training, most members of the 302nd went through HALO (High Altitude, Low Opening) School at Fort Bragg NC. The Military Free fall Course offers training in free fall techniques. In this course students learn to maneuver their parachutes with

HALO Jump

pinpoint accuracy, making a minimum of 35 individually-graded jumps. A number of these jumps are made from altitudes high enough to require bail-out oxygen.

The 302nd as a unit, took the Navy Combat Divers Supervisor Course. The course gives divers training beyond that of the combat diver, including work in para scuba and submarine operations. The course was conducted by the Navy at Chicago's Navy Pier. Unfortunately it did not qualify them as Special Forces SCUBA trained.

I enjoyed my association with the 3O2nd Special Forces. This was a professional hard charging unit. They took a back set to no one. This unit constantly trained to improve their skills. When they were not training, they volunteered for short active duty missions.

All Airborne Reserve units back in the late 50's had a hard time getting their jumps in. A lot of time was spent during Annual Training just jumping to cover the minimum number of jumps to keep you on jump status. One way to cover our jump requirement was to hitch rides with any active duty unit that may be jumping. Many times we loaded our automobiles and went to Fort Campbell Ky. and hitched plane rides with the 101st Airborne.

On one occasion the 82nd Airborne was refueling at O'Hare International, Chicago. They were on their way to South Dakota to make a demonstration jump for Governor's Day or something. When their aircraft left O'Hare Airport, ten members of the 302nd were with them. Bet your bottom dollar, I was one of them.

After the jump we assembled under a large shade tree while SGM Kerrigen arranged transportation home. In a short while our transportation arrived to take us to a waiting Air National Guard aircraft. Not wanting to leave the parachutes unguarded, we threw them on the aircraft.

Stealing you say. Not at all, we were putting government equipment under protective custody. Like magic the 302nd now had ten main parachutes and ten reserves on their property book. Our Rigger Olchivick now had ten deployed chutes to pack. Their Rigger Section took on a new look. We acted like someone gave us a million dollars. Unfortunately this jubilance would end abruptly.

Every time we requested permission to jump at our location, we were asked a battery of questions.

"Do you have a DZ (Drop Zone)? " We answered affirmatively. We could lease a farmers field for the drop.

"Do you have Medical and Rigger support?" Again we could answer affirmatively. Then the big question,

"Do you have equipment (parachutes)? " The negative answer would squash the deal every time. The parachutes now on our property book would turn that negative equipment answer to affirmative. We were sure we could get permission to jump at home station. We were ecstatic. The great Jump Master in the sky was looking favorably on us.

The 82nd would eventually realize their missing chutes were in Chicago. Needless to say, they wanted them back. Since I was a full time employee of the Reserve, I was given the task of returning the borrowed equipment to Fort Bragg North Carolina. Reluctantly I started the long trip south. The only positive thing was it gave me time to formulate a plan. A plan for what? I didn't have a clue.

"I finally found your parachutes. Those Reservists are foxy little devils.' I announced to the CWO in charge of the 82nd Rigger Section. "The chutes are in my truck. I need a hand unloading them." Without hesitation two members of the Rigger Section unloaded the parachutes.

A Walk With Giants 1957 - 1974

"I appreciate you returning the parachutes Sir. Thank you"

"It's not necessary to thank me. After all you have done for me, it was the least I could do." The Warrant Officer looked at me with a puzzled look. As though he couldn't remember doing anything for me. The fact of the matter is he hadn't. But he will.

I went into detail on how and why the 302nd acquired the parachutes. When I explained why they needed the chutes he was very sympathetic. Jumpers understand other jumpers desire to jump. Then came the magic words.

"You know they can get all the parachutes they need from us. I'll Hand Receipt as many as they need." Without knowing it this guy, just solved the equipment requirement to jump at home station.

Finally we got permission to Jump at a corn field near Cole City, in Grundy County Illinois. This would be the first time any Reserve unit ever jumped at home station. The permission was slow coming. Getting the Aircraft was easy. The Air Force Reserve is always looking for an excuse to fly. We took the Warrant Offices's offer and borrowed some parachutes from the 82nd Airborne.

The jump conditions were not very good. Normally the jump would have been called, because of high wind. We had too much time invested in getting permission to jump. There was no way we would call the jump. Everyone was told of the high wind. All decided to jump. At 08:30, on 25 March 1961, at 1250 feet, we hit the blast. Airborne.

About 50 present (30 jumpers) received injuries on the jump that needed treatment. Fortunately we had a doctor with us. About four needed a lot of care. The one broken leg was sent to a regional hospital. The emergency room was told he was in a auto accident. If we had reported the injuries, it would have been the end of Reservist jumping at home station.

Cpt Thompson and
302nd Medic McGinley

At the prop blast (airborne party) that night, all were bragging about their wounds. It was though they had a contest who's wound was the greatest. You never seen such a bunch, they were all Giants.

28

Chapter Two

SKY DIVING

In the winter of 1959, Oldrich Olchivick and I went to a small airport on the south side of Chicago to check on a sport parachuting activity. The sport, Sky Diving was just beginning to catch on in the Midwest and we wanted to be a part of it. An ex-paratrooper named Connie O'Rourke and about four other people were in the process of getting a Sky Diving club started. The fact that Rick and I were Airborne qualified and members of the 302nd Special Forces Reserve, opened the welcome door wide.

Olchivick, also being an Army Rigger, was given the duties of club rigger. It was unbelievable the way O'Rourke and the other were packing the parachutes. Rick without hesitation took over. We got along just fine with our new found friends. No big surprise, jumpers the world over, both Civilian and Military seem to have something in common. A bond that holds them apart from others, a strong brotherhood. Connie O'Rourks' request surprised me.

"Do you want to make a jump?"

"Sure, O.K. with you Mac?"

"Fine." I replied hesitantly. I was a little suspicious at this point, kind of thought maybe we should get a little training or at least a briefing. O'Rourke assured us that since we were airborne trained, any additional training would be useless.

Turned out that nobody was trained. One or two were ex-paratroopers and the others have not even, been in an airplane, never mind jumping out of one. As a matter of fact Rick and I, on our first day at the airport, were to be the first members to make a jump. The sky was clear, not even a small cloud. I remember thinking, an unusual day for Chicago in the middle of winter.

"You want to go first or do you want me to go first, Mac?" Thought to myself, if that big Czechoslovakian got in front of me, I wouldn't see a thing.

"I'll go first Rick." Rick got in the back seat of the waiting Cessna 172 and I followed. The pilot went through his cockpit checks of the aircraft. Connie ran up and yelled over the roar of the aircraft engine.

"I almost forgot. Throw this out when you get to altitude." He handed me a roll of toilet paper, so help me, a roll of toilet paper.

"What's that for?" Rick inquired.

"We're supposed to throw it out before we jump." Rick just shrugged his shoulders. Rick nor I understood why. Why were we throwing toilet paper out of an airplane? The combination of racing down the runway in an aircraft with a door removed, during a Chicago winter, was not the warmest place to be.

"What am I doing here?" I keep asking myself. "What am I doing here?"

The task seemed simple enough. Climb to a given altitude. Crawl out on the landing gear holding on to the strut, then push off when ready. Pull the rip cord then, gently float to the ground. Of course end up telling jump stories over a glass of cold beer. Simple right?

Wrong, as we climbed higher and higher, I tried to solve, what turned out to be a very important problem. Should I leave my gloves on, or should I take them off? Left on, my hands would remain warm. On the other hand I could get a better grip on the rip cord with the gloves off. First on, then off, back on, I kept this up until interrupted by Rick.

"What should we do with this?" Rick was referring to the roll of paper.

"Throw it out, O'Rourke said throw it out." Out it went. I found out later we were suppose to watch it. To get some sort of idea which way the wind would carry us.

"We are approaching the jump field." The pilot announced.

"What am I doing, have I lost my mind?"

Now jumping out of an airplane is no great thing. I have done it many times before. Let's see now how many? Nineteen times, including my carnival jumps. Maybe not many to you, but to me nineteen, at this point of my jumping career, were a lot of jumps.

A Walk With Giants 1957 - 1974

This one was to be different. This was my first free fall. The others were drag off's, where you pull the rip cord, then the open parachute pulls you off the airplane. Or static line jumps, where the static line attached to the aircraft, opens the chute. This time, if I were to have an open chute, it would be by my hand and my hand alone.

"What am I doing here?"

Holding the strut and pulling myself out on the step and wheel was not as difficult as I first imagined. Maybe because I had ridden outside of an aircraft before. On my drag off jumps, I stood on a small platform. The only difference, I was on the platform during take off. Don't know what the wind chill factor was. But I am here to tell you, it was cold, unbelievably cold. Not having goggles to protect them, my eyes were beginning to freeze.

"What am I doing here?"

"Now!" I yelled to Rick, he shook his head no.

"Now!" I yelled, again he shook his head, no. Why am I asking Rick? This is also his first free fall.

"Now!" Once again he shook his head no. The heck with it, I'm going. Later I found out he was just adjusting the chin strap on his football helmet.

Tumbling, head over heels, I remember thinking, "Now look what you have done?" I went in for the pull, my hands were frozen. I couldn't close my fingers.

"I have to pull, I have to pull." No time for a joke, but they say "It doesn't mean a thing, unless you pull the string."

Still tumbling, I managed to pull the rip cord with both hands. As the chute was deploying, I went through the modification, pulling the suspension lines behind me, then a tremendous jerk. It can be said, that jump had two jerks, one when the chute opened and one hanging in the harness.

Back in the fifty's, holes were cut in the parachutes, and toggle lines attached, enabling the jumper to steer the chute closer to a desired landing area. The holes or modification in the beginning, were very conservative.

Blank Gore

31

The modification in this particular jump was called a Blank Gore. Only one gore was removed, thus the name Blank Gore. I am sure someone told me the modification would be in the rear of the chute. When I checked the canopy, the modification was in the front. Oh well maybe, I misunderstood them. Turned out that I had a complete inversion, the chute turned inside out.

The view was spectacular, I could see for miles. Looked around for Rick but couldn't see the big Czechoslovakian anywhere. Hope he made it. I would miss him. It saddened me to think he may be a canceled Check. (That's a joke pal, just a joke.)

My sight seeing tour ended when I crashed into a corn field, that seemed to come from nowhere. Back in the 50's many farmers picked their corn by hand leaving the corn stocks standing. In Illinois corn stocks are eight to twelve feet high. This is a significant factor when you are five foot-six inches. I had no idea which way was up, never mind north or south.

Wow, this is a great sport, sure beats static-line jumping. My hands were still frozen, I had to start a fire before I could take my equipment off. Fortunately I always carried a Zippo lighter. Habit I picked up in Korea. My faithful Zippo served me well in Frozen Chosen (Korea). Started many fires with it. Now again in this sub-zero cornfield, it kept up to it's reputation.

After I picked up all my gear, and half of the corn field, I started the long search for a road that might lead to the airport, my car, and home. Took about an hour to find a road. No cars in sight, I started the long walk back to the airport. Finally a car, coming like a bat out of you know where, came to a screeching halt.

"Are you all right? I watched you all the way down, couldn't tell where your plane crashed."

When I told him that I jumped on purpose and that this was a new and growing sport, he got mad and drove off. The next and only vehicle I saw, was a fire truck heading to the corn field I just left. I'll bet someone was careless with matches (or Zippo). People should be more careful. Don't know what this world is coming too. It was getting dark when I finally arrived at the airport. Connie and Rick were sitting on the hood of my car.

Midwest Sky Diving Club

"We knew you would be coming back sooner or later, how did it go?"

"Great O'Rourke. I'll tell you one thing, it would help if you gave some sort of instruction before a person's first free fall."

"OK!" Connie replied in his Brooklyn accent. "Rick is the club's rigger and you can be in charge of the club's Training."

"Great Connie, the blind leading the blind."

"By the way Mac, waiting for you, we came up with a name for our club, "Midwest Sky Diving Club. How do you like it?"

"Fine, let's go somewhere, get something to eat and a cold beer. I have some jump stories to tell." We headed for the local watering hole, accompanied by John Coppie and Walter Huminsky and Walters brother Frank.

The Midwest Skydiving club grew very fast. The people drawn to the fairly new sport were quite unique indeed. That is not to say the occasional jerk didn't try to join. They were weeded out by our rigid training program.

I have been told many times that military jump school was a cake walk compared to our training program. I have to take credit for that. The truth of the matter is, I copied the Army jump school procedures and added a few of my own ideas. If the student could pass our ground school, they would be ready for anything. In fact, students were happy to jump from an aircraft in flight, just to be rid of my constant criticism of their half hearted attempt to follow instruction..

As I stated before, The Midwest Sky Diving Club, was located on the far south side of Chicago. As our numbers increased more and more members were from the north side of Chi-town. The decision was made to split the club in half. Midwest Sky Diving Club South and Midwest Sky Diving North. Rick Olchivick, Connie O'Rourke and I organized the north side club. Jokingly we were called the three Irishmen. How Olchivick became Irish, I will never know.

Chicago Sky Diving Club

In 1962 the three of us withdrew from the Midwest Sky Diving Club. The newly formed club was called, The Chicago Sky Diving Club. We found a private airfield north west of Chicago. Campbell Airport became our base of operation.

Verne Campbell, a retired businessman and pilot, let us have the use of his airfield free of charge. The paved runway and large jump area was ideal for our operation. Verne even threw in a large trailer to be used for a club house. This great man seemed to take pleasure in helping us. A finer person would be hard to find.

The rapid growth continued. Our training program was second to none and proved to all, Sky Diving was safe. To raise money for charities we put on demonstration jumps. The more demos we did, the more popular we became. The newspapers, radio talk shows, and TV stations were all writing articles or doing programs on our sky diving club. Sport parachuting was here to stay.

At that time Sport Parachute jumpers could be divided into three categories, Competitive, Training and Casual jumpers. Don't misunderstand me, I am not saying Competitive jumpers didn't help with training, nor am I saying Trainers didn't engage in competition. However, the Casual jumper was just out for the self enjoyment of the sport, and I surely don't find any problem with that. The new sport of Sky Diving, needed them all. Any advanced student of Sport Parachuting today probably knows more than we ever knew.

Back in the early days of sky diving. I like to think, "If it weren't for the vision of the yesteryear jumpers, the sport wouldn't be as safe as it is today." Now if that isn't true, please don't tell me. I might hit you in the nose with my cane.

Shangri-La

On clear days circling Campbell Airport, to reach jump altitude, I could see a field far in the distance that in my mind's eye would make a good jump center. I saw no reason why this great sport couldn't be turned into a profitable business. One day, I thought to myself, I'll drive over and take a look. Yes, one day I will have to take a look.

After about a year of procrastination, I jumped into my old Chevrolet station wagon in search of my phantom airport. After hours of searching, I pulled into a dirt makeshift parking lot. Unbelievable, I somehow knew I had just found my personal Shangri-La. Without stretching my imagination too far , I could see the sky filled with parachutes, plane's filled with jumpers taking off, empty planes landing to pick up more jumpers. The parking lot full to capacity, activity all over the place. And hovering over the entrance to this jumper paradise was a sign " Welcome to Hebron Airport, home of Land of Lincoln Sky Divers."

Walking into the smallest snack shop I have ever seen, I was greeted by a very sad looking gentleman.

"Want to buy a restaurant?"

"Sure," I replied (thinking he was joking) "How much?"

"One hundred dollars." All the equipment you see, one hundred bucks."

"Fifty and you got a deal," (still thinking he was joking) was my counter offer.

Handing me the keys, he informed me the new owner would probably be contacting me with regards to the amount of rent. Dumfounded I handed him fifty dollars. Am I still day dreaming? No, I wasn't dreaming. Fred and I talked for a couple of hours, seemed as though he was reluctant to leave. A very sad man indeed.

He explained he had owned the property for 20 years. At one time he had 30 planes based on the field and ran a flying school. Then a millionaire from Chicago opened a airport just one and one half miles down the road. One by one the airplane owners moved their planes to the new airport. Having paved runways, hangers, and a mechanic on duty was the drawing card. Grass strip airports were on the way out, and I call this my "Shangri-la".

A Walk With Giants 1957 - 1974

Land of Lincoln Sky Divers

Fred went on to explain that another old gentleman from Chicago, who loved grass strip airports, bought interest in his airport. As Fred needed more cash, Abe Marmel bought more interest in the airport. The only thing Fred had left was the small snack shop, and now that too, is gone. It is no wonder the man looked so sad.

Don't think for one moment Abe Marmel was a vulture, taking advantage of poor old Fred. On the contrary, Abe tried to help. Fred however, was living in the past, refusing to face reality. Hanging onto an old dream, unable to or refusing to get a new one. I will be talking a lot more about Abe Marmel as this story develops, I found Abe Marmel to be a very fascinating individual and indeed a friend.

"Stop by when you get a chance Fred." were my departing words. He didn't answer. Fred got into his pickup and drove off. Never saw the man again.

Looking around the ninety-acre field, it was very difficult to visualize that this unkempt property was once an airport. An old rusty iron wheeled tractor with a broken cycle bar stood in the head high weeds. It looked defeated by the very thing it once had the mission to control.

A Runway, hides beneath this grass

A Piper J3 with one wing missing, was home to a pair of robins. Even the twenty by thirty-foot snack shop (I had just purchased) although clean, showed signs of deferred maintenance. I couldn't help feeling sad for this apparent jewel of yesteryear. I vowed there on the spot to transform this forsaken property into a place of beauty.

This monumental task would require a lot of hard work. The sooner I started the sooner it would be completed. Plenty of daylight left in this beautiful August day. Unloaded my sleeping bag and tool box from my station wagon. Rolled up my sleeves, and proceeded to disassemble the ancient rusty tractor.

Three days later, I had the tractor overhauled and reassembled. Using the station wagon's battery, to my amazement, the old relic started. Somebody up there likes me, no doubt about it. I oiled the cutting fingers on the sickle bar and tackled the job of ridding the property of its head high weeds.

You may not believe this, but I felt the old tractor was smiling. Once again, acre by acre, it took charge of the overgrowth. Once again it was fulfilling its intended purpose. I was well into my mowing task when I noticed a car pulling into the driveway. A tall, graying hair, gentlemen started to walk in my direction. I turned the tractor off and dismounted.

Bob Arnold
If it had wings, Bob could fly it

"Good afternoon, did you come to help cut the grass?"

"It wouldn't be the first time I cut this grass." Reaching out his hand, "I'm Bob Arnold. I used to fly out of this field. Looks like some cutting fingers on the sickle bar need to be replaced." Maybe that's why its not cutting all the grass on the first run, I thought to myself.

We talked for quite a while. Bob knew the history of the property and seemed to enjoy telling me about it. When I told him I was going to restore the property to its Airport status, he was overjoyed. When Bob learned it would be a Jump Center his eyes lit up.

"Come over to the picnic table, my wife sent you a sandwich and some ice tea." For some reason that didn't surprise me, this was out in the country and country people are like that. We continued our conversation over a homemade bread and ham sandwich.

It was late. I decided to go to the local Motel, take a hot shower, and go to bed. Bob followed me. After his short talk to the Motel owner, $5.00 was taken off the price of the room. The Motel had two prices, one for locals and one for tourist. From that day on I lost my tourist status.

"See you tomorrow Dan." My new friend drove off.

I got up about 8:00 A.M.. I went to the motel office to get directions to the nearest restaurant.

"You don't need a restaurant, have breakfast with us. Any friend of Bob Arnold is a friend of ours." They wouldn't take no, for an answer. All through the meal they raved about Bob. Bob was a foreman in a small factory. He also was head of the local Rescue Squad. This man was loved by the whole community. This guy was a Giant long before I knew him and would maintain that status.

I arrived at the airport about 9:15 A.M.. Parked my station wagon close to the tractor, so I could jump start, the old relic. The tractor's battery had a cover on it. It didn't yesterday. Looks like the gremlins had been working. The tractor started as though it were new. I started cutting and noticed all the weeds were being cut on the first pass. The gremlins have really been busy. Every one of the missing sickle teeth had been replaced.

At 12:00 noon the gremlin drove into the parking lot. Bob Arnold and I had another lunch prepared by his wife. This lunch meeting and talk sessions would continue for the duration of the airport restoration. One of our conversations focused on the Hebron Rescue Squad. I was curious who supported them. All their money came from donations and an occasional fund raiser. I put that information in the back of my mind. If things went well, Land of Lincoln might be able to help.

"How long have you been flying Bob?"

"I went to flying school under the GI bill in 1945. I wonted to be a commercial pilot. I married my high school sweetheart and that kind of put my flying on hold. I only fly when the money is available. I used to fly for Fred when he offered sight seeing rides. When Art Gault built his airport so close, Fred's business took a nose dive. I was surprised to think anyone else would be interested in this place again."

"How about flying for me Bob? I can't pay much."

"I don't need any pay Dan." Bob interrupted. "I would be happy just to be able to fly. You can bet your bottom dollar I'll do whatever it takes to make Land of Lincoln successful." Time would show, Bob Arnold to be a man of action, not just words.

Working day and most of the night, in 22 days the new Jumping Center at Hebron Illinois, started to look really good. The once overgrown property looked like a golf course. I surveyed two runways and marked them with athletic field white chalk, mixed with water. One east-west (90/27) and a diagonal, northeast by southeast (15/33).

The jump target was also marked with a solid white circle, 50' to dead center and a broken circle, 100' to center. This helped to grade the student's accuracy. The chalk mixed with water resulted in the markings lasting a long time. An occasional thin coat kept them looking great. The view from the air was

Jump Center Hebron Illinois

spectacular, looked like a picture post card.

A good coat of paint and a few signs, turned the dull looking snack shop, into a fancy dinning facility. We added picnic tables with matching black and white umbrellas, to extend the dinning area for spectators. Later we would add a 20-X 48 parachute packing building.

My future expansion plans for Land of Lincoln Jump Center included the construction of a fly-in, ten room motel with a swimming pool and aircraft tie downs. The inclosed pool would have an entrance, from the motel or the outside.

Snack Bar & Class Room

Outside Dinning

Plans called for the motel be built on a foundation that could support a second story. All plumbing and electrics wiring would be extended to the roof and capped, waiting for the second floor. Future plans also called for expansion of our snack shop to a full service restaurant. There was no doubt in my mind that this dream would materialize.

I had no idea where the funding would come from. The fact of the matter is, every venture I had ever entered into (and there were many) was under funded. A situation that never stopped me from dreaming.

I have always felt, I was a lot better off than the person with more money then they need, but had no dream. What a sad life they must live. Wish they had my address, I could come up with a dream in a heart beat. It's not too late, look me up. I still have a few dreams that need funding.

ONLY IN AMERICA

At the same time I rented a building in Chicago, at 4358 North Milwaukee Ave near the Montrose Ave intersection. This was to serve as a Sport Parachuting School. Most would describe the building's condition as very poor. My budget forced me to look at the potential, not the present condition. Through my eyes, the building was beautiful and was an ideal location. I was sure with a lot of work this could be a show place. Work was no stranger to me. I started the transformation.

First task was to hang a very large sign "Future Home, Land of Lincoln Sky Diving School." Then I started on the office and reception area. My Sears credit card took care of the furnishings. Walking through the door, it was a sight to behold. It was like looking at a pearl in an oyster shell. The waist high wall separated the new from the old run down area.

I rented a sander and ground away at floors that haven't seen paint or covering for more than thirty years. When finished, the floor looked like a high quality gymnasium. The freshly painted walls with sky diving pictures transformed the old barn looking building to an absolute gem. Next task was to design and build training aids and devices.

"What's this going to be?" A voice interrupted.

"A Sport Parachuting School. Do you want to join?"

"Sure." One of the three visitors answered.

Bill Mellor, Dale Kosack and John Popendowski were to be Land of Lincoln's first students. The decision to hang the large sign outside was a good one. It drew a lot of attention to my new endeavor. Soon the first sport parachuting class was full.

I went on to explain to my new friends my intentions on improving the school area and future plans to build a member lounge and recreation area in the basement. I told them about my airport at Hebron; of my dream to build a Sport Center that had no equal

I received their undivided attention when I was explaining the training they were about to engage in. I emphasized that this sport took a lot of discipline and dedication. I informed them I had a hard nose, reputation in training. That I would never take it easy on a student. The nature of the sport demanded nothing less. I emphasized the safety of Sport Parachuting. This was a sport that could terminate a life, but only it you broke the rules. I closed with:

"The trip to the airport was far more dangerous than jumping from the plane." A true statement as a matter of fact.

'Can I help you fix this place up?" John asked.

"I'm working on a budget lad, can't afford to hire anyone."

"Oh. I don't want paid. I just want to help."

"I'll help to." Dale joined in.

"Me to." Bill followed suit.

This was the beginning of a long friendship. It was people like Bill. Dale and John and many more like them, which resulted in the rapid growth of Land of Lincoln Sky Divers. Giants every one of them.

The first training device built was a replica of a Cessna 172. The size of the door, angle of the strut and shape of the landing gear were cabin carbon of the real thing. Second device on the agenda was a Parachute Landing Fall (PLF) table that also served as a platform for our Canopy Control Trainer.

The Canopy Control Trainer was a device I was thinking about for a long time. I bolted an electric turn table from a Christmas tree to the ceiling rafters above the PLF (Parachute Landing Fall) platform. Then I attached a parachute harness to a metal hoop. The hoop was covered with parachute material, it looked like a miniature parachute.

Control Trainer

A student hanging in the harness could pull the right or left control lines which in turn would activate the electric turner and turn the miniature parachute in the same direction. The instructor could manipulate a miniature wheeled target on the floor that created canopy control problems for the student.

The canopy will turn in the direction it is pulled. It also will swing the jumper in that direction. Because of that fact, all students are thought to make all turns into the target and away from obstacles. If a tree or other obstacle became a problem, pulling on the opposite control line would move the student away from the hazard. We repeatedly told the student. Make all turns into the target and away from obstacles."

The last item needed was a parachute packing table. All students were required to be able to pack their own parachute before their first free fall. I packed all their

Charlie and Dan packing, Aircraft Mockup and PLF Platform in background

static line jump parachutes and reserves. In addition to building a packing table on the first floor I built one in the basement and at the airport. All in all, Land of Lincoln training center looked and functioned very well. There wasn't anything like it anywhere. Add the attitude of the talented people that joined Land of Lincoln and you end up with a win win situation.

42

Our first class consisted of nine students. Seven male and two female. The gender didn't matter. Everyone had to preform equally. No slack just because some were female. When you're alone in the sky, its you and only you that has to function. The worst thing you can do to a student is cut them some slack because they are female or for any other reason.

The class was ready for their first static line jump. I went to Hebron Airport to make sure the aircraft was laid on and to make any last minute preparations. Everything was ready to go, with the exception of the Snack Bar and empty Coke machine. Getting Land of Lincoln this far left me with $8.00 to my name. The airport looked good, but I was broke.

The coke machine, which came with the restaurant, held nine cases available for vending and four cases in the pre cool area. Maybe the Coca-Cola Co. will bill me for the coke. I called the area vender.

"Sorry we don't deliver on Saturdays to new customers. The earliest I can get to you is Monday morning."

"That won't do. I need 60 cases and I need them for tomorrow."

"Sixty cases, I guess I will have to make an exception for an order like that. What time do you want them?" The green-eyed monster greed, took over.

"I will need then no later than 8 A.M.. My only problem is 60 cases may not be enough for Sunday."

"That's OK Mr. McGinley, I can make another delivery on Sunday morning if you need it." I don't think I would have received the same attention if he knew, I only had $8.00 to my name. That took care of the beverage department. Now the restaurant.

"Let's see, give me four packages of hot dogs and two packages of hot dog buns. Also, a jar of mustard." That left me with a dollar and some change. On the way out of the little Hebron store I deposited it all in a Hebron Rescue Squad donation bucket. It seems I can't stand money in my pockets.

Bob Arnold was the first one at the airport. Next to arrive was Ken Haffer with a rented Cessna 172. I meet Ken at the school when he dropped in to see what we were doing. Ken held a commercial licence and looked forward to being our Chief Pilot.

"Ken, shake hands with Bob Arnold. Bob lives in Hebron and has been a great help getting the airport ready. Bob is also a pilot Ken"

A Walk With Giants 1957 - 1974

"How many hours have you logged Bob?" It seemed to me Ken was acting a little high brow.

"I really can't say. I guess I should log my time. Never seem to get around to it. It seems to me it's what you do with an airplane, not what you say you can do."

"Let's take a ride Bob. I'll see what you can do." Again Ken was a little high brow, bordering on sarcastic in his tone. "First we have to take a walk-around check" They proceeded with the check. "Everything looks fine Bob, let's take off."

"Just one minute, Ken." Bob went to his car and came back with a tool box. "You shouldn't be flying that aircraft with a loose manifold Ken." At the same time Bob tightened the loose bolt. Kens attitude immediately changed. They took off on runway 90 (east bound) and made a left-hand banking turn. When Ken and Bob got back from the check out ride, they seemed to be friends.

"Why did you make a left turn when we took off Bob? There is nothing wrong with a left-hand turn, I just wondering."

"If we made a right hand turn, we would have been in Galt's flight pattern." Ken didn't know that there was another airport less then one mile away. Some time after their first meeting I asked Ken how many flying hours he thought Bob had?

"A lot more than I have Mac. One day I hope to be as proficient as Bob." Talk about an attitude change.

The crowd was unbelievable. Our 20 space parking area overflowed to the road. We had to get a resupply of Coca Cola by 2:00 P.M. and another two deliveries on Sunday. With the money now in the register I stocked the Snack Bar. Monday morning I had more than $5,000.00 in the till for deposit. I felt like Rockefeller.

The jumping went well. By Sunday afternoon all but two students had made their five Static Line Jumps and their first Free Fall jump. I thought only Military jumpers could tell jump stories. The civilian jumpers are as good or maybe better. I was proud of each and every one of them.

My rule was that the student jumper had to pull three dummy rip cords on their static line jumps. Failure to do so would prevent them from going on free fall. Our two gal jumpers. Janice Dunkel and Gale Cortez, only pulled two. They were disappointed and it showed in their faces.

"Mac we can do it. We can pull the rip cord. Please let us make a free fall." I was tempted, two beautiful creatures clad in bikinis, pleading. Then the no compromise attitude took over.

"Another Static Line jump. That's the rule. If I see the red flag attached to the dummy ripcord, you'll go free-fall." I also added. "If both you gals were ugly that would be another story. I'm not going to take the chance on two beautiful women getting hurt." That mellowed them a little.

I applied for and got the school certified as a Federal Aviation Administration Parachute Loft. From time to time the FAA would use Land of Lincoln FAA Loft # 3157 at 4358 North Milwaukee to test new Parachute Riggers. Since I was a certified FAA senior rigger, I conducted the practical portion of the FAA Rigger Certification test.

Land of Lincoln Sky Divers was a for-profit business. It was unique because we had a club with dues paying members within the organization. If bad weather prevented safe jumping, members would work around the airport as though it was their own. Painting, cutting the grass, building training devices, helping with new students, whatever was needed everyone joined in.

Each member paid a $20.00 a year membership fee. The first five Static Line Jumps cost them $ 95.00. Land of Lincoln furnished all the equipment. If the student was kept on Static Line, the cost was the same as though they were on Free Fall, $4.00 per jump. We were able to keep the 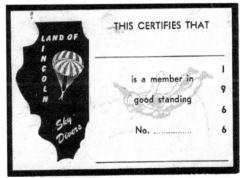 cost down because many people paid their membership dues and five Static Line jumps and we would never see them again. I guess it was worth that to them, to have a membership card. There are a whole lot of wannabee' in this world.

"See my Land of Lincoln membership card. I'm a Sky-Diver." I had no problem with that. Keep the $20.00 coming.

It was the spirit and friendly attitude of the membership responsible for the growth of Land of Lincoln Sky Divers. New members were greeted warmly. They felt at home from the start. I kept my hard nose attitude, but loved them as though they were my children. Like children they knew how to manipulate me to get their way. They saw through my hard nose act.

As the word got out more and more students joined Land of Lincoln Sky Divers. From a long list, potential Giants started to emerge. Ken Rorheim, Charlie Blomster, Don Figarrotto Harry Bucket, and Ed Halley, headed the list. The list kept growing.

The workload was not in proportion to our growth. The more experience the jumper became the more they helped with the new students. On rare occasions a jumper was in the sport for his or her personal gain and refused to do anything. No problem, I would let my "You're not welcome side show." Believe me they would be off the airport before the sun went down.

Not everyone was welcome. If they couldn't follow some simple rules, I forced them to leave. I didn't force morality on anyone. But while at the airport or our school area they were asked to keep any trashy life style away. Respect for everyone was paramount. Foul language had to keep under control. Positively no drinking while participating in the sport. The 24 hour no drinking before jumping rule was strictly enforced. I'm not a tea toddler. Drinking just doesn't mix with flying or jumping.

I really don't know why, but for some reason we had a lot of Policemen join our club. That was great. It kept a certain element away. One of these policemen was very active in scouting. Bob Curry was a very large guy. I'm sure it looked strange to see a guy my size chewing out a guy Bobs size. Something like Mutt, chewing out Jeff. Strange the power the guy holding the Static Line has over the guy at the other end.

Bob was an exceptionally good guy. No matter what, he would never get mad. He became a policeman because his father and his grand father and a couple of uncles were all policemen.

"Mac I won't be able to make it to the airport every week. I'm trying to get a BSA Explorer Post started. I have to spend some of my Saturdays with them."

"What specialty will your Post have? What company is sponsoring you?" Bob was surprised I knew so much about Explorer Scouts.

"We don't have a sponsor yet Mac."

"I'll sponsor your group Bob."

It started as simple as that. Land of Lincoln became the sponsors of Explorer Post 2905 with a Sky Diving Specialty. The first and only Sky Diving Post. Another achievement for this group of Giants. Robert Curry became the Institutional Representative and Committee Chairman and I their Advisor.

POST CHARTER

Explorer Post 2905

Like Bob the young men that joined Explorer Post 2905 were outstanding individuals. Eager to learn Sport Parachuting. As soon as they reached sixteen with their parents consent they made their first parachute jump. The twenty-five strong membership took a large part of the work load off the Land of Lincoln members. Odd, no one complained. I thought the members enjoyed working for me, without pay. (I'm not cheap, just conservative.)

"Mac our scouts are going to a parade downtown Chicago on Flag Day. Wouldn't it be nice if they all had uniforms?" Bill Mellor asked me a question but didn't wait for an answer. He went on to say the membership had a meeting and they decided they would come up with half the money if Land of Lincoln came up with the balance.

"Bill that's a good idea but we can't afford uniforms, maybe next year. Nobody bought me a uniform when I was a Scout." Bill walked away a little disappointed. He must have told the group. The airport became a little quieter than usual.

The next Saturday was very windy and jumping was put on hold. During the week I asked Bob to arrive at the Hebron Airport with his scouts at exactly 10:00 A.M.. Bob was sort of on schedule, At 10:05 two Vans turned into our parking lot. They looked good. Black coveralls with white embroidered letters, "Post 2905 Land of Lincoln Sky Divers." A Land of Lincoln patch on their right shoulder, black Cockerne jump boots, with white parachute suspension line, ladder laced. Of course their trousers were bloused. Topping their uniform off was their Green Berets, a gift from the 302nd Special Forces.

"Kill him!" The mob rushed in my direction. I experienced two chills that day. One from the high wind, and the other when they throw me in the cold creek water. Everyone followed our unscheduled swim.

47

Bob and I discussed uniforms earlier in the year. We had all the sizes in each Scout's record jacket. Land of Lincoln members just triggered the action. There was no way I would let them help pay for the uniforms. The members gave me something far more valuable than money, their friendship and loyalty.

Guatemala Invasion

I walked in the office while Harry Bucket and John Richter were involved in a conversation with Ronnie Mensizabal. It didn't seem they were getting any place, Mensizabal didn't speak English. Harry nor John spoke Spanish.

"Mac I think this guy wants to jump out of airplanes. Do you speak Spanish?"

"Not a word. Go see if Victor is down stairs, if he is, ask him to help us."

Victor Floras was from Cuba attending the University of Illinois. He was also one of many pilots that hung around trying to get some free flying time. In the ten plus years I ran Land of Lincoln I never had to pay anybody to fly our jump planes. There was never a shortage of pilots who would exchange their talent for flying time. Once the flying bug bites you, you're hooked. Victor was more than a pilot. He became friends with many of our membership, a clean-cut lad and a pleasure to be around.

"Victor this is Ronnie Mensizabal. Give him a run down on what we are about. Tell him the prices of jumping and equipment. If he wants to join us, the application packets are in the file cabinet."

There wasn't a member that wasn't knowledgeable about our business or who wasn't allowed in our files. If I didn't trust anybody, they wouldn't be around long. Victor was a dues paying member and trusted fully. Many people joined us who didn't jump. I left Victor with Ron and went back to my packing class.

"How did the interview go Victor?" I asked when Victor joined us downstairs.

"Great, Ron joined L of L, paid for his first five jumps. He purchased coveralls, a Bell Helmet, 3 Land of Lincoln patches, and ordered a parachute. He will start classes Monday night."

"I think I'm going to put you in charge of interviews Victor."

It didn't matter what night a student started. All classes regardless of the subject matter stood alone. Everyone in the class was hearing the covered subject for the first time. After a student showed proficiency in the subject, they moved to the next class. There was no beginning or ending date.

Ron was the son of a General in the Guatemala Army. At first that gave me a little trouble. It was evident Ron was not used to taking orders. Victor acting as an interrupter didn't help. I'm sure, Victor was not telling Ron, exactly what I was saying. Victor was too polite. Every time Victor would say something, and Ron would engage him in conversation. I didn't understand what they were saying, but the tone and expression on Ron's face indicated he wasn't pleased about something. The class was on body position, exiting an aircraft.

"Class, take a break downstairs. Victor and Ron, stay put." Sensing I was upset the class almost ran downstairs. "Victor I'm not mad at you. I want you to tell our friend from South America, to do more action and less complaining. If he doesn't like taking orders, I'll give him his money back."

Victor told Ron something in Spanish. Ron's facial expression showed signs of worry. As Victor talked, Ron kept nodding.

"Ron agrees to do whatever you tell him, Mac."

"Put your left arm like this." I bent my left arm and held my hand even with my head. "Put your right arm like this. Ron started to say something to Victor. I yelled out. "Put your right arm like this!" Ron snapped to it. "Arch your back, like this." I held my arms in position and arched my back. "More, more, arch your back more." Ron complied. In the process he fell flat on his face.

"Victor, go on down stairs and enjoy yourself, Ron won't be needing an interpreter. Before you go, tell Ron, to watch my expression. When he does well, I will smile. When he does badly, I'll frown. His job is to keep me smiling." Ron did a 180. I showed him and he mimicked me. Ron became better than the average student.

I was surprised to find out that the Guatemala Military come and go between the US and Guatemala at will. Flying under Radar, they come and go at will. Ron came in a WWII Navy (SNJ) trainer. The plane was given to Guatemala by the US. I don't think Uncle Sam intended it to be user for pleasure.

49   A Walk With Giants 1957 - 1974

On 24 June 1965 Ronnie Mensizabal completed his free-fall training. He did very well. After his 6th free fall jump, it was time for Ron to go home. We issued him a certificate showing he completed the training. I proclaimed him an honor student and gave another certificate. South Americans like certificates. Ron took off for Texas to pick up his plane. Then back to Guatemala via the same way he came, flying under the US radar.

Ron was back in three weeks (this time by commercial air) with an offer I almost fell for. General Mensizabal was so impressed with his sons training he wanted Land of Lincoln to come to Guatemala with our aircraft and equipment to train the Guatemala Airborne, free fall techniques. This sounded like the adventure of a lifetime. I'm a believer in the old saying,

"If it sounds too good to be true, it probably isn't."

Victor Floras was on summer break and volunteered to drive Ron back to Guatemala. I didn't know at the time, but Ron had told Victor he could get a surplus US Navy plane without charge. I figured it fell in that "probably isn't" category. With his head in the cloud's Victor went back with Ron to reconnoiter the area, and training offer. Victor was back in two weeks without his car. The story he told was frightening, just to listen to.

To start with, an inventory was taken of Victors Auto at the US/Mexican border and again at the Mexican/Guatemalan border. Many items of value were left off the list at the northern boarder crossing. Since the items were not on the inventory list, they were confiscated by the Mexicans at the second boarder crossing. That's what can be really called, free trade.

General Mensizabal wanted Land of Lincoln to teach free-fall but would never come up with a price. He told Victor we could work out the payment schedule at a later date. I guess he has been working with the US Government too long. Uncle Sam is a sucker on giveaway plans.

Another thing that was disturbing was the fact the drop zone was constantly changing hands. Some times it belonged to the rebel forces and other times it belonged to the Government forces. Like I tell my students, "turn away from obstacles." I turned away from this deal. It took about six months to get Victors Auto back to the US. I had to call in some favors, people in Government owed me.

Who's Airport Is It?

"Hebron Airport, 2727 Gulf, request wind direction and active." I was busy with students. One of the jumpers answered the radio.

"Welcome to Hebron Airport. Negative wind, runway 27 active."

I saw the plane come in but paid no more attention to it. Planes are always dropping in to watch the jumping. I was sure they would be given a warm welcome, and they were. Vivian (L of L's secretary) made room for them at one of our picnic tables and saw to it they were given a cold drink. About an hour later,

Abe Marmel

"Excuse me. My name is Abe Marmel. I was told you are in charge."

"That's what they say. I doubt it, they seem to do whatever they wont. My name is Dan, how can I help you?"

"Well, I think I own this airport."

"I'm glad to finally meet you, Mr. Marmel. I have to put this young lady on her first free-fall. We have an open seat, care to join us?"

"Oh yes, I would like that. Mama I'm going for a jump, watch for me."

"Excuse me Abe, your not jumping."

"Yes I know. I'm just teasing Mama."

We put a chute on Abe and loaded him into the plane first. I got in second and Gale sat on the floor in front of me. From Abe's vantage point he would be able to see a part of aviation, I'm sure he has never seen before. I don't know who was more excited, Gale on her first free-fall or Abe, my missing landlord.. I have occupied this airport for three years. This is the first time I had ever seen him. We climbed to 3200 feet and started our jump run.

"Get out." Was my command. At the same time I pointed to the strut.

Without hesitation Gale swing her legs out. Placed one foot on the aircraft step, turned and gave me a kiss. Then Gale reached out, took a hold of the strut. Pulling herself out she placed the other foot on the aircraft wheel.

All this time, Bob was holding the brake on. When we were over the exit point, I gave her a vigorous tap on the shoulder and hollered, "Go!"

My "Go's" can be heard on the ground. Her exit was perfect. Then she came in for the pull. Gale pulled that rip cord like she had been on free-fall for years. She had great body position for the opening. I'm glad I had a camera. Gales' first free fall was letter perfect. This gal is going to be a good jumper.

Bob banked the aircraft so we could follow her all the way to the ground. Abe Marmel was as happy as a kid with a new toy. I was sure, my strategy to soften him up for our first business meeting was working. (What strategy) Before we got out of the plane Abe asked me why Gale kissed me before she jumped. I was lacking an answer, I didn't know why. The gals just started the gesture and I did nothing to discourage it. The kiss had nothing to do with flirting or any thing like that. It was more like a good luck jester. Bob Curry and Bill Mellor had two more students waiting.

"Have one of our famous hamburger's Abe, I'll be right down."

Well I was back in just a few minutes. Again students were chuted up and waiting. I started to feel guilty after about five plane loads. I hope Abe is a patient man. I also hope he's not thinking I am trying to avoid him.

Finally I told Bill Mellor, Dale Kosack and John Ricter to

Bill Mellor, my back facing camera

chute up and put on a demonstration jump from ninety-seven-hundred (45-sec delay) with smoke. I had to talk to Abe.

"Where is your wife Abe?"

"She's inside doing your dishes. She doesn't do the dishes at home. She comes out here and you have her doing your dishes." I was glad he was smiling while he was complaining.

Sure enough when we went inside to talk, there was Mrs. Marmel behind the counter. Vivian our secretary, and Mrs. Marmel hit it off from the first. They became good friends. When Vivian was behind the counter, Mrs. Marmel went behind the counter.

"Mama, come we have to talk with Daniel."

"No Abe, we come for a good time. No business today. We will all go out for a business dinner one day next week. Vivian and I will pick a nice place."

The jump plane called in that it was on final. We all went outside to watch. Abe was afraid he would not be able to see the jumpers in free fall. As soon as the three jumpers left the aircraft they popped the smoke canisters attached to their legs. Abe was amazed with their performance. All three were very good jumpers and landed on the target.

The Marmel family became frequent visitors. They would bring their grand children and other relatives. To hear Abe explain sky diving to them, you would think he invented the sport.

Shirley & Abe Marmel

Our business dinner took place three days later. Vivian and Mrs. Marmel selected a very good but an expensive restaurant. This was no surprise to me. Vivian was a lady with class and expensive tastes. Vivian, the office manager for a large law firm in Chicago was no stranger to mingling with the affluent class. How she and I hit it off, remains a mystery to me. I'm more the Wimpy Hamburger type. It was because of this super gal, Land of Lincoln's administrative set up was second to none.

During the meal questions were fired back and forth about our private lives and backgrounds. It was a way of getting to know each other. Most questions were directed to answering the question,

"Who are we dealing with?"

I learned I was dealing with a man that loved the Airport Business. A man that just a few years ago, was almost broke. Abe owned Ravenswood Flying School located on Chicago's North-West side. Mr. Marmel built the grass strip airport and kept it going for more than thirty years. The close proximity to Chicago kept the airport active, in spite of not having paved runways. Then disaster struck, the City of Chicago built O'Hare International Airport across the road from Abe's place. The city started putting presume on Abe immediately. They tried everything in the book to close Ravenswood Airport.

They made it a requirement that all aircraft landing at O'Hare had to have radios with their Control Towers and Ground Control frequency. Abe had 36 Piper J-3's that didn't have radios nor a battery to run them. J-3's have a Magneto for a power source. No problem. Resourceful Abe installed a two-frequency radio. On the cowling just behind the propeller, he attached a small propeller. The wind from the aircraft propeller spun the small propeller which in turn generated power for the radio. Is this guy Marmel clever or what?

To rub salt into their wounds, Abe had all his students practice landings at O'Hare. The student would call O'Hare's tower and then start their slow landing approach. This infuriated O'Hare. The Piper J-3 has a landing speed of 30mph. O'Hare had to stack much faster Aircraft in a holding pattern. Abe's students made 50 to 60 landings a day.

The City of Chicago closed Ravenswood Airport. Then the legal fight began. Against all odds my new friend sued the City of Chicago and after a long fight, Abe Marmel won.

There was a Federal Law on the books that stated the first Airport in a given area, had the right of way. Ravenswood Airport was built years before O'Hare. The City of Chicago offered Abe 2-Million dollars for one half of his property. In addition they moved all Abe's hangers and buildings to Abe's half of the property. Chicago used their half to train police dogs. Abe Marmel disassembled all his aircraft and opened a used airplane part's business. I was fascinated with Abe's determination and resourcefulness.

Departing from my story for a moment. Abe Marmel's granddaughter, Lauren Knight sent me a newspaper article about an American Airline DC-10, Flight 191, crashing into the Marmel property on 25 May 1979. Killing all 270 aboard and two on the ground. Abe and his wife Shirley were injured by the crash.

Abe was tending his garden while Shirley was in the Hanger Office doing the books. Although injured, without hesitation, Abe rushed into the burning building to save Shirley. This act of heroism doesn't surprise me. Giants have a tendency to do such things. Back to my story.

Finally we got to the reason of our meeting.

"Daniel, I think you owe me some rent money."

"I find that strange Abe. I thought you owe me some management and development fees."

"Mama, can you believe this man thinking, I owe him money?"

"Yes Abe. Vivian has told me a lot about Daniel. I think you have met your match." I took that as a compliment. I felt Mrs. Marmel was on my side.

We went back and forth for hours. Abe made an offer, I countered his offer. The gals were getting tired and suggested we continue at another date.

"Who's going to pay for the meal Daniel? Don't tell me Daniel, I know." Reaching for his wallet, "How about the tip? Don't tell me, I Know. Mama, I think Daniel is Jewish." Then I asked the question, that sat us back down.

"Abe, what would have happened to Hebron Airpost if I had not come along three years ago?" With a strange look on his face Abe sat down.

"Vivian, come with me I know that look on Abe's face." The gals left I sat down with Abe Marmel. What happened next shocked me and everybody I have told this story to. Abe started talking a deal and I had no desire to interrupt. This great man (defiantly a Giant) told me I didn't owe him a nickel. The fact that I had turned a dying airport into thriving business amazed him. Hundreds of other grass strip airports were going under. He was equally amazed, I did it on very limited capital and without investors.

"Daniel, treat this property as though it belongs to you. One day it will be. If I ever sell, it will be to you. At a price we will agree to. I will finance the sale without interest. Daniel you have made an old man happy." I had nothing to say. At that moment, a kinship was born.

Land of Lincoln Flying School

Abe Marmel showed a lot of interest in the abandoned J-3 with one wing.

"Daniel, what will you take for that old J-3?"

"If you wont it Abe, take it." There was no way I would charge him for an aircraft I didn't own. All this time, I thought the aircraft in question belonged to Abe. The next time I came to the airport the plane was gone. Every time my new friend came to the airport, the question was the same,

"Daniel why don't you teach flying along with Sky Diving?" Finally I told Abe I didn't have an instructor nor the money to purchase aircraft. Abe was shocked to learn Bob Arnold wasn't a certified flight instructor. He had said many times he never saw a more qualified flyer.

"You don't have to purchase aircraft Daniel. Lease them from me."

Sounded good. A flight school would supplement our income when the wind was too high or the ceiling was low. As far as an instructor, we could hire one. The membership as a whole was excited with the idea of a flying school.

I negotiated a great deal with Abe Marmel. I leased five Piper J-3's from Abe at $25.00 a month per plane, dry. Dry meant I furnished the fuel. This was a way below market. Abe wasn't

Piper J-3

looking to make a profit. He wanted to help Land of Lincoln establish a Flying School

Our only difficulty was finding an instructor willing to travel the long distance to Hebron Airport. I solved that problem by guaranteeing three hours pay if they flew or not. We still couldn't attract the better pilots.

If a person was serious about learning to fly, they couldn't beat our offer. For $100.00 we would guarantee they would solo. Of course they had to join Land of Lincoln at $20.00 per year. There was no way you could solo for that price. Remember the wont-a-be's? Many paid their $120.00 and were never seen again.

56

Our first flying instructor was kind of a weird and grumpy individual. He was goggle eyed over our female students. He paid more attention to them personally then he did to their flying ability. On the other hand he was crabby to all our male students. He criticized every move they made. None of his criticism was constructive. Most of the male students didn't wont to take their second lesson. Time I checked this guy out.

"Clyde, take me up for a lesson. Since I'm paying for the aircraft, I might as well learn to fly them."

"I'll see if I can work you in Mac."

"You'll what? This is my airport buster, when I say it's my turn, you start propping the engin. I could tell he was a little angry with my tone. But again this is my airport and my anger has priority over all other anger.

I'm a little loud when my feathers are ruffled. I don't know if it's because I'm hard of hearing or just a show off. Maybe a little of both. Regardless, all attention was directed to our little chat. Dale and Bill even held up the jumping so no one would miss the outcome of my instructors' evaluation. We started taxiing down the runway. Over the roar of the engine, Clyde launched his complaint.

"You embarrassed me in front of everybody. If that ever happens again, I'll quit. I throttled back and stopped the aircraft.

"Get out of my airplane. You're fired." I never saw anybody exit a Piper J-3 as fast as he did. As soon as he was clear I turned the plane around and taxied back to the starting point.

Taxing was not new to me. During winter months, to supplement income I worked at Palwawkee Airport refueling aircraft. Single engin, twin engin, it didn't matter. I couldn't fly them, but I could taxi them all. Clyde got into his automobile and departed the area. The students were jubilant. Not one would miss Clyde, the grumpy flight instructor.

"Mac, I have a friend that is instructor rated. He hangs out at Du Page County Airport.

"Call Du Page Ken. Ask him if he can come out today. Tell him, we will pick him up." Ken Hafer made the call, then took off for Du Page Co. Airport with one of our J-3's.

Kens friend turned out to be a fine instructor and liked by most students. His only draw back, he was a professional student. This guy was 32 years old and would travel the world, for a particular class he thought he needed. His parents always footed the bill. He hadn't worked a day in his life. I guess flying wasn't work for him. Beatnik or hippy probably describes this guy's lifestyle the best.

I enjoyed having the Piper J-3's at Hebron Airport. Every time a new student would sign up I would ask them if they wanted an airplane ride. The answer was always yes. I would make sure they secured their seat belts and then would taxi to the end of the runway. Then go through the pre flight procedures like I was going to take off. I have never flown, nor did I have a licence. I taxied back to the tie down area with a disappointed passenger. I pulled this joke over and over. I got a lot of fun out of my prank. All the new-be's got was disappointment.

"John, want to take a plane ride?" I hollered as I taxied by a group of students.

"You have already pulled that on me Mac." I continued taxiing to the west end of the runway.

"I think he is going to do it this time. Macs going to take off." John Popindoski was hollering.

I could hear him over the sound of the idling engin. I don't know what came over me. I gave the plane full power. In a very few feet the plane was airborne. I have been around airplanes long enough to know,  whatever you do, follow through. Survival is more likely, if you crashing straight ahead rather than turning around trying to get back to the airport. Another thing, most small aircraft (if trimmed properly) will almost fly themselves. Pilots trying to override this natural state, get into trouble.

As soon as I broke ground, I knew I had to follow through. Observing pilots on hundreds of flights I was fairly familiar with aircraft controls. I made a slow banking turn to the left. The airport was looking smaller and smaller. When cutting the airport grass the property was huge. Looking at it from the air, it seemed like a postage stamp. I knew I had to get this contraption back on the ground.

58

The windsock indicated the wind was coming straight down our diagonal runway. I decided to line up on Runway 33. I was doing a great job. I couldn't have done a better job of alignment if I had a thousand hours of flying time. The only problem I was at 100 feet.

I swear, if I had a parachute on, I would have jumped. I kept trying to muster enough nerve to bring this baby home. I was running out of daylight. The people on the ground were also getting nervous. A few turned their headlights on to illuminate the runway. The lights blinded me. I made a low pass and used my jump command voice.

"Turn the light's off." This was my last chance. It would be now or never.

The line up was good. I had enough altitude to clear the wires at the south east end of the runway. I made a perfect three point landing. I was so proud of myself. I applied full power. I was airborne again.

"Why did you do that fool?" I asked myself.

The lineup on my second landing attempt was good as the first. That's where the comparison ended. I barely cleared the wires. I hit the ground and bounced three times finally coming to a stop. My knees started to shake uncontrollably. That was without doubt, the closest one can get before its classified as a crash. Luck of the Irish? No, more like 'God watches over fools. And this fool keeps him busy.

I flew every clear day after that. Takeoffs and landings, takeoffs and landings, hundreds of them. The farthest I got from Hebron Airports landing pattern, was Galt Airport, one mile away. At that point, navigation was not one of my strong points.

Harry Hanson one of the many pilots associated with Land of Lincoln decided to purchase a Cessna 175, and lease it to Land of Lincoln. Per agreement the aircraft was to be used by Land of Lincoln exclusively. The aircraft was to be housed at Galt Airport in a hanger, L of L paid for. Like the J-3's, I couldn't resist flying this beautiful aircraft. One day when Bob Arnold and I were at the airport alone I wonted to get Bobs reaction to my flying the 175.

"Bob lets take a ride." I got in the left seat of the Cessna 175. Bob got in the right side, without saying a word. I started the engine and took off. Still Bob didn't say a word.

"Aren't you surprised that Im flying the Cessna Bob?"

"I have known from the first day Mac. Your questions about the 175's stalling speed, and other questions, tipped your hand."

"Bob if this 175 was your plane, would you let me fly it?"

"Yes I would Mac. You're a safe pilot, I would let you fly it."

That's all I needed. If your flying could please Bob Arnold, you could please anybody. Like the J-3's, I flew 6565E every time I got a chance.

I was landing a J-3 on runway 27 (heading west) when I noticed a car entering our parking lot. I didn't recognize the vehicle and decided to check it out.

A Piper J-3 is a tail dragging aircraft. It is impossible to see the runway in front of you while taxing, without using a zigzag pattern. That is unless a pilot of Bob Arnold's qualification shows you his method. Bob applies just enough power to keep the tail of the aircraft off the ground. In this position the runway is visible making straight forward taxiing possible. I use Bob Arnold's method when taxiing a tail dragger.

I held my left brake on. Applying a little power, I turned the J-3 into the wind. Pulling back on the power, the tail was lowered slowly to the ground. I got out and approached the visitor's automobile. As I got closer, the gentleman opened his door. There on his door, in bold letters, for the world to see, 'United States Government. Our visitor was from the Federal Aviation Administration (FAA). The real shocker was his opening statement,

"Am I glad I caught you." Fear filled my body. Not only didn't I have a pilot license, I didn't have a learning permit. "It's important we teach our students to fly by the seat of their pants." Our Visitor continued. "How many flying students do you have enrolled at Land of Lincoln?"

"About fifteen, we try to keep our enrollment between ten and fifteen. How about a cup of coffee?" He declined. I wanted to change the subject from flying to jumping. "Bring you family by this week end. I'm sure they will enjoy watching the jumping. It will be a good opportunity for our flying students to meet a representative from the FAA." He thanked me and departed.

I'm sure he thought I was Land of Lincoln's flight instructor. On all Airport Directories under the Hebron Airport heading, I was listed as owner, operator, and instructor. I was an instructor, Sky Diving Instructor not Flight Instructor. I jumped into my station wagon and drove to Gault Airport to see Art Gault.

"Art, I got caught by the FAA. They caught me flying."

"Mac it's a perfect day, and you're within your license limitations."

"Well, you see Art, I don't have a license."

"What, you have been flying all over the place and you don't have a licence. Well you're within a student permit."

"Art, I don't have a student permit." I could see the disbelief in his face. Every Sunday Art and I would take one of my J-3's and fly to different Airports for fly-in breakfasts. This guy was a millionaire. In addition to owning Gault Airport, his family owned Maywood Park Race Track. Although Art owned a twin engin Beach, he loved flying our vintage Piper J-3's.

"Harry, take this baldheaded guy up and don't come down until you're ready to sign his student ticket. Arts Flying school manager asked,

"You're plane or ours Mac?

"Let's take my Cessna 175. Without bragging I could handle that geared prop Cessna as good as any. The aircraft looked like a Cessna 172, but handled a lot differently. The geared prop allowed the plane to take off at lower rpms making it a lot easier on the engine. In fact if you gave it full power, it could cause the engine to suck a valve. Which in turn would result in castle repairs.

In less than an hour Harry got out of the aircraft to observe three takeoffs and three landings. A requirement before an instructor sings off on a student ticket, to fly solo. I went to Gaults ground school and passed with flying colors. This opened the door to a lot of cross country flying. The sky belonged to me.

Should Have Charged by The Pound

I probably have a million stories about Land of Lincoln Sky Diving School and the great members that were associated with our organization. Unfortunately, a few were not so great. One in particular comes to mind. We were sitting around waiting for the wind to die down. A fairly large individual approached us.

"What does it cost to jump out of an airplane?", a lad of large proportions asked.

"What kind of shape are you in lad? Can you pick up that log?" I was referring to one of the 10 foot logs blocking cars from driving on our grassed picnic area. Concerned about his size prompted the question. He just stared at me.

"Charlie pick up that log." Charlie Blumster was an averaged height very thin guy.

Without hesitation Charlie picked up the log like it was a tooth pick. Another thing about Charlie, he was an ex-Marine. Tell a Marine something and it's done. Charlie would have picked that log up, even if he had to buy an elephant to do so. Marines are funny that way. Heavy Drop not to be out done, after a lot of struggle, picked up the log.

Surprisingly our large friend did quit well in training. He had a positive attitude change and seemed to be looking forward to his first jump. Because of his size I decided to use a larger parachute on his jumps than regular jumpers use. Jumpers less than 200 pounds use a 28-foot diameter chute. He would be using a 34-foot diameter parachute. In addition to being larger the chute was parabolic in shape. This reduced oscillation, resulting in a softer landing.

Safety is paramount in Sport Parachuting. Having emergency procedures that can be activated immediately will enhance the overall safety record. At Land of Lincoln we had safety reaction plans, for ground or air emergencies.

All members were required to attend a 20-hour first aid class to include CPR, given by the Hebron Rescue Squad. That took care of most ground emergencies that might occur. In the event a jumper was in some sort of trouble, we had immediate action plans to match the problem. An example. In the event a jumper got hung up on exit, the Jump Master would declare an emergency. The pilot would immediately fly our Jumper's in Trouble Pattern. In addition he would radio the airport. Depending on the wind direction, the pilot flew into the wind following one of our designated emergency roads. This pattern was only used in emergencies. Anyone seeing the aircraft flying that pattern knew a jumper was in trouble. Immediately our emergency vehicle would be dispatched.

I put Roberto in the aircraft first. He would be the second static line jumper out of the plane. I got in second and sat beside him. Heavy Drop was instructed to back up to the aircraft door so I could hook up his static line. He then sat on the aircraft floor in front of me. We took off and flew to 2800 feet static line jump altitude.

"Get out!" Was the command as I pointed to the aircraft step. For a large man, heavy drop got out quite fast. He stood on the aircraft step and wheel, hanging onto the strut looking straight ahead. He didn't blink an eye. "Go!" His exit was good. However, his canopy maneuvering was poor. The jumper made no attempt to steer to the target nor showdown for landing.

The amount of force a jumper hits the ground with is determined by the velocity of the wind plus the speed generated by the parachutes modification. The descent of the chute forces wind out the modification (holes we purposely cut into the rear of the canopy). This gives the parachute a built in forward speed. We also attach two control lines to give the jumper absolute control. Pulling on the right line, the parachute will turn to the right. Pulling on the left line, the parachute will go left. The parachute will continue turning in whatever direction as long as the control line is pulled. A 360° turn is possible.

This same parachute speed can also be used as braking device. Say the wind is 15 mph and the canopy speed is 10 mph. Turning the parachute so you are facing, the wind will result in the landing of 5 mph. Heavy Drop didn't attempt to use the control lines. He rode it to the ground. In spite of this error he landed 12 feet from the target center. He received a slight sprain of his right ankle.

I hooked up Roberto's static line and directed him to the floor in front of me. He seemed a little nervous. I grabbed his head and turned it so he could see me.

"Sure you want to do this?" Roberto nodded his head affirmative.

"Get out!" With some hesitation Roberto climbed out on the step.

"Go!" As fast as lightning, Roberto turned and grabbed the static line.

"We have an emergency! Jumper hung up." Bob started flying our 'Jumper in Trouble Pattern. A bad situation. I had a jumper refusing to jump. Hanging onto the static line for dear life. The static line was hooked to a "D" ring on my harness.

I had two options. Try to pull the jumper back into the aircraft. Or jump and pull. The force of my chute opening would jerk Roberto's static line out of his hands, allowing his static line (still attached to me) to deploy his chute. I used my first option, with a slight modification. I had a firm grip on Roberto's harness. Without a little help from him, there was no way I could get the lad back in the aircraft.

"Fly 150 feet north of the road." Were my instructions to Bob. "I've got you lad. Leave go of the static line." His eyes were four times greater than normal. "Let go of the static line!" Roberto let go. With all the strength I could muster, I pushed Roberto away from the plane.

"Go!" We circled following the jumper all the way down. By the time Roberto landed the ground crew was on site. It was good to see our emergency plan worked so well. Bob and I needed a break. After we finished our coke, we headed back to the aircraft. Bill Mellor had Roberto chuted up.

"Mac, Roberto says he can do better. OK with you?"

"Sure, who am I to stop a man from doing better." The second jump was letter perfect. Roberto Johanson went on to be a very good jumper and a loyal member. His help with students, especially slightly nervous students, was unmatched.

Interrogative

"Sign here, please." The postman requested. "The sender requested a signature."

The letter was from the Illinois Court. The letter ordered me to appear at the Court to answer interrogatives. I didn't know what an interrogative meant. I was kind of shook up.

"Charlie, take a look at this?" Charlie Blumster wasn't a lawyer. However, he worked for the State of Illinois Legal Aid. Charlie was in and out of court quit often.

"Your being sued Mac. I can't believe Heavy Drop is suing you. All they are asking you, come to the Court and answer some questions.

"Do you know any good, inexpensive lawyers, Charlie?"

"Let me take that summons to work and ask an Attorney what we should do."

I'm purposely not using Heavy Drops name in this story. He might read it and sue me again. Start making a little money and everybody wants part of the action. Whare were they, when things weren't going so well? It seems to me people are sue-crazy. I have to admit this summons had me a little worried.

Suddenly a story Vivian told me came to mind. Vivian told me a client came to her law office bragging about the amount of money he was going to get from an injury he received at an airport. Pointing to his bandaged ankle with his cane,

"You're looking at a few hundred thousand-dollar Vivian." Vivian didn't associate his story with our airport, nor did I. In fact I put it out of my mind until now.

"Hi Mac. I called to see if you are going to be in the office for a while?"

"Sure, I'll be in all afternoon. What's up Charlie?"

"Tell you when I get there. Have to run now." Charlie didn't keep me waiting long. In less than an hour he was parking his state-owned vehicle in front of our school on Milwaukee Avenue. He wasn't alone.

"Mac this is Jim Atworthy. Jim is an attorney for Legal Aid. Jim this is Dan McGinley, owner of Land of Lincoln." We shook hands. As a matter of fact, that's not all that was shaken. I was really concerned about the pending law suit. Jim got right down to business. He asked for Heavy Drops application and any training records on file. After a long silence,

"Are there any witnesses. People who observed the jump up close?"

"We had 40 to 50 people on the ground and two in the aircraft the yo-yo jumped from." I replied

"That's good. Will any of them give you a written statement?"

"Sure, they all will." Was my rapid reply.

"I don't think so. You'll find people are funny about giving statements. They don't wont to get involved. You'll be lucky to get five or ten." Then Charlie jumped in,

"Not this group Jim. Land of Lincoln members are close. Mac could probably get statements from members that weren't even at the airport." After another short period of silence,

"You will not be needing an attorney Mac."

I liked hearing the words, but it didn't help my worrying. I have never been sued before and wasn't looking foreword to the court proceedings. Jim Atworthy gave me a list of things I should accomplish before my court date.

He suggested I get all the notarized witness statements I could. Bring all the documentation I had attesting to my capabilities of running a Jump Center. He suggested a letter from the FAA (Federal Aviation Administration) and the PCA (Parachute Club of America) would help.

That was no problem. I was a certified FAA Parachute Rigger and FAA Parachute Loft Owner / Manager. In addition Oldrich Olchivick and I both gave our views when the FAA upgraded Part 5 of the FAA's regulation covering Sport Parachuting. In addition Olchivick was the Area and I the club's Safety Officers, appointed by the Parachute Club of America. Oldrich and I were called on as expert witnesses on many parachute-accident investigations.

I was also to bring all Heavy Drops training records, application, and hold harmless agreement. As Jim stated, the hold harmless agreement isn't worth the paper it's printed on. The Courts won't let an individual sign their rights away. However it shows intent and indicates the student is aware the activity they are engaging in may be dangerous if caution was not observed.

I arrived early wearing a suit and tie and carrying an attaché case with one folder in it. A few minutes later, Heavy Drop arrived with three lawyers. The clown was in a wheelchair with his leg in a cast. Finally our case was called. Standing in front of the judge wasn't that bad. My nerves settled down.

"Mr. McGinley is your Lawyer present?" Asked the judge.

'No your honor. I won't be needing a Lawyer. I have full confidence in the decision of this court." Jim Atworthy told me to say that.

"The court appreciates your confidence Mr. McGinley. Never the less I strongly advise you engage an attorney."

Heavy Drops Attorneys stated their client suffered severe bodily injuries do to faulty equipment and unsafe conditions. They also stated their client suffered unmeasurable mental anguish when he was tricked into leaving an airplane in flight.

"Your honor, the bodily injury will heal in a short time. The mental trauma will linger for many years to come. We ask the court to award damages to compensate our client's inhumane treatment and gross negligence by Land of Lincoln Sky Divers Incorporated."

"What is your response Mr. McGinley?"

"Your Honor, something is wrong here. This gentleman didn't receive injuries that would require a cast and a wheelchair. He received a very simple sprain. To avoid him from getting injured, we had him use an extra large parachute. Although he did nothing to steer the parachute, the wind was so gentle, injury of the magnitude they clam, would be impossible."

"Your honor, does Mr. McGinley claim to be an expert on injury?"

"You don't have to answer that Mr. McGinley. I'm prepared to continue this case for 10 days. That will afford you time to retain an attorney."

"Your honor, the US Army thinks I'm an expert. I have been a medic in two wars. World War II and Korea."

"I have heard enough. This is just a preliminary hearing. I'll hear this case on 15 August. Mr. McGinley, I advise you to seek advice from an attorney." The gavel came down. The hearing was over.

I waited for the second elevator. I didn't want to be any place near my friend in the wheelchair. I might make it his permanent method of transportation. One of Heavy Drops attorneys also waited.

"Can I buy you a cup of coffee Mr. McGinley?"

"No thank you. You better save your money. You won't be making any money on this case."

"Our client is an outstanding individual. We have a good case."

"Your client is a phoney. He's pulling wool over your eyes." We continued our conversation in the lobby. Do you want to add a piece of apple pie to your coffee offer?" He agreed.

We talked for the better part of an hour. I gave him a mini course on Sport Parachuting. He was surprised his client had a fully opened chute on landing. When I told him Heavy Drop played a few games of bad-mitten after the jump he really looked upset.

"Why don't you have a lawyer Mr. McGinley?"

"I have a lawyer. He's sitting on the side line. This case is too small for him. He tells me what to do and not to do."

A few days later Heavy Drop was in Vivien's office again. This time without his cane. My pal Vivian engaged him in a tell all conversation. He admitted he wasn't injured. He also said it was his brother-in-law, the lawyer he worked for, that gave hin the idea about a lawsuit. This guy was a clerk for a small law firm. Vivian's company of Income Tax Lawyers did their returns.

I looked foreword to going back to court. I couldn't believe it. Just two weeks ago I was worried sick about going to court. Now on the 15th of August I can't wait for the court to open. Heavy Drop and two of his lawyers joined me.

"Good morning gentlemen." I started shaking their hands. "Isn't this a great day to lose a case?" They all gave me a strange look. The court opened and our case was first on the docket.

"Good morning gentlemen." Everyone returned the judges greeting.

"Mr. McGinley, have you retained an attorney?"

"No your Honor, I haven't. I don't think I will need one." The judge read the complaint from the court transcript. Then asked if they were correct. Heavy Drops attorneys agreed they were.

"As I remember Mr. McGinley, you were responding to the charges."

"Yes sir. Many things have been revealed since our last appearance."

I proceeded to unmask Heavy Drop. I told the judge the exact story Vivian told me. I emphasized the fact Heavy Drop was walking without a cane. And that his lawyer brother-in-law talked him intoa lawsuit against Land of Lincoln.

"Your Honor, this man admitted he wasn't injured. I have a notarized statement to that fact. I also have **35** notarized statements of eye wittiness who observed the plaintiffs jump. Thirty-three from the ground and two from the aircraft. In addition sir, I have a picture of the plaintiff playing bad-mitten after his so called horrible injury."

I laid all my documents on the bench to include a picture of Bridget in a bikini playing bad-mitten with Heavy Drop. The picture was the weakest evidence. No one would feel pain playing bad-mitten with Bridget. Especially if she was wearing her bikini.

"Your Honor, may we have a 10 minute recess?" Heavy Drops attorney requested.

"We will recess for five minutes." The gavel slammed down. I think the judge was mad. In about three minutes we were back. Standing in front of the man with the power.

"Your Honor, my client wish is to withdraw the law suit."

"Mr. McGinley, you're correct, you don't need a lawyer. Case dismissed."

Mr Juice Man

To help meet the expenses of maintaining a Sport Parachute Center I would quite often look for a job during the winter months. During the winter of 1966, I worked for Island of Snow Juice Company. My Route was on Chicago's near west side. Rumor control had it that Martin Luther King was bringing his civil rights crusade to Chicago. He vowed to wage war on slums and inequality during his first Northern Crusade.

1550 S. Hamlin
Chicago Illinois

On January 26, 1966, Rev King and his associates from the Southern Christian Leadership Conference moved into 1550 S Hamlin Ave. The apartment was chosen as a typical, West Side ghetto apartment. At this point in time I had no idea who Martin Luther King was, nor how famous he would become.

The newspapers reported that King occupied a $90 a-month, four-room apartment on the third floor. They also reported that when the landlord discovered that the civil rights leader intended to use the apartment, he had an eight-man crew refurbish it, against Rev Kings wishes. Not quite accurate. Kings associates supervised the remodeling of the whole building, two months before the move in.

I had customers at that address and they were thrown out of the building and relocated four or five buildings south. The King group occupied the whole building, not just the third floor. King and his family lived on the third floor. His administrative personnel occupied the second floor and his large security force occupied the first floor.

My orange juice route took me past the construction daily. I watched the decayed building slowly emerge to a spotless gem. Living with the poor is fine if you don't have to live like the poor. This whole process struck me as phoney. It didn't seem to bother them, they uprooted six families. When the building was finally occupied in 26 January 1966, I knocked on the front door to see if they needed any of my product. I promptly was advised that all solicitations and deliveries had to be made at the rear door. I couldn't believe it, here I was working in the ghetto and they were acting like high society

The new tenant ordered a lot of orange juice and seemed to like our product. Now getting them to pay for the product was another thing. After trying to collect several times, I finally had to put my foot down and demand payment. I have to admit I get a little loud when I'm upset. Anyone trying to cheat me out of what is rightfully mine, upsets me, the most. This argument involved Kings security guard and got louder and louder. It really didn't matter to me that I was outnumbered and in a hostile environment. The fact that most of them were armed didn't even enter my game plan to collect what was mine.

"Mr. juice man, you know we are only fooling with you," one of the guards announced. At the same time the rest of the security guards became quiet.

"I pulled this one off, I told myself, then I saw the reason for their change of attitude. Dr. King had come down stairs to see what all the commotion was about.

'What's the problem here?" He asked..

I told him, his clowns were trying to cheat me out of money owed. "Pay this man," King ordered, and give him an additional ten spot for his trouble." The long and short of it was, I got paid what was owed. From that day on, I delivered the juice to the front door, on a pay as you go basis.

I had delivered orange juice in this poor neighborhoods for some time. I have never been cheated by any of my poor customers. I believe basically most people are honest. I also believe all of us desire a lot more than we can afford. In the poor manes case, his money runes out sooner than his desire, leaving the impression they are trying to cheat. I had no problem extending credit to my customers. I had no problem being at their homes late evenings hours on their payday to collect monies owed. It is a simple fact, the first one in line will be paid. Your chances on getting paid diminish proportionally with the number of collectors in front of you.

My short encounter with Dr. King impressed me. There was something about his mannerism that earned respect. His rise to prominence through the years didn't surprise me. Surely this was an outstanding American whose ancestors were from Africa. When his life was taken, I was sad.

Something Wrong

I never thought the day would come when I would do more flying than jumping, but it did. Armed with a learning permit, I was ready to fly anything that had wings. Now don't misjudge me and think I'm a bragger. The fact is, I was very good at takeoffs and landings. That's about all I ever did. Over and over again, takeoffs and landings. However when I got five miles or more from the airport, I got lost. Navigation was not on the list of things I did well.

Many of Land of Lincoln's jumpers liked to come to our Jump Center during the week. Not burdened by students burden, they could hone their own jumping skills. The fact that it was hard to get a pilot, during the week was never a problem. Without fail, a Phantom Pilot would suddenly appear. Some say the Phantom, looked like me.

Some sports put a strain on marriages, if the spouse is not also participating in the sport. Gulf, rock climbing, hunting, and fishing are classic examples. Sky Diving can be added to this list that can turn a wife into weekend widow,. Surly a source of unrest.

One of our members was having domestic problems. I'll not mention his name at this point. I think they are back together. It's better to leave well enough alone. Telling this story, I will call him Jim.

Jim's wife packed all her belongings and went home to Pennsylvania. I got along good with his wife Dora. Many times she requested my opinion on personal matters, knowing they would be kept between her and I. So when Jim asked me to accompany him to Pennsylvania and help persuade her to come back to Illinois, I wasn't surprised.

"Dan if you fly me to Johnstown Pennsylvania I'll pay all the expenses." A long cross country was very tempting, I jumped at the chance. I was really getting into this flying thing. Dale Kosack asked if he could join us;

"Sure why not, you can be the stewardess." I jokingly replied.

As I stated before, navigation is not on my list of talents. Map reading was, using Road Maps in place of Aeronautical Charts, should not be hard to understand. The way I figured it, the Engineers that built the roads must have known what they were doing. I started plotting my course on a Road Atlas.

To avoid flying around Chicago, I decided to head for the Great Lakes Navel Training Center, on the shores of Lake Michigan. Lake Michigan third largest of the GREAT LAKES, fifth largest lake in the world. It is 307 mi long and 30-120 mi wide and a maximum depth of 923 ft

Because of Lake Michigan's size, the FAA required pilots to file a Flight Plan. Flight Plans can be filed at any time in person or by phone. To activate (open) the plan, you must radio the FAA advising them of your exact starting time, type of aircraft and destination.

During the flight over large bodies of water, pilots are required to radio their status every twenty minutes. In turn the FAA will mark your location on a chart. Failure to call the FAA will automatically trigger an Air-Sea Rescue search. The search will start at your last reported location. If they find you in the water, no problem. But if you arrived at your destination but forgot to cancel (close) your Flight Plan, guess what? You pay for the search plus whatever other penalty they might decide on.

About three minutes out I called the FAA Control at O'Hare International, and opened the Flight Plan I had filed earlier.

"FAA Control, 6565 Echo. Open Flight Plan 074." Number 074 I was assigned earlier.

"Roger 6565 Echo, 074 Iopen. Reporting station O'Hare Tower. They gave me a frequence to monitor and report to. Every twenty minutes I reported;

"O'Hare Tower, 6565 Echo, high and dry."

From the Great Lakes Navel Training Center I plotted a course to South Bend Indiana. The nervous lake crossing began. It was a clear day, flying conditions couldn't have been better. Everything was going great until we reached the point of our flight when I couldn't see a shore line on either side or in front of me. I got to the point where I looked for ships. If we were to go down, I thought it might be a good thing to crash land as close to a ship as possible. I was glad when it came time to check in. It took my mind off horrible thoughts.

"O'Hare Tower, 6565 Echo, high and dry."

" Roger 6565 Echo. Turning you over to Fort Wayne Tower. Enjoy your flight."

O'Hare gave me Fort Wayne's frequency. Twenty minutes later I started my radio relationship with another FAA Tower. Finally a beautiful sight, Indiana Sand Dunes, in all its glory, straight ahead. As I approached South Bend I radioed the FAA and closed my Flight Plan. I was over land now. My shy as a lamb attitude, which developed while I was over water, was replaced with my normal cocky attitude. From South Bend we headed for Fort Wayne Indiana and then Pittsburgh, Pennsylvania.

I like a lot of gas in my tanks when I'm flying. I look at a half full tank as, half empty. Traveling over the rough, thickly wooded, mountainous Pennsylvania terrain increased the desire for a fill tank. I could hear the radio traffic at Pittsburgh International but didn't have them in sight.

"Pittsburgh International, 6565 Echo."

"65 Echo, Pittsburgh International, what's your intention, Go."

"Pittsburgh, I would like to refuel. I do not have you in sight. "

"65 Echo, turn right, turn left. I complied. "65 Echo I have you 5 miles south of our location."

"Pittsburgh, I'm sorry I do not see you. I'm a student Pilot maybe I'm missing something."

"You're a what?" I repeated the fact that I was a student Pilot. "6565 Echo, turn your head to your left, now look down." Holy mackerel Plaines were flying all over the place. I found out latter Pittsburgh International, was the third busiest airport in the US.

Looking out left side window   Looking out and down

"65 Echo what is your intention?"

"Pittsburgh Tower, I'm coming down to gas up."

"65 Echo, don't be nervous. You are cleared to land on runway 33, wind out of the West at 12mph. If you prefer you can use runway 27, we will hold traffic."

What the heck is this guy talking about, nervous. He apparently doesn't know he is talking to one of the world's greatest airplane landers. I may not do a great job finding airports, but once found, my landing skills take over.

"Pittsburgh Tower, runway 33 will do fine." I had a runway 33 back at Hebron Airport.

"65 Echo, switch over to ground control (he gave me the frequency). When your aircraft is secure 65 Echo, would you mind stopping by the Tower? You have made our day. We will send a car for you." Of course I agreed, I like VIP treatment. It's the Ham in me.

"Pittsburgh Ground Control, 6565 Echo."

"6565 Echo, Pittsburgh Ground, good landing. We have been waiting for you. Take the East Taxiway to the Tie Down Area. A government Car will pick you up. Be careful, America Airlines loading." Another guy doesn't know who he is talking to. I could taxi circles around that American Airline plane, that was loading from the ground. Then a terrible thought. How am I going to explain passengers? Student pilots are not allowed to have passengers.

As soon as I entered the Tie down Area, I instructed Jim and Dale to get out and start walking to the terminal. I know sooner tied the aircraft down, when the government car arrived.

"Good afternoon, I'm supposed to give you a ride to the Tower." I thanked him and jumped in the front seat. Halfway down the taxiway, we caught up to, my clandestine passengers.

"Slow down driver." Hanging my head out the window, "You guys need a lift?"

Dale and Jim got into the rear seat. All the way to the Terminal we conversed as though we were strangers. I have seen worse actors nominated for the Academy Award. Dropping our passengers at the Terminal, the driver and I continue to the Control Tower. As soon as I got off the elevator the friendly greetings started.

They restated that I had made their day. Student pilots are encouraged to use busy airfields but most shy away. When I asked why, they couldn't tell me. When a new flyer decides to use their facility, a certain amount of excitement fills their day. I thought about that for a while. Maybe new students are given too much knowledge about busy airfields, and it frightens them or at the least makes them shy away. I'm not smart enough to be scared and never have been shy. After a short tour of the tower, I said my goodbys.

"Give us a call when you are ready to go to your aircraft. We will drive you back to the tie down area.." I thanked them.

After a quick lunch with Jim and Dale, I called for transportation. Like before my pals were walking along the Taxi way and like before, I asked them if they needed a ride. When the car was out of sight, we boarded the plane.

"Pittsburgh Tower, 6565 Echo permission to taxi."

"6565 Echo, taxi to end of 270. Follow United Airlines.

"Pittsburgh Tower, 6565 Echo Negative United Airlines. Request permission to follow Twin Beach on Taxi way." I had read a lot about Jet Aircraft creating Vortex on the runway during their take off. I wanted a prop driven aircraft to break up any possible problems.

"65 Echo, permission granted. Follow Twin., hold short of runway. We followed the Twin Beach and held short. Th United Airlines took off followed by the twin Beach. We were given permission for immediate take off. I turned on the main runway and applied full power. Goodby Pittsburgh International. Then a horrible thought, I forgot to top off my gas tanks.

"Pittsburgh International 6565 Echo. Permission to leave pattern on 090 heading. I was taking off to the West and wanted to change direction to the East without flying their long pattern.

"65 Echo, roger 090 heading. Thanks for making our day. Pay us another visit.

I was told at Pittsburgh to use Runway 27 when I landed at Johnstown. I was also told to land with a little power to override the updraft at the end of the runway. There was a steep drop off at the end of approach 27. I followed instruction and landed without incident. The meeting with Dora produced mixed results. She promised to come back to Chicago in thirty days. Of course Jim wanted her to fly back with us. That was not to be.

I had enough of flying over large bodies of water to last for a while. On the way home I plotted my course from Johnstown to Colombus Ohio, then Hammond Indiana. I made a wide circle around Chicago to avoid O'Hare Traffic then I headed for Gault Airport.

By this time darkness had snuck up on us. I didn't have enough sense to be nervous. Flying around Chicago at night was beautiful. The auto lights, traffic lights, street and building lights made Chicago look like a Christmas Tree. Suddenly, there it was in front of me   Pal Waukee Airport, my last check point. A slight turn to the north and I was headed home.

It was at this point I started asking myself some concerning questions. How am I going to see to land?   How will I determine which way the wind is coming from?   Then the question without an answer. What am I doing flying at night with passengers?   Truly my concern was for my passengers. I was an extraordinary lucky person. I think it had something to do with being Irish. Jim's luck hasn't been too good lately, and Dale seemed to be accident prone.

Then I remembered Art Gault had his runway lights rigged to be turned on by radio frequency. A click of the mike and the runway lights would turn on and remain on for thirty minutes. I could see a storm beginning far on the horizon. That would generate westerly winds. That left the unanswerable question. What am I doing flying, at night with passengers? I figured two answers out of three wasn't bad.

I maintained seven thousand feet until I got a lot closer. Altitude, especially at night is your friend. I was sure I spotted the town of Hebron on the horizon. Now the only question where is Gault Airport? Then came the dawn. Turn the runway lights on. I clicked the hand mike, oops wrong frequency. I made the correction. Clicked the hand set and there she was, a jewel sparkling in the night.

It was my first night landing, but it was a good one. During the whole landing process for some reason or another, my passengers were quiet as a mouse. I taxied to the wash area, didn't want to put this baby to bed dirty. If I waited until morning, the work load would have been all mine. Not being a selfish person, I wanted to share. After her bath we pushed 6565 Echo into her hanger. When nobody was looking, I kissed her nosecone and whispered,

"Great job sweetheart."

I learned a lot during our long cross country flight to Johnstown. The paramount lesson, I needed a lot more knowledge about flying. I signed up for Gault's Advanced Ground School. I finished the course, scoring 100. No surprise, I studied hard and did each assignment several times.

"Art, when is the FAA Examiner coming to test your students?"

"Next Monday Mac, thinking about getting your licence? I answered in the affirmative.

You only have to have forty hours solo time to take a Privet Pilot Examination. A couple of hours under the hood (simulating instrument flying), a few cross country flights and, an instructor to certify the requirements. After you pass a check out ride, with an FAA Examiner, you have earned your Private Pilot Licence, in the class of airplane you took your test in.

Qualifying for a pilot licence is largely on the honor system. Your cross country flights are verified by a licenced piolet signing your log book, at the distant airport. Your daily practice building up solo time, doesn't have to be verified. Stupidly, many students add flying time they haven't made. They are misguided thinking they will look better to the Flight Examiner.

Say you go for your check out ride, with one hundred hours logged. Let's further state that sixty of the hours are phoney. You have just shot yourself in the foot. That examiner is expecting to see one hundred hours of experience. Your phoney hours will not fool him. A better plan would be to have more hours under your belt then you have logged. A student with forty hours logged but flying like a pilot with one hundred hours surely will be in your favor. When I went for my check out ride with the FAA, I had more than two hundred hours. I had only logged fifty. Keep in mind most of my hours were bootleg, acquired before I had a learner permit.

I arrived at the airport about an hour before my test flight. Shortly after, a US Government car pulled into the parking lot. Getting out of the vehicle was the same FAA examiner that caught me flying a few months earlier. If he remembers me, my goose was cooked.

"Good morning, great day for flying." Was my greeting.

"It sure is." He replied..

After a few questions during our pre-flight, we took off for the test flight. We did a few power-on and power-off stalls. He gave me a few compass headings. After successful execution, he pulled the oldest trick in the book.

"Fly into that cloud, I want to check your reactions under instrument conditions."

"No thank you, student pilots are not allowed near clouds."

"It's OK, you have my permission. Fly into that large cloud to our right." Again I refused.

"What's the problem?" He asked.

"You might be an examiner, but you don't have the authority to change the rules." He smiled and we landed. The test was over.

Over coffee I told him what I thought about him trying to trick a student to violate. A younger student might be intimidated by his position and be talked into violating the, "stay clear of clouds rule." I told him it was like entrapment and not good for relationships between the government and the flying public. Far too often, government employees think they are the government. Not true, they are employees, they work for you and me.

In less than a week I had my Pilot (Single Engine Land) Licence. Being legal didn't make me a better pilot. It just made me legitimate. To tell you the truth it took a lot of the thrill out of flying. Oh well, I'll just have to live with it. The phantom pilot has been unmasked.

All flying is great. Some just have special elements that make them more memorable. We were returning from a cross country. Ken Haffer was flying. Ken needed to build hours for his Commercial Licence. A little south of Indianapolis Indiana the whole plane shook violently. Needles to say it got our undivided attention. Ken applied a little carburetor-heat which seemed to clear it up a little. A short while later the violent shock struck again.

The decision to land at Indianapolis was easy to make. We checked into a Holiday Inn and left a call at the desk to wake us early. Not being able to sleep I went back to the airport and looked for a mechanic. An extensive examination of the aircraft failed to turn up the cause for our trouble. The closest the mechanic could come up with was carburetor icing. That was our original thought. We probably didn't leave the carburetor heat on long enough.

The weather was deteriorating by the minute. I was busy putting my new found skills to work. Frantically I was searching the charts for an airport. Kankakee Airport wasn't that far. As navigator I chose Kankakee. I grew up in Saint Anne Illinois and I knew the Airport was on the Kankakee River. Visibility was less than a mile we were in deep trouble.

"Follow that river Ken. When you get to a large bend, make a ninety degree turn to the left, give her full flaps and land this baby." Ken didn't question my directions. I had convinced him I knew the area. We came to the bend. Ken's left turn, put us dead center of runway 270. It was extremely hazy, but the airport was in sight.

It was a fast-moving front. In less than an hour the sun came popping through. While I was fueling, Ken went to check the weather.

"We are all set Mac, shouldn't have any problems."

"What about the clouds west of town? Looks like another storm front."

"We will be home before it arrives." I had a lot of respect for Ken's flying, and had no cause to doubt him. We took off and headed for Chicago.

In less than an hour we were socked in. Visibility was zero. At one hundred feet we could barely see the ground. I was worried about the many towers indicated on the chart. We needed to land, and land now. The conditions forced me to revert back to my road navigation techniques. The chart indicated a private airport off a two-lane road. I spotted the road then the grass strip.

"Make a left and land Ken." Ken made the turn in a timely manor but couldn't land. The cross wind was extremely high. Ken froze. I took over the control of the aircraft. We were going to land, a crash-landing maybe, but we were going to land. From this point on we were on instruments. Relying fully on the aircraft instruments, we went around for another approach.

I could barely see the grass runway. No matter, we were going in. I came in with power on, right wing tipped into the cross wind. As soon as I felt the ground, I turned the engine off. 65 Echo dug into the water-soaked sod. I thanked God and saved a little thanks for my pal 6565 Echo. After taking a few minutes to recover, Ken and I headed for the hanger like building at the end of the runway. The door was open so we walked in.

A Walk With Giants 1957 - 1974

"What are you guys doing here?" It was apparent, we startled the occupants.

"We just landed on your airstrip"

"This is a private strip. You can't land here."

"There is no such thing as a private landing strip during a storm buster. If there is any damage to your property I'll pay for it."

I decided not to ask for a ride to town. I don't like to ask favors of people I don't like. After a bite to eat we hired a car to drive us back to Hebron Airport. Ken went home looking very sad. It was obvious, he was ashamed of losing it on landing. I headed for Bob Arnold's home. I needed a better pilot to get 65 Echo out of that field than the one that put her in.

Bob got a kick out of the story. The next day at sunup, we loaded a truck up with ten inch wide planks, a couple of rope pulleys and went about our recovery mission. There she was, a little dirty but otherwise in good shape. I can't prove it, I swear, 6565 Echo smiled when she saw us. Surprisingly we backed the plane out the same way it went in. With the help of ropes we inched the aircraft back a little at a time. We cleaned about ten tons of mud off the landing gear.

We checked the prop out thoroughly. The engine started without hesitation. In two hours Bob was flying 65 Echo home. I left a note on the hanger door to contact me to pay for any damage to the runway. I drove the truck back to Hebron. The old saying, "if you're in a hurry don't fly." Proved to be true.

Growing Pains

To stay in business the business has to show a reasonable profit. The Sky Diving business is no different. An additional problem in the Sky Diving business is you are working with high cost items. Airplanes, fuel to run them, the cost of maintenance and inspections, all high ticket items. Add the cost of property (airport and/or drop zone) to conduct your operation and the cost of parachute equipment. All will make a normal person think twice before engaging in Sky Diving as a business. But then I have never considered myself normal, therefore it didn't stop me.

The student, beginner jumpers, is where the profit is, if there is going to be a profit. They pay more for their jumps and it doesn't take all day to reach jump altitude. As soon as they advance to free fall jump status, the cost skyrockets in direct proportion to the length of their free fall. For that reason it never bothered me if an advanced student left Land of Lincoln and went to another jump center.

However, the jumpers who stayed with Land of Lincoln and helped with the students, created a situation that obligated me to help them get the necessary jumps to qualify for different type of Sport Parachuting License. That included longer free fall delays (30 to 60 second), night and water jumps. In addition to that if they were to advance in their chosen sport, they would need to engage in competition jumping and relative (jumping with other jumpers) work. Bottom line we needed to put more jumpers in the air at the same time. The search for another aircraft began.

A guy in Amarillo Texas, who I am going to call Dan Blue (not his real name) advertised two airplanes for sale. One would carry twelve jumpers and the other six. Although they were both very old planes, it didn't matter. His claim was they were both freshly overhauled and in top shape. Aircraft are judged by how many hours since their last major overhaul. FAA regulations require all damage and repairs be logged in the aircrafts log book and certified by a licenced aircraft mechanic.

Although the twelve jumper plane sounded tempting, it was out of our budget range. The six jumper was more in line. At present our jump plane carried three jumpers. Six would double our jump load. I decided to take a trip to Texas and look at the 1940 Gull Wing Stinson. If it showed any promise, Bob Arnold would fly down by Commercial Air and fly the Gull Wing back to Hebron Airport.

I have never passed up an opportunity to make a buck. I answered a newspaper-add to, drive a Cadillac to Amarillo Texas. The owner would pay one hundred dollars plus pay for all the gas. In addition he would allow six days to make the trip. I jumped at the offer. This provided me with free transportation and the use of the auto for a couple of days. Ken Rorheim offered to go with me. This was no surprise Ken was Johnny on the spot if you ever needed help. Unfortunately for Land of Lincoln Sky Divers, this would be Ken's last help mission. Ken joined the Air Force. Soon after Ken was selected to join the Air Force Parachute Team. He made demonstration and competition jumps all over Europe and the Far East. Ken was a credit to his country and the sport of Sky Diving. Again no surprise, giants are achievers.

We lost a lot of members to the armed services in 1967. The Vietnam war triggered the patriotic feeling in our Giants. Along with Ken (Air Force), Bud Bemmet (Army), Bud Henry (West Point), David & Robert (Marine Corps), Art Liskie Phil Kerrigen, Paul Slazak, and Bill Gates went to (Special Forces.) I am sorry to admit there were more whose name I can't recall. Back to our trip;

We drove nonstop to Amarillo Texas and checked into a motel close to the airport. After making contact with the aircrafts's owner to meet with him the following day, Ken and I headed for the airport to get a sneak preview of the vintage Gull Wing.

I was surprised to see a large hanger with a sign stating it belonged to The Moody Bible Institute. Moody Bible was a Christian College on Chicago's near north side. I was familiar with the school. My brother Jack was a student at Moody, and he managed their Book Store. I entered the huge hanger in the hopes of getting information about the airplanes for sale.

I introduced myself to the shop foreman and told him about my brother being a student at Moody's. I told him of my surprise to see Moody had its own airplane. He promptly replied they had several aircraft. The Amarillo operation was their fleet maintenance section. They took care of all aircraft supporting Moody's mission throughout the world. The shop foreman was very friendly. When I asked about the Gull Wing Stinson, he told me it was behind the hanger. He was quick to point out that Moody nor he had anything to do with the plane. I was eager to see the vintage aircraft. I almost ran out of the hanger.

1940 Gull Wing Stinson

Some might say it was the ugliest plane they have ever seen. I would be the first to agree. The dull faded green would never win any beauty contest. But looking beyond that, I saw a beautiful flying bird. One look at the shape of her wings, I understood where the name, Gull Wing came from. They're so named because of the unique wing construction that puts a hump in the wing about a quarter span outboard, combined with the beautifully tapered wing profile. The entire aircraft was made of canvas, which trembled slightly when touched, (like the surface of a taut drum.) It was love at first sight, a love that would be short lived.

I was pleased to find the large doors were not locked. Opening them revealed a plush leather interior. The back seat could accommodate three adults, with room to spare. Attached to the rear of the front seats were two additional fold down seats. The abundant leg room added to its majesty. I had to climb three stairs to enter the

cockpit. The woodgrain dash was loaded with instruments and radios. Surely this was the Cadillac of airplanes in her day. In my mind's eye I could visualize a new paint job and the Land of Lincoln logo proudly displayed on her sides. This plane was going to be mine, even if I had to tow her home.

"Are you thinking of purchasing the Gull Wing?" Moody's foremen asked.

"Yes I am. It will make a great Jump Plane."

"Be careful. Dan Blue is a slick dealer. Study the plane's log books." He went on to explain.

The owner who happened to be the local Weather Forecaster was a religious man. He wouldn't cheat any one of his religion. All others better look out. I immediately dismissed his statement. I didn't want to get involved in a "my religion is better than you religion debate." This guy knew a lot about the Stinson. He went on to explain it was powered with a Lycoming 680, 9-cylinder, 300 HP, Radial Engine. The 43' 3" wing span was great for heavy loads. The aircraft was 27" long and 8' 5" high. She looked like a baby airliner. The 18 gallons per hour fuel consumption gave me very little concern. I figured the pay load would justify the consumption.

We had a face to face meeting with Mr. Dan Blue at 12:30. He listed all the repairs he made to the Gull Wing and asked if I wanted to see the plane's log books. When I answered in the affirmative, he stated he would bring them to the airport tomorrow. Strange I thought, aircraft log books are to remain with the plane. This was the first of many strange things I would encounter with Mr. Dan Blue.

"Mr. Blue, I know you are asking five thousand for the Gull Wing, it's probably worth every cent of that. 1 have a cashier check for four thousand. If the plane checks out, that's my offer."

To my surprise he agreed. I went on to explain. Bob Arnold could be in Amarillo in two days for the check out ride. Again he agreed. Ken and I went back to the motel and called Hebron Airport. Bob sounded almost as excited as we were. Dale Kosack would take Bob to O'Hare Airport for his trip to Texas. This would be the longest two-day wait in my life. I didn't know Dan Blue other than he was a Cheap Charlie. Didn't even offer to by a cup of coffee. We don't do business like that back in Illinois.

Upon Bob's arrival, I called Dan Blue. He stated he couldn't make it today but would try for the next day. I couldn't believe the delay. Maybe he is having second thoughts about selling. His tomorrow came and went. In fact, his procrastination caused a couple of tomorrow's to cone and go. I got fed up and went to his TV Station and gave Blue one last chance.

"We fly that Gull Wing tomorrow at 08:00 or Bob, Ken and I were leaving on the 10:00 Flight to Chicago." He became very apologetic, and offered to take the checkout flight in one hour.

"We are on my schedule now Blue, not yours. Tomorrow at 08:00." Dan Blue was very close to losing the sale of his aircraft. Bob and I arrived at the Airport at 07:30. Dan Blue was waiting for us.

"Did you bring the log books Dan?"

"Oh! I forgot, they're on my desk back at the station."What's your problem Blue? You act like you're afraid of a check out ride. This old goose fly's doesn't she?" With that he started the pre-flight.

Everything he did was in slow motion. He wanted to show me how clean the oil was. I wasn't interested. I checked the oil three day's ago. He attempted to show how clear and free of water, the gas was. I showed no interest. That also was checked three days ago. Finally we were on the taxiway, heading for the active runway. That also took a long time

All tail-draggers are taxied making "S" turns in order for the pilot to see what's in front of him. His "S" turns down the taxiway were three times as large as the needed to be. Blue called the Control Tower for permission to take off. When they came back announcing there, was an 8-mph cross wind, old Dan Blue got very upset. There was no doubt in my mind, this baby airliner intimidated him.

Our original plan was, Dan Blue would run the aircraft through a few maneuvers. When he was finished his sale-flight, Bob would take over. If Bob Arnold was satisfied, we had a deal. I suddenly knew we needed a change in plans.

"Bob take over. See if this thing flies." There was no way I was going to fly with anybody that taxied like an (no disrespect intended) old lady. Blue didn't mind the crew change. As a matter of fact I think he was relieved. He asked Bob if he wanted to change seats. Usually the pilot in command sets in the left seat.

"Don't worry about it Blue. Bob could fly this plane from the back seat."

We barely got rolling and we were airborne. This baby was born to fly. Later Bob told me the plane wanted to fly at 40 mph. He had to force the plane not to fly until 50 mph. This was a surprise, being it was such a large aircraft. I was tickled with the Gull Wing performance. The smile on Bob's face indicated he was also. We had a done deal. N87E has a new owner. We followed Blue to his office and went over the logbooks. The books indicated the aircraft just had a major overhaul and the fabric was in the High-Green. The best rating the fabric could have.

"I'm afraid you will have to take a cab back to the airport, I have a ton of work to do. I hope you don't mind."

"No, we don't mind. I had you figured as a Cheap-Charily from the beginning." I know I embarrassed Bob, but it was what I felt. People that know me will tell you, I am not always tactful.

If you custom ordered a day for flying it couldn't have been better. A windless day and not a cloud in the sky. I must have been acting like a kid with a new toy. Bob and Ken kept laughing at me. I played with every gadget on our new aircraft. I really got Bob's attention when I opened the door and slipped around the front seat to get to the lounge like rear seat with Ken.   I don't know why he was surprised. I have done the maneuver many time before. Of course I always had a parachute on.

The amount of room in the rear seat amazed me. The AM, FM radio had individual head sets for each passenger. The inch and a half carpet looked new. The soft glove leather seats gave the feeling of luxury. It was hard to believe this aircraft was built in 1940. I stayed in the rear seat for a couple of hours listing to the radio. When I got board, I switched seats. Then the news came on.

N 87E Interior

The Vietnam news was so depressing, I turned the radio off. The only thing more depressing than the war, was the report of thousands of antiwar demonstrators. What an insult I thought. Scumbag's rioting and tearing our cities up, while young Americans are dying on the battlefield every day. That's carrying freedom of speech a little too far. Dam them draft dodging, flag burning, SOB's. I crawled over the front seat on my return trip to my copilot position next to Bob. Ken remained in the luxurious back seat.

About an hour out of Wichita Kansas the plane started to vibrate. The vibration would come and go. While Bob tried to smooth the engine out, I started my search for an airport to make an emergency landing if necessary. Every time I found one we could make, I reported the fact to Bob. Then I would look for another one. We kept this routine up. Finally we decided to land at Wichita. Knowing Wichita National would have mechanics on duty.

"Wichita Tower N87 Echo, request dead in approach, power-plant problem."

"N87 Echo, N87 Echo, clear to land Runway 36, winds from the North at 10. Do you need emergency equipment?"

"Wichita Tower, negative emergency equipment. Appreciate a guide to repair facility."

That short transmission accomplished a lot of activity. First it gave us priority landing over all aircraft in their flight pattern. At the same time, all aircraft on the Tower Frequency became aware of our situation. They offered but we declined emergency equipment. Fire Truck, Ambulance and the like. Lastly they dispatched a ground vehicle to guide us to a repair facility. The great thing about flying is, it exposes you to a lot of dedicated people, when you find yourself in an emergency situation.

The mechanics worked on the Gull Wing more than two hours and didn't find our problem. I had them change oil anyway. We toped the tanks and decided to stay the night. Flying an aircraft with possible mechanical problems at night, isn't the smart thing to do. We got up before dawn and headed for Hebron Airport. We had plenty of time to be at home base in time for most of the busy Saturday jumping. We had a whole bunch of jumpers waiting to try our new airplane out, including our third passenger Ken Rorheim

"Hebron Airport, Hebron Airport, N87 Echo." No answer. Bob kept trying with the same results, no answer. Hand me that mike Bob.

"Hebron Airport, Hebron Airport, Pick up that mike Harry!"

"Oh! Is that you Mac?"

"That's not the proper radio procedure Harry, try again."

"Aircraft calling Hebron Airport Go." Apparently I shock Harry. That was Dale's voice.

"Hebron Airport, this is N87 Echo, fifteen minutes out from your location. Have five jumpers prepared for immediate takeoff."

"Roger five jumpers 87 Echo, out." I got a kick out of Dale Kosack's haste to get off the radio. Dale was a jumper not a radio man.

It was natural for Bob to put on a little aerial show. We buzzed the field, everybody was waving and cheering. As far as they were concerned, this was their new aircraft. It didn't belong to the Corporation. Our Club within a business, was the cement that held the operation together. I was fully aware we were flying over a large group of Giant's. They have proved their Giant status over and over again.

I was on top of the world watching the Gull Wing coming down the runway with her first load of jumpers. Before the plane reached midpoint of the runway, she was about one hundred feet in the air.

I'll bet we could have put another two jumpers on board. Bob turned South to gain altitude. This was a little strange, our usual pattern was to the North. That kept us  away from Galt Airports approach pattern.

While they climbed the rest of us headed for the picnic table area so we would have choice seats for this historical jump. I took a while for me to realize, Bob was flying our emergency pattern along side Galt Airport Road.

"We have an emergency. Curry get a couple of cars south of Galt." Nothing more had to be said. We had practiced emergency runs many times. Bob took off with a couple of his Explorer Scouts and their aid kits. I ran to the office and got on the radio. As I approached the office door, five jumpers left the aircraft. Bob Arnold started a very steep dive toward our location. To late for radio contact now. Bob had his hands full. When he got closer, we could see the prop wasn't turning. Bob was coming in dead stick. Only Bob and his Copilot God, could pull this one off.

At the southwest corner of Hebron Airport was a clump of trees about 25 or 30 feet high. As Bob got closer to the ground, the trees hid the plain from our view. After a few seconds of extreme worrying, N87 Echo, popped over the trees and made a perfect landing. Not only did Bob and his Copilot God, execute a perfect landing, the aircraft came to a dead stop in front of the gas pump. Bob got out of the plane as though nothing happened and stated;

"I think I ran out of gas."

That demonstration of flying, was testimony of our "Giant Pilots" flying ability. I have never meet, before, nor since, a pilot more qualified than, my friend, my brother, Robert Arnold. John Rickter climbed the ladder to reach the Gull Wing gas tanks. Then his horrible announcement.

"The tanks are half full."

You could have shot me. It wouldn't have hurt as much. Our whole expansion program hinged on this aircraft. Without doubt this was a setback that would be hard to recover from. It took ten of us to push 87 Echo to the aircraft tie-down area alongside the building. The jumping went on. The only ones missing from the activity were Bob and I. We were busy removing the Gull Wing 's Cowling.

The rusty bolts created a major problem removing the cowling. To examine the Radial Engine, the protective cowling had to come off. We had no choice, had to use a hack saw and cut the rusty bolts. It was apparent, the bolts were replacement bolts. Bolts used on aircraft don't rust. Another major

N87E 68, 9 Cylinder 300 HP Lycoming

factor, this cowling hasn't been off for quit sometime. There was no way this aircraft had been worked on recently.

The more we worked on the Gull Wing the madder I became. Thank God, Dan Blue was so far away. If he were closer, I would have spent a night or two in jail. With the cowling removed the aircraft jugs (individual firing chambers) were exposed. Like the cowling, they haven't been worked on for a long time. Without saying a word Bob got in his car and left the airport.

When he returned, Bob had great news. He convinced the bank manager to stop payment on the check we gave to Dan Blue. Normally that doesn't happen on certified checks. Those funds are pledged to the payee. Since there was apparent fraud connected to this sale, an exception to the rule was possible. I don't believe anybody else could have convinced the bank to freeze funds on a certified check. Bob Arnold had the respect of everyone in Hebron Illinois and that included the banker.

Further examination of the airplane confirmed Bob's suspicion. We had blown a jug on 87 Echo's radial engin. Madder than a hornet I decided to call Dan Blue. After several attempts I finally reached him. My opening words;

"Pick up your aircraft, I don't like the color."

"A deal is a deal." He fired back. Then he hung up.

On the following Monday he called back. "Mr. McGinley, can we talk?" He must have found out payment on his check was stopped.

"I'll talk Blue, you listen. Pick up your aircraft. By the way I am charging one hundred dollar's a day for storage." I hung up.

Five days later Dan Blue arrived at Hebron Airport. His mode of transportation was a Ford pick-up truck. Its cargo consisted of a radial aircraft engine, a motor hoist and several boxes of tools. The funny thing about this story, I hadn't told him about our engine trouble. Dan was either a mind reader or he knew he sold us a faulty engine. My money is on, he knew.

"You owe me $500.00 for storage Blue." When asked if he could plug into our power so they could see to repair the plane. "That will be another $100.00, cash that is." They worked on replacing the motor all night. When they asked to use the toilet, I replied ;

"That will be another $100.00." He didn't pay.

I trusted Dan Blue about as far as I could throw a piano. For that reason I stayed at the airport. At day break, he was at my office door asking for the log books. I dumped the papers contained in a large manila envelop on the counter. I wanted Blue to know I had a copy of the logbook, and closeup pictures of the supposedly overhauled engin.

"Why did you copy the logbook?"

"Dealing with a crook, I thought a copy of the log books, might be a good thing to have." I had no problem talking to Blue this way. I know several Texans whom I am proud to call friends. In fact most of them are Giants. This poor excuse of a human falls far short of any Texan I have ever meet. I'll bet, twenty to one, he's not from Texas.

This slob had the nerve to tell me he was going to test-fly the Gull Wing before he headed back to Texas. They would probably head for Texas early Sunday morning. I am sure my answer startled him.

"As soon as you break ground, head away from Hebron Airport. I charge a $500.00 landing fee and my storage fee has just increased to $300.00 a day. In other words you are not welcome." The crooked small man from Texas departed. It didn't surprise me the procrastinator from Texas didn't do the flying. The mechanic flew, the crook drove the truck.

I would say we broke even on the deal. Our storage fees replaced the money we spent on transportation and lodging. The stop payment on the four thousand dollar check, saved the day. The only negative thing, we had to continue our search for another airplane.

An Offer They Can't Refuse

Hebron Airport was about fifty miles Northwest of Chicago. By auto, not a bad ride. When Tony arrived by Motor Scooter with a passenger, it surprised me. I am sure that wasn't the safest way to travel. I always tell people that the trip to the airport is more dangerous than the jumping. A Motor Scooter, almost makes that a fact.

Tony thought he could come to the airport, be given instructions and make his first jump the first day. When I informed him, he had to go to a six day or more Ground School, before his first of five Static Line jumps he was shocked. Shocked, not only by the Ground School requirement but by the Static Line Jumps. He was under the impression he could hop in the aircraft and make a free fall the same day.

"I'll give you $200.00 if you let me jump." I declined. "How about 300.00." My reaction was the same. He and his female companion watched the jumping for a while. Had something to eat, then disappointed, he left the airport. So I thought.

Our next class started the following Wednesday. First to arrive was our Italian friend Tony. As the instructors and regular members arrived. Tony would call them by their first name. I asked Bill Mellor how this guy knew everybody. Bill told me how hard Tony worked at the airport. He worked behind the grill, helped with packing the student chutes. Would bring jumpers a cold coke after their jump. All at his expense. Bill was surprised I didn't know. I guess I was to busy with the students.

At first our new student, with Italian heritage, let his short temper show. I corrected that problem by showing him our door worked both ways. He got the message and dedicated his energy to learning. Tony became a good student. He followed training instructions to the letter.

After class most students went home. Not Tony, he joined the regular members to our club house, on the ground floor. Without hesitation he jumped behind the bar and served everyone's beverage of choice. He not only served as bar tender, he furnished the beverage to be served. Tony owned a restaurant at 22 East Jackson, downtown Chicago. Simply named "22 East."

Many jumpers offered Tony a ride to the airport. He declined all offers. He preferred to take his motor scooter. Like always, Tony was an early arrival. Without asking he got behind the lunch counter and started the coffee and turned the grill on. While the grill was heating, Tony went to his scooter and came back with a box of groceries he had strapped to the rear seat.

People started arriving earlier than usual. They didn't stop for breakfast. Tony had informed them he was going to serve breakfast at the airport. And what a breakfast it was. Home made Italian sausage, eggs anyway you wanted them to include, egg benedict ham bacon, and hot home made rolls. Tony wasn't a cook, he was a chef. I had the jump manifest made out and made the announcement.

"First two loads are static line jumps. First load, Bob, Tony. Second Load, Bill and Janet. The other loads will be posted on the Bulletin Board." Tony was busy cleaning the grill.

"Are you a fry cook or a jumper Tony? Get chuted up."

"Mac I still have three more days of training. There must be a mistake."

"I have made one mistake in my life. It was so long ago I forgot what it was. Chute Up."

Tony almost tripped over himself he was so excited. I go over every student's progress with the instructors. All were in agreement. Tony was ready.

"Mac I didn't bring any boots. I didn't think I was jumping until next week. Besides Gene (his female companion) wanted to see my first jump."

"There is a pair of boots in the Packing Shed that will fit you." At that point Gene walked in.

She rode out with Gale Catrez. Gale called her earlier in the week and told her Tony was going to make his first jump. Of course we make her promise not to tell Tony. As Tony walked to the waiting aircraft, he had a smile that went from ear to ear. Our Chef Bor-Dee, would soon be airborne.

"Get Out!" The command for the student to put one foot on the step and the other foot on the braked, aircraft wheel. Pulling himself out, hanging onto the strut, looking straight ahead, waiting for further commands.

"GO." Tony's exit was great, Arms extended, back arched, head held high looking at the horizon. If I didn't know better, I would have thought, he had done this before. Although he didn't have to on his first jump, Tony came in for a dummy ripcord pull. That gave him an excellent grade on his first jump. His second jump of the day was a carbn copy of the first. Now that he was on jump status, Tony's bond with the other members became stronger and Land of Lincoln as a whole became stronger.

Being a businessman, Tony knew, better than most, Land of Lincoln's charge for jumping wouldn't support the business by its self. He understood the importance of raising money through other means. Fund raising Air shows. Demonstration Jumps, Equipment sales, proceeds from our small restaurant, and of course Charity Jumps to keep Land of Lincoln in the public eye.

All demonstration jumps and to a larger extent jumping free for a charity, generated front page newspaper coverage. Coverage that couldn't be purchased at any price. Adding TV and Radio coverage with live interviews kept Land of Lincoln on prime time. Full page picture lay outs, in the Chicago Tribune, Sun Times and the Daily News, kept students flocking to our door.

Tony was very friendly with the owners of Chicago Fire Works. It was my understanding they were the biggest fire work's company in the industry. They held the contract with both Chicago major ball clubs. Every time a home-run was hit, the scoreboards would explode with a firework display.

Every 4th of July, the Chicago Fire Works Company would put on several extensive shows throughout a four-state area. One of the larger shows was held on Mississippi River, on barges, anchored between Davenport Iowa and Moline Illinois. Tony got them to offer two thousand, five hundred dollars, for two jumpers to parachute and land on the barges. The contract called for them to furnish the aircraft. I accepted their generous offer.

Normally there are no problem getting volunteers to jump at shows' or whatever. When the jumpers were told they would be wired with explosive devices, they took off for the woods. The free fall and landing on a barge in the middle of the Mississippi didn't bother them a bit. Firecrackers exploding, during the free-fall portion of the jump didn't produce any candidates for the first time ever jump.

I was left with a problem, I needed a good jumper. A risk taker, that could keep his cool while the world around him was exploding. The big question, who? I didn't have to wait long, my answer drove in the parking lot.

Rick Olchivick was an old friend. I first meet him when I joined the 302nd Special Forces. He was their Parachute Rigger. Rick and I started Sky Diving together. An excellent jumper, but more important a loyal friend.

"Rick I have a deal for you." I announced as he approached. I went on to tell him about our fireworks jump on the Mississippi. He jumped at the chance to be part of it.

My Czechoslovakian friends' acceptance didn't surprise me. He was no stranger to risk taking. As a twelve-year old lad, his whole family was taken to a German Concentration Camp. On the way to the Camp, Rick's Brother Stan escaped and made his way to America. At the camp, men were separated from the woman and children. Oldrich, hasn't seen his Father since.

While watching Russian Soldiers, digging their own graves, then being kicked in the head and buried alive by drunk German Guards, triggered a violent response. Oldrich picked up a Guard's rifle leaning against a tree, then shot the two German Guards. Rick hid for a couple of days. When the Camp Commander announced, he was going to take reprisals. Rick turned himself in.

The Camp Commander, impressed with Ricks bravery, made it possible for Rick and his mother to escape. Apparently the Commander did not condone burying people alive. Rick and his mother made it to England, then the United States. Rick joined the 11th Airborne, then Special Forces.

Mrs. Olchivick, told me on several occasions, she didn't hold any grudge against the German people. She refused to blame the many for the acts of a few. Stan, Ricks brother had also joined the US Army. He had several Airborne assignments that included Commander of

A Walk With Giants 1957 - 1974

Special Forces Berlin Detachment. Working his way through the ranks, Stan retired with the rank of Colonel. Now if that isn't a story about three Giants, I don't know what is.

The only difficulty about our 4th of July jump, was limiting the amount of explosions the firework experts wanted to attach to our bodies. If they had their way, we would have gone into orbit. We allowed everything except the rockets. Didn't want any missiles shooting holes in our canopies. Tony was to arm the device as we left the aircraft. That seemed appropriate, an Italian guy named Tony, acting as our trigger man.

On our approach to the Barges we flew over a large Dam. I remember feeling anger when I saw old cars dumped into the otherwise beautiful water. To me it looked like someone got rid of their old Volkswagens by throwing them over the bank of the river. They probably didn't figure the Dam would prevent them from being carried down stream.

As we got closer to the target, I started concentrating on an exit point. We didn't have any jumpers on the ground. I relied on smoke coming from a factory to determine wind direction. Everything appeared favorable for an uneventful free fall to celebrate our nation's birthday.

As I climbed out on the strut, Rick close behind me, I nodded to Tony. He pulled the pin on the explosive's safety device. You might say we got off with a bang. I had barely let go of the strut before the first explosion went off. At that point I was glad we decided to use a Scuba Diving Wet Suits for flotation (in case we missed the barge) gear. The thick material protected us from multiple small bums. In spite of the padding, I could feel the multiple bursts of heat. Whoever agreed to this jump should have their heads examined. Or at least, they should be watched closely.

We were right on target. When we left the aircraft, it triggered the start of the ground fireworks show. What a spectacular view from our vantage point. This topped any fireworks show I had ever seen. Well it did, until I saw Rick.

Rick was free falling in a frog position. Hundreds of explosions popping off his body. I couldn't believe the number, it was great. We laid there for a few seconds watching each other. I was almost sad when it came time to open our chutes. How time flies by, when you are having fun. I was exploding all during the opening of the canopy, to the landing on the barge.

I couldn't see a thing. The smoke from the expended ordinance filled the air. In addition to, not being able to see, I couldn't breath. Using the quick releases on my risers I ditched my canopy and jumped into the Mississippi. Rick followed suit. They say, God watches over fools. He had his hands full this night. Rick can't swim.

Back in the 302nd Special Forces, as reservists, Rick and I went to a Combat Swim Course, conducted by the US Navy at Navy Pier on Chicago's lake front. To qualify for the course, each student had to swim (free style) three lengths of their pool. Watching from pool side, I saw Olchivick jump in the deep side of the pool. Making his way along the bottom, Rick preceded to the shallow end. Made his turn and headed back to the deep end. It was at this point, I pushed the panic button. I excitedly told the instructor, my pal Rick couldn't swim. When one instructor hit the water, all the instructors hit the water. They swooped on my pal and brought him to the surface.

"What's a matter? What's a matter?" Rick asked with his Czechoslovakian accent.

Realizing he was OK, the instructors let him go. Back to the bottom he went, to finish his qualification swim. I should say crawl. Rick Olchivick cannot swim. The ability to hold large amounts of air enabled my pal to execute three laps (free style) of the pool to qualify. The balance of the course, using snorkel, fins and air-tanks was a cake walk.

I was startled when I heard the splash behind me. As luck would have it the scuba wet suit keep Rick afloat. We made our way to the Iowa side of the river and enjoyed the balance of the fireworks show. The Volkswagens dumped into the river by the dam upset me all evening. I was telling Rick about how I felt, when I was interrupted by a native Iowan.

"Excuse me sir, those are not Volkswagens, they are fish, oversized over fed Carp."

They can't be fish, I thought to myself. He went on to explain, they have been there for years. Too large to swim, they just waller around in the mud, eating everything insight. He went on to tell us, although they don't bother people, scuba divers stay clear. If one would roll on top of a diver, it would be the end of the story. I had a hard time believing it all. I chocked it up as just another exaggerated fish story.

Tony rode back to Chicago with Rick and I. We never did find our chutes we left on the barge. I think it upset Tony more than it did Rick and myself. He saw to it that Chicago Fire Works added a five hundred-dollar bonis to our paycheck.

I became obsessed with the idea of getting a larger aircraft. I considered getting another Cessna. Maybe a Cessna 180 or 182, both were good jump planes. Land of Lincoln could not grow without putting more jumpers in the air.

When Tony offered me a bar  tending job at his restaurant, I had no trouble accepting. The extra money would shorten the time to acquire another aircraft. I didn't know much about tending bar. Tony insisted that didn't matter, he would teach me anything I needed to know.

22 East Jackson was a unique restaurant. The thirty by fifty-foot, three story building was one of the few buildings that survived the Chicago Fire. The building was the Coach House of then the Governor of Illinois, making it a land mark. The building was situated down a three hundred-foot long alley that just added to its uniqueness. Needing more seating capacity, Tony had a local artist paint murals on the buildings bordering the alley. He added two rows of umbrella tables that gave the otherwise ugly alley, a French Café look.

The full service bar at 22 East was on the first floor. All available floor space was jammed full of small tables. The second floor was the main dinning area. It to was jammed full, with small tables. The third floor was reserved for private parties. Its furnishings were quite extravagant. At first that puzzled me. After meeting some of Tony's clients I understood. If you didn't have big bucks, you didn't eat here. No elevators in this old building, a winding staircase serviced the clients. A rope operated, dumb waiter, connected all floors to the kitchen located in the basement.

The most unusual thing about the whole operation was the opened end menu. It didn't matter what type of food you desired, what country it was linked to, or how exotic the preparation, you could order it at 22 East Jackson. Tony was a Specialty Chef, I emphasize the word Chef. This man could prepare any food on this earth. With a forty-eight-hour notice, a feast that would please royalty, would be waiting to please your pallet.

The big problem Tony had, he wasn't good around people. His hot temper would run customers and staff off. The business flourished as long as Tony stayed in the kitchen. Tony was well aware of this flaw in his character. He did his best to stay out of sight. Gene, the gal he brought to the airport was the manager of the restaurant. She was also the bookkeeper and did all the hiring. As Tony put it, Genie does the hiring and he the firing.

In the beginning I thought Tony had something going with Gene. That turned out not to be true. Gene was married to Tony's partner and friend who was in prison. Tony took on the job of protector. Some said he over protected her. Gene went nowhere by herself. She lived in the same house with Tony and his family. When they went out, Gene went out. If Tony's wife had something to do that didn't involve Gene, Tony took her with him. That explained the trips to the airport, on the back of a motor scooter. The fact of the matter is, Tony hired me because he fired the last Bar Tender. They say he was a very well trained bar keep. It made no difference. He made a play for Gene and became history.

Gene and I didn't hit it off from the get go. There was something about the gal I didn't care for. She wasn't a bad looking gal. But as soon as she opened her mouth, it became evident her brain and lips had a compatibility problem. There wasn't a day, when she and I didn't clash. My stay at 22 East Jackson, would be short lived.

The clientele that frequented 22 East was as unique, as the Restaurant itself. The noon crowd was composed of office workers and small shop owners. Their arrival time, what seat they would occupy, and bar order was as predictable as the four seasons. I had their first drink poured and waiting. The first drink held them over until their food arrived. Another drink to wash the food down. A third drink and they were on their way, back to the grind stone. What a boring routine I often thought to myself.

The evening crowd a little less predictable but still caught up in the rat race, to earn a buck   Most just stopped by to have a couple of drinks before their long journey home. By six thirty the bar was empty, and remained that way until seven thirty, when my favorite crowd started to arrived.

Reporters from all three major Chicago Newspapers, TV and Radio News personnel, to include a couple Talk Show hosts. This was a fun group. A close-net group, loaded with remarkable stories. 22 East Jackson was their watering hole, a club house so to speak.

It was the Monday night before Labor Day week end. Traditionally Labor Day is a slow news day. The Market, Government Offices, Schools and Businesses are closed. Yet the media guys and gales have to stand by waiting for a possible breaking story. Everyone was in agreement, this was going to be a boring week end. Then the idea came in a flash.

"What do you mean, boring week end? Land of Lincoln Sky Divers are making a water Jump in Lake Michigan, followed by their annual picnic. What can beat that for excitement?" At that moment I had everyone's attention.

"What Beach are they jumping at Mac? How many Jumpers? What altitude are they jumping from?" The air was fall of questions that were in need of answers. Land of Lincoln's water jump came to me in a flash, out of nowhere. I should be able to get the answers from the same place.

"The jump is scheduled for Montrose Avenue Beach, at ten o'clock Saturday Morning. There should be fifty jumpers or more." The news hounds showed a lot of interest, however all were in agreement, the jump site was to far from downtown and their offices. They had to stand by or be close in the event of a breaking news story. I made an, on the spot adjustment.

"How about the Chicago Avenue Beach?" Thay're to far from the home office attitude didn't change. "OK, Oak Street Beach. You can't get any closer than that guys." That got their attention. I spent the rest of the evening adding to my on the spot, water jump plan. Oak Street Beach was directly in front of the Tribune Tower, across the Outer Drive, on the very edge of downtown Chicago. The Tribune Tower was a land mark that housed the Chicago Tribune Newspaper's office.

"OK Guys, listen up. Now that I have adjusted the jump site to suit your schedule, does anyone have any idea how Land of Lincoln can get permission to jump at Oak Street?"

"Who gave you permission to jump at Montrose Avenue Beach Mac?" I ignored the question. The idea of making a water jump was just a couple of hours old. I haven't mentioned a water jump to anyone before.

"Colonel Riley, in the Mayor's Office of Special Events, is the guy that makes all the decisions on what happens at all of Chicago's Parks and Beaches. Riley rules with an iron hand. Even Mayor Daley doesn't go against him. If Colonel Riley doesn't give the go ahead, it just doesn't happen." Was the long informative answer to my question. At nine o'clock the next morning I was at Mayor Daley's office, requesting to see Colonel Riley.

"I'm sorry, Colonel Riley is on vacation, We don't expect him back until the first of October. Can I help you?" A great thought flashed through my mind that make it easy to decline her help. I departed the Colonel's office with one thing on my mind. This water jump was a go.

If the Colonel was the only person that could approve an event, he has to be the only one that can reject an event. I went to my office and called every jumper I could think of and informed them I was having a special meeting at our school on Milwaukee Avenue. When I informed them the purpose of the meeting was to formulate plans for a water jump at Oak Street Beach, I could feel their excitement through the phone.

Their excitement was well justified. One of the requirements to get a Class C licence from the Parachute Club of America, was to have a water jump logged. This was a golden opportunity to fulfil the requirement and have a great time doing it.

The big winner was Land of Lincoln itself. The publicity we would surely get had no price tag. You can't buy the front page of a major city's newspaper nor the picture page. Chicago had three major papers at the time. The icing on the cake was all three Chicago Television Stations promised coverage. Add Radio stations, and Talk Show Host, we had a winner.

The only thing that could bust our bubble was bad weather (it would have to be very bad) or a breaking news story that could top ours. That was not likely to happen. Sky Diving was fairly a new sport and drew large crowds. A story to top Sky Diving would have to a major one, like a War or some other devastating happening.

Our hurried meeting produced a manifest of fifty jumpers. One of our jumpers had a brother who belonged to a boat club. We invited them to retrieve jumpers from the cold waters of Lake Michigan. Another member had a friend active in Ham Radio. Still another member who were also members of the 302nd Special Forces Scuba Team, promised their help with our water jump project. In less than two days, this spur of the moment idea, was up and running. I am here to tell you folks, this could only be accomplished by Giants. Soon to be wet Giants I might add.

There was only one thing left to be checked, the Drop Zone. Of course flying over Chicago Beaches at one hundred feet is not allowed. No problem. We made a few landings and take off from Migs Field.

Migs Field was just south of Oak Street Beach on Chicago's lake front. Bob Arnold flew while I took pictures of the beach. Bob's long approaches on landings and slow increases in attitude, on take off, afforded me all the time I needed to take pictures we needed for planning.

Migs Field

After I finished our clandestine picture taking, Bob and I had lunch at Migs Field Coffee Shop. We were careful not to mention the water jump planned for the next Saturday. I sure didn't want the Mayor's Office of Special Events, and more particularly. Colonel Riley to be advised of our plans for his sacred beach. Some might say that is a little dishonest. I say it was very considerate. I didn't want to spoil his vacation.

Show Time

It was all in the timing. To eliminate the possibility of someone putting a damper on our Oak Street Jump, we decided to meet at Land of Lincoln's School on Milwaukee Avenue. From the school, our plan called for the use of a bus to transport jumpers and equipment to Migs' Field on Chicago's Lake front. Bob Arnold would bring the jump plane, 6565 Echo. Bob was to arrive at Migs' Field at exactly 8 A.M.. The Jumpers would arrive at exactly 9 A.M.. This would have everyone in place for the scheduled, 10 A.M jump. The tight schedule was paramount. It didn't leave much time for anyone to ask the question, "what are you doing here?"

I met Bob at the Aircraft Tie Down Area. It was apparent he was nervous. He didn't have the foggiest idea how I was going to pull this stunt off. At that point, neither did I. I had one thing going for me, experience, I had a lot of experience pulling solutions out of the fire at the last minute. I am living proof, you don't have to have brains to accomplish, seemingly impossible tasks. Some people that know me say, I was hiding behind the door, when they passed out the brains. Other say, I wasn't in the room. As soon as the aircraft was secure, we headed for the Control Tower.

"Good Morning. We sure picked a great day for our Sky Diving Show. I can't tell you how much we appreciate your cooperation putting this thing together. You can be assured, Colonel Riley will hear about your effort. They gave me that 'What are you talking about, look'. Before they could respond, I fired another question.

"If it's OK with you, we will set up next to your Tie Down Area." Again I eliminated their response time. "What frequency should we call when we are on Jump Run?" Armed with the contact frequencies, I thanked everyone again and shook their hands. As Bob and I departed the Tower, someone asked the 64-dollar question.

"O'Hare Tower know about this jump?"

"You have to be kidding me. Who in their right mind would be putting 50 jumpers in the air, over Downtown Chicago without permission? You must be kidding." Time to get out of Dodge. Bob and I departed.

Chicago O'Hare Airport and Land of Lincoln Sky Divers had a great working relationship. We have jumped in their controlled airspace all over Chicago and surrounding areas.

In the beginning, one of their approaches was directly over Hebron Airport. On all aviation charts of the area, Hebron Airport was listed in the Note-Tarn to Pilots section,

"Be aware of Sport Parachuting in the vicinity."

After a couple of years, O'Hare moved the approach twenty-five miles to the East. We had an outstanding relationship with the FAA and the Control Tower at O'Hare. Regardless where we jumped, all we had to do was notify them one hour before the jump, when we were on final for a jump and when we had jumpers in the air. The Jump at Oak Street Beach would follow the same pattern.

I went over the manifest with Bob and asked him to pass on a few last minute instructions to the jump master of each load. Then I headed for Oak Street Beach. As planned, the non jumpers were busy setting up the picnic area. The Boat Club, Radio Club and Scuba support people were waiting for instructions. The odd thing, they were accompanied by a couple of Chicago's finest, Park Police. I was greeted with;

"Mac we have a problem." Jerry Richards who was also a Chicago Policeman was having an argument with a Park District Police Sergeant.

"This guy claims we need a permit to run our Boats. "

"Of course you need a permit Jerry. Colonel Riley requires a permit for any Park activity. You should know that." I have never met the man, but I got a kick out of using the Colonel's name. "The Boat permit is probably with our Jumping Permit. Colonel Riley wouldn't allow a Water Jump without a safety backup."

"What Jumping Permit." Asked the Park Police Sergeant."

Time to Tap Dance,

"Colonel Riley was on vacation and couldn't issue a hard copy.

Call his office Sergeant, I am sure they will give you his hotel phone number. He can tell you first hand if we have a Permit or not. I'll bet you will look good, back on the Bicycle Patrol." This guy was stemming.

"Jerry, have the Boats form a circle a couple hundred yards out. The jumpers need a target. Put a radio in each boat." Jerry took off to accomplish the mission.

"If I see one Jumper leave the aircraft, I'll through the whole Club in Jail.", the almost out of control Park Policeman yelled.

"Clean out your Jail, I have 50 jumpers on the way."

A moment later our jump plane 6565 Echo, was on final jump run. The Park Policeman almost ran to the single phone booth at Oak Street Beach. By this time the Fire Boat and Chicago Police Boat Crew's arrived. They too, headed for the phone. After their phone calls, they headed in my direction. The Fireman was the first to speak.

"My boss doesn't know what to do. He said I should cooperate with you, how can I help?" The Police Boat Skipper announced the same.

"Take a position at the impact area. Help them create the target circle. Thanks for your help." The Park Police Sergeant didn't say a thing. Can you believe it, a minute ago I was threatened with jail, now I am despatching Police and Fire Boats.

Oak Street Beach

Bill Mellor was the Jump Master of the first load. He made a pass and dropped a wind direction streamer, then chose an exit point. Bob radioed, the exit point was the Tribune Tower. The plane began its jump run. Bob flew 65 Echo directly over the exit point, but no jumper left the aircraft. Another pass and still no jumper. What in the heck is going on here?, ran through my mind. I tried to signal one of the boat drivers. I needed a ride to Migs' Field.

"Can I help." To my surprise, it was the Park District Sergeant.

"Yes, I need a ride to Migs Field."

We hit the Outer Drive at top speed. Lights flashing, an occasional beep on the horn. If I didn't know better, I would have thought the Chicago Fire had rekindled. One thing was certain my Park Police Sergeant was a fast driver. I started to wonder if he was a good driver. I didn't have time to evaluate him any farther. We arrived at Migs' Field. All the jumpers were laying on the ground under the Cessna's wing, using their parachutes as pillows. Bob seeing me coming headed in my direction.

"O'Hare won't give us permission to jump Mac." I didn't answer. I headed for the Control Tower. I had just won a battle on the beach, and felt very good about it. I wasn't about to let some Tower Jockey ruin my day. As soon as I approached Mig's control panel, I was handed the mike. At the other end was the Yo-yo who stopped the jumping.

"This is Daniel T. McGinley, the owner of Land of Lincoln Sky Divers. By what authority did you stop my people from jumping? Your job is to keep aircraft separated to avoid collision. You do not have the authority to approve nor disapprove the use of air space. Who is your supervisor?"

"Mr. Edward Halley Sir." When he called me sir, I knew I had him ducking.

"Put Ed on the wire." Ed Halley used to fly for us. Ed, his sister, and his father, whose name is also Ed, are all members of Land of Lincoln. I'm playing with a pat-hand here. This sure has been one heck of a day.

"Mac, this is Ed. Sorry for the mix-up. Phil is a great guy, but new at the job. Take it easy on him OK? Get your jumpers back in the air. I'll see you tonight at the party." A little more chit chat and we signed off.

By this time, the Park Police Sergeant, Mig's Tower operators and anybody else that doubted I had permission to jump at Oak Street Beach, were converts. As I left Migs Field on my way back to Oak St. Beach, the jumpers were boarding the aircraft.

The balance of the day was great. I remember thinking to myself, (when I saw the first jumper hit the water), how easy things are when you bypass the bureaucracy. Many worthwhile things could be accomplished, if only Government, kept their control to a minimum. Of course we need Laws to protect others. What we don't need is, big government running the show. People shouldn't forget, the United States of America is a Republic, not a Democracy. A Republic established under GOD. The pledge of allegiance to our Flag will prove my point.

My turn to jump finally arrived. I was to be the only Jumper in the aircraft. That gave plenty of room for a TV Cameraman. The selection was easy. First all cameramen had to promise to share the jump film with the others. All in agreement drew straws. NBC won the draw. To insure Land of Lincoln would get the maximum coverage, I wore a Jump Suit with a Land of Lincoln Patch, bloused-boots and all.

The cameraman was all smiles as we loaded the aircraft. Setting behind Bob adjusting his camera, he was happy as a lark. I sat on the floor next to Bob. As we speed down the runway with the right door removed, his smile faded. I love the color green, but not the shade beginning to show on his face. For a few minutes I thought we might have to land and get another cameraman. This guy was about to barf.

"Are you OK?" I asked before we turned on final. He nodded.

"Take a couple of deep breaths, it will help to relax you. Don't worry, you're strapped in, you can't fall out." I was going to tell him a couple of jokes. Decided not to, some people say many of my jokes make them barf.

On all jumps, when we are taking off at an airport the same altitude as the jump area, we set the aircraft altimeter and the jumper's altimeter to "O." This affords the jumper a reliable source to check the exact distance they are above the impact area. Knowing this, they can calculate how long of a free fall they can make, before opening their parachute.

My altimeter read 5200 feet. I didn't believe it, those buildings looked close. I requested an altimeter check. Bob came back affirming 5200. I put my legs outside the aircraft. One foot on the step and the other on the aircraft wheel. I grabbed the strut and pulled myself out. We had drifted a little to the right. I signaled Bob to steer left. Old Robert made the correction. I turned to the cameraman, gave him a salute and started my plunge to the ground, or should I say water. Those buildings still looked close.

Normally the 5200 feet jump allowed me a 20-second delay before it was time to open. The law states you must have a fall canopy at 2200 feet above the ground. Because of the buildings, we raised the opening altitude to 3000. The buildings still looked close. I started my favorite jingle, as I went in for the pull. "It doesn't mean a thing unless you pull the string."

I was hanging over Michigan Avenue, brakes on (facing the wind) and I was still was moving backswords 15 to 20 MPH. The ceiling was dropping all day. Now apparently the wind is picking up. There was no way I was going to hit the target circle created by our Boat Club friends. No problem, I noticed a boat breaking formation to pick me up. I sat back and enjoyed the ride.

My scenic ride was interrupted when I looked down. I was passing directly over a sailboat. Laying on her deck, were two sunbathers, female type, topless. I wasn't 20 feet above their mast. I am sure I startled them. When they saw me the quickly grabbed towels to cover up and started to wave. At least I think they were waving. Maybe they were shaking their fists? I waved back. In fact I was still waving when I made contact with the water. The wind prevented the parachute from hitting the water. The 28-foot diameter canopy, drug me across the lake, like a motorboat pulling a water skier. Then things started to happen and happen fast.

My bloused jump suit, filled with lake water and started to drag me under. At this point I was concerned about surviving. There is only a certain amount of water a person can drink. I had my fill. About then a couple Scuba Divers were pulling me to the recovery boat. At first they couldn't get me on board. The weight of the water filled jump suit was too much for them. Both Scuba Divers were from the 302nd Special Forces. Both were airborne qualified, shortening the time it took them to figure I had my trouser bloused. Bloused trousers is an unbreakable habit of anybody airborne qualified. As they un-bloused the boots, the water rushed out of my jumpsuit and I was pulled aboard. I was safe on board, but not breathing well.

As a child I had Asthma. This bout with the lake must have triggered an attack. There was no way I wanted the spectators, nor the press to see me in this condition. The exaggerating press would turn this into a near drowning. That would

Navy Pier

be negative reporting, taking away from the achievements of the otherwise perfect day. I gave them instructions to drop me off at Navy Pier. From Navy Pier, I took a Taxi-Cab home to fight this temporary condition without spectators or fanfare. Being a Ham at heart, made this a difficult decision. But this ham was over cooked.

The news coverage was better than I could ever imagine. Every TV Channel I turned to had pictures and interviews of jumpers. It became very apparent, I wasn't the only Ham at Land of Lincoln Sky Divers. The newspapers had fall page photo spreads of Land of Lincoln's finest day. All articles were upbeat, not a single negative remark in any newspaper. My decision to go home and keep out of the lime light, was a good one.

The positive results didn't end with the news coverage. It generated a couple of live interviews on Radio talk shows. We received several invitations to put on Jump Demonstrations from surrounding cities and other public gatherings. It seemed like overnight. Land of Lincoln Sky Divers, came of age. Membership application started to flow in. Unknown at the time, this notoriety would eventually hurt us.

At most Sky Diving Shows, I assumed the role of Master of Ceremonies. It wasn't because I was the best person for the job. It was more like, when you were a kid playing baseball. The guy that owned the baseball could play any position he wanted. Master of Ceremonies, particularly at a jump show is an important job. It is the only communication between the crowd and the jumpers. Can you imagine, being at an airport waiting for a jumper to appear in the sky? At best you would go home with a very stiff neck. Not to mention the boredom waiting for something to happen.

Having a MC, the crowd is kept advised on the status of the jump. While waiting, you will be given a brief history of the sport. The purpose of your organization and what their donated money will be used for. You can be assured of a few corny jokes mixed in, hoping to entertain them. Of course a little interaction between the MC and the crowd is always helpful. Usually that takes the form of questions and answers. Without fail, the question that always pops up is,

"What if the chute doesn't open?" At that point we tell them the importance of the reserve chute.

Land of Lincoln was jumping at an airport near Waukegan Illinois. I was preforming my task as MC. At the question and answer portion of my presentation the predictable, "what if the chute doesn't open," question was asked. I answered the question in the usual manner, only this time I explained different types of malfunctions.

A Streamer, where the parachute unfolds, the lines are fully extended, but for one reason or other, the Parachute doesn't inflate. Regardless of the cause, it was reserve time.

Blown Canopy, large holes, blown in the canopy at opening increasing the jumpers decent to an unsafe rate. Probably caused by age of the canopy, faulty or poor packing. Same results, reserve time.

May West, the most likely seen on flat circular canopies. This one got its name from an old Film Star and Stage Show Queen. May West was a very well endowed, voluptuous woman. Some say the malfunction looked like her brassier floating from the sky. The May West is caused by the chute trying to invert (turn inside out). Most likely caused by the jumper in a head down, tipped to one side position on opening. The complete inversion is interrupted at a point, by the inflating canopy. Now it looks like you have two canopies, affectionately called, a May West. Again, reserve parachute time. To reinforce my mini lecture I had large pictures and drawings.

When it came my time to jump, I turned the mike over to another jumper. When I got to jump altitude, my stand in MC would tell the crowed to watch the red smoke. On all my jumps I had a smoke grenade bracket attached to my right foot just above the heal. As I left the aircraft, I pulled the pin on the smoke grande. When my chute opened, presto, a May West. When I was sure I would land close to the crowd I would pull my reserve parachute.

After I was sure I had a fall canopy, I released the malfunction. I hung on to the main canopy (it dangled at my side) until I was close to the ground. This eliminated the time and effort it would take looking for it.

When I got back to the platform, the audience had a million questions. Most relating to, how much fear I had experienced. When I told them, I didn't have any, that I had full faith in my reserve parachute. I don't think they believed me. I emphasized the fact that a Parachute Rigger, licenced by the FAA had to inspect and pack every jumpers reserve and had to be freshly packed every 90 days. They started to understand my belief in my reserve.

"Who is the FAA Rigger at Land of Lincoln?" Someone asked.

"I am." Was my reply. That always got a laugh.

When it was my turn to jump again, I popped the smoke at 7200 feet above the crowed. At 2200 I went in for the pull. Same results, May West. By this time the crowed began to doubt my jumping expertise. When my third jump of the day was duplicate of the first two, they knew they had been had. The malfunctions were intentional. Everyone got a big kick out of the show. Well everybody except the FAA. Have you ever noticed anybody working for a Government Agency, doesn't laugh much? A good example is the IRS.

Let's See How Good They Are

The Lake Geneva Sport Parachuting Group decided to host a Jumping Contest. I knew that my Land of Lincoln Jumpers would win big against the Lake Geneva Group. I trained most of their jumpers and knew their limitations. I also knew that with a little fine tuning the Land of Lincoln Team would give all others a run for their money. On a Sunday afternoon after jumping I called a meeting in our Snack Shop.

"How would you guys like to enter the Lake Geneva Competition?" This was not a quit group, but for a moment, their silence was synchronized. Finally Bill Mellor spoke up.

"Mac we can't beat those guys. All they do is competition jumping."

"I agree with you Bill. They do a lot of competition jumping, but very little winning."

"A few of us were talking about this last night, Mac."

"I know you were Bill, that's why we are having this meeting."

Bill Mellor was the most advanced jumper we had at Land of Lincoln. His loyalty and friendship was unquestionable. Yet I knew deep inside Bill would be one of the first to leave Land of Lincoln. Bill had learned all he could at a facility that was dedicated to the student jumper. In search of advanced training and opportunity in is believed sport, Sky Diving, Bill Mellor would have to leave.

I ended my meeting with a promise. If they would follow my instructions to the letter, I would guarantee, they would come back with trophies from the Lake Geneva Parachute Meet. This was an easy to execute guarantee. The advanced jumpers at Land of Lincoln were above average compared to others. Every single jump they made, was an accuracy jump. They were graded on how far they landed from dead center of the target. To assist that grading, we had a broken circle that was 100 feet from dead center and a solid circle that measured 50 feet from dead center. Without fully realizing it, they were practicing accuracy jumping from their first jump.

It was no surprise they agreed. They had a lot of experience following instructions. The fact they were still jumping at Land of Lincoln was testimony to that. I ran a tight ship. I was obsessed with student safety. There was no room at Land of Lincoln Sky Divers for the uncontrollable rule breaker.

We were allowed to send, three, 3-man teams. The ten members at the meeting fulfilled that requirement. The extra team member would act as backup.

"Gentlemen, Hebron Airport will be open every day for two weeks. Weather permitting, regardless how many show, we will conduct jumping exercises."

"Can Bob make it out every day?" Seemed to be the major question.

"I don't know I haven't asked him yet. But I have it from good sources, the Phantom Pilot will show." That was a private joke, between the members and me. I stayed at the airport Sunday night. Didn't bother taking 6565 Echo to our hanger at Gault Airport. She would be needed early Monday, the start of our team training program. Bill Mellor and Dale Kosack also stayed at the Motel in Hebron. By 10:15 Monday morning, all ten jumpers were at the airport.

Like all my classes I started with a short lecture. We gathered at the target area. This would be the class room for the next two weeks. Our final goal was to hit dead center. I figured we should get used to being in close proximity to our goal.

I have never told any of our members, I had any experience in competition jumping. They knew Connie 0"Rourke, Rick Olchivick and I started Sky Diving together, and each of us, in our own way, contributed to the Sport's growth in Illinois. They were surprised to find that Connie, Rick, and I were members on the same Competition Team and participated in many Sport Parachuting Contests, throughout Illinois, Iowa, Wisconsin, and Indiana. I didn't want them to think that they were getting instructions from Joe the rag man.

"Gentlemen, I am going to divide you up into three, 3-man teams." Bill Mellor interrupted.

"Mac, Dale, John and I would like to be on the same team. OK with you?" It would have been Ok, if this was a Democracy.

"Bill, that would be taking the Team Captains from Team two and three. Sorry, but my answer has to be no." The negative answer didn't bother them. They wanted to jump as a team, but they liked the idea, all three would be Team Leaders better."

The rest of the afternoon was devoted to practicing three man exits. Every jump would require the Team Leader to throw a wind - streamer out at 2200 feet (legal opening altitude).

Select an exit point, and give the command for the rest of the team to follow. All were warned not to go for dead center. Three jumpers going for the same spot on the ground, at the same time, will almost guarantee an injury. Dead center training would come later. The goal now was to learn to jump as a team.

The wind-streamer consisted of a fifteen foot long, 12 inch wide, piece of crape paper weighted at one end with a piece of welding (4 oz) rod and then rolled. Flying into the wind, the Jumper, throws the wind indicator out when the plane flies directly over the target. The welding rod will assist the crape paper to unroll. Fully open this home made wind-indicator will experience all the wind (wind can be coming from different directions at different altitudes) directions an open canopy experiences. In addition the crape paper, weighted properly will fall at the same rate as an open canopy. The Jumper then can draw an imaginary line from where the indicator landed, to the target. Heading into the wind, going the same distance beyond the target and select an exit point. Couple that with the steerability, of the parachute and you have the potential of obtainable accuracy. Rocket science, no, just an indicator.

They managed to get in three team jumps. We topped the gas tanks on 65 Echo and called it a day. These guys are full of surprises. They all decided to stay at the Hebron Motel. When I asked them about going to work, I was given every excuse under the sun. I'll call in sick, they owe me some time off, I work for my Father, he doesn't care. The best one was from our State Policeman, he would pick up his patrol car and monitor his radio from the airport.

"Listen up guys, get a good nights sleep, the first jump tomorrow will be at seven. Bob has to be at work at eight, he'll fly the demo jump, then go to work. I'll contact the Phantom Pilot and have him fly until Bob gets off at 15:00."

"What kind of demo? Who's making the Jump? What are you talking about?" Questions were being fired from every angle.

"Don't worry about it. You will recognize the jumper. You all have meet him several times. Just watch him closely and hopefully you will learn something about competition jumping."

Bob and I (the Phantom Pilot) were the first to arrive. While Bob got the aircraft ready for jumping, I loaded my main chute and reserve in the back seat of the aircraft. I put my jumpsuit on, then Bob and I had a cup of coffee while we waited for the teams to arrive.

Normally they stagger in a few at a time. Not this time, nor the rest of the two week training period. They came in convoy formation. After parking their vehicles, they laid their jump equipment on three matching parachute packing mats. Byron Palsun had the packing mats specially made for the meet in Lake Geneva. The 30 foot long 30 inch wide mats were white canvas, veinal covered on one side to keep moister from the equipment. On four comers and on each side, garments were installed allowing the mat to be staked down. When they were all set up, they called me over to get my reaction.

"I have never seen a packing-mat as good as this one. Byron ordered a dozen for the club." Byron went to his car and came back with 10 mats for Land of Lincoln. With a cup of coffee in hand we headed for the target area class room.

Then I started with my traditional short lecture. I asked them to recall the hours they spent hanging in the canopy training harness. That brought a loud reaction from the group. Hanging in a parachute harness while an instructor moves a wheeled target on the floor, is not known for its comfort. The students called the procedure, " Suspended Agony," a term borrowed from Army Airborne Training.

I asked what it meant, while facing the target, the target seemed to move away from them? All agreed it meant they were falling short of the desired landing area. Their agreement continued when I pointed out the fact that if the target seemed to be moving toward them, it meant you were going to land past the desired point.

"Gentlemen if the target is not moving away from you, nor moving to you, that in fact it seems to be standing still, and increasing in size, your going to hit that baby. Competition, canopy manipulation, is as simple as that."

"If it's that simple Mac, the other teams can do the same thing. We won't have a chance."

"Believe me, at the Geneva meet, most teams will enter the aircraft as a team. As soon as they open, it becomes an individual race for the target."

"The Land of Lincoln Teams will do it different. You will be a team when you enter the aircraft, when you exit the craft, and when you go in for the target. Each Team Leader will call all the shots. If he holds, you all hold. If he decides to run for the target, you all rum. Keep your eyes on the Team Leader. Do your best to duplicate his actions at the same place, he imitated the maneuver. It the Team leader starts a turn over a tree, bush or whatever, each team member makes the turn as close to that spot as possible. It doesn't matter where you land. Land as a Team. I uncovered an acetate covered, aerial picture of Hebron Airport and the surrounding area.

"Gentlemen, from this day forward, I don't want you on the Drop Zone without this chart. When you go to Lake Geneva I will furnish a chart of their area. You will also note I have three Magic Markers in the attached pouch. Green for Team 1, Red for Team 2 and Black for Team 3." I went on to tell them it wasn't their responsibility to keep the chart update. That would be done by an assigned Chart Keeper. However it was their responsibility to report everything they experienced during their jump. Wind direction and estimated velocity they experienced at different altitudes. The exact exit point for each jump. All information was to be preceded with the jump number and time of jump. The color would identify the team making the entry.

The Meet Promoters had the responsibility to drop a wind indicator before the first jump and again in the afternoon. Nevertheless, I wanted the additional information available to our teams. They were new to Competition Jumping and needed whatever information obtainable.

It was my intention to send a support team to assist Land of Lincoln's Jumpers. The support team would consist of eight Explorer Scouts. Of course they would be wearing their Land of Lincoln uniforms. Two Explorer Scouts would be assigned to each team. The plan called for them to lay out the opened parachutes for re-packing, or whatever else the jumpers needed help with. Two Scouts were to enter the data on the Area Chart. In addition they would monitor the ground wind direction, using a hand-held wind-indicator. These were outstanding, polite, young people, gentlemen all. The feedback I received after the Meet, from Connie O'Rourke was very complimentary.

"What I am about to tell you, is not to be discussed in front of students. Likewise what you are about to see, is not to be done nor demonstrated while students are present. I have to have your promise guy's, or this class is over." Without exception they promised. I chuted up while Bob started the aircraft.

"Watch every move I make. From the time my chute opens to the moment I hit dead center." Of course that got a laugh. Just before getting into the aircraft, I reached inside my jumpsuit and retrieved a 6" diameter heavy aluminum disk, painted bright red.

"Put this on Dead Center." I announced, tossing the disk, to the class.

We made a pass over the target at 2200 feet and dropped a wind indicator. At the time the FAA rule was, have a full canopy at 2200 feet above the ground. As we climbed to 3600 feet, the altitude all teams were to jump from at the Geneva Meet, I selected an exit point.

At this point it was important to perform the same way I will be asking the teams to perform. Free of the aircraft my first task was to check to see how close I was to the exit point. Satisfied, my next task was to locate the target area. At the same time keeping tract on any movement my body might have in relation to the target. Finally, a turn into the wind to open my chute. I had ten seconds to preform my simple tasks.

After checking my canopy, to see it was intact and it was steerable, I unhooked the left side of my reserve. Having a reserve on your chest obstructs the view of the ground. Hanging on one side enhances your chances for accuracy. Slight problem, the reserve and the attached instrument panel, could slap you across the face when you land. There is a defense against this happening. You can be assured our jumpers would be taught this technique.

Student jumpers are taught to turn and head for the target area, after they check their canopies. The competition jumper doesn't make an unnecessary move unless they are convinced the move will bring them closer to the target area.

With my reserve out of the way I had an unobstructed view of my feet in relation to ground movement. Facing into the wind, my first check was to see if the built in speed of my canopy could cancel out the prevailing wind speed. It didn't, that prevented me from facing the target at this point. My next check was to check the Target over my shoulder to insure I was heading toward it. I was, and with a combination of holding (facing the wind) and running (facing the Target), I worked my way to the red disk. I hit so soft, I had to force myself to the ground. Then with a lightning fast move, I got away from the red disk as though it was on fire.

116

The answer is "both."

The question, "who learns during a period of instruction, the student or the instructor?"

I have been teaching parachute maneuvering for more than nine years. Hitting the target disk didn't surprise me. The reaction of the class was overwhelming. One would think I had just discovered the cure for baldness.

"When did you know you had dead center Mac?" Bill Mellor asked.

"At one thousand feet I knew I was going to be close. When I came over the north fence, I was about two hundred feet. At that point I knew, the red disk was mine. That's what we are going to talk about now. Final setup to hit the target." At that point Charlie Blumster showed up with cold refreshments.

I moved the class-location to the point on our North fence line where I crossed on my way to the target, just a few minutes ago. I went over my jump procedures' step by step, emphasizing the importance of a jumper, constantly knowing their exact movement in relation to the target, even while they are free falling.

I pointed out that the big difference they would have to overcome was facing the wind when opening. It didn't matter much when you are fun jumping, if you face the wind or not. In competition jumping it just might be the difference between winning or losing. The wind velocity plus the built-in speed of the canopy might use up distances that can't be recovered.

"After checking your canopy, do not, I repeat, do not turn toward the target until you are sure you are falling short of the target. If the target seems to be moving away from you, then and only then, turn and use the wind to make the correction." Of course Byron being Byron, had to change the subject.

"Mac did you know, your reserve unhooked?"

I unhooked my reserve after I checked my canopy. That enabled me to have an unrestricted view of the ground. That's taking me ahead of my story Byron, more about unhooking the reserve later. I continued.

"If you recall when I was crossing this fence line, I made two turns to face the wind. On both turns, my canopy not only canceled the wind, it carried me back into the wind. At this point I knew I was in complete control. As you witnessed, I steered my chute, a little to the right of the target. Just as I passed the center I made my final turn into the target. With a little foot adjustment, I bagged that little red rascal."

I asked them to recall me telling them about O'Rourke, Olchivick and myself jumping in competition. I continued the story by telling them, although we entered several competitions, we never came home with many trophies. Every loss could be traced to the last canopy turn in the target area. About 90 percent of the time, a turn was made, to avoid hitting our fellow team mates.

"At the Lake Geneva meet, jumper in the air, hit the team member that just landed. Jumper that just landed, move out of the way."

"Mac we can't do that." Seemed to be the group reaction.

"Sure you can. If your Team Leader makes a left hook into the target, the Team Members following, make a left hook into the target. Upon landing, the Team Leader roles to the right. Just follow his lead. The separation you had during the jump is still there. It just looks a little closer because the jump is terminating. Practice this over and over. When you get to Geneva, it will all come together. This class is over, meet me in the packing shed in thirty minutes."

"What about unhooking the reserve?"

"Byron the class is over." Byron was a nice kid, but for some reason he aggravated me.

I used the packing shed meeting to summarize previously covered subjects and to issue equipment. I had just modified ten, fresh out of their storage cans, U S Air Force orange and white surplus canopies. Each was modified five gore TU's. Each had never used surplus B-4 Back Packs and new Land of Lincoln black and white striped sleeves.

"I want you all to practice what we have covered during the last few hours. However, not in front of students. You all know student attempting any thing we have learned today would put them in harms way. I'm serious about this, not in front of students."

The day of the meet, they all gathered at Hebron Airport. Lake Geneva was only about twelve miles down the road. This was their first Parachute Meet. I think they needed the support from each other. They not only looked good, they were as good as they looked. They have been practicing hard.

"How many trophies are you bringing home?" My question was directed to the whole group.

"How many do they have?" Was the group's answer. Two weeks ago this same group, didn't think they had a chance. Now they are thinking of destroying the opposing force. I guess that's what happens when Giant's gather."

"One thing before you go guys'. It will be up to the individual to unhook his reserve or not. If you decide to unhook, you unhook the left side only. I went on to explain that would insure the reserve ripcord was on top and less likely to be accidently deployed.

"One more thing. Remember, that loose reserve will have a tendency to slap you in the face upon landing. Use your right arm to prevent that from happing.

I was a little concerned, our Explorer Scouts had not arrived. Then Bob Curry drove in the driveway. He was alone.

"Where is the ground crew Bob?"

"At Lake Geneva Mac. They camped there last night." Bob went on to tell me that the people in Lake Geneva wanted to use the Explore Scouts to man their vending stands and control traffic.

"I told them no way. Their specialty was Sky Diving, not hot dog and soda peddlers. Is that OK Mac?"

"You did great Bob. The scouts are there to assist the Land of Lincoln Teams only. Bill Mellor will see to that. I was thinking about breaking you in as a Jump Master today. Feel up to it? Most of our Jump Masters would be at the Meet."

"Sure Mac, I can do it." Bob Curry, a mountain of a man with a heart as big as the outdoors. I have never seen him get mad, nor would I want to. This was one big guy. I almost had to stand on a chair to chew him out when he made training mistakes. His concern over student training and promoting Land of Lincoln, earned him high marks on our favorite people list. Bob Curry would make a great Jump Master.

Before our teams departed, I wished them luck. I told them that we would have a little victory celebration at the club house in Chicago. I knew we would stop jumping early. Most of our members would be at the Lake Geneva Meet cheering our teams on. I kind of wish I could be with them. Unlike most jumping organizations, Land of Lincoln was trying to be a profitable company. I had to stay at Hebron Airport. Accounts payable, were in complete control of my schedule.

I earned my keep that day. I didn't realize how important my advanced jumpers were to the operation of Land of Lincoln. In spite of the heavy work load we finished jumping about 5:00 P.M., we headed for Chicago. That is everybody except Bob. Bob Curry wanted to see how his Scouts were doing in Lake Geneva.

Several members had arrived at the School on Milwaukee by 8 P.M.. A few that had been at the meet didn't have much to say about how our guys had done. I found that a little strange, and it kind of ticked me off. This was the first competition Land of Lincoln had ever participated in, a little enthusiasm would be in order.

Everyone was downstairs in the Club House, I was doing some book work when I heard the Teams arriving. Byron Pulson was the first in the door carrying a damaged canopy. Walking to the packing table, he hung the apex on a hook and draped the canopy on the packing table.

"Sit here Mac." I couldn't believe my ears. Byron giving me orders. Byron's ability to get my goat was on target. Reluctantly I sat on the packing table.

Byron gave the signal and our three Competition Teams filed in, each carrying the Trophies they won.

One by one they placed them around me. I couldn't believe my eyes. They took all Team awards, first, second and third.

In addition Bill and John took second and third individual awards. I have never been prouder of their accomplishments.

"Go on down stairs guys, the members have a little victory celebration planed for you. I'll join you in a bit, I have a couple of things I have to do.

Alone, looking at the trophies, my mind was filled with mixed emotion. I was happy because they won and sad because the will soon be leaving. An old song filled my thoughts;   "How are you going to keep them down on the farm, after they seen Pari?"

Demonstration jumps and jumping to help raise money for charities are great for public relations and truly a pleasurable experience. Our members loved them. Unfortunately there is a down side. In addition to tying up the aircraft, there is an associated cost that pays havoc on the budget.

I was good at juggling money. But the rob Peter to pay Paul strategy was bound to backfire. A smart person seeing the hand writing on the wall would have discontinued all Demonstration Jumps. I have never been accused of being smart, clever but not smart.

Sending jumpers to competitions didn't cost the company any money, jumpers pay their own entrance fee. However when your best jumpers, who are also your instructors, are away from the airport, it adversely affects the training program. Land of Lincoln's main source of income was its student program.

Time to Leave the Nest

I have no problem getting rid of the "hurray for me the heck with others," kind of jumper. As soon as they went on free fall, if they didn't show signs of helping Land of Lincoln Sky Divers grow, they were history.

There were parachute clubs in the area that weren't trying to build a business. Groups just organized for the fun of jumping. Chicago Sky Diving at Campbell Airport, east of us was one of the better ones. Connie O'Rorke ran an operation just outside Lake Geneva Wisconsin. In fact most of my throw always ended up with Connie. If I found a person undesirable, more likely than not Rick Olchivick the president of Chicago Sky Divers, would rate them the same. Connie was easy going and would give you the shirt off his back. Believe me the people I kicked out of Land of Lincoln, would take the shirt, then complain it wasn't freshly laundered.

The jumpers I kept at Land of Lincoln were top notch, eager to learn. Giants, or potential Giants. Their loyalty to Land of Lincoln triggered my obligation to them. As they grew in their jumping skills, their desire to achieve kept pace. There was no way I would be able to afford the high altitude jumps they needed for their licence requirements. I knew down deep that one-day they would leave the nest.

The request for exhibition jumps increased monthly. With the increase of demonstration jumping our ability to handle large beginner jump classes diminished. To stay afloat Land of Lincoln had to do some drastic readjustments.

The first casualty was our Flying School. Although it was holding, it's own. The flight school was more of a convenience to our members than a money making endeavor. Closing it didn't seem much of a loss. That turned out to be wrong. The moment an organization stops going foreword, it is at that moment decline sets in.

To deal with the declining number of student jumpers I decided to move our Chicago based jump school to a smaller location. That also was a mistake. Eventually I moved the whole operation to the airport. With that move the planes for a Fly in Motel and swimming pool moved off the drawing board. Then one Saturday morning, the final blow.

"Mac can we have a talk?" Bill Mellor asked.

"Sure Bill, what's on your mind?" Bill started the conversation by stating he and four other jumpers were working on their Class C Parachuting License and needed higher jumps to satisfy the requirements. He didn't have to mention their names. I knew he was talking about my top five people, the very heart of our organization. Bill went on, explaining they were going to Lake Geneva. Lake Geneva had two twin engine aircraft capable of high altitudes.

"Mac this will be our last week end at Hebron Airport. I hope it will not hurt our friendship. We all owe a lot to Land of Lincoln."

"Bill, look at that sky. Not one cloud, don't waste it. I would go to Lake Geneva now, if I were you." That ended the conversation, I went about the business of training new jumpers.

I was on a final run to drop a new student when I looked down to see three cars leaving the parking lot, heading for Lake Geneva. I watched them as long as I could. Maybe they will change their mind and come back. That didn't happen. Back to the business at hand.

"GET OUT!" Then over the exit point, "GO!" It was a hard Summer, but Land of Lincoln hung in there. Before I knew it, December was upon us. It was a cloudless day, cold but a good jumping day. I was in the packing shed packing some student chutes. Suddenly a familiar voice;

"Hi Mac." It was Bill Mellor. I didn't get a chance to answer.

122

"Mac Connie was just killed in a parachute jump." I couldn't answer, Cornelius O'Rourke was a very personal friend. I felt I had just been hit by a train.

'How is Sarah doing?" Sarah was Connie's wife and also a personal friend.

"She is taking it pretty hard Mac. She asked me to tell you about the accident. If you get the time, I am sure she would appreciate you paying her a visit."

"There will be an investigation Bill. Lake Geneva will be closed until it is completed. Tell your team mates they are welcome to come back to Land of Lincoln."

"They're out in the parking lot. We kind of thought you would let us come home. Mac what about." I didn't let Bill finish. I knew he was going to ask me if the other jumpers from Lake Geneva were welcome. The answer would have been no.

"Take care of the place Bill, you know what to do. I'm going to see Sarah.

"What are you guys doing sitting around in your autos? Can't log jumps that way." As they unloaded the vehicles, I could see a smile on every face. My prodigal children have come home. I took off for Lake Geneva.

Rick Olchivick, PCA's area Safety Officer had already arrived by the time I pulled into the main entrance to Lake Geneva Drop Zone. Connie's accident really tore us up. The three of us were very close.

"Mac can you give me a hand on this investigation for PCA?"

"Sure Rick." Like Rick, I was a certified FAA parachute rigger. My input would be important to the overall safety investigation.

While I examined the faulty equipment, Rick interviewed some of the Lake Geneva Jumpers. The plan was to meet after lunch and compare notes. Because of our close relationship with Connie, this became a monumental task.

I was about finished with the equipment examination. I was removing the altimeter from Connie's reserve, when Sarah walked in the equipment room. I was putting off seeing her. I didn't know what to say that could give her comfort nor express my true feelings. As she got closer my arms opened. We stood there for some time not uttering a word. The only sound was Sarah's weeping. Words were not spoken but surely reverent communication was taking place. Rick walked in and joined our circle. After a while, we walked Sarah to her car and promised her we would have dinner with her that night. Just before Sarah drove off, she uttered words that would start to reveal the reason for such a tragedy.

"Mac Connie didn't want to make that jump. He couldn't get anybody to take his place."

Connie was making a Santa Clause jump at a Mall. When his main chute malfunctioned, he deployed his reserve. The reserve tangled with the malfunction. Connie rode both entangled chutes to the ground. All his efforts to get a replacement for Santa's jump failed. It was then Connie decided to make the jump himself.

Cornelius O'Rourke had no business jumping at a Mall or any other hard service landing zone. In all the years I have been jumping with Connie, he had never jumped before he asked me to bandage his ankle's with elastic bandages. Connie has had problems with both ankles since his jump at Normandy in World War II. Bandaging his ankles was as important as rigger checking the jump equipment.

The meeting with Rick Olchivick after lunch was short and to the point. I reported the condition of the main parachute was questionable. It had a damp feel and musty smell. This was no great surprise. Lake Geneva didn't have a packing table one, nor did they use packing mats. One could easily visualize a parachute picking up moisture from the grass. Especially if the chute was packed in the early morning or late evening when the dew is the heaviest. Storing the parachute, then jumping a wet chute could affect its opening properly.

Because of Connie's weak ankles, he was hesitant about coming in on a reserve parachute. Not only are reserve parachutes smaller in diameter, reserves have a tendency to oscillate, insuring a hard landing. Because of this Rick and I came to the obvious conclusion, Connie waited to long before he deployed his reserve.

Most of Connie's members at Lake Geneva were rejects from Land of Lincoln Sky Divers. Knowing them I could understand them not wanting to help Connie with his demonstration jump. What puzzled me was Bill or one of the other four, new arrivals from Land of Lincoln not making the jump for Connie. Asking around I was happy to find out Connie took off for the Santa Claus jump before they arrived.

The large crowed at Connie's funeral was a tribute to his popularity. Cornelius O'Rourke was respected and liked by most who meet him. I paid my respect to Sarah, then went looking for the person in charge. I had let my feelings known that I wanted to be one of the pallbearer's. I saw Rick standing with several other jumpers and headed in their direction.

"Hi Rick, who's running this show?"

"No one Mac. Six of us will carry the casket and we have twelve honorary pallbearers' that will follow behind."

"Gentlemen, I got news for you. I will be carrying Connie to his final DZ. One of you will have to join the honorary group."

"What makes you think you can take over and give us orders? This isn't Land of Lincoln."

"Well, look who's acting like he has a spine. You just volunteered, Johnny boy." John C. was one of a group of three I expelled from Land of Lincoln, for moral reasons. He and two others tried to force their attention on fourteen year-old girl who lived near our school on Milwaukee Avenue. The young girl had learning difficulties, which made her an easy target.

I can honestly say I didn't push hot lips out of the way. I held his arm firmly, guiding him in the direction I wanted hin to take. John C. knew not to resist. The night I caught them, I demonstrated my ability with fisticuffs. There was something about John C that gave me pleasure to pound on his face. Like the good book say's, "turn the other cheek." I did one better, I turned him around and kicked the other two.

We buried more than Cornelius O'Rourke PCA licence # D 200 at Lake Geneva. We buried part of the Midwest area Sport Parachuting history. I'll bet ten to one, Connie is teaching the angles how to improve their free fall technique.

They say time heals everything. This wasn't true in my case. I had two very depressing things going on in my mind. The first, how to save my dream of a Sport Parachuting Center. The second, a deep feeling of guilt, not being part of the struggle America was having in Vietnam. Going back in the Army and volunteering for Vietnam, became a thought I lived with. Some say I was looking for an easy way out. Those who would say that, don't know Mrs. McGinley s' son Daniel.

I don't think going to war is the easy way out. Going to war is a soldier's obligation.

Chapter Three

The Fight Begins

The news from Vietnam was worsening daily. The feeling of not doing my part was dominating my thoughts. Television brought the horror of war to our living rooms. I watched an Army Captain propped up against a tree going into shock. "Lay him down, raise his legs, you fool!" I yelled at my  television set. Of course nobody could hear me. Though to myself, if I was there, he wouldn't have died.

"Well, why aren't you there?" I asked myself. Second guessing a medic under enemy fire is like being a Sunday afternoon quarterback, all show and no go.

It was the first week of July 1966. I was on the return leg of a cross country flight in my Cessna 175. I got as far as Rockford, Illinois, before the weather made it impossible to continue. I wasn't a great pilot but I was a safe one. The decision to lie over in Rockford was made without hesitation. I didn't know it at the time but this decision would change my life and countless other lives.

The sun was shining bright as I departed the hotel. Looking up and down the street for a restaurant, I noticed an Army Recruiting Office. I felt it won't hurt to talk to them. Forgetting breakfast, I headed straight for the Recruiting Office.

I was greeted by SFC (Sergeant First Class) Robert L.Adams. SFC Adams was quite confident that I would be able to enlist in the Army. Adams stated that the Army would be glad to have someone with combat experience join their ranks. The fact that I had been in two wars and was volunteering for Vietnam would improve my chances greatly. Both of us knew my age might be a factor.

"No problem, we'll ask for a waiver. My God, people are burning their draft cards on the White House steps in protest to the Vietnam War. Others are going to Canada to avoid being drafted. Yes sir, the Army will be glad to have you Mac. Let me shake your hand." Adams might have been feeding me propaganda. I had no problem with that. I was eating it up.

Adams told me the 101st Airborne was going to Vietnam. It might be a good idea (since I was Airborne) to fly down there and have a talk with them. Who knows, maybe they could pull some strings. It surely couldn't hurt. Sounded good to me, beside I needed to log more cross country flying time. I plotted a course to Outlaw Field, a civilian airstrip on US 41, across from Fort Campbell, Kentucky home of the 101st Airborne Division. Thank you, SFC Robert L. Adams.

Landing at Outlaw Field, I was greeted by a gentleman that seemed quite upset with me.

"Did you know you just flew through the Military air space?"

"Of course, I know air space is controlled around Military Reservations. Do you think I'm some kind of dummy?"

I called Ft Campbell Base Operations and requested transportation. A staff car was sent to pick me up. I'm sure the airport manager was convinced I knew what I was doing and I was probably a VIP. I entered the 101st Airborne Division Headquarters. I told the receptionist the nature of my visit and asked to see the Command Sergeant Major. The receptionist made a few phone calls.

"The CSM is in the cafeteria. He invites you to join him."

Over lunch I told CSM Butler my intention of volunteering for Vietnam. I told him I knew the 101st Airborne was going to Vietnam and wanted to join them. I had a great interview with the CSM. He made me feel welcome. I informed Sergeant Major Butler, of my slight difficulty at Outlaw Airport.

"No problem." Then he made a few phone calls. The CSM managed to get my flight in approved and logged in. I also was given permission, to return by the same route.

"Call me when your enlistment is approved. I'll do all I can to make you a Screaming Eagle.", were his departing words. Flying home my head was in the clouds, even though the sky was clear as a bell. Soon I would be back in uniform, fulfilling my duty to country. All is well.

No Time to Waste

Convinced the Army would be calling me any day, I started to get my personal life in order. My biggest problem was to figure out what to do with, Land of Lincoln Sky Diving School at Hebron Airport. A lot of people, stuck with me in the early years while I was developing my Sky Diving School. I just couldn't leave them hanging. I decided to Incorporate. I'd made them a deal they couldn't refuse.

Ten of my loyal associates jumped at the chance, to own Land of Lincoln Sky Diving Inc. I was pleased the school would be in good hands until my return from Vietnam. We had no sooner completed the stock transfer when SFC Alman, called with the disappointing news. My enlistment was disapproved.

Land of Lincoln Club Patch

"Not favorably considered" they put it. Exception to age requirements contained in paragraph 3.e(20), AR 601-210 is not made. I considered this denial an insult. I vowed to fight this decision to the bitter end.

Sometimes our government is hard to understand. During this period a large portion of our population was protesting the US involvement in Vietnam. Draftable individuals were burning their Draft Cards and went to Canada to avoid being drafted. Would you believe after the war, they were given a pardon and received the same benefits given to the patriotic Americans who served their country?

The fight would last sixteen months, with an expenditure of five thousand dollars of my personal funds. The campaign was started with a letter to the Secretary of Defense Robert McNamara. I figured he worked for the American citizens and this citizen demanded an answer.

Dear Sir

I have been trying to join the Army since10 April1967, to serve my Country in Vietnam. Not thinking it was possible for my country to turn down my request for active duty, I sold my Sky diving Business, put all my personal affairs in order, to be ready when my enlistment papers returned.

"Not Favorably Considered," Sir, this is my country, and when she in engaged in a conflict, it becomes my conflict. I respectfully request that you reprocess my papers and enlist me in the Army as Staff Sergeant E6, for service in Vietnam. I hope to receive a favorable reply from you at your earliest convenience.

Resentfully Yours

Daniel T. McGinley

P.S. I am available for personal interview, in Washington or any other place, on date and time you specify.

McNamara didn't have the courtesy to answer my letter himself. I received a reply from a Lt. Colonel Leo J. Martineau, the Chief of Personal Action Division. He stated they appreciated the spirit which prompted my offer and desire to serve my country. Never-the-less, they could not break, the regulation on age. Someone should have told this misguided officer, regulations are just guide lines, and that is all they are, guide lines.

If I wanted a letter from an LTC, I would have written to an LTC. I later learned that the Secretary of Defense, was having some personal problems. McNamara resigned his Secretary of Defense position shortly after. No loss I say. If you can't stand the heat, stay out of the kitchen. An old saying but a true one. I'll have to try another approach. I will go to Vietnam, and that is a fact.

This letter angered me. But what angered me the most was every time you turned the news on, the main story was about Anti War demonstrators protesting the Vietnam War.

The leader of the anti American activity was Jane Fonda. Fonda began her participation in antiwar activities around 1967, allegedly after meeting with Communists while in France and with American citizens who were revolutionaries. Her activities included active participation in demonstrations, rallies, radio broadcasts and plays.

In 1972 Jane Fonda, Tom Hayden and others traveled to North Vietnam to give their support to the North Vietnamese's Government. When she returned to the United States, she advised the news media that all of the American Prisoners of War were being well treated and were not being tortured. She

Jane Fonda applauding NVA Gun Crew

went out of her way in supporting our nation's enemy. Her trip to North Vietnam angered many Americans.

I am a strong believer in freedom of speech. I also believe strongly that it can be carried too far. We had young Americans dying in Vietnam serving their country. Yet the gutless are given permits to demonstrate against their noble sacrifice. The place to demonstrate is at the ballot box. Demonstrating in the streets, disrupting. and destroying everything around, is mob action and nothing more. Thank God, most Americans appreciated the sacrifice of the patriotic Americans serving their country.

More Than One Way to Skin a Cat

The situation in Vietnam continued to deteriorate. Not only were they calling up reserve units, individual reserve members, could volunteer for a fifteen-month Vietnam tour. I had only been out of, the 302nd Special Forces Reserve, for a short period of time. I decided to try that approach.

The 302nd went from a Special Forces Detachment, to a Special Forces (12th) Group Headquarters. That really didn't surprise me. The 302nd had a lot of talented people, very capable of their new mission. I went to see them at their new location in Cicero, Illinois.

It was like going home. First to greet me was CWO John Condage. John was the 12th Group Administrative Officer. I was glad of that. John had the reputation of making seemingly impossible administration tasks workable.

"Come to join us, Mac? " John greeted me holding out his hand.

"In a way, yes, John." I replied as we shook hands.

"I'm trying to get to Vietnam, and the only way left is activating myself, through the Reserve."

"Oh, yes, the fifteen-month program. Sure that will work. Let's go see the Commander." I felt better. I was at home surrounded by friends.

"Look who's paying us a visit Sir."

"Mac, glad to see you. Have you come to join us? Your slot is still open, with an increase in rank."

"Congratulations on your promotion Sir. That Major Leaf looks good." I wasn't just buttering him up, it did look good. If anyone deserved a promotion, it was Captain, now Major Hoffman. This great officer turned down a promotion to Major in the old 302nd. The 302nd didn't have a Major slot. The promotion would have triggered a reassignment to another unit. There was no way this talented soldier would leave Special Forces.

"As far as joining Sir, as I told Warrant Officer Condage, in a way yes. I'm having a little trouble getting to Vietnam. The Army has an age cutoff they won't budge on. However, if I was a Reservist, I could activate myself for what they call, a fifteen-month Vietnam tour." I went on to explain the program. The fifteen-month tour, allowed three months, for in and out processing, and twelve months in Vietnam.

"If anybody can pull it off Mac, it will be you." Our conversation was interrupted by CWO Condage entering with a hand full of papers. He went behind the desk and laid the paper work in front of the Major.

"Sign here, and initial all the crossed out words' Sir." I couldn't help wondering how in the world could my enlistment papers be ready for signing. I had only been here ten minutes at the most. Condage was good, but not that good. As though the CWO was reading my mind,

"Wonder how we did this so fast Mac? Tell him Sir."

"SGT Mac, when you left us to build your Sport Parachuting Center, we knew you would be back. CWO Condage suggested and I agreed, to keep your enlistment papers on file. We knew you would come home.

"Sign above your name, welcome home." The CO was shaking my hand when CWO Condage butted in.

"Sign here Major. This is Mac's request for active duty, under the Fifteen Month Program." OK, the Major explained the enlistment papers being ready. How in the world did the activation papers appear so fast? When I asked John, he replied

"Magic Mac, just pure magic."

In less than an hour I was sworn in the 12th Special Forces Group, as a Staff Sergeant (E6) with a request for active duty. John's reputation of making seemingly impossible administration tasks workable, was on target.

Special Forces had a great friend in the Army Assignment Branch. Mrs. Billy Alexander was in charge of Special Forces assignment's world wide. I called her. After about ten minutes on the phone, I felt I knew her all my life. Calling her a great lady, would not begin to describe her. Special Forces truly had a person who cared about them. A female Giant if you please. Mrs. "A," as everyone called her, said it might take a few months to get me a Special Forces assignment in Vietnam. She also informed me, if I could get to Vietnam, regardless of the unit, she could get me to a Special Forces assignment without any problem. OK, Mrs. A, Airborne all the way. I read you loud and clear. I packed my bag, rented a car and hand carried my activation papers to the Pentagon in Washington, D.C.

Mrs "A"

I was promptly informed, my paper work had to be taken to the Chief of Personal Actions. This was the same officer, who wrote the letter for McNamara. Thank you, but no thank you. Trick me once, it's your fault. Trick me twice, and it's my fault. To date I had wasted sixteen months, and spent almost five thousand dollars, trying to serve my country, enough is enough. Time to see the main man. LBJ I'm on the way.

I guess I'm a pain in the neck sometimes. But if I feel strongly about something and it's not against the law, I don't let go. I felt very strong about going to Vietnam. As far as I was concerned, all elected officials work for the people. Going to see the President didn't bother me a bit.

132

Himself LBJ

I waited three days, to see Linden B. Johnson. The afternoon of the third day the large doors opened, and there was himself, the President of the United States. Following close behind the President, was a very nervous looking Army Colonel. I started to get second thoughts. If he turned me down, I don't know what I would do. The President's secretary was the first to speak.

"This is the Sergeant I told you about Mr. President." I jumped up, and the President reached out his hand. As we shook hands, I had to look up, Lyndon B. Johnson was a very tall man.

"Sorry it took so long for you to see me, Sergeant McGinley. As you probably know, I have a lot of irons in the fire."

"Yes Sir, I have come to help you with one of them." The words popped out of my mouth. I didn't want to sound like a smart aleck, but I really felt I could help.

"Colonel, get this Sergeant in my Army." The little puppy dog perked up.

"Yes, Mr. President. Yes sir, I'll take care of that right away sir." The President pulled the string and the puppet jumped. My departing phrase was a classic. I was quite good at opening my mouth before engaging my brain.

"Thank you again, Mr. President. I won't let you down." (Like I was doing this for him.)

"You better not, Sergeant. I'll see to it you're a Private faster than a cow can knock over a bucket of milk." Seemed like the President had the same, mouth and brain engagement problem. He followed that statement, with a hardy "Ha, Ha." I'm here to tell you, I was on cloud nine. Thank you God, thank you, thank you.

A sad look came over the President's face. He turned, said something to the Colonel in a low voice, and excused himself. We shook hands again, and he walked away. The President, suddenly didn't seem so big. It was obvious he was carrying, the world on his shoulders. I'm not a Democrat, but I liked the man. I don't know about you, but I have always found, the higher you go to solve your problem, the easier it becomes.

"How long will it take you to pack Sergeant McGinley?" Now the question didn't startle me, but the tone of voice did. Less than a minute ago, the puppet was meek as a lamb. Now the President was out of sight, the Colonel was talking like he was the king of the roost.

"I'm ready now Sir."

"It seems a little unusual to me, a person would be ready to go to war at the drop of a hat," The Colonel replied with a voice, that had a tone of disbelief.

"Sir, let me tell you something. I have had, bureaucracy up too here," Holding my hand palm down under my nose. "I have been trying for sixteen months, to go to Vietnam. Unusual, is not the word sir, determination is the word you should be using. If seeing, the President didn't work Sir, I would have had to use my contingency plan."

"What was your contingency plan?"

"Classified Sir, classified." He smiled.

"Go to the Pentagon, see Lieutenant Colonel Martineau. Do you know Lieutenant Colonel Martineau?"

"Oh yes, Sir. The LTC and I correspond frequently." I had my fingers crossed. This was the same LTC who answered my letter to McNamara.

"I'll let him know you are coming. I'm glad I was able to work this problem out for you." I had to pause before I answered.

"I appreciate your help Sir." Gave him a salute and got out of there, before I told him what I was thinking about. Who worked out what?

As soon as I opened the door, I knew that I was needed in the Army, and needed bad. An over fed, sloppy looking excuse for a soldier opened the conversation.

"Yes, what do you need? "

"First of all, Specialist, my name is Sergeant. What I need is you to button up that uniform. You're sloppier than a draft dodging, flag burning hippie, on his way to Canada." I knew I could replace this clown, and look better doing it. Have you ever felt someone was behind you, you couldn't see them, you just felt their presence? As I was talking to this slob, I had that feeling.

"Do you have a problem Sergeant?" a friendly voice inquired. Turning I replied,

"Is this guy on our side Sir?"

"Unfortunately yes. " LTC Martineau replied. "I had a call from the White House, informing me you were on the way. Seems you're the kind of a person that can't take no for an answer. How about a MAC-V assignment in Vietnam?" I didn't have the slightest idea what a MAC-V assignment was. I surely didn't want the LTC, to know of my ignorance.

"What part of Vietnam will that take me to Sir?"

"You will go to a replacement center in Saigon. Then you'll be assigned to a unit." The reply, didn't answer my question. I dropped the subject. The fact I was going to Vietnam, was good enough for me. I saluted the LTC, and departed. I drove the rented car back to Chicago, said a few hasty goodbyes. Ten days later, I was on final approach, to Tan Son Nhut Airfield, in Vietnam. Mrs. A, I love you.

Tan Son Nhut Airfield Vietnam

Welcome to Vietnam

Now the test, does Mrs. A have all the power everyone claims? How will she pull this one off? Here I sit wearing a baseball cap, heading for a leg (non airborne) assignment with MAC-V. Of course, I had a Green Beret in my pocket. In the back of my mind, the question remained . . . How in the world will Special Forces pull this one off? As soon as the plane came to a halt, a friendly voice, came over the loud speaker.

"Welcome to Vietnam." A slight pause then, "SSG McGinley report to the rear of the aircraft." Hey, this is great. Just arrived, already I'm being paged. Told them, they couldn't win this war without me. The aircraft door opened, standing on the ramp, was SGM Richard Campbell.

"Hi, Mac. Take that baseball cap off, you won't be needing it anymore." At the same time, SGM Campbell handed me a Green Beret.

Dan 1968

"No thank you, Sergeant Major. I appreciate the offer, but I won't be needing that Beret, I have one of my own." He smiled, as I threw the issued Army baseball cap to the wind. I put on my Green Beret.

I was taken to, a Special Forces Safe House in Saigon. The plan was to keep me there until Special Forces convinced MAC-V to give them my records. At 10:45, 30 January 1968, I boarded a C-130 (classified, specially equipped) Blackbird flight to, 5th Special Forces Headquarters in Nha Trang.

The Vietnamese New Year (TET), Year of the Monkey, began 31 January, while we were in flight to Nha Trang. Tet is Vietnam's major holiday. It is like our Christmas, New Year and Thanksgiving, thrown into one week long holiday. Tet is celebrated in both North and South Vietnam. There was a truce, the North and the South had agreed that there would be no offensive operations conducted during the Lunar New Year celebrations.

The North Communist government chose as usual, to betray their word. The North Vietnamese and Viet Cong, launched a massive attack country wide. By the time we landed, the fighting was almost over. Six of us arriving on the Blackbird, were rushed to a waiting truck. Our destination, was a makeshift bunker, downtown Nha Trang.

The Bunker was, at an intersection, down the road form, the Nha Trang Hotel. Across from us, another bunker, occupied by American and Vietnamese MP's. There wasn't much fighting going on. An occasional shot now and then but nothing, really exciting was happening.

Downtown Nha Trang

In 1968, all new arrivals, assigned to Special Forces, were required, to go through their COC (Combat Orientation Course) conducted at the SF Recondo School in Nha Trang, just down the road from Group Headquarters.

5ᵗʰ Group Hdq

Recondo School

The course served two purposes. It familiarized new troops with enemy weapons and booby traps, and as a refresher course on, US weapons, M-79 & 81 motors, Map Reading, Requesting, Tactical Air & Artillery Support.   It also afforded them time to get used to the Viennese weather.   The climax of the course was a joint search and destroy operation with both, a Vietnamese and American Special Forces A Teams.   I thought I was in good shape until I met up with these guys.   I was hurting but didn't want them to know it. I fooled everybody except a very large Native American, MSG Pahael Leanna. He noticed I was having difficulty.

"Give me your rucksack Mac." I hesitated, but finally gave in. I knew I was getting close to heat stroke. I'm telling you this was one strong guy. Carrying both rucksacks, his in the back, mine in the front, Leanna charged through the jungle like a tank. I trotted behind taking advantage of the hole he made in the foliage. MSG Leanna was being assigned as the new Team Sergeant of Plateau Gi A-243.

In about two hours I got my second wind. At the next break I took my rucksack and we continued our force march through the triple canopy. It seemed the Vietnam Team and the American SF Team were having a contest. Each trying to outdo the other. Maybe they were just trying to impress us. Whatever the reason, they impressed us.

In the back of my mind I was hoping we would make contact with the enemy. That would give us an excuse to stop and catch our breath. Anything would be better that this mad race through the jungle. We bedded down by a small river for the night. I was too tired to sleep. The thought came to my mind. Maybe I was too old for this war stuff.

B-24 Kontum Vietnam

My next move was to a Special Forces B-Team in Kontum, located in Northern II Corps. I was greeted by their CSM (Command Sergeant Major).

"I'm assigning you to the B-Team McGinley. My medic runs the club."

"First of all, it's SSG McGinley. I'm not your medic Sergeant Major." I replied in a highly ticked-off tone. "I didn't come to Vietnam to run a bar. I'm a medic and a good one. I came here to practice medicine. Do I make myself clear? Don't misunderstand me SGM Henge. I'm not disrespectful to your rank. You see, I fought for two years and spent a lot of my own money getting to Vietnam. I came to use whatever medical skills I have and save as many lives as I can. That is exactly what I'm going to do."

I could tell by the glare in his eyes he wasn't used to anybody talking to him in this tone. For a few moments, I thought he might take a swing at me. That wouldn't have mattered. I was ready to do battle with the enemy. As far as I was concerned, the enemy was standing in front of me.

"SSG follow me." The frustrated CSM blurted out. We walked across the hall to the CO's office. "This SSG questions my authority on assignments' Colonel, I think we had better straighten him out."

"McGinley" LTC Marques began.

"That's SSG McGinley Sir."

"SSG McGinley, you seem to have an attitude problem. The CSM makes all the enlisted assignments at B-24. I support him and have confidence in his judgement. You're walking on very thin ice. What do you have to say in your behalf?" Giving me a chance to speak was his first mistake.

"Sir, I have been associated with Special Forces since 1956. I'm very familiar with the SF mission and SF-TO&E's. Please show me a slot for a bartender, on any Special Forces Table of Organization."

"It's an additional duty." The CSM butted in,

"Sir, can I finish?"

"Go ahead." Replied the Colonel with some hesitation. His second mistake.

"Sir, I was told three things during my in briefing in Nah Trang. First, there is a country wide shortage of trained Special Forces Medics. Second, B-24 had some deep rooted problems. And third, if I had any suggestions on how to resolve any of them, I should not hesitate to bring them forward. Sir, many people were glad I won my battle to come to Vietnam, including the President." I didn't get a chance to finish. The LTC broke in.

"SSG McGinley, I didn't know you were a Presidential appointee." His third mistake. I wasn't, but why tell him. "I think we all should take another look at this misunderstanding, you agree SGM?"

"Yes Sir." We returned to the CSM's office. This guy was as hot as a two-dollar pistol. It's obvious we were not to be friends. It wouldn't surprise me, if he didn't send me a Christmas card. "Exactly what assignment would satisfy your desire to serve, SSG McGinley?"

"On an "A" Team, Sergeant Major. As far from the flag pole as I can get." I was assigned to, A-245 Dak Seang. A Special Forces Camp, on the tri borders, of Cambodia, Laos, and Vietnam.

Dak Seang A-245

As I boarded the chopper for Dak Seang. The CSM reached out his hand.

"No hard feeling's, Sergeant Mac. You sure are a determined trooper."

"SGM, that is the under statement of the year." We shook hands. I boarded the waiting chopper. We headed, North West to Dak Seang A-245.

Helicopter to Dak Seang

I cannot say that the HU-1B helicopter trip to Dak Seang was uneventful. I was the only passenger. For a short while, I felt very important. Following the winding Dak Poko river, skimming the trees at ninety miles, an hour got the adrenalin pumping. It was like riding a roller coaster. I don't mind admitting that I was not at ease.

Every so often the door gunner would fire his 30 caliber machine gun. When I asked what, he was shooting at, he answered,

"There might be VC in the area."

"There also might be friendly forces. If you don't stop shooting, I'll take your toy away." You hear about jerks like this every so often. They call it friendly fire. Murphy's law states, "Friendly fire isn't."

We made a sharp turn to the left. Before us in an open valley, lay camp Dak Seng (A-245). I remember thinking to myself, Why did they build this camp in the middle of a valley? I would think, one of the surrounding hills would be a better place.

Dak Seang A-245

When we got closer, I realized, the two-mile wide valley, was too large to cover from any of the hills. The valley extended five miles westward to the Laos, Cambodian border. The camp location was ideal. It served as a blocking obstacle. Any enemy invading from the west, would have to tangle with the Dak Seang defenders. Dak Seang had been tested in the past and will be tested again.

We circled the camp while the pilot-made radio contact. A smoke grenade was popped on the runway indicating it was safe to come in. The pilot acknowledged the color and started his approach. The acknowledgment of the smoke color was extremely important. The VC (Viet Cong) and the NVA (North Vietnamese Army) popped smoke trying to fool pilots. As an aircraft came in, they would blow the craft out of the air.

"I see red, (or whatever color) smoke." Also, the acknowledgment.

"Roger red," At the expense of repeating myself, is extremely important.

We landed at my new home. This would be the start of a great adventure. From this day forward, life took on a new meaning.

Without saying a word, SFC Anthony Dodge, the teams Intel Sergeant, ran up to the chopper and grabbed my bags, and ran back to a waiting jeep. I followed, just cleared the aircraft, and the chopper took off, gaining altitude as fast as possible. I had no sooner got in the jeep, when Tony executed his fast

Dak Seang Runway, North Side of Camp

departure. Dodge getting out of Dodge, (pun intended) you might say. Tony informed me, the enemy liked to drop in a mortar round or two when aircraft land at the camp. It's best to get off the air strip ASAP.

"It's about time they sent us a medic. We haven't had medical support for about four months." Well I'm glad to meet you too, I thought to myself. Dodge got a little friendlier when we got to the team house.

SFC Dodge introduced me to the team members sitting around a large table. My timing was excellent (as though I had anything to do with it). Most of the team was gathered to have their evening meal. As we approached the table, a SFC stood up reaching out his hand.

"I'm Tom Weeks, welcome aboard." While we were shaking hands he continued, "What do you know about mortars?"

"A little, plenty room for improvement."

"Good, I will teach you a few tricks. In no time at all you will be an expert." SFC Tom Weeks was the team's, Heavy Weapons Sergeant. A great one, I was soon to find out.

"I'm Lt Robert Kreger the team XO (executive officer) and acting Team Leader. If you need anything to accomplish your mission, just ask. If I can't get funds for it, I'm sure the team will steal it for you."

"We don't steal, LT." Weeks broke in. "We liberate equipment and keep it safe from thieves." Everyone laughed.

The Team's, Vietnamese cook handed me a plate full of oriental food. This was the second greatest oriental food I had ever tasted. It was only surpassed by a beautiful Thai gal waiting for me in Bangkok.

SSG Crushfield, the Team Engineer and Demolition man, was introduced by Lt. Gillet. Crushfield didn't have much to say after the initial welcome. This lad was responsible for most of the camp's improvement, above and below ground. A good engineer is an asset to the overall mission of an A-Team. It was evident SSG Crushfield was a good engineer.

"I'm Albright, what did you do to deserve assignment to Dak Seang?" The statement came from the Jr. Radio Operator at the far end of the table. I didn't understand the statement. I answered with,

"Just lucky I guess." I withheld judgment on this Team Member. Glad I did, SSG Albright turned out to be a good soldier. That took care of the introductions.

Two team members were missing. The Senior Radio Operator Al Heber who was on radio watch and SSG Robert Schrag, the team Intelligence Sergeant, who was on operation. The Team Leader, Jr Weapons, and Jr Medic slots, were not filled.

All though the meal we talked about a variety of subjects. All were targeted to bring me up to speed on camp operations. SFC Anthony Dodge described how the camp was divided into three sections. This insured control over everyday operations and command and control, when the camp was under enemy attack.

The American Team was in the center surrounded by a sandbagged wall and barbed wire. Within this area were several buildings. The Team House, that was used for planning operations, eating, or just

American Team House

sitting around watching TV. It even had a bar, where you could enjoy your favorite beverage. You can be assured beverage intake was done in moderation.

"Let's take a walk." Dodge suggested.

The tour started at the communication bunker beneath the Team House. This was the nerve center of all A-Team missions. The walls were covered with situation maps, showing enemy locations and possible avenues of attack. Al Heber the Sr. Radio operator didn't say a word. He was busy decoding a message. I was introduced to him later. Al Heber and I became life long friends.

Next stop, a long building just in front of the team house. The building contained a latrine, shower room, laundry area and at one end, above ground, living quarters. It was hard to believe, a building in the heart of a jungle, had hot and cold running water, two washers and two dryers.

Continuing down a cement path. On the left, was the entrance to the below ground sleeping quarters, underground medical bunker, and several other rooms connected by tunnels. This enabled the team to be fully operational no matter how large the attacking force. It also had an escape tunnel in the event the camp would be overrun by a determined enemy.

At the end of the path, on the south end of the American area, was a building used to house the team's 12 man Security Guard. The building had a large red cross on the roof. It was apparent that at one time this was a dispensary. I didn't tell my guide that this was soon to be a Treatment Facility. A new landlord had arrived, the present tenants were to be evicted.

Next Tony showed me the 4.2 mortar pit and its ammunition bunkers. The pit was four feet deep, with reinforced cement and steel walls. The heavy base plate was set in cement. This improved the weapons accuracy ten fold. In a regular Army unit, the 4.2 Mortar, is a crew-served weapon. In Special Forces, the 4.2 Mortars, are usually operated by one person.

4.2 Mortar Pit West Side of Dispensary

Our tour continued to a large warehouse building. It was filled to the brim with rice, canned fish, uniforms, and weapons. If it was needed, it was in that building.

"Aren't you afraid of this building being hit?" Dodge smiled as he opened a trap door. Like the rest of the camp, this building had its underground component.

Further down the path was the team's 81mm Mortar pit. It also was reinforced with concrete and had its own ammunition bunker. This turned out to be my favorite weapon. I made the unsubstantiated claim that if you are on the run, I could drop a round in your hip pocket. Nobody took me up on this claim.

The Vietnamese SF Team (LLDB), had their own walled area. It paralleled the US Special Forces Team.

LLDB Area on left, American Area on right.
Looking North. Runway on other side of gate.

A twenty-foot wide road leading to the runway separated the areas. It was said jokingly, that if their underground area was any deeper, they would have struck oil. The "LLDB" stands for, Luc-Luong Dac-Biet. Tony Dodge insisted it stood for, "Look Long Duck Back." The US Special Forces Team, and its counter part LLDB, did not get along very well at Dak Seang in 1968.

Surrounding the US Special Forces and the LLDB's areas, were underground live-in bunkers. The bunkers formed the outer perimeter of the camp. Four Companies of CIDG (Civil-Irregular Defense Group) soldier, occupied the bunkers encircling the camp. The 400 soldiers plus their families, brought the camp population to a little more than six hundred, men women and children. This Montagnards strike force was predominantly from the Sedang Tribe, with a few from the Jai Tribe.

This underground city was all the Montagnards (DEGA People) had to call home. There were no villages around Dak Seang, nor anywhere in the camp's area of operation. This was in the bonnees folks, on the Vietnam, Cambodia and Laos border.

I had my choice of bunking underground with most of the team or occupying a room above ground. I chose to stay above ground. I unpacked my gear and then took a stroll back to the medical building. I entered the east door. I was surprised no one was in this area of the building. The room was cluttered with unpacked crates and boxes, most with medical corps markings. The two large rooms would be ideal for a dispensary I thought to myself. They needed a lot of cleaning to get rid of the overwhelming smell. Otherwise, this building would do just fine.

I suddenly became aware of the great silence that fell over the building. When I first entered, I could hear the guards next door, now nothing. I went outside, around the building to the other entrance used by the guards. Not a soul was in sight, where did everyone go?

My attention, was attracted to the Team House. Eight or ten very upset people were standing around SFC Dodge. I walked toward them thinking this may be a camp uprise or something, Dodge might need my help. As I got closer, I could see these little guys were unhappy about something. They looked like they were afraid of something, as though they had seen a ghost.

They didn't see a ghost, they heard one. The ghost turned out to be me. The medical portion of the now guard quarters, was used as a morgue to hold camp defenders, who were killed in battle. Sometimes they were held for days awaiting transportation to their home village. That explained the overwhelming smell of death. Montagnards are a very superstitious people. When they heard me, they were sure a ghost of one of their departed friends was in the building. When I told Tony it was me in the building, he smiled.

There was no way the guards would go back to that building. When it was time for them to move to another location, they wouldn't go back for their personal items. We had to retrieve their belongings. The Yards know that ghosts are afraid of Special Forces. They must have been, they didn't show.

The sun had set, but there was plenty of daylight left. No use wasting it. I went to work going through the large pile of boxes. One of the first boxes contained light green disposable, surgical drapes. I lined the walls and ceiling with the heavy paper drapes. The transformation was like magic. The once dirty, dull looking rooms, became bright and cheerful.

The distinctive smell of decaying bodies would not go away. I unpacked box after box. It was like opening presents at Christmas. Each box was full of surprises. I ended up with a well equipped and supplied medical facility. A treatment facility that would hold its own with the very best.

Special Forces A-Teams were authorized very sophisticated surgical instruments and laboratory supplies. During the Vietnam War, they were also authorized a large variety, of prescription drugs, to include Code-R (narcotic) drugs. This insured the new Treatment Facility would be able to handle a variety of injuries and medical problems, limited only by the experience of medics assigned. I was interrupted by SFC Tony Dodge.

"Mac, you're on radio watch, in a half hour. You have to take Bob Schrag's watch, he is on operation, and won't be back until tomorrow morning." Who in the heck is Bob Schrag? I thought to myself. With a little practice I could learn to hate this guy, I have work to do. My thoughts were interrupted again by Tony.

"Forget the radio watch. I'll cover for you. This place looks great, keep on with what your doing. I can't believe what you have done to this old morgue."

All through the night, Dodge would pop his head in and make positive comments. I didn't know if he was sincere or just keeping me working with compliments. It didn't matter, the dispensary was looking good and I knew it. By 06:30 the next morning, I was ready for patients. Two questions came to mind. Both pertained to my proficiency in medical treatment,

"Do I know enough to make a difference? Do I have the talent to use this sophisticated medical and lab equipment? Tom Weeks, the team's heavy weapons' man, was in the Team House having breakfast. I sat down and told him, I was ready for patients.

"Good, I'll pass the word to the Companies. What time will sick call begin?"

"Give me time to shower and get a bite to eat, I'll be ready to go." The fact that I hadn't slept all night didn't bother me. Last night was a labor of love. A labor of love is not tiring.

They Won't Come

I was ready at 08:00 to see my first Montagnard patient. I was little apprehensive, but ready. To this point the only Montagnards I had seen were the security guards. I scared them half to death the night before. Time passed, first one hour than two. Not a single person showed up. Tony finally came to give me the bad news. The Montagnards refused to come to my new Treatment Facility, fearful of the ghost they knew dwelt within. I understood, the place did have a strong odor of decaying bodies. Very disappointed, I opened the door to leave. Squatting on the ground, were three young Montagnards. I greeted them with a nod and a hardy,

"Good morning, can I help you?"

They jumped to their feet bowed at the waist and said something in their native tongue. In broken English, one stated they were Company Medics. All had worked for Bac Si (doctor) Johnson, the previous medic. After a brief silence I asked,

"Are you good medics?"

"Yes Bac Si." Replied one of the yards in broken English." He continued. "This man name Ek, he number one medic, this man Bual not number one, me think number five."

"Bual, number ten!" Ek blurted out, everyone laughed.

"My name Yet, me number one, number one."

I guess the double number one put him in charge. Throughout the Orient you find they use a numbering system to rank events or individuals. Number one, being the best or highest, and number ten, the lowest. If a person or thing, is really disliked, zeros are added to the ranking number. Number ten thousand, is lower than the low. The person given this number would have to stand on a rock to look a snake in the eyeball.

I extended them an invitation, to come in and see their new dispensary. They hit the squat position again. It looked like a race to see who could squat first. There was no way this group would go into a ghost inhabited building. I went in the dispensary and returned with four M-5 medical treatment bags. I laid one by each of them.

"If the patients won't come to us, we will go to them." To my surprise they didn't make a move or sound. Could it be they are also afraid of the medical bags? I was not getting any place and getting there fast. I squatted in front of them. I asked what the problem was? I really wanted to be accepted by the Montagnards. I have heard great stories about them. I wanted to learn more. In the best English he could muster, Yet asked,

"Why Bac Si no like Montagnard."

"I love the Montagnard."
Was my reply.

"Why you no have Montagnard Bracelet? Friend wear bracelet. How many bracelets, show how many friend." They all held out their arms adorned with brass bracelets. I explained I had just

Montagnard Bracelet

148

come from the United States and they were the first hill people I had
ever seen. I also told them I was sure, one day I would have
Montagnard friends. Yet continued his interrogation,

"Why Bac Si come to bad place like Vietnam?"

"For you, to meet the Hill People and help them."

"You want me friend?" Yet inquired.

"It would make me happy to be your friend." My speech, that
I'm sure, would have matched Lincoln's Gettysburg Address was
interrupted. All three of my new friends put bracelets on my right arm.
Today, those bracelets are among my most cherished possessions. My
three new friends picked up the M-5 Medical Bags. We started our
pilgrimage around the outer perimeter of the camp.

At first only a few Montagnards showed any interest.
Eventually we were surrounded by a large group of smiling people.
One would think this group of shabbily dressed, undernourished people
had nothing in this world to be happy about. Still, their childlike trust
and sense of inner peace were bubbling over.

The Montagnard
(DEGA People) have a
strong resemblance to
our Native Americans.
Scholars studying the
migration of man have
proven, people migrated
from the Himalayas to
Alaska when the two
continents were joined.
Then from Alaska to
Canada, then, to the Americas. This sure would account for the
resemblance.

Like the ancestors of our Native Americans, the Montagnards
life is influenced by spirits. The Yang spirit, who governs the sky,
earth, mountains and river. The Kanam who are spirits of their
ancestors. The Kanam rule the forest and demand appeasement. If not
pleased, the Kanam will bring untold misfortune to the people. In all
my travels, I had never met people, like the DEGA People. This was
the beginning of my love affair with the Montagnard.

All had medical problems that would take more equipment than we could carry in our M-5 medical bags. Out of nowhere a strange looking old lady, wearing some sort of ceremonial gown appeared. As the camp's sorcerer got closer I could hear her chanting something. The glare in her eyes gave me the impression, I was not welcome.

"Bac Si, we go now, go now." Yet insisted. "This old lady medicine women, she number 10,000, no like American Bac Si." We departed. Walking away I knew if I were to have any impact on the Montagnard health, I would have to deal with this sorcerer. I would have to win her over. The battle lines were established. This medicine woman and I would have to come to terms.

It was quite evident, the DEGA People, would not come to the dispensary as long as the ghost and spirits were in residence. I could almost understand their point of view. The place did have the smell of death. If I were to have patients show up for treatment, I would have to get rid of the decaying body smell. I put together a concoction of ingredients which no ghost, with self respect would stay around. It contained; calcium chloride, household bleach, wintergreen, surgical soap, gasoline, lighter fluid, and a few other ingredients I don't remember. Then the thought came to me.

"Why don't I solicit the help of that glaring Medicine Woman?" She claimed to have control of the spirit world. Well here's her chance. I sent Yet, to request her assistance to rid our treatment facility of ghosts. To help influence her, I sent gifts and food.

Within the hour I could hear chanting outside the dispensary. I dumped my ghost chasing concoction on the floor. Hurriedly I swished it around with an old broom. The strong odor took my breath away. I hoped it worked as well on the spirits. It did, the smell of death was gone.

When the chanting stopped, I went outside. Using Yet as an interrupter, I thanked her for her great job. I went on with my praise and told her I had never seen anything like this before. The fact of the matter is, I haven't, and hope I never will.

I also offered her an area just outside the dispensary to practice her witchcraft, or whatever she called it. My final gesture of goodwill, was to invite her inside. To my surprise she went in followed by 50 or so Montagnards.

The work load at our now "ghost-free" dispensary increased daily. In less than two months, we were averaging fifty to sixty patients a day. I strongly suspect that many were coming just for the attention. It didn't matter. I enjoyed working for my new love, the Montagnard people.

Our Montagnards at Dak Seang lived underground in damp, cold, lower than standard, sanitary conditions. Because of their environment, we treated everything from a simple cold, to malaria, tuberculosis and a few cases of the plague. When the Team went on operation and made contact with the enemy, we treated the resulting war wounds.

Tren Bren

The DEGA (Montagnard) People in all of Vietnam were treated like second class citizens by the Vietnamese and sometimes by the Americans. When wounded, they had no priority on Medical Evacuation. One of the questions asked when calling for a Med-Evac, was to state the wounded soldiers nationality. I got around this by stating the wounded person was an American, regardless of his or her nationality. Of course when they arrived at the targeted hospital the second class citizen treatment came back into play. Because of that, I kept as many injured as I could. The duty of everyone associated with medical treatment, is to get the patient to the best treatment possible. For the Montagnard that was the Special Forces Medic.

I had just finished supper, and was about to make my nightly walk around the perimeter. The purpose was to check on patients that were confined to bed rest or needed dressing changes or whatever. Yes, Mr. civilian doctor, in Vietnam we made house calls. Suddenly, there was a loud commotion at the front gate. Our counterpart the LLDB were returning from one of their few (not accompanied by Americans) patrols. They had a prisoner who they claimed was a Viet-Con. The lad turned out to be a Montagnard. This upset our yards. Although he was not from their tribe, they knew he was no Viet-Cong. I headed toward the commotion.

As I came closer to the disturbance the crowd parted and I was face to face with the Vietnamese Camp Commander. It was time to tap-dance. Tap-dancing is what Special Forces call, stalling for time.

"What do we have here, Sir?"

"My team captured VC," I felt Captain Luan was glad to see me. He needed a way out of this situation, without losing face.

"Good, let's string him up," I insisted as I approached the prisoner.

"No, Bac Si, we no can do. We send to prison camp in Pleiku."

"Hold it Sir, this is no VC. I know this Montagnard, he worked in the CIDG Hospital in Nha Trang." Don't prejudge me. This was no lie. Maybe a stretching of the truth, but surely not a lie. I think you will agree, stretching the truth, is far better than stretching this lad's neck.

"This for sure Bac Si?"

"Yes, Sir, this lad worked for the Americans at the CIDG Hospital in Nha Trang. Let's call Nha Trang Sir. I'm sure the CIDG Hospital, will vouch for him. Sir." I kept Siring the Vietnamese, they love it. Sir, it's a lot better than calling them what I really want to call them.

"In the meantime Captain Luan, let me take charge of the prisoner. I'll make sure this guy earns his keep. I'll work his tail off in the dispensary."

One week prior to this incident, I treated Captain Luan's three-year-old daughter for suspected Malaria. On one of my evening perimeter rounds his wife asked me to look at their three-year-old. The child had a one hundred and four temperature. I rushed her to the Dispensary. I soaked the kid with cold wet towels. I drew some blood and started her on pediatric liquid Tetracycline. The body temperature came down in a very few minutes. The blood work didn't show any signs of malaria. In four days you couldn't tell this kid was ever ill. Surely that influenced Luan's granting my request, of having the so-called VC work in my dispensary.

"Follow me kid, if you try to run, I'll shoot you between the eyes."

"No Bac Si, no shoot this man, I get in much trouble."

"Don't worry Sir, I don't have my gun with me."   A fact that I didn't bring to his attention was, there is no CIDG Hospital in Nha Trang. The CIDG Hospital is in Pleiku, Vietnam.

I asked Yet to accompany us to the dispensary. Yet was to be my interpreter. It was important I find out just who this captured guy was. What was he doing in an area that has no villages? I had a host of questions that needed answers. I had no problem rescuing this lad. If he gave me any trouble, I could always put hin back into custody, turn him over to the team for delivery to a US Prison Camp. At least he would arrive safe and be treated humanely.

I wanted this interrogation to be as pleasant as possible. I have always found you can get more out of a person with kindness than you can with meanness. We sat around a table drinking a coke. Yet asked him his name. Simple question right? Wrong, it took Yet about twenty minutes, to inform me the lad's name was Tren Bren. Yet was from a Sedang Tribe and this lad from a Jai Tribe. The Sedang and Jai tribes do not understand each other fully. In fact, they fought for years over misunderstandings. A friendly greeting in Jai, like, good morning, was an insult in Sedang. The Jai good mornings translated to, "Your parents are decedents of pigs," in Sedang.

Six hours later all I knew was, the lad's name was Tren Bren or Bren Tren. He was from an area called Dak Sut. Special Forces had an A-Team at that location in 1966. The A-Team and village were destroyed by the NVA (North Vietnamese Army). Tren told Yet, he was visiting his mother's grave when the LLDB captured him.

"I'm going to bed. Yet find this lad a place to sleep. I'll see you both in the morning."

"No, no, Bac Si, you no go. This man Tren have to make friend you." Yet insisted.   I followed them to the perimeter, then down into the Montagnard sleeping bunkers. It was 02:00 and the bunker was set up for a party.

There were at least sixty Montagnards, gathered in this very large, underground bunker. It looked more like a cave, a very dirty cave at that. It was no wonder the camp defenders were in such poor health. At that moment, sanitation and personal hygiene were moved to the top of my priority list, of things to improve the Montagnards life.

In the center of the damp floor, was a stretched out parachute, covered with food. At one side a large colorful, ceramic jug, with a bamboo stick protruding from  the center. In a far corner, over an open fire, four young women were cooking something hanging from long bamboo sticks. I was soon to learn gourmet cooking, Montagnard style, and the power of home made Rice Wine.

Everyone present shook my hand, then Tren's. I mean everyone. I couldn't understand a word they were saying. It was clear they were happy about me removing Tren from the LLDB's control. I later found out that Tren, being from a Jai trib, didn't fully understand our host who were Sedang. It didn't make a bit of difference. Everyone seemed extremely happy. A thought crossed my mind, maybe the world would be a better place if all people listened with their hearts and judged people by their smiles. With the same enthusiasm we were ushered to the waiting Rice Wine, for the friendship bracelet ceremony.

Yet explained that first Tren would have to become a friend of the Sedang Trib. Then he would have the power, to welcome me as his friend. I was glad Tren would go first. I wasn't overly excited about drinking an unknown liquid from an old clay crock. By all means Tren, go first and take your time . . . please take your time.

While they were welcoming Tren to the Sedang Tribe, my curiosity about the open fire cooking got the best of me. I walked over to the cooking area. Lying across the hot coals were, some sort of animals. All with Bamboo sticks through their bodies. I wondered if this was the Montagnards equivalent of our Shish-kabob style of cooking?

The Montagnard gals were delighted, I was taking an interest in their cooking. Without hesitation they offered me a taste. Not bad, tasted something like wild rabbit or maybe squirrel. The cooked meat was removed from the coals to make room for a new batch. Without hesitation, I took another large piece of meat. I wanted something in my stomach, before the Rice Wine ceremony.

Talk about making a person feel welcome these gal's take the cake. I was convinced they wanted me to help with the cooking. First they would point at me then at the fire, back to me, then the fire. OK! I replied.

OK must have been a universal word. One Montagnard gal handed me, a live rat and a long piece of bamboo stick. Yes, the rat was alive. She went on to demonstrate how to place the pointed bamboo stick just under the rats tail. For you City Slickers, that is the solid waste eliminating opening. Then, push it through the body, until it came out, just under the rat's head. At this point she laid the (I'm sure) very unhappy rodent, on the waiting hot fire. I wanted to change my OK to NO, but I didn't have time, it was my turn at cooking.

The rat's hair and everything in it, like lice and other parasites were the first to go. The rat's stomach started rising at a rapid rate. In a few minutes a slight popping sound, followed by the rat's stomach collapsing. What a time saver I thought. We take a lot of time and waste a lot of effort cleaning our meat before we cook it. I'll have to tell my friends about this method when I get back to the States. The truth of the matter is, I lost my appetite, somewhere between the hair burning and the rat's stomach popping.

"Bac Si, you be Tren's friend now,"

Why not? I thought. Nothing could top the rat eating experience. I squatted in front of the ceremonial jug. Everyone gathered around all talking or laughing at the same time. I didn't know if they were laughing at me or with me. It didn't matter, they were happy. As we all know, happiness is contagious. I caught the happiness bug.

Lying across the top of ceremonial jug, was a piece of bamboo, with a one and one-half inch splinter, hanging down into the rice wine. In addition, a bamboo straw protruded from the dirty yellow, liquid. The object was to keep sucking on the bamboo straw until the liquid level was below the splinter. Why not, anyone that can eat rats can do anything. Nothing could be worse than eating a rat. I was wrong.

I was ready and reached for the straw. Before I could get started, Tren reached in his pocket and pulled out some clear plastic tubing. He replaced the bamboo straw. Tren was immediately the center of attention. It was as though he discovered a new computer chip. Surely this was the Montagnards equivalent to high technology. Hamming it up, Tren handed his hosts' two more of the miraculous devices. From that day on, Tren Bren could do no wrong in the Sedang Tribe. Not only was he their blood brother, time would prove, he was their very smart blood brother.

Equipped with this high technology device, I started removing the fluid from the ceremonial jug. This stuff was terrible. The attack on my taste buds, was so violent, they gave up without a struggle. I couldn't taste this horrible potion anymore, but I could still smell it. I had to go on, accomplishing the mission was paramount. I had to lower the fluid level,

What a man has to do for his country

exposing the bamboo splinter. The rules of engagement called for a repeated effort, if one failed the first attempt. It's amazing what a man has to do for his country. As soon as the fluid level was below the splinter, my newly found friends cheered. It turned out I was the first American that accomplished this task on his first try. Tren put a Montagnard bracelet on my left arm, they all cheered again. Time would prove that this was not just a ceremony of friendship. It was a commitment for life.

"How you like Montagnard Rice Wine Bac Si?" Yet inquired.

"Not too bad young man, not too bad. The only problem was the smell, smelled like something died in that jug."

"Oh, yes, Bac Si, he die now." At that point Yet reached to the bottom of the jug and retrieved a dead rat. He must have died happy. I swear it looked like the rodent had a smile on his face.

For any of you that would like the recipe on how to make Montagnard Rice Wine, I submit the following Rice Wine Formula

Put 2 pounds of unwashed rice in a 5-gallon ceramic jug
Place one live rat, wrapped in banana leaves on top of rice
(Be sure to tie rats' legs to his body to prevent movement)
Fill jug with river water (draw water before your bath)
Seal top of jug with banana leaves covered with old cloth.
Store Jug in a dark, cool area for several weeks.
(Be sure to check with your local authorities for a permit)

For the rest of the party I tap-danced. I managed to keep clear of the Rice Wine. My main excuse, I had to be in good shape to hold sick-call. The truth of the matter, it is very poor policy, to drink anything that has an alcohol content, while serving on a Special Forces "A" Team. Too many lives are depending on each Team member performing at top proficiency.

It was about 06:30 when I left my new friends. The morning light hurt my eyes as I departed the dark Montagnard bunker. I was tired, but a quick shower, and a bite to eat should perk me up, to conduct the medical tasks at hand. I'll catch up on my sleep later.

"Mac how about some 81 mortar firing, to help digest our food?" Tom asked after we had finished dinner one evening.

"Great, I have been looking forward to that." As a matter of fact, it worried me knowing I was not up to speed on all the weapons. On a Special Forces "A" Team, everyone is Infantry. Individuals specialty training,

81 mm Mortar Dak Seang East Wall

medical, communications, demolition or whatever, is just that, specialty training. To defend an isolated A Camp, it takes everybody to engage the enemy.

We went to the 81mm mortar pit on the east side of the camp. About 250 yards out was an old dead tree. The tree became the target for Tom's training. Weeks made an adjustment, then dropped a round in the mortar tube. A direct hit. The white-

phosphate round filled the tree like snow on a Christmas tree. Tom went on pointing out how to adjust the mortar. Turn a calibrated dial, right or left (traverse), to follow a given target, right or left. Turn a crank, to rase or lower the tube's (elevation).

"Go ahead, give it a try." With that invitation, Tom changed all the settings. I cranked the elevation adjustment to 70 degrees. I moved the dial that controlled the right and left position of the tube, to about mid position. Holding the WP Shell above the mortar, I hollered,

"Fire in the Hole." Then I dropped the round and put my hands over my ears. Like Tom's, my shell illuminated the tree.

"That's great Mac, are you sure you only know a little about mortars?"

I didn't tell Tom, I watched every move he made. I knew he set the tube at 70 degrees. I also knew the mortar was in line with a chip on the mortar pit wall.

"It might have been beginners' luck Mac, try another one." Like before, Tom changed the settings, then handed me another round. I positioned the tube, in line with the chipped cement, then set the angle to 70 degrees.

"Fire in the hole, the round was on it's way." This time the tree didn't illuminate. The round exploded far beyond the target. Where did I go wrong? With a big smile on his face, Tom asked

"What if I repaired that chip in the cement? Stand aside, watch this." Without changing my settings, Tom dropped another round in the mortar. The round exploded at the base of the tree.

"A WP Round is heavier than a regular HC round Mac. To make the HC Round land in the same spot, I had to remove some of the powder bags, at the bottom on the shell." Tom's explanation cleared up my wondering, what all the paper powder bags were at the bottom of the shell.

"How do you know how many powder bags to take off Tom?"

"There's no particular formula. Many things affect the value of each bag. The humidity, condition of the tube, and temperature. You have to play it by ear."

"What about the numbers, painted on the walls of the pit Tom? They look like compose directions."

"Exactly, 36 due north, 9 east, 18 south and 27 west. Mac you will be firing the mortars often. Each time you fire one, try to pick out an imaginary target. Critique yourself each time. You'll find your proficiency improving rapidly. It boils down to, knowing your weapon's limitations and the terrain around you."

Dak Seang had a good assortment of defensive weapons. Two 105 Howitzers, manned by the LLDB. One on the North East and one on the South West side of camp. One 4.2 mm and an 81mm Mortar on the East and South West sides. In addition we had two

105 Howitzer

50 Cal Machine Guns, about 10, 30 Calabar Machine Guns, and two jeep mounted 106 Recoilless Rifles. Adding to that arsenal, the camp had about 400 Montagnard armed to the hilt with, M16 Rifles. M79 Grenade launchers, 60mm Mortars and plenty of hand grenades.

In the case the Camp needed help, a host of people and weaponry was standing by. By far the greatest assistance, was the Mike Force. The Mike Force was composed of Special Forces and CIDG personnel whose main mission was to come to the aid of an A-Team in trouble. It mattered not how large the apposing forces were. These fearless fighters of the forest would take them on. Withoutt hesitation this highly trained force would engage and destroy any enemy surrounding a camp. Retreat was not an option, they would fight until the besieged camp was freed.

Also on call were gun ships like the converted C-119 nicknamed Stinger. Stinger had Gatlen Guns that fire 2000 rounds per minute and 40mm Cannon that fired out of the tail section of the aircraft.

Then there was Spector a converted C-130 affectionately called Spooky. Her 7.62 mini gun and 20mm cannons gave out a hideous sound, Spooky was a good name for this killer.

Spooky

Additional air support like the B-52 Bomber with her Arc Light and F-4 Phantoms Jet armed in various configurations were but a radio message away. A-Teams had top priority in Vietnam. Yes, we had our necks on the chopping block. We also had a lot of top notch warriors standing by. Gods bless each and every one of them.

All A-Teams were paid visits by Artillery Forward Observers. The would plot areas surrounding the Camp, then assign a Fire-Mission number to that particular area. If during an attack, the enemy occupied any plotted area, all the camp had to do was radio for that Fire Mission by Number. That area and everyone in it became history. Both track mounted and fixed Artillery stood at the ready.

Support and resupply folks played a special part in the survival on any camp under siege. Supplies were brought in by Chopper, Fixed wing Caribou and 130's, or anything else that could fly. In the event the aircraft couldn't land (which was most of the time), supplies were dropped by parachute. On many occasions resupply was done by convoy under heavy fire. Many resupply personnel lost their lives in that endeavor. They were truly our comrades in arms. And without question, Giants.

A group that quit often wasn't given the credit due them was our fearless Med-Evac Units. When an A-Team is under siege, they have no choice but to stay and fight regardless the size of the enemy force. Hopefully putting a price (in lives) on a particular parcel of real-estate, the enemy will not want to pay. The Dust-Off Team has a choice. They know the enemy is all around the camp, well armed and in large numbers. Without hesitation they will come in and get your wounded. Truly super acts of courage and dedication. All soldiers appreciate and admire them.

If you are a soldier that was ever wounded, you appreciate and love them. To this day every time I see a Dust-Off Team, I want to salute them. Giants all.

Tom Weeks gave me a class on weapons every night after dinner. There was never a time that Tom criticized, my lack of knowledge about a particular weapon. Tom was aware I had breaks in service between WWII, Korea and Vietnam. As Tom put it, "Weapons change constantly. It's my job to bring you up to speed Mac." He never got tired of my questions. In little over a month I was holding my own on all weapons.

Dust-Off

This was my first experience with a Special Forces "A" Team in a combat area. Until this point all my experience with Special Forces was in training. The composite talent of this A-Team was unbelievable. Being three men short of a full Team didn't slow them down. Their only complaint was, the day's were not long enough. Unlike conventional units, Special Forces didn't have support units to help improve their camps. If anything was to be accomplished, the A-Team had to do it, and do it between battles.

Camp fortification was priority one. Dak Seang got high marks for that. The enemy, attacking with superior forces never were able to take the camp. The Special Forces (most of the time under-strength) A Team and about four hundred Montagnards repelled thousands attacking their beloved Dak Seang. This real estate was not for sale. On several occasions the enemy dead had to buried with bulldozer. The enemy kept trying, and they kept dying.

The Cover Up

I heard them before I saw them, choppers and a lot of them. A large air-assault I thought, I'll bet the 4th Division is going to hit the NVA, and hit them hard. The 4th Infantry Division was the major conventional unit in our Area of Operation. I should say their Area of Operation. The Central Highlands were under their control or lack of control, depended on how you looked at it. When they came into view,

I could see they were heading straight toward us. What in the world are they up to? A horrible thought entered my mind. I started toward the Dispensary. When I got close, I hollered for Yet. Yet and Tren came running.

"VC come Bac Si, VC Come?"

"No, worse than that. American soldiers are coming."

I told Yet and Tren to get the other medics, go around camp and tell all the women to cover their tops. The dress for the Montagnard women at Dak Seang, were long black, wraparound skirts, without a top. Special Forces was used to this attire. But large groups of conventional troops, tend to act like animals. Worse yet, a large proportion, think they are God's gift to women. Disrespect for our Montagnard women, would not be tolerated on my watch. I knew I spoke for the Team.

A cardinal rule, is not fraternizing with the indigoes' women. The mission of an A-Team is to, teach them how to defend themselves against anyone that would do them harm. Romancing their women, does not fall under that category. The best way to turn a Montagnard friend, into an enemy, is to mess with their women. That's kind of universal, isn't it?

While Lt Gillet greeted the 4th Division brass, the rest of the Team had an emergency meeting in our como-bunker. The meeting was in progress when I arrived. MSG Dodge brought me up to date.

"Mac, we decided we won't let the 4th Div. inside the camp."

"Can we do that?"

"Sure, this is a classified camp, under the LLDB control.

We all agreed, we are not going to use the shower while they are in our AO. We would use the river. We don't want them to know we have showers with hot and cold water. We also agreed, we would send a guard with the Montagnard women, when they go to the river to bathe.

"I wish they would cover up, while the 4th is around, but that is not likely to happen."

"Tony, the gals are covering up as we talk. My medics are spreading the word."

"They won't do it Mac. We tried that before." After the hurried meeting, we went outside to greet our visitors. As though it was planned, Yet passed us, followed by about twenty Yard women, with their long black skirts raised to their armpit. Tony Dodge summoned Yet.

"Yet, how did you get them to cover their boobs?"

"Yet tell them Bac Si get mad if American GI see Montagnard girl with no clothes. Only Special Force can see." Tony Dodge was not one to laugh often, but this cracked him up.

By the time we got to the airstrip paralleling our camp, the 4th had moved out. Lt Gillet, explained that the 4th ID was going to establish a 105-Artillery Fire Base on Nuiak (Hill 247), just North West of our camp. From that vantage point they could give artillery support, to our camp, Ben Het to our south, and Dak Peck to our north.

"I will believe that when I see it," MSG Dodge, a true skeptic, announced.

Three and one half hours later, the 4th ID loaded on their waiting choppers and departed Dak Seang. Sergeant Albright, our radio operator, rushed in the team house.

"Everyone outside, especially you Bac Si."

"Now what? Don't tell me the 4th is coming back." Something is funny here. First, why is an E5 ordering everyone outside, we all out rank him? Second, why especially me?

We were greeted by a large group of women. All with their skirts still raised to their armpits. Yet, who was acting as master of ceremonies, was laughing, almost out of control. He told the group something in Sedang. All the gals lowered their skirts to their normal position. Everyone got a big kick out of this performance, even the straight faced LLDB. I gave them a thumb up. In a while, everything settled down. It was late, I headed for the dispensary.

My first surprise was the activity. Every medic was working on patients. Tren, had taken over my area in the treatment facility. With a stethoscope hanging around his neck, he was pointing to the ceiling, apparently trying to explain something to his Sedang patient. I just stood there and watched. Finally the patient shook Tren's hand and departed.

"Yet get over here, ask Tren what he was telling the patient."

"Bac Si why you call me speak Tren, Tren speak American." This was a day full of surprises.

"Tren why didn't you tell me you could speak English?" Tren didn't answer. "Am I speaking too fast?"

"No Bac Si, you no speak too fast. I thinking what tell Bac Si, not want Bac Si mad me. I like Bac Si. Mac"

"I never get mad at Montagnards Tren. You can tell me anything."

"For sure Bac Si, for sure?"

"Yes Tren, for sure."

"Me not VC Bac Si, I work Special Forces Camp Dak Sut. VC come camp, kill American and Jai people. I run away, work for Montagnard Army FULRO. Bac Si, Vietnamese no like Montagnard people. I no like Vietnamese, come from north, come from south, all same same, me no like." Tren continued his story.

"I work American, he name Master Sergeant Smith. Me think, Smith like me work him. He teach me speak American. I like work for American. I work for you Bac Si. Tren stop work Bac Si Mac when Tren die. I didn't know how to respond to that. I changed the subject.

"What were you telling that patient, when I walked in?"

"Sedang people no understand Tren. Me tell man take medison, three times one day. He no understand. I show him. Sun come morning this way, (Tren pointed to the east) take medison. When sun (pointing straight up) this place take medison. When sun go sleep (Tren pointed to the west) take medison. Sedang man understand, he go. Even I understood the three times a day direction. From that day foreword, we used Tren's pointing formula.

Tren just created a couple of challenges for me. One was, how was I going to get permission from the LLDB, to have a suspected VC added to the strike-force payroll? Second, how was I to get Tren assigned to me. I had faith in myself. I'd make it work. SGT Albright, our radio man, was coming out of the Team house as I approached.

"SGT Albright I need a favor."

"You've got it Mac. If I can do it, consider it done. If I can't,

I'll get it done. Talk about a positive attitude. Not a surprise though, the whole team shared that, "We can do anything spirit." That's what so special about Special Forces. As the old saying goes, the difficult we do immediately. The impossible takes just a little longer.

"I need a radio message from the CIDG Hospital in Nha Trang."

"There is no CIDG Hospital in Nha Trang Mac. The CIDG Hospital is in Pleiku."

"I know that Albright, but the LLDB doesn't. I want the message to verify that Tren Bren, not only worked for the CIDG Hospital, he was one of the best workers the hospital ever hired. You know what I mean Albright. Make it a walk on water message."

"Can do Bac Si. I'll get on it ASAP."

"By the way SGT Albright, deliver the message to me only when you see me and the LLDB Commander together." That took care of the first challenge.

Two days later I was talking to the Vietnamese Camp Commander about the shortage of trained medical personnel. I was explaining how I was about to start a medical training program that would improve the efficiency of the few company medics he had. In addition, his medics could cross train non medical troops. He was expressing his agreement with the plan when SGT Albright approached.

"I have a message for you Mac. It's from Nha Trang, I think it was the one you have been waiting for." As I reached for the message, I thanked Albright and hinted that it might be a good idea for him to go back to his radio bunker. I didn't want any witnesses to what I was sure to be a star performance. I'm a firm believer in the fact, "if a person cannot handle the truth, don't burden them with it."

I read the message and then handed it to CPT. Luan. SGT Albright did an excellent job, This was truly a walk on water endorsement. Now all I have to do, is sell the idea. This will take a star performance.

"Sir this is your lucky day. Faith has provided you with a hospital-trained medic. Now you will be able to improve the health problems, you have been wanting to do for such a long time." He had the dumbest look on his face I have ever seen on a human. What in the world are you talking about? look. What medical problems?

165   A Walk With Giants 1958 - 1974

"Sir, I promise you, I will provide all the assistance you and Tren need, to carry out your medical programs. With your guidance, and our hard work, Dak Seang will be among the healthiest LLDB run "A" Camp in all of Vietnam." I didn't give him a chance to respond, I was on a roll. "Sir, I consider it a great privilege working for a Commander that puts the well being of his people above all." At that point I saluted him, then walked away.

To this day, I don't believe the LLDB Commander had the slightest hint of what I was talking about. Although he could speak very good English, he didn't have the foggiest idea of what he was agreeing to. Surely I had just performed an Academy Award performance. My audience was spell bound. I took Tren to LT. Gilbert and had him put on our payroll, with duty station at the dispensary. That took care of the second challenge.

Tren was an extremely fast learner. With a little instruction and guidance, he soon could perform any given task. Perform them at a level, of any Special Forces trained medic. Truly Tren Bren was one of a kind. We became very close. If you saw me, you would see Tren near by. I loved Tren like a son.

Tren Bren

A-245 was conducting a large operation, in the mountains surrounding the camp. A couple of hours into the operation, contact was made with an enemy force estimated to be about a Company in size. The enemy was routed, but not before three Montagnards were wounded and one killed.

Tren and I just finished working on the last of the wounded, when the Montagnard KIA (killed in action) was brought into the dispensary. The gaping hole in his chest and missing portion of his skull made verifying, if he was alive or dead unnecessary. I wondered why they brought him to the dispensary. I told a couple of my medics to take him to the morgue, forgetting this building used to be the morgue. Nobody moved..

At that point, Yet appeared with a weeping grief-stricken Montagnard girl, the striker's wife. Through her wailing and crying the young girl was trying to tell me something. Interpreting, Yet spoke,

"This woman want Bac Si bring husband back. She no want him die." I never felt so helpless in my life.

I don't know what came over me. I suddenly knew I must do something. I cut off his bloody tiger fatigues. Then I started an IV in our diseased friend's abdominal cavity. I needed a place to hold the IV fluid. Then I filled the gaping hole in his head with surgical 4" x 4" gauze and covered the area with a bandage. The same procedure was used on the chest wound. At the same time, Tren had washed all the blood from his body. What in the world are we doing, this man is dead.

My attention was suddenly focused on the extreme quietness that fell over the dispensary. No more crying and wailing. Everyone stood quiet with a peaceful look on their faces. I had a sudden urge to place my stethoscope on our comrade's chest in search of vital signs. Knowing I wouldn't find any, but I went through the procedure anyway.

I walked over to the Montagnards young wife. When I was in range, she grabbed my hand and held it close to her face. Words were not being spoken, but communication was taking place. What a wonderful moment this was in my life. I asked Yet to tell everybody to wait outside. We would keep them informed. As they walked out, I headed back to my patient.

The "if a person cannot handle the truth, don't burden them with it" approach is not going to work this time. What in the world am I hoping to accomplish? Then it became quite clear. I was preparing her, buying her time to handle the truth. If I'm successful, the truth will be less of a burden to her. I continued my stethoscope procedure for another few minutes.

"Yet, I want you to tell this man's wife we are very sorry, we did our best, but can do no more. Her husband went to see his ancestors."

"Please wait Bac Si." Yet then called a couple of medics who rushed in with a set of new tiger fatigues. With the clean clothes, absence of blood, he was ready for his journey.

The Montagnards wife, was now accompanied by a young child. Yet gave her my message, she grabbed my hand again, this time she kept bowing and repeating something over and over.

"What is she saying Yet?"

"Bac Si, this man thanking you all her heart, she never forget you."

"Nor I her," I replied in a low voice.

The Montagnard people don't expect you to perform miracles. They only want you to try. From that day forward, dead or alive, we treated them all. Did we do any good with this practice? I don't really know, but I sincerely hope we made the burden of dying a little easier. These little people gave us so much and asked so little from us in return.

The Vultures

When a Montagnard is killed in action, his survivors receive a year's pay and transportation to their home village. We are not talking about a lot of money, but it helps them a great deal. It is important to remember that Americans were doing all paying and providing the transportation. However our wonderful counterparts, the LLDB, impose a tax on this pay. They also charge the grief-stricken family for the transportation. They would make good candidates for employment, in our Internal Revenue Service.

Team members of "A 245" decided this time it was to be different. This young lady was paid and the team called for a chopper to take her to a village near Dak Pek. While waiting for the chopper, we hid her from the LLDB vulture.

This infuriated the LLDB, widening the cooperation gap. The gap grew daily. The LLDB didn't appreciate the American Special Forces Team protecting the Montagnards. On several occasions the friction between the LLDB and the Americans almost reached the boiling point. I was told of many incidences that happened before my arrival. As time passed, I witnessed many more conflicts that eventually resulted in an armed conflict between the two teams.

On one occasion, SFC Dodge sped by the team house with our Jeep mounted 106 Recoilless Rifle. He came to a screeching halt 20 foot away from the LLDB,105 MM Artillery pit. Jumped out of the

Jeep and aimed his 106 directly at the LLDB's 105, which was pointing directly at our area. Anthony Dodge would respond to a threat without hesitation.

The LLDB's 105 pointing to the American Team, was all quick draw Dodge needed. This was a threat. I witnessed this event from the Montagnards perimeter. I became very concerned. This was surely a lose, lose situation, and had to be defused. I walked between the two weapons and started shouting orders for them to back off. I didn't know if they would listen. I did know, they both had painted themselves in a corner. I hoped they were looking for a way out.

"Dodge, get away from that weapon. Back off"

I then turned and walked straight at the LLDB hot head, pointing and motioning to turn his 105 away. Lucky for me they both took this opportunity to back off, without losing face. I was no stranger to giving orders, especially when scared. This was my third war. I had witnessed dumb acts before. This was a classic dumb act.

Another time, the commotion was so loud I thought we were under attack. I rushed toward the disturbance with my M-16, ready to do battle. SGT Albright was engaged in a very heated argument with three of our counterpart, LLDB. Three against one was by no means, a fair fight. Wayne Albright had a size fifty chest and about a twenty-six waist. Wayne held a Marshal Art Black Belt and was instructor qualified. This would not have been a fair fight. Albright could have handled six or more LLDB. Fortunately for the LLDB, SGT Albright had exceptional control over his temper. By the time I arrived, the LLDB Commander had the situation under control.

"What's this all about Wayne?"

"Bac Si, they killed Sergeant Major." Albright was referring to a puppy he was raising. The K-9 was the unofficial Team Mascot.

"We'll have to walk away from this Wayne. You know as well as I, higher Command will take the LLDB's side." We walked away.

After we were a short distance away, the three LLDB's started with their sarcastic remarks. The further we got, the louder and more threatening the remarks. I was successful in getting Albright, to promise me he would stay put, until I returned. I walked back to the jeering group. Very firmly I asked the LLDB Commander to get his people under control. I pointed out, by walking away, SGT Albright was displaying tremendous control. My closing remarks were,

"A lesser Man would have broken all three LLDB skinny necks." I turned and joined Albright, together we went to the team house.

The Team had to be brought up to date. This would not be the last of this situation. The time of total retaliation, was drawing near. Both the LLDB and the American teams were getting dangerously close to a point of no return. To make a very bad situation worse, the Montagnards would probably stand with the Americans. That would guarantee the total annihilation of the LLDB Special Forces Team. Everything humanly possible had to be done to avoid this. Wrong or right, the American Team would be blamed and suffer the consequences.

I've Got You Covered

Most Special Forces missions are in remote areas. It is imperative, all members of an A-Team are well trained in medical procedures. Being able to start an IV (intervenes) to administer, blood plasma or albumin is high on the priority list. The SF Medic knows he can take care of the Team. The question is, can the team take care of the medic? A good policy is to have, each Team Member demonstrate their ability to start and stop an IV. I carry the policy one step further. All indigenous personnel working in medicine for SF must also demonstrate this ability.

"Tren, I have seen you give many shots to your patients. You do it very well I must say. Can you start an IV?"

"Yes, Bac Si, I can do."

"Good. Start this IV on Yet. When you are through Yet will start one on you." Without hesitation Tren started an IV. Then Yet started an IV on Tren.

"Yet, who taught you, how to start an IV?" I knew I hadn't.

"No Bac Si, Tren teach me how. Tren #1 IV man." Another surprise from my new friend, Tren.

"Tren, start an IV on me." The silence was deafening.

"Tren, did you hear me?"

"Yes, Bac Si. Tren hear, no can do American."

"What if I get wounded, who's going to take care of me?"

"Yet, VC shoot Bac Si, you take care Bac Si, OK?" Tren passed the buck

"No, no Tren. You no can do American, I no can do American." Without hesitation, Yet replied.

"Tren, pick up that IV. Plug it into my arm and do it now." Reluctantly, Tren picked up the needle. After a long hesitation he started, the slow plunge into my arm. I'm glad I wasn't armed. I felt like shooting him. I never had anything hurt like that slow motion puncture.

"Try it again Tren. That was too slow. Start the IV on me just like you started one on Yet. We will keep at this until you get it right." Again Tren failed the task. It was quit obvious, Americans, intimidated him.

"Do it again, Tren." By this time we had a crowd watching. Twelve attempts later, both my arms aching, I gave up. "That's all, Tren. I'm really disappointed in you." I pulled the misplaced IV out of my arm.

"No, Bac Si, no get mad Tren. I can do Bac Si." At the same time Tren pulled my arm back to the table. With one easy smooth stroke the IV was in my arm. The small group of spectators gave out a cheer.

"What are you guys cheering about? One week from today, you will all be tested. Anybody not able to start an IV, in an American will no longer be working in this dispensary. Do I make myself clear? One week from today."

Big Ugly Fat Fellow

The B-52 was informally named by its crews, "BUFF," or Big Ugly Fat Fellow. This aircraft would play a major role in the Vietnam War. The B-52 bomb runs were given the name of 'Arc Light'. A name that filled the enemies mind with fear. By the spring of 1966, all of the B-52Fs were replaced in the field by B-52Ds, each of which was modified to carry more conventional weapons than the F model. These modifications were termed the "Big Belly" B-52D. A single D Model could carry more than 108 of the deadly 750 pound iron bombs.

My first encounter with this powerful, devastating weapon was in 1968. One of our sister camps, Ben Het A-244 was under attack by two Battalions of NVA Regulars. They called in an Arc Light (B-52 Raid). Three B-52's responded to the Arc Light request. That's a pay load of more than 220 bombs, each

B-52 (Arc Light) Raid

weighing 750 ponds. The B-52's flew a V-formation and released their deadly cargo at the same time.

The individual bombs exploding were not audible by the human ear. It sounded like very loud, roaring thunder. Dak Seang was 23 miles from the impact area. The earth trembled as though we were in an earth quake. Arc Light raids continued, despite some misgivings within SAC (Strategic Air Command) regarding the use of high altitude radar bombing against the Viet Cong, by all accounts a scattered guerrilla force. The effectiveness of mass area bombing however, was soon proven and the plane went on to play a very successful role supporting ground forces in combat. B-52Ds flew out of Andersen AFB on Guam, U-Tapao in Thailand, and Kedena AB on Okinawa, hitting targets across Southeast Asia, including Laos and Cambodia, as well as the famous Ho Chi Min Trail. To further beef up the force, B-52Gs were also deployed to the combat zone.

When the North Vietnamese pulled out of the Paris Peace talks, President Nixon ordered B-52 raids on North Vietnam. The BUFF played a decisive role to encourage them back to the negotiating table. The entire campaign would last just eleven days. It was punishment enough to convince the North Vietnamese to return to the Paris table and negotiate seriously. In all, Operation Linebacker II saw 729 B-52 missions flown, dropping 15,287 tons of bombs on 34 targets. Damage across North Vietnam was extensive. In all, 1,600 military structures were hit, three million gallons of petroleum had gone up in smoke, and 80 percent of the country's electrical power production had been destroyed. The Vietnamese had learned the hard way that the B-52, given enough time, really could "bomb them back into the stone age." "Big Ugly Fat Fellow," the name surely fits.

The Miracle

My assignment to Dak Seang "A" 245 was a high point of my life. The experience acquired as a Special Forces, A-Team Medic changed my life dramatically. There was no such thing as a routine day. Each day was unique and had its own adventure. When my memory recalls some of the happenings, every emotion I have is taxed.

When a Montagnard woman has a child, she goes into the forest accompanied by the Tribe's Medicine Man or Woman. A thick vine is tied between trees. The expecting mother squats, hanging onto the vine and delivers her child. After the birth the mother goes into isolation. The Medicine Woman determines the length of time.

In the event of a multiple birth, one child is given away. If one child of a multiple birth, is still born both children are buried together. A disfigured child is not permitted to live. All these decisions are made by the Medicine Man or Woman. Having knowledge of this primitive behavior influenced my decision of letting the Medicine Women use the outside area of my Treatment Facility. Tren tied a climbing rope, between two poles in the Medicine Women's area alongside our dispensary. Three days later the sorcerer's skills were to be tested.

"Bac Si, you take care this man." Tren was referring to the young, Montagnard girl he was carrying in his arms. Montagnards refereed to all people as man, regardless of gender.

"Tren you know that all pregnant women go to the Medicine Woman. Take her there." Tren surprised me by bringing the pregnant girl to our dispensary, he knew better. What was he thinking of?

It was imperative, we kept a good working relationship with the Camp Sorcerer. Bringing new babies into the world was her area of responsibility. It was the price we paid, to keep harmony in the camp. I didn't like it for one minute. The sorcerer had the power to shut us down. All she had to do, was tell her people, the ghosts have returned to our building, presto, we would have been out of business. In less than five minutes Tren rushed in shouting, cervix

"Bac Si! Bac Si! you come. This man want to die." I followed Tren around the side of our building. Laying on the ground with one hand still hanging onto the delivery rope, was our young expecting mother. Protruding from her Vagina was a tiny foot of her unborn child. A thousand thoughts ran through my mind. I haven't got the talent this is going to take. To this point in time, I have only assisted in one normal childbirth. A breech presentation is difficult even for the experienced. I'm going to need a lot of help on this one. "God please help me."

As I gloved, Tren opened the KY-Jelly, then saturated my gloved hand. At first I tried a gentle approach. It didn't work. Time was against us. I forced my hand alongside the baby's leg. It seemed to help. Half of his little buttock popped out. At this point it became evident, his other leg was in front of the little guy's face. I moved the leg to the side of the head. Again this seemed to help. The other half of the buttock was exposed. The little guy's gender was also exposed. We were working on a man-child.

I looked up for a moment, to my surprise, we were surrounded by Montagnards. Out of the corner of my eye I could see the Medicine Woman rushing toward me, waving a large piece of wood. A few of the yards grabbed her and latterly threw her in the barbed wire fence separating the American area from the rest of the camp. At this point SGT Albright appeared.

"Mac they won't come"

"Who won't come?"

"Med-Evac, I called them and they won't come." Albright went on to explain, they told him the birth was too far along to transport the patient. However they have a doctor standing by if I need advice.

I continued with the delivery. I removed my hand to relieve a cramp in two of my fingers. Half of the baby's trunk followed suit. I reentered placing my hand between the baby's face and the Vaginal wall. His little leg popped out like he was trying to kick me. I was thrilled. The crowd gave out a cheer. I guess they were also thrilled. The balance of the delivery went quite fast. Before the arms were fully delivered, Tren, was clearing the child's nose and mouth with a suction bulb. Then the greatest sound in the world.

"Yell out little guy. We have a live birth. Thank you God."

I had never felt so great in all my life. I didn't know whether to cry or sing. I have been privileged to be part of a miracle, the miracle of life. I had the feeling that some Devine power brought me to this place, at this time, to perform this task.

I tied the umbilical cord in two places, then cut between the ties. A Montagnard woman took the child from me. Two other women gently pushed me away. It was evident they were going to deliver the balance of the umbilical cord and the placenta.

"Tren, have them save the placenta, I need to examine it. Also, bring the patient to the Dispensary ASAP." I then walked over to the barbed wire to supervise the removal of the Medicine Woman.

There wasn't a person in the crowd that wasn't mad at the Camp Sorcerer. Some were suggesting she be removed from this earth, with a crossbow arrow through the heart. Others demanded she be expelled from the camp. All were in agreement. Her medicine was worthless. I understood their frustration. Surely many have died because of her witchcraft. However, her removal from Dak Seang would not be operational smart.

In 1968 we knew there were at least two individuals that were sympathetic to the enemies cause, within our walls. Getting rid of them would not eliminate the problem. They would be replaced. At least we knew our two spies' identities. Knowing and monitoring your enemy is half the battle. A lot of Intel can be gathered watching their behavior. Now it seemed like we had a candidate for the third.

The Medicine Woman knew too much about the camp's defense. She knew the types and number of weapons. In all probability, she could come up with the exact amount of ammunition and supplies we had on hand. Expelling her from the camp would be unwise. Killing her would make us no better then the people we came to fight.

Another factor came into play. A lot of the older Montagnards believed in witchcraft. They would be very upset with her removal. Fortnightly at a meeting on the Soccer's deposition, I was able to expand on my point of vew. She was allowed to stay. I saw to it she would have no part in medical treatment. Her area beside our dispensary was dismantled. From that day forward the Sorcerer kept out of my way. How's that for turning the table?

I had just finished cleaning up when Tren, the new mother, and her husband arrived. They were accompanied by a crowed of people. The DEGA people don't do anything by themselves. If they go to war, the family goes to war. If they work in the fields, the family works in the field. The same is true about going for medical treatment or going to the hospital, the family tags along. The examination went well. The little gal, and her new son were in great shape.

"What are you going to name the baby?" Tren, explained my question to the new parents. That triggered a conversation evolving the entire group. After about five minutes Tren asked,

"Why this man, need name now, Bac Si?"

"What are the mother and father's name, Tren?"

"This man Bo, this man Mi." Tren answered, referring to the husband and new mother.

"Why do they have names, why do you have a name Tren?"

"Oh yes Bac Si, this man get name. This man get name at big celebration. Maybe one month, maybe two months."

"Why do the Montagnard, wait so long, before naming their babies?"

"Bac Si, maybe this man no like us, maybe he no stay." I knew Tren was referring, to the high, infant mortality rate among the DEGA People. I stopped my questioning.

Another group conversation erupted.   Then the little mother put her hand on my arm, and asked me something in Sedang.

"This man (referring to the mother) want to know your name, Bac Si. Know you Bac Si McGinley, want to know other name. "

"My first name is Dan. I was named after my Father." Another group conversation started. This time everyone seemed joyful, and were nodding their heads in agreement. Then my friend Tren announced.

"This man, we call Dan. This OK you Bac Si?"

My dear Montagnard friends never cease to amaze me. What an honor I thought. Is it OK with me?

"You bet it's OK with me Tren. Tell them I'm honored to share my name with this little man." I was on an emotional high, as the words were leaving my lips.

The name giving celebration took place thirty two days later. Of course the baby had to give me a bracelet. I survived another bout with Rice Wine and another dead rat banquet.

Mi brought her son to the dispensary at least three times a week. There was nothing wrong with the little guy. Mi just wonted toshow him off.

Wheeling and Dealing

Special Forces, had the reputation for pulling off some great deals with other units. Most conventional units, are hindered with red tape and regulations. This is not to say Special Forces doesn't have regulations governing their actions. It just means SF, interpret regulations a little different. The mission comes first. All Special Forces Operatives are obsessed by that fact. This often means adjustments to the rules have to be made from time to time. Not many top brass or regular Army units like to come to where we operate (thank God). That's why adjustments are easy to make and not often challenged. Speaking of God, I'll bet he wears a Green Beret.

Unlike conventional units the Special Forces Supply system only furnished weapons, ammunition, and other non consumable supplies. Special Forces Teams didn't have supply lines that furnished food, beverage, and personal items. Each team was given an operational fund to purchase those items and anything else they might need. All nonissue items were purchased from, local Vietnamese vendors. The fund also paid the food bill for the camp defenders. This was a great idea. The plan insured Team self reliance. It eliminated the so-called expert trying to run the show from a distance. The best part was, the team had complete control over the fund.

The icing on the cake was any surplus was put in an unaccountable slush fund to be spent as the teams saw fit. The principle is as old as time itself. The amount of money which can be saved is in direct proportion to the extent of your wheeling and dealing. The more a team could negociate, borrow, scrounge, or appropriate, resulted in a larger surplus in the team's operational fund.

In the old days you weren't SF unless you had a Rolex Watch, a Sapphire Ring and a Demo Knife. All paid for out of slush funds. Special Forces Teams, became the world's best negotiators, scroungers, and appropriators.

The Team came up with some great ideas to assist our negotiations. We had our Montagnards make Cross-Bows. A Sedang Cross-Bow would bring a case of T-bone steaks from the Air force. A Viet-Con flag

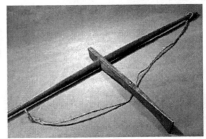

Cross Bow

177

with bullet holes, splattered with chicken blood, could be traded for cases of canned goods from the 4th Infantry. Montagnard bracelets would bring unbelievable amounts of food.

The policy at Dak Seang was to (when enemy activity permitted) send one man off the site to conduct the team's business. The team member was given money to purchase items that couldn't be acquired by other means. When finished with the team's business the team member could take another day for personal needs.

A Caribou (A two engine aircraft resembling a C-130) buzzed the camp. It shook everything in the dispensary. I was sure the plane was crashing. The perimeter was filled with Montagnards. Most of the American and LLDB Teams had joined them. I didn't have the foggiest idea, what was taking place.

"What in the heck is happening Schrag?"

"It's Dodge returning from a Team scrounging trip."

"Why are they bussing the camp?"

"Get over here Mac, we are about to see an airborne qualified water buffalo"

I thought to myself, did he say an airborne buffalo? I didn't get a chance to ask Schrag to repeat himself. The Caribou was on it's five hundred-foot final approach. When the aircraft was about mid-runway, the pilot gave his motors full throttle and pulled the nose of the aircraft up. A bright red parachute pulled its  payload out of the aircraft. I couldn't believe my eyes. Floating to the ground was a live buffalo cow. I read about the Cow that jumped over the moon. A Cow jumping from a plan was a new one for me.

If I were asked, to grade the Buffalo's performance. I would give good marks on his aircraft exit. Average on the descent to the ground. However, the landing was very poor. He should have put more effort on keeping his feet (legs) together. A good well executed, parachute landing fall, will lessen injuries. It was apparent the water buffalo needed more training.

As the Buffalo cleared the aircraft, the plane made a sharp turn to the right then dove to the runway. Looked like the pilot was trying to beat the cow to the ground. I later found out, that was exactly what he was trying to do. Aussies like to add adventure to their flying. That may be one of the reasons why Australians get along so well with Special Forces.

The decision to drop the Buffalo was made because the aircraft was overloaded. The over loaded plane was too heavy to land on our dirt runway. Australian pilots flew Caribous (Wallabies, as the Australians called them) for Special Forces. They were great pilots that would fly in any weather day or night. Their two engine Caribous were the perfect choice for SF operations. Caribou aircraft look like a miniature, C-130. The Australians claimed if an item could fit in their craft they could deliver it. They proved that time and time again.

Meat has to be brought to the camp alive. Montagnards will not eat fresh packed or frozen meat. If they are not permitted to have a ceremony for an animal, they won't eat it. This custom was handed down from their ancestors. No one could convince them to change. As a matter of fact, I don't think we should.

Holy Cow

The slightly wounded buffalo was carried into camp in a cargo net. The fifteen load bearers gently placed the cargo net on support poles. The support poles were high enough to prevent the buffalo's weight from further damaging its legs. The decision to hold the slaughter ceremony on the spot, was a good and humane one. Surely the poorly trained airborne animal was in pain.

Suddenly there wasn't an American in sight. Before I could figure out what happened, my Montagnard medics ushered me to the buffalo. The Yards were extremely happy. It was evident they were pleased with the new supply of fresh meat. Something was missing. I didn't see any ceremonial rice wine jug.

The buffalo was raised by tying a rope, around its hind quarters. A makeshift pulley, supported by three large bamboo logs, was used to raise the buffalo. In a very short time the animal was in the final head-down ceremonial position. Just before raising the animal was given a very large ration of Rice Wine. I thought to myself,

"I'll bet that rice wine, make the cow look forward to death."

Speaking of death how were they going to terminate this reluctant jumper? The method of termination was revealed when the Sorcerer picked up the ceremonial sword. With one quick motion the animal's throat was cut. A little more cutting and the head was removed.

Very gently, two Montagnards laid the cow's head on a waiting table, a place of honor. Every drop of the emerging blood was captured in a large clay jug. Then the Medicine Woman added a little rice wine to the blood. A little primitive but interesting ceremony I thought. Then I decided to go back to work.

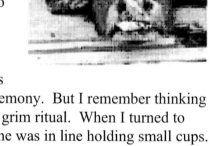

"No, Bac Si, you no go. Tren have present for you."

I wasn't aware giving presents were part of an animal dedication ceremony. But I remember thinking it was a nice addition to an otherwise grim ritual. When I turned to rejoin the gathering, I noticed everyone was in line holding small cups. The Sorcerer was issuing everyone some of the rice-wine-blood mixture.

"Bac Si, sit this place." Yet instructed pointing to a black cloth-covered seat. "Buffalo say, give to Bac Si." Tren handing me an empty cup.

"Thank the Buffalo for me Tren. I always wanted a cup like this."

Yet translated what I said to the crowd. The gathering broke out in a laugh. I was so occupied with the crowd's reaction to my statement I didn't notice the line forming in front of me.

"Bac Si, you hold cup this way." Tren instructed, demonstrating with his cup. I did as he asked. Then everyone started putting drops of blood into my cup. In my mind I was wondering, what in the world was I going to do with a cup of blood? Oh well, I'll go along with this act of friendship. I didn't want to hurt their feelings. My cup runneth over. Well not quite, almost running over. Everyone was gathered around me with most of them siting on the ground. Tren broke the silence.

Montagnard Hunter

"Bac Si, we drink now." Everyone put their cups to their mouths. I had to follow suit. First Rice Wine, then a dead rat, now warm cow-blood. What have I gotten myself into?

As I was drinking the warm blood, I noticed Weeks and Dodge looking out the Team House door. They seemed to be enjoying my blood drinking baptism. I was suddenly aware of the fact, this was a set up. At that exact moment I started planning my payback operation. After the ceremony the rice wine party started.

Revenge Is Mine

A drainage ditch ran along the side the American area. Someone filled the ditch with expender, 105 shell casings. The idea was to help filter the drainage water. Their plan was to have the casings act like rocks in a stream. The plan didn't work. In fact, the shell casing, half filled with water were great breeding places for mosquitos. I identified this problem to the team upon my arrival. Everyone assured me that when I was ready they would all help to get rid of the problem. I would be ready tomorrow morning.

Selecting the day to clean the ditch was no accident. I picked a day when everybody was off site or busy. Bob Schrag was on operation. Crushfield was on a scrounging mission. Albright was on radio watch. Tom Weeks, Tony Dodge, and I were the only ones available for the clean up. When I asked Tom and Tony to help, I knew they would both say yes.

"We better get an early start. It's going to be hot tomorrow." Tony mumbled.

"An early start is a good idea. I'm going to bed." Tom replied.

"Mac, are you going to ask the Yards for some cow-blood to give you strength while your digging tomorrow?" Tom added followed by a Ha Ha. I almost felt sorry for them. Little did they know that tomorrow was payback time.

"Goodnight gentlemen see you in the morning." Were my departing words. I didn't go directly to bed. I had some preparations to take care of.

We all had a shelf in the laundry room. When the laundry girls finished cleaning our clothes, they put them in our assigned areas. My first stop was the medical lab set. I picked up a bottle of powered red stain. Laboratory stain doesn't become active, until it is exposed to moisture. Armed with the red stain I stopped at the laundry room. Carefully I powdered the left inside jacket of Tom Week's fatigues. Folded the jacket and replaced it on Tom's shelf. I duplicated the same operation on Tony's jacket. I knew they would put on clean fatigues. They both held company formations and had to look sharp in front of their troops. You can't expect your troops to look good if you dress like a slob.

We got up at o-dark thirty. Our Viennese cook had breakfast waiting. I had an extra cup at my place. Dodge and Weeks seemed to be waiting for me to say something about the contents of the cup. I didn't say a word. I picked up the cup it was my intention to drink it and ask for more. I didn't get a chance.

"Don't drink that Mac, its chicken blood. That's all the cook could find."

I got up slowly, picked up the cup and walked to the kitchen area. The Vietnamese cook was laughing so hard he couldn't talk. I pulled out my 45, then handed the cook the cup of chicken blood.

"Drink this," I demanded. His eyes were as big as the plate I was eating off of. He grabbed the cup and drank every drop. I really enjoy jokes Americans play on each other. When the Viennese enter the game, I get hostile.

"Mac we didn't want you to get mad."

"I'm not mad Tom. I just don't like Viennese in the game."

"I'll see you guys at the ditch. I have to check the dispensary first." It was about two hours before I went to the work-site. Tom and Tony had quite a lot of work completed.

"We thought you weren't coming Mac, are you still mad at us?"

"I'm not mad Tony, how many times do I have to tell you that?"

"What's wrong with your chest Tom? Open your jacket, let me have a look."

Both Tom and Tony had sensitive skin. Both sunburned easily. They worked with their jackets on no matter how hot they were. This was the ideal condition for the red lab-stain. They're hot sweaty bodied was all it took. The red stain produced all kinds of weird patterns. Tom really looked bad. The stain was doing a great job. Pay back was going to be better than I had hoped for.

"Mac! I caught it too. What is this stuff?" Tony yelled.

"I don't know guys', I have been in three wars, I have never seen anything like this. It looks like it may be contagious." I set the stage, and my payback plan was on target. I went on to explain it might be a good idea if they moved in the empty room above ground. Both Tony and Tom hated to sleep above ground. They felt safer in the underground bunker. They were correct. It was safer underground. Reluctantly they entered the vacant room.

"I'll contact the 71st Hospital in Pleiku, and see if they have any ideas. In the meantime, don't let anybody in this room. I'll send the house girl with some food. Don't let her in, have her put the food on the ground then when she leaves you bring the food into the room." I left leaving them with plenty to think about. I returned to my red stained comrades in about forty minutes.

"I have some bad news for you guy's." I announced in a low sad voice. "The 71st, hasn't the slightest idea what you have. They are going to contact the Center for Disease Control in the US. They should be getting back to us in a day or so."

"A day or so!" Dodge shouted. "We could be dead."

This was starting to get out of hand. These guys are really worried. I decided to call off my pay back plan. The only problem, how to accomplish this without getting killed?

"I'll be right back, I have something in the dispensary that may help."

I returned with a bag containing two bottles of lab stain. One red and one violet.

"Tony, remember how we caught the LLDB stealing from the warehouse?"

"Yea, we dusted the boxes with your lab powder. When they washed their hands, they were purple." I handed them the bag.

"I want you to remember that when you open the bag." I made a rapid exit to the team house. I was bubbling over with delight. I didn't get a chance to finish my explanation to the team leader on what I had done. I was interrupted by an unpleasant sound.

"McGinley we are going to kill you."

"You got us Mac that was a good one." Tom got a kick out of my payback.

"I didn't think it was so good." Grumbled Dodge.

"Dodge, that was a lot milder than telling the Yards I loved to drink cow blood. If you can't take it, don't give it. We had better put a screeching halt, to this activity." Everyone agreed, that was the last of our horsing around. Well almost the last.

Test Time

"Mac I'm going on operation tomorrow. We are going to look at an abandon village south of camp. We have to make sure the NVA hasn't occupied it. I want you to cover me on the 4.2 Mortar." Tom's request terrified me. It's one thing, firing at the enemy or an imaginary target. Firing in support of an American operation, is another ball game. I had to tell him what I was thinking.

"Tom, I don't think I'm ready for this yet."

"You're ready Mac. I would rather have you supporting me with the 4.2, than the LLDB with their 105 Howitzer." Tom sounded like he meant what he was saying. However, it didn't help me stop worrying. On radio watch that night, I fired the 4.2 mortar eight times. All in the direction of the abandon village. Tom and his company of Montagnards left camp just before sunup. I picked up a PRC-25 radio and headed for the 4.2 mortar pit. I knew it was early, Tom wouldn't be at the village for an hour or so. I just wanted to be ready.

"Tren take care of sick call. If you need me, I'll be here in the mortar pit. SFC Weeks might need some help."

"You can do?" Tren asked with a slight smile. "I tell Yet, Bac-Si fight VC." Tren ran to the dispensary.

What's gotten into that Montagnard I wondered? He returned in less than three minutes. "I help you fight VC Bac-Si." Tren jumped into the pit with my M-16.

"What are you doing with my weapon, Tren?"

"Bac Si, shoot papa gun. Tren shoot baby gun." I had to laugh at his reply.

"Northern Dancer, Northern Dancer, Dancer One, Go." That was Tom on the radio. Northern Dance was Dak Seang's call sign.

"Dancer One, Northern Dancer, Go." I acknowledged.

"Fire mission, one round, predetermined target, go." Tom wanted one HC round Fired at the village. Oh God, the enemy has occupied the village.

"Dancer One, ordnance on the way, Go" I advised Ton, the 4.2 round was in flight. I had my fingers crossed.

"Northern Dancer, on target, fire one WP for effect." Tom was advising me we hit the target. He also was requesting, a 4.2 white-phosphate round.

I almost dropped the round in the mortar tube. I realized, the WP round was heavier, and would not reach the village. I really got shook. If I had dropped the round, I might have hit Tom. I had no idea where Tom was in relation to the Village.

Suddenly I remembered one of Tom's classes. The 4.2 round, had an extension that screwed into the bottom of the round. The extension provided additional distance. I attached the extension and dropped the round in the tube.

"Dancer One, ordnance on the way, Go"

"Northern Dancer, Dancer One, on target. Good job, close fire mission, Out" Tom acknowledged we hit the target. He also requested we stop firing. The "out" indicated he had nothing else to say.

"Dancer One, roger close mission. Northern Dancer, Out." I acknowledged.

Tom Weeks returned to camp before night fall. I went to greet him. I wanted to get more compliments, this time in front of other team members.

"How many NVA were in the village Tom?" Tom acted like he didn't hear me. I was about to repeat my question, when Tony Dodge broke in.

"NVA? In what village." Tony asked with a puzzled look on his face.

"Albright told me you radioed in and reported the village clear."

"Mac, we were west of the village when I called for mortar support. I wanted to test you. Mac, you passed with flying colors." I was glad I passed Tom's test. But disappointed, I wasn't firing on a live target. That would change soon.

SFC Robert Schrag was from a little town South of Aberdeen Kansas. Bob spent all his military career in Special Forces. If you wanted a great field soldier on your team, it was SFC Robert Schrag. Quite often Bob would take another Team Members turn to go on operation. The Team's Intelligence Sergeant would rather be in the field, than in camp.

Bob and I spent many hours, debating any subject, that might come up. We weren't always in agreement. However, before a debate ended, somehow we arrived at common ground, leaving us both with a respect

SSG Robert Schrag

for the other's opinion. We became friends. Five months after I arrived at Dak Seang, Bob Schrag tour, in Vietnam was up. Schrag received orders to return to Fort Bragg. We all said our goodby's. Bob departed for the states. At least that is where we thought Schrag was going. Thirty days later, Bob Schrag volunteered to return to Vietnam. If you have to have a War, you just can't keep a good soldier away.

SFC Schrag was assigned to CCN, in northern I Corps. CCN (Combat Control North) was one or the three, similar classified projects, Special Forces was engaged in. The other two were CCC (Combat Control Central) and CCS (Combat Control South). All three were involved in gathering intelligence in denied areas. Twenty days after SFC Robert Schrag return to Vietnam, we got the word. Bob was killed in action. A deep sadness fell over our Team.

Above and Beyond

I was shocked when I learned the LLDB was going on operation without an American. This was a rare occasion.

"What prompted this move Tony?"

"Higher Headquarters is putting pressure on the LLDB to do more. This is their war. HQ feels they should do more. It's about time. The sorry SOB's want us to do all the fighting." I had to interrupt Tony. He was going on and on. Dodge was very vocal, about his dislike for the LLDB.

"Where are they going, Tony?"

"I don't know. You can bet that it won't be far."

It took the LLDB most of the morning to get ready. They were used to the American SF Team doing all the work. They checked everything four or five times. They were not sure of what was needed. Their pride kept them from asking for help. The LLDB's nerviness was apparent. The Yards were getting restless. Finally the operation departed camp four hours behind schedule.

"Look at them stupid jerks, their heading north. The NVA will blow them away." Tony was at it again.

"They don't have the experience nor the equipment to engage the NVA. They're going to get our Yards killed." Tony cared less for the Vietnamese, but he loved the Montagnards."

Less than two hours after the LLDB departed camp, they were in trouble. The LLDB Camp Commander came running to our Team House. My people in trouble. Too many NVA, my people in trouble." He didn't have to ask for help.

Dodge was on the radio requesting air support. Tony disliked the LLDB, but he hated the NVA.

"Show me the exact location of your operation Sir." Weeks asked the LLDB Commander, handing him a map.

"Top this hill. My people stay top this hill." The point the LLDB CO was pointing to, was just one mile from our location.

Dodge briefing his Reaction Team

"Told you, they wouldn't go far." Tony, blurted out. Then he ran out of the Team House as though it was on fire. His fast departure startled the LLDB Commander. Didn't seem to bother Weeks, he kept studying the map. Then almost as fast as he departed, Dodge returned.

"The Reaction Team will be ready in ten minutes." Then Tony joined Tom. Together they formulated their rescue plan. When the plan was completed, the argument started.

"I'll go by air," Tony stated in a loud voice.

"The hell you are, I'm going in by air," Tom insisted.

I was amazed. In less that five minutes a rescue plan was formulated. Tom Weeks was to be air lifted to the top of the hill to link up with the trapped LLDB and then fight their way down the hill. Tony Dodge was to lead a 20-man Reaction Team, to the bottom of the hill. Then engage the enemy from behind. This would open a gap in the NVA's circle, allowing Weeks and the LLDB to escape.

To a conventional soldier, this would be considered a suicide mission, not to Tom and Tony. Although socially they were not the best of friends, militarily they were a perfect match. Both respected the other's professionalism. Both knew they could count on the other's maximum effort. Both knew that failure was not an option. The Reaction Team was outside waiting.

"Drop your back packs. The only equipment you will need is your weapon, two bandoleers of ammunition, and a bag of grenades. We are not going far, but we are going fast. We are not going to double time, we're going to run." The Reaction Team didn't seem happy about something. Finally one raised his hand.

"Why we no take knife, SFC Dodge?"

"Of course you can take your knife. Montagnards never leave home without their knife." They all drew their knifes, holding them high, cheered. A Montagnard without his knife, is a Montagnard lost. As SFC Dodge and his team departed camp. SFC Week's helicopter arrived. Boarding the chopper Weeks gave the LLDB Commander, some final instructions.

"Make sure you radio your people. Tell them to follow my commands exactly, and without hesitation. I won't put up with their usual BS. Do you understand me?" The LLDB nodded his head, indicating yes. I often wondered why he didn't volunteer to go on the mission. If those were trapped Americans', you would have to fight Special Forces officers, to keep them off the mission.

The chopper took off. Weeks wanted to monitor Tony's progress on the ground. After a short period we could see the chopper on final approach to the hill. Dodge and his team held their fire. The plan called for Weeks to initiate the attack. Suddenly we saw the chopper make a sharp turn to the left. Something must be wrong. The chopper was heading back to our location. Horrible thoughts went through my mind as I ran to the dispensary. I could hear our radio operator yelling. "Their bringing in wounded Americans!" I readied an IV and opened a surgical pack. I wanted to be prepared, regardless of the severity of the wounds.

"Tren, set up the other treatment table. Set it up the same as this one." I didn't have to tell the other medics a thing. They were on the chopper pad with litters.

The first litter entered followed by the chopper pilot. Quick examination revealed a gun shoot wound to the right chest. I instructed Tren to make the wound air tight. In case there was internal bleeding, I inserted a chest tube. It was a severe wound, but not life threatening. I plugged in an IV, just in case.

"Will he be OK Bac Si?" The pilot was concerned about his Door Gunner.

"He'll be fine Sir. We'll clean him up a little and give him something for pain. He will be fine."

"Where is the other patient Yet?" I knew, it had to be Weeks.

"Only one man, Bac Si."

I turned to ask the pilot about SFC Weeks. He was gone.

"Tren take over. I have to check on Weeks."

I could tell that the Door Gunner wasn't happy about being treated by a Montagnard.

"Dr. Tren, if this patient gives you any trouble, cut his throat. I'm only kidding lad. Dr. Tren is a graduate of Harvard Medical School. I'm his understudy."

"No kidding? That's great." Our Door Gunner was happy again.

The chopper took off for the second attempt to land at the LLDB's position. This time Ton was the acting door gunner. I almost felt sorry for the NVA. SFC Tom Weeks was an expert on the machine gun. Dead eye Weeks surely would make some . . . dead eyes, this day.

We saw the chopper assault the hill again. Like the previous attempt, the chopper made a sharp left turn. Only this time he didn't head back to our location. The pilot touched down then gained altitude and circled the engagement area. We had our radios on their frequency and monitored the activity. From his vantage point the chopper pilot was able to assist the teams on the ground. It also provided us with a blow by blow report on the action.

"I don't believe it. This guy has to be crazy. The NVA are burning the hill. Tom is leading the Vietnamese through the fire." It sounded like the pilot was thinking out loud. There was a pause in his reporting. Finally the transmissions started again.

"Northern Dancer One, Northern Dancer One. Be advised, large enemy force approaching you head on. Sky Angle out. Dancer One, they're coming fast." Then another pause.

"Northern Dancer One, disregard last transmission. Bad guys' on the run. Sky Angel out." That was great news. We where positive Tony was doing his thing.

"Northern Dancer Base, Northern Dancer Base, Dancer One and Dancer Two united., Sky Angel out."

"Roger united, Sky Angel. Thanks for the help. Come on home and have a cool one."

"Thanks Northern Dancer. Think we will stay on station for a bit. Wanna make sure bad-guys don't follow. Sky Angel out." Nothing like a successful mission to brighten up the day.

First to come into sight, was Tony and his team. Tony had them double-time home. When they arrived at our watering hole, they all jumped in. Splashed around a short while, then doubled-time back to camp. Dodge wanted to be at the gate, when the LLDB arrived.

Tom Weeks and the liberated LLDB arrived twenty minutes later. Tony and his reaction force started their harassment. Tom got a kick out of it. The embarrassed LLDB didn't say a word. They headed to their underground bunkers.

"How is my man doing?" Were the first words out of the pilots' mouth.

"Great. " I replied.

We loaded the Door Gunner on the chopper. He acted like he didn't want to go. During his short stay he became friendly with our Montagnards. The Montagnards enjoyed him also. They particularly enjoyed him calling Tren, Dr. Tren. We said our goodbys, and thanked them again for their outstanding job. Then in a cloud of dust, our new comrades departed.

The LLDB Commander and his Team were invited to the mission debriefing but declined the invitation. They didn't have the courtesy to thank Tom or Tony, for getting them out of a life threatening situation. Tony's interpretation for "LLDB" was correct. Look Long Duck Back, fits them to a tee.

A burst from an M-16, alerted the US Team. Someone was spraying the American Team area with bullets. My quarters were alongside the sandbagged wall between the LLDB Team area and the US Team. It didn't take me long to man my position on the wall. Then another burst of fire. This time I could see the shooter.

"He's on top of the LLDB's Team House!" I yelled. "I have a clear shoot."

"Hold your fire, Mac!" Tom insisted.

Then there was a lot of Vietnamese chatter. It was apparent people were trying to convince the shooter to lay down his weapon. Finally one of his team members got behind him, and took him down.

"Thank you not shoot." The LLDB Commander announced. "This is bad situation, very bad."

Things started to settle down. Most of the team went to the Team House to get a cup of coffee. I headed back to my quarters. SGT Bill Gordon, Bob Schrag's replacement collapsed at the Team House door. A couple of guys moved him into the Team House. Then I was summoned to look him over.

"Mac, Gordon has been shot!" I cut away the right leg of his trousers. Bill had two wounds. An entrance wound and a very large, gapping exit wound.

"We need a Med-Evac!"

"On the way Mac." Al Heber radioed for help.

"Who put this tourniquet on?" No one answered.

"Who put the tourniquet on? I have to know how long it has been on!" Again no one answered. Further examination revealed Gordon used his belt to control the bleeding."Why didn't you tell us you were hit Lad?"

"I didn't want to bug out. You guys needed all the help you could get. Is it bad Bac Si?"

"Nothing we can't handle. It's going to hurt a little Lad. Let me know if you need something for the pain." Unfortunately the tourniquet wasn't doing the job. Bill was losing a lot of blood. My final diagnosis; Gunshot wound right upper leg. Femoral Artery involvement. No apparent Femur damage.

Because of the amount of blood loss, this became a Priority One Med-Evac. I clamped the major bleeders with hemostat's. The bleeding didn't stop. I had to reapply the tourniquet. With the bleeding under control, I dressed the wound and gave Bill a shot of Morphine.

We could hear the Med-Evac approaching. Gordon was taken to the chopper pad. I briefed the medics on board of Gordon's condition, making sure he understood I applied a tourniquet. Bill was on his way to the 71st Evac Hospital in Pleiku. What a stroke of bad luck. Bill Gordon just arrived two day's ago. One heck of a guy.   He tried to hide his wound to prevent medical evacuation.

On several occasions, I have witnessed Special Forces personnel concealing their wounds or medical condition. Staying on, or going on operations, had a higher priority. Conventional troops would use the same situations as a ticket home. And they should, any normal person would. Nobody has ever accused Special Forces of being normal.

It's The Americans Fault

"We have to talk Captain! Come to our Team House." It didn't sound like a request, sounded like Lt. Gilbert was giving the LLDB CO an order. This was kind of shocking. Lt. Gilbert was a laid back, quiet guy. The LLDB Commander and the Lieutenant, had an hour meeting. After the meeting, both Commanders notified their higher. headquarters. This was a very serious situation, heads were sure to roll.

At first light, two choppers were at our location. One from the LLDB's B-Team and one from our B-Team in Kontum. An hour later, choppers from both

Pleiku C-Teams arrived. Initially, separate meetings were held. My guess was they wanted to get their stories straight. Then the joint meetings started. About three hours later, a C-130, from Ne Trang arrived and picked them all up. The only officers left behind, were the LLDB Commander and his Montagnard Officers. Something strange was happening. At this point we didn't know what.

Three days later, Lt. Gilbert returned. He was accompanied by our new A-Team Commander. Captain Sherman, held an emergency Team meeting to explain the situation.

He started by telling us the LLDB officer, that fired on the Team House, was drunk. He went on to say, he only wanted to scare the Americans, not hurt them.

"We have to put this behind us, and march on." He continued. "The LLDB Lieutenant, will not be coming back to Dak Seang, he has been reassigned."

"You mean to say, that's all that is going to be done, to that chicken livered slob?"

"Losing face is punishment enough, SFC Weeks. Remember we are in their country."

"Sir, how long have you been in Country?" Tony inquired.

"I have been in Vietnam, about 30 days. This is my first SF assignment. However, I have studied, Oriental Culture in college. I consider myself an authority on the subject."

"You got to be kidding me!" Tony got up and left. He was soon followed by other Team Members.

The Captains meeting, kind of dissolved itself. He just sat there, with kind of a dumb look. The expert on Oriental Culture, didn't understand, SF culture. There was no way this guy would make it on an A-Team. We all agreed he would make a good staff officer. Nobody listens to them anyway.

We were finishing with the last patient.

"Tren, close the place down. I'm going for a cup of coffee. When you are finished, come join me."

As I entered the Team House, I couldn't help noticing, the strange look on Captain Sherman's face.

"What's the problem captain? Can I help?"

"I can't believe that they walked out on me."

"Sir, they didn't walk out, they had things to do. We are under strength. They had to get back to work."

"I'm the Team Leader, when I call a meeting, I expect everyone to stay."

"That will never happen on an A-Team Sir. Rank is not important. We all share the work load. Loosen up a little Captain. You have to earn their respect."

"How do you coordinate your efforts, without meetings?"

"We conduct all Team business over supper. That is, if it's not classified." Our new Team Leader was gone in two days.

Half of my Reserve activation enlistment, had passed. I had a lot more that I wanted to accomplish. That made my decision to extend my Vietnam tour an easy choice to make. The shortage of Special Forces Medics, guaranteed approval. I was on the next Caribou heading for Nha Trang, to sign my extension.

"Why are you extending McGinley? Why not take a short discharge from the Reserves and join the Regular Army?" Asked the Administration Officer.

"I can do that?"

"Sure we do it every day. I'll have your enlistment papers ready in one hour.

"Hold it Sergeant McGinley. Better make that two hours. You have an enlistment bonus coming.

Reading from a list of critical MOS's he informed me a Special Forces Medic was entitled to a $4,000.00 re-enlistment bonis. I was beginning to like this Admin Officer. I tried for two and a half years to join the Army in the States. Now I can join the same Army in two hours? And be paid a bous to boot. Seems to me the right hand doesn't know what the left hand is doing.

"Make that $5,000.00 Sergeant First Class McGinley. Your promotion came through yesterday, congratulations.

Return From The Dead

I hated to spend time in Nha Trang. My aircraft wasn't leaving until 0530. I had no other choice. I decided to see a movie at the SF Headquarters theater. About halfway through a very boring movie, I was paged over the theater's

5ᵗʰ Special Forces Hdq Nha Trang

intercom. "SFC McGinley report to the lobby." Great I thought, maybe my aircraft is departing early.

Half way to the lobby the theater door opened. For a moment I thought I recognized the person blocking the entrance. No, it couldn't be, he's dead. As I got closer my eyes getting used to the light surrounding the person in question were able to focus. My heart was suddenly in my mouth.

"Bob Schrag! You're supposed to be dead."

"I don't think I'm dead Mac. If I am, I wasn't notified."

When I got closer, I gave my resurrected friend a bear hug. Before we went to the NCO Club, I stopped at flight operations and cancelled my flight to Kontum.

Bob and I had a lot to talk about. Boy was I glad to see this guy. Another thanks to the man upstairs. We talked about everything under the sun. We solved half of the world problems. In fact we solved some problems the world wasn't aware of yet. Finally we got to the big question.

"Why did they report you killed in action, Bob?"

"This club is too crowed Mac. Since we are both E7's now, lets' go over to the Top 3 Club, it's quiet there." We paid our bar bill and departed for the, top three club.

Bob was right the place was quiet. We were the only ones in the place. The Vietnamese Barmaid was a knock out. But she will have to wait. I had to get my question answered.

"Why did they report you, killed in action?"

"They didn't Mac. We were over the fence, can't tell you where. The extraction chopper tried, but couldn't get us out."

Bob went on to tell me how they hid in the jungle for six days. Then walked out without incident. By that time rumor control engaged. First rumors had them captured, finally, killed in action. The bad thing about rumors they're easy to start and almost impossible to stop.

"The gang back at Dak Seang and the B-Team are going to be glad you are alive. You can bet your bottom dollar, I'll spread the word."

"How about your family Bob. Do they know your OK?"

"The rumor didn't reach them."

Time flew by fast, it was 03:00 before we knew it. Bob had an early flight to catch. We went to our quarters. At 07:00 I saw my good friend off. I remember hoping he would stay out of harms way. But knowing my warrior friend that was not to be.

On my way back to Dak Seang I stopped off at the CIDG Hospital in Pleiku. Members off sight never miss a chance to scrounge something for the Team. Pleiku was a fairly large city. It was the home of the 4th Infantry Division, the 71st Evacuation Hospital and several other large units. Ideal targets for a good negotiator on a scrounging mission. Without bragging, I considered myself one of the best. The CIDG Hospital was not on the target list. We never scrounge from our own. Well almost never.

I was greeted by SFC Owen Wright. Owen was one of the best Special Forces medics I have ever met. His specialty was surgical procedures. This outstanding American, of African heritage was a dedicated professional.

SFC Owen Wright

"Hi Mac glad to see you." Then in a loud voice. " Nail everything down, McGinley's in town." We both laughed.

All new Special Forces Medics arriving in, II Corps, were first sent to the CIDG Hospital for an evaluation period. I was pleased to find that three medics were coming to Kontum. Owen introduced me to them all. One in particular impressed me. He had an outstanding attitude. In a few weeks Gary Beikirich would be recommended for our nations highest award, for valor, "The Medal of Honor."

"Owen how about letting me borrow a jeep?"

"Mac we only have two. One is redlined and the other is dispatched."

"No problem. Have your ambulance driver drop me off at the 4th Division. I want to do a little shopping." That brought a smile to both of our faces. Shopping indeed.

I thanked the driver for the ride. Entering the 4th ID's dispensary, I headed straight for their supply room. I was no stranger to the 4th. Their welcome was friendly. Then we got down to business.

"SGT Frank how would you like two Cross-Bows, three NVA Battle flags, and six pairs of, VC, black pajamas?"

"Great, what do you want for them?"

"As good as you have been to me in the past, I should just give them to you. But the fact remains, I have to feed my people. How much of this can you spare?" I handed SGT Frank a list I had prepared earlier. He studied the list for a couple of minutes.

"If you could dig up another Cross-Bow, I could add to your list."

"Like what Frank?"

"Two cases of canned turkey, canned bacon, and sausage."

"Throw in a couple cases of fruit, and you got a deal." He agreed.

"Drop the goodies off at B-24 the next time you go to Kontum SGT Frank. They will give you the trophies. SGT Frank went to Kontum twice a week. The 4th ID had a camp just south of the city.

"SGT Frank, I need transportation back to the CIDG Hospital."

"No problem. Pvt. Williams take SFC McGinley anywhere he wants' to go." I spent the night at The CIDG Hospital. Taking the first chopper the next morning, I headed for the B-Team in Kontum.

Professional courtesy demands checking in with the Command Sergeant Major. Quite often the CSM has information that could benefit the Team. In addition it affords one an overview of the total B-Team operational area.

"Where are you going on your enlistment leave Mac?" The SGM inquired.

"I Didn't know I had an enlistment leave, Sergeant Major."

"You sure do. Thirty days anywhere in the world." That was great news. However I didn't think I would be able to take a leave. I was the only medic on sight. I didn't want to leave the Team without medical support. I headed back to Dak Seang, on the first aircraft flying. During the flight I convinced myself a 30-day leave was out of the question. Tren could probably handle sick call. The thought of an American being lost because of my absence convinced me. There would be no 30-day leave.

I could feel the tension. Something was wrong. What in the world could have happened during my 3-day absence?

"Tony, what in the world is wrong, did someone die?" Tony didn't answer. He walked away.

"Tom what's the . . . " I didn't get a chance to finish. Tom walked away. A red headed Sergeant First Class walked toward me holding out his hand.

"I'm SFC Max Schaft the new Team Sergeant. You must be McGinley the teams pill pusher." The statement and the Ha, Ha, after it, ticked me off.

"Correction, I'm Sergeant First Class Daniel T. McGinley, the Senior Medical Supervisor of this team. You and I are not getting off to a good start SFC Schaft."

"Didn't want to tick you off. I used to be a SF Medic. I was always called, a pill pusher. Sometimes a Bed Pan Commando. It was all in fun." My mind was working a mile a minute. Schaft a trained SF Medic. Good, maybe I will take that 30-day leave.

"Didn't you know about this Mac?" Weeks asked.

"Know about what Tom? What's going on here?"

"We thought you knew. Tony and I are being reassigned. In fact we were sure you knew Mac. You never leave camp. As soon as the Captain arrives, you're gone." No wonder Tony and Tom gave me the cold shoulder. I probably would have thought the same thing.

Weeks and Dodge spent most of their remaining time at Dak Seang, bringing the new Team Leader and Team Sergeant up to speed on camp operations. In two days Tony Dodge was gone bag and baggage. His new assignment was an A-Team at Fort Bragg NC. While at Bragg, Tony volunteered for the Son Tay Raid. A plan to free POW's in North Vietnam. Tom Weeks was assigned to Camp Dak Pek, as their Team Sergeant. Within three days I was the only member left from the old A-Team.

"Why wasn't I reassigned Sir?"

"The LLDB Commander, asked the B-Team that you be permitted to stay." The Captains reply almost made me feel guilty. I had the same feeling for the LLDB as Tony and Tom.

Every time America sends troops to help a nation survive, we end up letting the nation being helped, run the show. If in fact they are that competent, why send our troops to do the dying? This incident between the American Team and the LLDB is a good example of that policy. Probably lack of policy would be closer to the truth.

"SFC Schaft, how are you and Captain Sherman on mortars?"

"Maybe little rusty, but I would say pretty good."

"If you would like, I'll pass on to you a few tips I have learned from SFC Weeks. Believe me, Tom was one of the best." I couldn't believe my own words. A few months ago I couldn't hit the side of a barn now I'm offering instruction. Immediately after dinner we gathered at the 81nn mortar pit.

"Why don't we make this interesting gentlemen? I'll bet a case of beer, I can come closer to a target than either of you." Schaft and Captain Sherman took the bet. They knew that they could beat a Medic on an 81 mortar.

"Let's see now, what should we use as a target? See that old bare tree? That's the target gentleman." I picked up, an 81 round, removed a few powder bags, and adjusted the Mortar settings to the exact settings Weeks used when he instructed me.

"Fire in the hole." The shell hit the bottom of the tree. I quickly removed my mortar tube settings. Next to fire was SFC Schaft. His round hit short and a little to the right. The Captain's round didn't come close.

"Thank you gentlemen. Make that Coors Light."

"Lucky shoot.", Schaft insisted. I went on to explain luck had nothing to do with it. I rubbed salt into the wound by stating,

"After Tom Weeks, I was probably, the best shoot in Vietnam." They both laughed. They were not buying that statement at all. "I'll tell what I'm going to do, double or nothing. Forget my first shot, I'll put a white phosphate round in the center of the tree."

"That I have to see, you're on." I couldn't believe this was coming from the guy whose round hit, so far off the target. I picked up a WP round, and adjusted the tube settings.

"Fire in the hole." I dropped the round in the tube, turned and walked away. Glancing over my shoulder, I could see the target lit up like a Christmas tree. I never told them that I was using predetermined settings. To this day, they think I'm a great mortar man. Who am I to spoil this image.

Around The World

Tomorrow will be the big day, I start my 30-day extension leave. When you put in for a leave, you are required to name a destination city and an address you can be reached. Thanks to Owen Right, I named the US Embassy, Copenhagen Denmark as my contact address.

The only way to get to Copenhagen Denmark from Vietnam, was through the US via, TWA. Flight 101, was a continuous fligh around the world. First to Hawaii, then a

TWA. Flight 101

stop at San Francisco, Denver, Chicago, then New York. The flight continues to Frankfort Germany. At Frankford, you had to change airlines to reach Copenhagen. The same airline returned to Frankfort to catch the next TWA flight 101. Then the round the world flight continued to Tel Aviv Israel, Bangkok Thailand, then back to Vietnam.

I will be taking this round the world flight, four times. TWA Flight 101 was made to order. My brother and sister lived in Colorado, I had dear friends in Chicago, the stop at New York afforded me the opportunity to see a Broadway show. The icing on the cake was, you could get off of Flight 101 at any scheduled stop, spend a few days, then catch the next Flight 101.

I got off of Flight 101 in Denver Colorado. It was relatively easy to catch a Military flight to Colorado Springs. I spend a couple of day's with my brother Jack and his family. Jack and his wife Joan had five great children, Susan, Karen, Cathy Jo, Keith, and Bryan. Jack and I remained very close over the years. A little surprising, considering the stunts, I played on him when we were growing up. Jack's wife and five children, were in a class by themselves. I didn't get a chance to see them as much as I would like. Seems as though I always have

Jack Joan and 5 gifts from Heaven

something in the fire occupying my time. Time spent with them was quality time, I wouldn't trade for anything.

From Jacks, I went to Denver to visit with my sister Sarah and

Vernice, Sal, and Verne

her husband Vern, and daughter Vernice. By this time their son's Dan and Steve were out of college, away from home, presuming their individual careers. Visiting Sal and her family was always a meaningful experiences. It would have been a plus if I saw Dan and Steve more than I did. Vern and Sarah's children are great examples what a Christian home can produce.

Uncles are not supposed to have special nephews or nieces. Vernice forced me to break that rule. Her letters to me in Vietnam brightened up many a sad day.

June 1968, I was in a very serious situation in Viet Nam. We had just lost two Montagnards of our six man team. The NVA had us surrounded and to make thing worse we were low on ammunition. Chances on any of us making it seemed at least questionable. Then in the distance we heard a helicopter. The chopper couldn't land but they did manage to drop small arms ammunition and hand grenades. Attached to one of the ammo boxes was a mail bag. The B-Team thought we might need something for our moral, we did.

While we waited for darkness to make our escape we read our mail. I opened the large envelope containing a homemade card from my niece Vernice. She had cut words and pictures from magazines, papers or what ever and made cute phrases out on them. All pertained to Airborne, Special Forces and directed at me. Words can not express the uplifting that card gave me. Like magic, the card had taken me from the lowest moral point I have ever experienced, to a feeling of invincibility. At that moment, I proclaimed Vernice my favorite.

I have always used my sister Sarah and her husband Vern as a measuring device, a blueprint for marriage. My goal was (if I ever married) I would want a union like theirs or I wouldn't get married. I achieved my goal in Bangkok, Thailand when I met my wife Chomeyong.

From Denver, I took another layover in Chicago to visit with old friends. Then I drove to Hebron Airport, 50 miles northwest of the city, to visit the Land of Lincoln Sky Diving Club. Turning into the airport, was like entering your home after a long absence. A lot of me was put into building this Sport Parachuting Center. The like my home feeling was justified.

The jump plane was taking off as I got out on my rented car. I watched them climb to jump attitude. First one jumper out then the second and the third. What a beautiful site. I'll never lose the thrill of seeing jumpers in the air. I went out to the target area and waited for them to land. Dale Kosak landed about two feet from a dead center.

"Did you forget everything, I taught you?" I hollered.

"Mac! How are you?" Then Bill Mellor landed two inches from a dead center.

"Not bad, for an older man." My mouth was at it again.

"Put a chute on, show me how it's done." Bill jumped up and gave me a bear hug. Charlie Bloomster was so busy waving and welcoming me home, he forgot to turn his parachute, to slow down for landing. He flew past the target. Bill, Dale and I shot the breeze until Charlie, made it back to the target area. After a warm welcome from Charlie we all headed back to the Snack Shop.

No one realized I was at the airport, until we came close to the team house. Then they came out. It was like an old home week. They may have been faking it but all seemed happy to see me. I wasn't faking it. I was very glad to see them.

I didn't have to ask who was flying the jump plane. I could tell by the landing. Bob Arnold was the only pilot I knew that could land with such precession using less then half of the runway. We talked for over an hour.

"We can finish this talk latter guys. I'm keeping you from jumping."

"Put a chute on Mac." Bill Mellor insisted.

It had been more than two years since my last free fall jump. The thought of jumping didn't scare me. Let's say it put me in the extreme caution mode. With a little reluctance I chuted up with borrowed equipment. We left the aircraft at 7200 feet for a 30second free fall. Bill Mellor left the Cessna 175 first. He was followed by Dale then, with a slight hesitation, I followed. Our goal was to make a three-man hookup before opening.

Bill and Dale hooked up within 10 seconds. I overshoot my first attempt. Would have probably made it on the second try but ran out of altitude. The rule was you have to have a fully opened canopy at 2200 feet. We were at 2100. I was a little disappointed not making the three-man. The disappointment was overridden with the pride I had for my two friends. I trained and put both Bill and Dale out on their first free-fall. Watching their performance filled my heart with pride. Of course my beautiful thoughts

Bill Mellor and Dale Kosack

were crumbled by the harassment I received from both my superstars. I combated the ribbing by saying I didn't want to show them up.

"You staying for the week end Mac?" Bill asked.

"Sure if the motel has a room"

"They have a room, you're old room." A familiar voice announced.

I could recognize that voice anywhere. I turned and gave Bridgitte a big hug and kiss. Bridgitte was Bill Mellor's girl. They took over my room at the motel when I went to Vietnam. While we were talking, Bridgitte called the Motel, advised them I was back in town and would be staying the night. She had the motel move their belongings to another room and advised them I was in town.

We made one more jump (missed that 3-man again) then headed for the Hebron Motel to clean up. Over dinner we exchanged stories to bring us all up to date. What a great evening, this was a tight group we were like family. The evening tightened the bond of our relationship. I considered myself very fortunate having so many friends at Land of Lincoln.

Later in the quiet of my room, a sadness fell over me. What was I doing? People are dying back in VN. My wife and son are waiting for me in Bangkok. Suddenly I felt guilty for enjoying myself. I left a goodby letter in the Motel office and departed for Chicago's O'Hair Airport. I caught the next TWA Flight 101 to Bangkok Thailand, to spend quality time with my wife Chome and our son Johnny.

My wife Chomeyong was waiting for me at Don Maung Airport. I was tired after my long trip and had a lot on my mind. After snuggling up to an angel for a few seconds, suddenly everything was peaceful. I didn't have a worry in the world. It was great to be home.

Chomeyong

Bangkok is a very large and busy city. It is almost impossible to get around in the city's heavy traffic unless you have your own driver.

Lek had been driving for Chome's family for many years. In addition of being a good driver, Lek had a Mercedes that he kept spotless.

"Take us home Lek, let me know when we get there. I'll have my eyes closed."

I wasn't kidding. If you want a good scare, just go to Bangkok and watch how they dodge in and out of traffic. When they get to a traffic circle, it is one great game of chicken. First one at the circle has the right away. Thailand has a lot of peculiar traffic rules we will be talking about later on.

It was time to get out of the Mercedes. We weren't home yet. We still had about a half of mile or so to walk. It was a very pleasant walk. A winding path through the jungle like vegetation. Over a  few foot bridges, down another path that led to a large clearing surrounding our modist home. Waiting for us was our son Johnny, Chome's Mother, and Aunt.

After the customary formal Thai greeting. A lot of bowing with hands held together and a few Sawadee's, we settled down to a great meal. All through the meal well wishers kept popping in with gifts. I think the best thing I like about leaving Thailand, is the great welcome home's, I like the attention. The only thing I would change is the formality of Thai greetings. If I had my way, I would jump in with a lip-lock on that sweet gal.

"Oh Mack! I almost forgot tell you. I have a message for you." Chome unfolded a copy of the logged radio message.

"Where did you get this message?"

"Wayne gave to Dang, Dang gave to me, now I give to you." Sounds complicated doesn't it? It's not really. Wayne is a friend who works at the US Embassy in Bangkok Dang is his wife and childhood friend of Chome. Of course, 'the you', Chome is referring to, is me. Still sounds complicated doesn't it? I think we lost something here in the translation.

The message was from, CSM Richard Campbell. He asked I get in touch with him ASAP. If only Chome gave me this message at the Airport. We passed the Embassy on our way home. I kind of wished Chome hadn't remembered the message until morning. I was dog tired. Besides I wanted some private time with the Dragon Lady. That is not a sarcastic remark. Chomeyong Kemtong is my personal Dragon Lady. The D.L. in Terry and the Pirates, couldn't hold a candle to Chome.

The 'ASAP' in the message gave some concern. I decided to go to the Embassy and have Wayne radio patched me to CSM Campbell. Back over the bridges and down the paths to the little Market area where Lek was waiting. Lek has the patience of a Saint. Unless you release him, Lek will wait all night. This was one loyal and dedicated driver. I was radio patched to Saigon in about ten minutes. Finding CSM Campbell took a little longer. Finally contact was made.

"SGM Campbell, McGinley, Go."

"Hi Mac. Glad you called. Need to see you on your way back Kontum, Go."

"Roger that. I'll call as soon as I get in country, Out"

"Roger. Out." That was short and sweet. I wonder what he wants? By this time traffic had died down. Lek got me back home a lot quicker.

Time flies when I'm with Chome. Before I knew it, Lek (our driver) was taking me to the airport to catch a plane back to Vietnam. I called CSM Campbell as soon as I landed in Saigon.

"Mac, there's a black Chevrolet in front of the terminal. You can't miss it. It has Diplomat Plates. Tell the driver to bring you to this location." I spotted the driver before I saw the car. All the people working for SGM Campbell are Chinese Nung's. This mammoth guy stood out like a neon sign.

"Take me to the Special Forces Safe House." He didn't have the slightest idea of what I was talking about. "Take me to see SGM Campbell."

"Oh yes, Special Force." He opened the door and we were off.

I take back what I said about the drivers in Thailand. This guy drove like a mad man. He cut people off and then cussed them out for being in the way. His best trick was when he bumped into the rear end of a Vietnamese Police car. He got out of the car shaking his fist at them. They just drove off. I would have put this clown in the monkey house. This guy defiantly wasn't dealing with a full deck.

I was glad to see CSM Richard E. Campbell again. He impressed me at our first meeting a year ago. Because of him, I was able to get my assignment changed from Mac-V to Special Forces. I didn't know what he wanted. But if it is within my power to return a favor, I was prepared to do so.

"Mac I have something to tell you in strict confidence. I need your promise not to breathe a word to anyone." Of course I promised.

"Lieutenant Cornel John Hennigan is going to be the new B-24 Commander. LTC Marquis is going back to the states. LTC Hennigan asked me to be his Command Sergeant Major. I worked for LTC John Hennigan in the past. He is one great CO." I kept wondering what that had to do with me. "When you get back to B-24, they are going to ask you to be the B-Team Medic. I know there are some at B-24 you would rather not work for, never the less I want you to take the job."

I knew because of my new rank I would have to be reassigned. Although I had planned to go to the CIDG Hospital in Pleiku, I agreed on B-24 in Kontum. I was looking forward to working for CSM Campbell. I caught a C-130 flight to Pleiku, then a chopper to Camp Dak Seang. Circling the camp I saw a lot of activity along the river leading to Dak Seang's bathing area. Not again I thought to myself.

"Their building a shanty camp alongside the river." Every two or three-month's Montagnards from scattered villages high in the

Cardboard Shacks

mountains, try to move in close to the SF Camp for protection. They build lean-to shakes out of cardboard or whatever they can find. We have been moving them out as fast as they can build them. You have to give them credit though, they keep trying. The harmless looking shelters become very dangerous to the SF Camp and its occupants.

First they become health hazards for their occupants and anybody around them. But most important they become safe havens for the enemy. Before every attack on the camp, the NVA position forward observers in the shacks to direct they're artillery fire. They cannot be allowed to stay. Their very survival depends on moving them out. One day the Camp defenders would be forced to open fire on them to silence the enemy observers. I told the new camp commander what I observed. It didn't seem to matter to him if the built a village or not. I went on to explain how the enemy would use the shacks for cover.

"I don't think they would be that stupid," was his reply.

"I hope you're not stupid enough to at least consider the possibility." I was suddenly aware of the fact I was talking to a person with a whole lot of smarts, laced with threads of stupidity. I was pulling for the smarts to overcome.

Chapter Four

B-24 Kontum

I didn't get a chance to unpack. The radio message was short but to the point. I was to meet with the B-Team Commander LTC Andrew J. Marquis and CSM Eugene Henge. The message didn't state the purpose of the meeting, it didn't have to. My meeting with CSM Campbell in Saigon tipped their hand. The message stated the meeting was to be at my convenience. To me that meant ASAP. I headed for Kontum (the B-Team's location) that afternoon.

"Didn't expect to see you this soon SFC McGinley." CSM Henge called the B-Team Commander to inform him I had arrived. "The CO will see us now McGinley." We headed for LTC Marquis' office. After the preliminary greetings, LTC Marquis got to the point of our meeting. He explained that because of my promotion I was the ranking medic assigned to B-24. He went on to inform me he was assigning me to the B-Team. The Colonel emphasized that I would have complete control over the B-Team Medical Mission.

"What Medical Mission?" I thought to myself. The LTC went on to explain although the CSM Henge was in charge of all enlisted assignments, he would consider my recommendations on assignments of Medical personnel.

"I know our first meeting left something to be desired. We will put that behind us SFC McGinley. B-24 has but one mission, support the A-Teams." That should come as a surprise to the A-Teams. To this point, that hasn't been apparent. I was glad the LTC wasn't a mind reader. "Your assignment to the B-Team is effective immediately SFC McGinley. Welcome aboard." The LTC reached out his hand as he stood up.

"Sir, what choices do I have?" A frown replaced the smirk the LTC used for a smile. It was evident the gentleman didn't appreciate my question.

"With your record, probably any assignment in the 5th Group."

I wasn't about to reject the assignment to the B-Team. I just wanted the LTC to know, I knew he didn't have the authority to reassign senior medics. That job belonged to the Group Surgeon. Besides CSM Campbell and I had a deal. At this moment I knew LTC Marquis wasn't aware he was being replaced as the B-Team Commander. I shook the LTC's hand and thanked him. LTC Marquis put the B-Team Chopper at my disposal to pick up my personal belongings.

Although Dak Seang was a remote site, it was a tough camp. An enemy trying to occupy this piece of real estate would have to pay a big price. It was more than a Special Forces A-Camp. It was home to a proud people, the Montagnard. I suddenly realized it was also my home. I was sad to be leaving.

Good Bye Tren

It didn't take me long to pack. An old rule in Special Forces "if it doesn't fit in your rucksack, you don't need it." I follow that rule as close as I can. Not because I follow rules to the letter. More like, because I'm lazy.

Tren was conspicuous by his absence. All the medics were helping me. Where was Tren? Of all the Montagnard medics, I figured Tren would be close during my last few hours at Dak Seang. My inquiring thoughts were interrupted by the camp's only Montagnard Company Commander Captain R-Com. R-Com entered the medical bunker.

"Bac Si, time for celebration, you go celebration." Celebrate my leaving? Does this mean they are happy I'm going? If I didn't know better, my feelings might have been hurt.

The only strange thing about the invitation was who it was coming from. I had little to no contact with this Montagnard Captain. In fact nobody had much contact with him, to include the LLDB team. This guy was definitely a loner.

I was pleasantly surprised to see the elaborate layout. The tables were full of Vietnamese, American, and Montagnard food. The beverage to wash it down, was as varied as the food. Vietnamese Ba mui Ba (33Beer), and American Beer and of course my favorite Montagnard Rice Wine. The LLDB donated some Vietnam

Dak Seang A 245

whiskey. It looked like everyone in the camp showed up to say goodby. Tren was still conspicuous by his absence.

I had an hour to wait for the chopper to pick me up and take me to B-24. I took my last walk around the Dak Seang perimeter. Unlike my first walk, most of the Montagnards were outside sitting on top of their underground living quarters. I stopped at every family group and bid them farewell. A heavy sadness fell over me. I would miss my beloved Montagnards.

I was surprised and a little hurt as most of the Yards who were closer to me, to including Tren and Yet were no where to be seen. To make myself feel better I entertained the thought that maybe they were too sad to say goodby. I didn't know if that was true or not. It just made me feel better.

I could hear my chopper approaching. I headed for the runway. Another surprise, Yet was standing by my baggage with a big smile on his face. Apparently he had a change of heart and decided to say goodby. Still, no Tren.

"Bac Si you come, Tren want see you." I followed Yet feeling a lot better.

As we approached the river, I could see a group of Montagnards gathered near the camp's bathing area. When we were closer, I recognized the smiling faces of my missing Montagnard friends. I felt really good. It would have been terrible to leave Dak Seang without being able to say goodby to my special group of friends.

"Bac Si you stand this place." Another order from Yet.

On the far side of the river a band of armed Montagnards emerged from the jungle. They were headed in our direction. The group stopped short of the river. The Montagnard leading them crossed to our side. I couldn't believe my eyes, it was Tren.

"Bac Si Mac, Tren come tell you good luck. I very happy Bac Si Mac friend me." As we shook hands, it was evident, I was viewing a side of Tren I have never seen before.

"Tren why aren't you at the dispensary? In my absence I hoped you would take over until another American was assigned .

"Bac Si not work Dak Seang, Tren Not work Dak Seang." Our conversation shifted to the real reason for our meeting at the river.

Tren informed me that he was a Dai Wie (Captain) in the FIHPM \ FULRO movement. FIHPM \ FULRO (In French, Front de-Iteration des- Hant-plateaua Montagnard DEGA) a DEGA military force that was organized during the French involvement in the Central Highlands. Tren's involvement in FULRO didn't surprise me. I suspected it for some time.

Just to mention the name FULRO was not permitted. At one time it might end in a court martial for US Forces. The Vietnamese government feared the FULRO and executed anybody belonging to the movement   The Vietnamese knew FULRO was capable of fulfilling their mission of regaining complete control of the Central Highlands and return the area to its rightful owners, the DEGA People.

"Bac Si, long time now you be FULRO Lieutenant Surgeon. Now before Bac Si go, Bac Si be Dai Wie (Captain) Surgeon in FULRO. This OK with you Trung Shi (Sergeant) Bac Si?"

Why not, I thought to myself. An officer in the FULRO movement with the status of Surgeon, why not. I welcomed the offer as a very friendly jester from a very good friend. Of course I wouldn't be able to tell anybody about my lofty position. If Command got wind of this, I might be Private McGinley. I'll just have to stick by my old defensive rule . . . Admit to nothing, deny everything and file counter accusations.

The armed Montagnards that accompanied Tren, crossed to our side of the Dak Poko river. In a very short while The Montagnard Company Commander from camp Dak Seang joined us. The ceremony was short but very military in structure. After a few words in the Jeh language, Captain R-Com pined Captain Bars on my lapel. He saluted me and I returned his salute. Without hesitation, Tren removed the captain bars from my lapel and put them in my fatigue jacket pocket.

"Now nobody know Bac Si Dai Wie Surgeon." Tren smiled as he buttoned my pocket. I was impressed. I felt like a Dai Wie (Captain) Surgeon, what ever that was. I said good by to everyone and shook their hands. I took Tren aside and let him know how much I appreciated his friendship and loyalty. My attempt to get him to change his mind about not working at Dak Seang failed.

"Bac Si not work Dak Seang, Tren not work Dak Seang." His mind was made up. I boarded the waiting Mai Dai wop-wop (helicopter) and headed to Kontum and B-24.

What Medical Mission?

I went straight from the chopper pad to CSM Henge's office and reported in. Before we got too far into our conversation, I made my request.

"Sergeant Major, how about me looking around a bit before you give me my briefing?" Henge agreed. I wanted to get a lay of the land so to speak. I needed first hand information on any positive or negative situation that was to confront me. Attending an in briefing with one person holding all the cards would have put me at a disadvantage. You can't negotiate without knowing what you're up against. Something was wrong at B-24. I just couldn't put my finger on it. I started my fact-finding tour at B-24's Dispensary.

"Good Morning, my name is McGinley, Sergeant First Class McGinley." The clown laying on the cot looked startled, I must have woke him up.

"I have two questions for you son. What are you doing in bed at this time of day and why are you sleeping in my dispensary?"

"I worked late last night Sarge. We had a promotion party at the Club."

"My name is not Sarge. It's Sergeant. Was someone injured at the party?"

"No, I'm the Club Manager."

"That's, no Sergeant. What time is Sick Call?"

"We don't have Sick Call Sergeant McGinley. I just handle emergencies."

I couldn't believe my ears. We were short Medics in Vietnam and this clown is working as a club manager. I had better cool off before I have my meeting with the B-Team CSM. Meeting with him now would not help our already shaky relationship.

"Pack your bags young man. I want you out of this Dispensary within the hour."

"I'll be leaving the B-Team on Saturday Sergeant McGinley. I don't see why I can't stay. What difference will three days' make?"

"What parts of GET OUT OF MY DISPENSARY didn't you understand? You now have 30 minutes to vacate this building." I departed the Dispensary by a door leading to the B-Team's S-I (administration office).

"Good morning SFC McGinley, I'm Captain Shackleton, the B-Team S-I. I thought we were under attack. Good luck, but I don't think you will be able to move that medic out of the Dispensary. That E-5 has a lot of pull with the CMS."

"He'll move Sir, believe me he will move. By the way Sir, are those your file cabinets alongside the Lab-table? They will have to go also." I left, Captain Shackleton with a bewildering look on his face.

I went to B-24's open air patio to get a cup of coffee and jot down items I wanted to bring up at my meeting with the B-Team CSM. This turned out to be a monumental task. I had no problems listing items that needed improvement and ways to correct them. The hard part was coming up with positive items. It's one thing criticizing, but a pat on the back or compliment makes the criticizing pill easier to swallow. That was the problem not much was good about the medical mission or more correctly, the lack of one.

SSG Al Lipson

"Hi my name is Al Lipson, are you the new Bac Si?"

"Dan McGinley, glade to meet you Al. Guilty as charged."

I didn't know it at the time, but SFC Al Lipson and I were to become life long friends. Al explained he didn't belong to the B-Team. He and about nine other Special Forces Communication Specialists belonged to the 403rd SOD (Special Operations Detachment) an intelligence gathering unit.

They occupied a small classified area within B-24's compound. Just to be near their area you had to have a Top-Secret plus Clearance. Neither the B-24's Commander nor the CSM was allowed in their heavily guarded sandbagged bunker. Al Lipson was a friendly outgoing individual. Al's Degree in Electrical Engineering was just the proverbial tip of the iceberg. This was a multi talented individual always willing to give a helping hand. His enthusiasm in offering help, left you with the feeling, he really was sincere about offering.

We were shortly joined by other SOD Team members. Al went around the table introducing everyone. First, SFC Bob Courchaine his Team Leader, SGT J. B. Fuller, SGT's Lorin Pacini, SSG Roger E Smithand and Mike Sitterfield all SOD Radio Operators. A missing member of their Team that would play an important part in my life was SSG Glen Watson. SSG Watson was on operation with the Mike-Force. The 403rd SOD, in addition of monitoring enemy radio broadcast at B-24, took their intelligence gathering talent to the field with the Mike Force and A-Teams in our A O (area of operation). The SOD Team and I hit it off great. In a short time I was coming in and out of their Team House as though I was a member of the team

"Sergeant Major, are you busy?"

"Come on in SFC McGinley, I thought you got lost. What do you think of our Medical operation?"

"Not a heck of a lot Sergeant Major. Your Dispensary is in poor condition. After I meet your medic, I understood why."

The CSM didn't respond. CSM Henge has been around Special Forces for a long time. The CSM had a reputation of being a good Special Forces Operative. Just because he and I didn't get along, doesn't make him a bad guy. I'm sure the CSM knew my assessment of B-24's Medical Mission was on target.

The CSM went on to explain that my assignment to the B-Team would involve the supervision of ten A-Team Medics. He went to a wall map and pointed out their location. "Camp Dak Peck A-242 is our most northern camp in II Corps. They have one medic on site. Our A Team at Dak Suit was overrun nine months ago. We will never rebuild it."

"Wasn't MSG Bucky Smith the Team Sergeant when the camp was overrun?" I just had to get my two cents in.

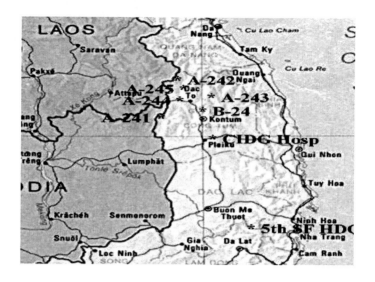

A-242 Dak Pek, A-245 Dak Seang, A-244 Ben Het
A-243 Plateau Gi, B-24 B-Team at Kontum
C-2 C-Team at Pleiku, CIDG Hospital at Pleiku
5th SF HDQ at Nha Trang

"Yes he was. He got out OK as did the rest of the Team." I
didn't think that was correct. Someone had told me they all didn't
make it. My information was second hand. I chose not to challenge
the CSM. This was one of the few times I wished the CSM was
correct, and I wrong.

"I don't have to tell you about this camp." CSM Henge was
referring to Camp Dak Seang (A-245). The thought of not taking my
promotion and going back to A-245 crossed my mind. But that
wouldn't be to smart. On the other hand no one has ever said all of
Mrs. McGinley s' children were smart.

"Plateau Gi A-243 as you can see is north east of our location.
It's difficult getting in Plateau Gi at times. They have a fog problem.
The fog also limits air-support during attacks by the NVA. Ben Het
A-244 is about 12 K (K= 5/8 mile) south west of Dak Seang and about
30 K from our location. They also only have one Medic. This was the
only A Team that was assessable by vehicle. "Camp Polie Kleng A-241
is at this location." The CSM was pointing to an area on the map that
was about 20 K south of Ben Het. "At Present we also have the
responsibility of Camps Mang Buk, Plei Djereng, Plei Mrong, Duc Co,

and Plei Me. However, they are being transferred to Vietnamese control. The increased enemy activity will keep us busy supporting the five northern camps.

As you can see we only have one medic at each camp. Now that you have been reassigned, Dak Seang doesn't have any. The TO&E calls for two medics per camp. We could use three per camp." The thought ran thru my mind, why are you using a medic as a bartender? Later I found out the part time medic was not Special Forces Qualified, the B-Team borrowed him from MACV.

"McGinley, I know you will have a problem with this. I assign the duty station of all enlisted personnel in B-24 and that includes medics."

"Henge I'm fully aware of a CSM's authority." The CSM jumped in like a bolt of lightning.

"You're not much on military courtesy are you? Put a rank in front of my name."

"I'm a strong believer in military courtesy. Put a SFC in front of my name and I'll extend the curtsey by putting a CSM in front of yours." I have no problem bringing the worst out of a person. The CSM was hot.

"As I was trying to tell you CSM Henge, of course you have the enlisted assignment authority. In the case of medical assignments, your Senior Medical NCO should have input. What in the heck does an infantry CSM know about medical assignments?" This did nothing to cool him off. I thought I saw steam coming from his ears.

At this point in my life I was not a career soldier. I volunteered to come to Vietnam to do medicine. Hopefully to save a few lives. I chose Special Forces because they are the best. If you must go to a war, go with the best, your chances of surviving are increased ten folds.

I had fully intended to go back to civilian life after the Vietnam war ended. What a hot-headed CSM thought of me didn't bother me a bit. I made up my mind he was not going to interfere with my mission. As far as I was concerned he could shove this job where the sun doesn't shine.

"CSM Henge, I decided not to take the B-Team assignment. As I see it, we have two choices. First send me back to Dak Seang A-245 or I'll go back to the C-Team Surgeon for assignment to another area. I'm sure there is another A-Team somewhere that could use a medic."

"SFC McGinley, the Colonel has assigned you to B-24 and this is where you will stay."

"Negative Sergeant Major. Your Lieutenant Colonel doesn't have the authority to assign Senior Medical NCO's. The 5th Group Surgeon alone has Senior Medical NCO assignment authority. Send me back to Dak Seang or I'm out of here." The CSM didn't get a chance to respond. LTC Andrew Marquis entered the room.

"I couldn't help hearing this unprofessional conversation. Both of you gentleman are lacking in communication skills. I am disappointed in both of you." This LTC was out of line correcting his CSM in front of another NCO. The little respect I had for him was lost at that moment. "I fully agree, all medical personnel assignments should be made with the recommendation of the B-Team Senior Medic. If I'm not mistaken, we talked about this before. If you two can't agree come to me. Do you understand?" We both answered, yes Sir.

I suppose I owed CSM Eugene Henge an apology. Maybe he is not such a bad guy as I thought. I put the apology on hold. I'll take a harder look at this guy. In the mean time I'll try to ease up on my abrasive attitude toward him.

He Walked All the Way

"If you are not part of the solution them, you are part of the problem." I don't know who originated that statement. The fact of the matter it is true. There was no way I would be part of the B-24's medical problem. I looked at this lack of Medical mission as an opportunity. With or without commands help, I made my mind up to build the best treatment facility in all of II Corps. That is nor bragging or patting myself on the back. I am just stating a fact. It was noon so I headed for the patio to get lunch and formulate my plans. Halfway through lunch a familiar voice filled the air.

"Good afternoon Bac Si McGinley. I come work you. OK?"

"Tren, how in the world did you get to Kontum? I'm really glad to see you." Another thought entered my mind. How did he get on a classified post?

"Tren walk three day now Bac Si. If Bac Si McGinley work Kontum, Tren work Kontum. This OK Bac Si?."

"Sure it's Ok Tren. We have a big job to do Tren, a big Job."

"Not problem. Bac Si Mac, Tren can do."

I didn't have the heart to tell Tren I had no authority to hire him to work at the B-Team. In fact I didn't have the authority to hire him at Dak Seang. Come to think about it, who needs authority. I'll work it out. I'll pay him out of pocket if I have to. How glad I am to see my friend.

I took Tren to see the dispensary. It was shabby but had great potential.

"This very nice Bac Si. We make this look like hospital."

Hospital? Why not, I'll bet, this could be a hospital. The hospital idea was born. The idea became a goal.

"I have to find you a place to sleep Tren."

"Tren sleep brothers house this night, brother stay near airport."

At that point SFC Johnny Hollis walked in. SFC Hollis was in charge of security at B-24. This was one heck of a soldier. Hollis recruited and trained forty or so Montagnard reaction force. They were responsible for B-24's security and manned the perimeter at night.

"Who do we have here Mac?"

"I'm sorry. Tren this is SFC Hollis, John this is Tren. Tren worked for me at Dak Seang. I'm going to try to get him a job here at B-24."

"They're not hiring anybody now Mac. I'll carry Tren on as a guard for as long as I can. We have room in the guard shack, Tren can stay there.

"Thanks John. I owe you one." SFC Hollis sent one of his men with Tren to get an ID and show Tren his bunk.

"Now you have two of my men Mac."

"Negative John, I don't have anybody working for me." It turned out there was a man assigned to the dispensary. However, they kept him working at the club. That got my Irish up. I excused myself and headed for the club. The front door was locked. I went to the side door. Sitting at a table with three of the bar-girls was B-24's Mess-Stewart / Bar-Manager.

"Do you have a medic working here?' The slob pointed to a young Montagnard sitting on the floor cleaning ash trays. I walked over to the lad and moved the Stack of ash trays with my foot. Needed to make room for the lad to get up. Later the slob told the CSM I kicked them across the floor. Not true. They did fall over and make a little noise, but they were not kicked.

"Go wait for me in the dispensary kid, I'll be there in a minute."

Then I turned to the Mess-Steward. I should say messy-Steward. This guy looked like a pig. Needed a shave, hair was too long to be working around food and beverage, slob was the only name for him. I went on to inform that my Montagnard Medic didn't work for him anymore. My departing words were;

"When was the last time these girls had a medical check up?" I found Tren and my new Medic deep in conversation. Tren saw me enter the room.

"This man think you want to kill him Bac Si. This man name Pirie. I tell man name Pirie, Bac Si no kill Montagnard, Bac Si love Montagnard."

Pirie could speak English a lot better than Tren. Not surprising, being raised in a village near Kontum afforded him the opportunity to have more exposure to Americans. His medical knowledge fell far short of Tren's. That presented no problem. Tren was a good teacher. This guy would be up to speed in a short time. How fortunate I was to have both of them on my team. The only potential problem was Pirie seemed to be afraid of me.

Evaluating additional assets available to accomplish the mission is something that is drilled into every Special Forces Operative. It doesn't matter if you are in a jungle, desert or populated area. Additional assets, human and materialistic can influence the mission in a positive way.

I started my asset search at the MACV (Military Assistance Command Vietnam) compound. MACV was on the west side of B-24, separated by a barbed wire fence. It was immediately apparent, MACV was not an asset. Their one doctor and six medics operated out of a small poorly equipped dispensary. Over staffed, under trained was my critical impression. Like most conventional units MACV medics including their doctors were restricted on what medical procedures they are allowed to perform. As a result all of their patient load that needed lab test or more than simple care, were sent to the 71st Evac .

MIKE FORCE and B-24 Compound   MACV Compound

On the east side of B-24 also separated by a barbed wire fence was the Special Forces Mike Force compound. Their main mission was to assist A-Teams that were under seige or heavy enemy attack. Many Special Forces soldiers were saved by this gallant band. I respectfully labeled them, "Fearless Fighter of the Forest."

The Mike Force had a full issue of Special Forces Medical equipment and supplies. In addition they had a 20 by 40 building that housed their medics and small dispensary. This was a gold mine. I would be revisiting this asset.

Three miles south of the river, that was the southern border of Kontum, was MACVSOG FOB-2 (Foreword Operational Base) compound. The FOB compound occupied both sides of the road going to Pleiku. At night they blocked the north and south ends of the road and became a strong blocking force for any attack on the city of Kontum from the south.

Although FOB-2 were all Special Forces Operatives, they were under the Command and Control of MACVSOG. These were high speed, hard-hitting troops, that conducted top-secret missions in areas occupied by the enemy. There were three camps like this in Vietnam. FOB-1 (southern-south VN), FOB-2 (in central-south VN), and FOB-3 (in northern-south VN). Later their names were changed to CCS (Command Control South), CCC (Command Control Central, and CCN (Command Control North).

221   A Walk With Giants 1958 - 1974

Fob-2 had a well-equipped dispensary. Unfortunately like most Special Forces Units they were short of medics. In addition to running their dispensary they had to Fly Chase. Every time a SOG Team was infiltrated, a medic riding in another chopper stood by. Entering hot-LZ's (landing zones) to extract the wounded resulted in the loss of many SOG Medics.

FOB-2/CCC Kontum had a difficult time getting medical supplies in a timely manor. All their orders went through MACV, and of course the MACV bureaucracy kicked in. I was looking for assets for my mission. I ended up being an asset for FOB-2 and later CCC. No problem, we were all Special Forces. I took this unit under my wing. I could get them anything they wanted and then some. The icing on the cake was I could get it in a timely manner.

SF Medica at FOB-2 told me there was a Leper Colony down a dirt road paralleling the FOB-2 compound. Since I was so close, I decided to pay them a visit. My new friends insisted I take two of their armed Montagnards with me.

Leper Colony Kontum Vietnam

Security in the area was questionable.

The Colony was run by Sister Marie Lowise and a staff of six French Nuns. When the French were forced out of Vietnam all the doctors were sent back to France. Sister Marie and her loyal nurses oped to stay behind. All were from the Order of The Sisters of St. Vincent de Paul. Their dedication to their belief, devotion to the Montagnard people, ranked them among the tallest of Giants.

Sister Marie gave me a tour of the grounds and beautiful buildings. The dormitories had bunks stacked five high. On one of the top bunks, laying on his back, an armless young Montagnard boy was painting a boarder at the top of the wall. The skill this lad had, using his feet to manipulate his paint brush was a beautiful sight to behold.

"Master Gui has done all our walls Sergeant McGinley. Aren't they beautiful?"

"They sure are Sister." The young Gui had a big smile. I think he knew we were praising his work.

From the dormitory we went to the livestock area. There in a pen (I can't call it a pig pen it was immaculate) was the largest sow I had ever seen. The best estimate I could give was seven hundred pounds. This gigantic hunk of pork was housed in a roofed, cement floored, small pen. Would you believe this animal gets a bath twice a day? When I asked why the pen was so small. I was informed, to keep him from losing weight. This guy was for pig picking. Not an ounce was to be wasted by exercising.

I heard them coming around the barn. Five of the finest show horses you could find anywhere, trotted over to where we were standing. Sister Marie Lowise said they were brought from France during the French involvement in Vietnam.

"We use the horses for therapy SGT McGinley. Our beloved Mountain Guards get a lot of pleasure grooming the beautiful animals." I didn't tell Sister Marie we now call her beloved people, Montagnards. The fact they were loved was good enough for me. By this time a large crowd was gathering around the Colonies main building.

"It's treatment time. Would you like to observe this activity Sergeant?" Sister Marie Lowise asked.

"Yes, Mame, I would. I'll give you a hand if you like."

"Are you in the medical care business, Sergeant?

"You could say that. I'm a Special Forces Medic." By this time we were at the treatment area. Sister Marie handed me an apron and explained, dressing a Lepers sores, are no different from dressing any other kind of sore or wound. She went on;

"When you come back, we will teach you how we treat the disease."

"How do you know if I'm coming back Sister?"

"You're Special Forces, Sergeant. After Special Forces Medics see our situation, they always come back." Sister Marie had our number.

There were two treatment areas. One was used to treat facial, neck, and upper body sores. The other for lower body, legs and foot involvement. Each treatment area had a very large, (16' plus) polished marble slab. The patients would sit on the slab, between each others legs forming a long line. The person conducting the treatment sat at one end with all the dressings needed. One by one the patient would scoot up and receive their treatment. When finished another patient would scoot into the treatment position. This continued until everyone received a dressing change.

The Vietnamese fear and treat Lepers similar to the way they did in biblical times. On the other hand, Montagnards treat them as normal people. They keep them in a designated area of the village, isolated from the non-leper population. They also require them to harvest their rice separately. Other than that, they want for nothing.

Leprosy is a devastating disease, causing the bone and cartilage to gradually deteriorate developing sores' The body seems to melt away. The distortion is most apparent in the hands, and feet. In extreme cases the hands and feet become lumps with nail tipped stumps of fingers and toes. Fortunately the disease can be prevented and controlled. Dapson was the medication of choice in Vietnam.

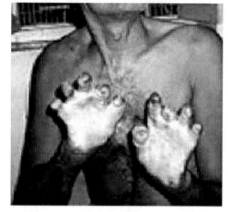

Leprosy is a devastating disease

Again while looking for assets, I became one. I drew an inward strength from the lepers. In spite of their devastating affliction, they manage to smile. As a Special Forces Medic I had the pleasure of working with Montagnards with Leprosy. A humbling experience that I will never forget.

On the east side of Kontum was another Montagnard hospital run by Dr. Patricia (Pat) Smith. This dedicated lady was loved by all DEGA people. She spoke their language and dedicated her life to their care. On occasion Pat had a problem getting medical supplies and food for her Montagnard patients. This problem was solved by Special Forces. Bac Si (Doctor) Smith appreciated all the assistance she received. Nevertheless, she kept her distance from Americans.

Her Montagnard Hospital was in an isolated area. When the sun went down it was VC (Viet Con) territory. As long as Dock Smith wasn't too involved with Americans the VC left her alone. Pat Smith, was a doctor not a politician, she treated everyone. It didn't matter what the patient's political beliefs were. If a human being was in need of her services, extremely talented Doc Smith would jump at the chance to relieve the suffering. The indomitable, blunt-talking woman the Montagnards call "ya pogang tih"-big grandmother of medicine, has experienced 13 years of terror, disease, squalor, frustration and triumph. Her love for the Montagnards gave her the strength to carry on.

Dr Pat Smith

Dr. Smith narrowly escaped death in March 1968, just after the Tet offensive, when North Vietnamese troops invaded Minh Quy Hospital. They shot up the labs and X-ray room and captured Renata Kuhnen, her German nurse. A human blanket of more than 30 Montagnard staff and patients lay on top of the doctor and hid her, while enemy troops ran through the wards tossing grenades, shooting women and children in the legs and demanding, "where are the Americans?"

I spent several hours a week at Doctor Smith's Montagnard hospital. On one of my visits Dr. Smith greeted me with a little more enthusiasm than usual.

"Sergeant McGinley I have something exciting to show you follow me!" I had a hard time keeping up. This gal had her walking device in full gear. Stopping at the bedside of a new arrival without hesitation Doc Smith removed the sheet covering a forty-five-year-old Montagnard.

"This gentleman has Bubonic Plague. This is the first case I have seen since sixty-six. Have you run across any Plague in your travel's Sergeant?" I didn't get a chance to answer. Doctor Smith handed me a pair of examining gloves then proceeded gloving herself.

"I suspected plague when I saw the swollen lymph node in his groin. Their glassy shine and dark center plus their sensitivity to touch heightened my suspicion. The lab work was the confirmation. I was praying the test would be negative. Very gently feel the left node."

"Seems to have a very hard core." The patient was in extreme pain when touched.

"If you ever see anything like this Sergeant McGinley please let me know. We might have a problem on our hands. I'll give you a copy of my findings. If you would give it to the MACV Surgeon, I don't have communication lines with them.

"I'll give a copy to our Special Forces Surgeon in Pleiku if you don't mind."

"I thought you were under MACV?

"No, Mame. Special Forces have their own Surgeon. Not only a very good Surgeon, Captain Shetler is one heck of a guy. They don't come any better than Paul L. Shetler. As they say Doctor Smith, you can take that to the bank."

"I would like to meet this one heck of a guy."

"I'll make sure that happens Mam. The next time Captain Shetler comes to Kontum, we'll put him in some civilian cloths and we will pay you a visit." Every time I went to Dr. Smith's hospital, I wore civilian clothes. Didn't want to wave a red-flag in front of the (VC) bull. Of course I left the area before sundown. I found it really sad having to sneak around to help the needy.

Conventional US forces didn't want me to help Pat Smith. My Commander and CSM had the same attitude, keep away from Dr. Smith she treats the enemy. No problem, if it bothers them to know what I was doing, I won't tell them.

Pat Smith's Montagnard Hospital treated Montagnards period. I acknowledge the fact that some of the Montagnards from remote areas, were forced to work for the enemy. That did not make them Anti-American nor my enemy. Having to sneak around to help Pat Smith would soon end. Our new Commander and SGM saw to that.

VIP Treatment

I started my B-Team assignment by visiting the five northern most A-Teams in B-24's area of operation. We left Camp Polie Kleng A-241, heading for Ben Het A-244 when the chopper developed motor trouble. We were at mid point between the camps when the pilot decided to make an emergency landing in a jungle clearing. Fortunately we had radio communications with the B-Team. They dispatched another chopper to pick us up.

226

Since we were in hostile territory, they also sent a Gun-Ship to fly cover. The Gun ships with 7.22 mm Mini guns, could fire more than 2,000 rounds per minute. It also had 2.75 Rockets, that could fire one at a time, in groups or all at once. That mean looking baby hovered right above us until everyone was on the rescue ship. Just

Gun Ship standing guard

as we were taking off, a Company of Montagnards arrived to guard the downed bird until she could be lifted out of her jungle resting place. My plan was to continue on with the A-Team visits. We headed to Camp Ben Het   A-244.

"It's for you Sergeant McGinley, Sergeant Major Henge." At that point the Co-Pilot handed me the head set.

"Poker Spools, Poker Spools, Buddha go."

"Buddha, Poker Spools, I have some bad news. Your Mother passed away. Your emergence leave will be ready when you arrive at this location."

"Thanks for your help Poker Spools. Be at your location 010, Buddha out." The Pilot monitoring the conversation headed for Kontum and B-24.

Dam death. No matter when it comes, you're never prepared. I surprised myself. I didn't have a deep sadness within. My mind was filled with memories of a great lady loved by everybody that knew her. A lady that would go out of her way to help others, even if it meant doing without herself. They say heaven is a place of beauty and happiness. A perfect place . . . well it is now. Sergeant Major Henge was waiting at B-24's chopper pad.

"I brought your shaving gear and a few things in this bag. There is a Caribou in Pleiku waiting for you." Handing me an envelop. "The B-Team took up a collection for you. Have a safe trip." The Pilot took off like something was chasing him. Things were happening fast and would continue to do so. The Caribou was waiting at Pleiku Airport. From Pleiku to Nhi Trang and a waiting C-130. When we landed at Tan Son Nhut Airfield in Saigon, an MP Jeep took me to the main terminal and ran (and I mean ran) me through customs. Back into the MP Jeep to a waiting civilian aircraft. The aircraft door was open with a small ladder hanging down. The MP's drove close to the ladder and I boarded. Would you believe, TWA Flight 101?

"Have you been waiting long?" I asked as I sat on the floor with my back resting on the cockpit door. Everyone cheered. It turned out the Pilot was giving them a blow by blow description of my progress as he heard it over the radio. Their plane was on its taxi run to the takeoff ramp as my C-130 was landing. At that point they were asked to wait for one more passenger. Lucky them.

"You won't be cheering when I occupy a seat next to a few of you after I catch my breath. I haven't had a bath for four or five days."

"Sit here Sergeant. After we get to altitude, your bath will be ready." I quickly took a seat next to the beautiful speaking doll.

"Good evening ladies and gentlemen, this is your Captain. Sorry for the delay. We had to wait for you know who." Everyone booed.

"The weather ahead is great, we have a slight tail wind, that should shorten our flying time. Relax and enjoy your flight."

"Follow me Sergeant your bath is waiting." I followed the sweet flight attendant to the rear of the aircraft. She opened the door and pointed to the nine inch-round wash basin.

"Thank you kind lady. I don't suppose you would care to give me a hand?"

She didn't answer. Her response was handing me a towel.

I took inventory of the items the Sergeant Major packed for me; Clean set of Fatigues, socks, handkerchiefs, shorts, T-shirt. Great he packed my Corcoran Jump boots, brass and ribbons, and of course my Green Beret. Off came the extremely soiled cloths and into the trash can, boots and all. After the sponge bath and dressed in clean clothes I felt like I was on top of the world. Cleaned up the mess I just created, then joined my fellow travelers.

The cabin lights had been dimmed by the time I was finished. I took a seat about mid-plane and tried to get a couple of Z's. I wasn't successful, had too many things on my mind. There would be no sleep this 7 November 68 night. The sun filling the cabin with its golden rays interrupted the nightlong self evaluation. Weighing all the pro and cons, the remaining conclusion;

"I could have been a better son."

When we landed a Travis AFB in California, the hectic pace started again. The Buses in waiting were not for me. The Red Cross was standing by with a sedan. I was quickly taken to a Taylor and measured for a class A uniform. While I was waiting for the alterations, I was provided with a two inch thick T-bone Stake.

"What size shoes do you wear Sergeant?"

"I don't wear shoes' Sir. I have spit shined, jump boots. "

"You airborne are all alike."

"As a matter of fact we are not Sir. Some of us wear Green Berets."

By the time I finished a very hot shower, my uniform was ready and the Red Cross speed me to a civilian Airport across town. Twenty minutes later I was on my way to Chicago. Every thing was great. I was given VIP treatment all the way. That is until I got home. Then the contempt some civilians had for the Vietnam Soldier started showing through.

"Good morning, I would like to rent a car for five days."

"What Credit Card will you be using?"

"None, young man, I'll be paying cash."

"You will need a Two hundred-dollar deposit." I couldn't believe it. I reached for my check book.

"That has to be cash. We don't accept checks from the military."

I was ready to tell this individual a few things that were on my mind. But knowing me, I would have followed through with a jab to the jaw. I was late for my mothers funeral and needed a car. I'll go and cash a check, I thought to myself. Then came the dawn. The envelop the Sergeant Major handed me. I hadn't opened it yet. I made a quick motion and opened my kitbag and retrieved the envelop. I think the jerk behind the counter thought I was reaching for a gun. His eyes were full of fear and his mouth wide open.

Another example of Special Forces taking care of their own. The envelope contained a little more than six hundred dollars. I paid my deposit and hit the road. This incident bothered the heck out of me. I didn't expect any special treatment being a member of the Armed Services. By the same token I didn't appreciate being treated like a second class citizen. America what's wrong?

It was great seeing relatives, I haven't seen for years. The sad part was it took a funeral to bring us together. I guess we all can take the blame for that. Of course we all have hundreds of excuses.

The tears shed and expressed sorrow, of Mary Anna Wilson McGinley passing, were genuine. This great lady was loved and will be missed by all.

My tears didn't leave my eyes. They were absorbed by the blotter of regret. This wonderful lady deserved better treatment from me, than was given . . . for that, I am sorry.

I didn't stay long. Like always when I am hurting, I run to my comfort haven. I departed for Bangkok, to Chome and our son Johnny. After a few hours, her magic powers lifted the heavy bourden of guilt from my shoulders. All to soon it was time to return to Vietnam.

I was a little disappointed, neither the new Command Sergeant Major nor the new CO had arrived yet. With the present people in charge, any plans for developing a medical facility at B-24 would have to be put on hold. Maybe by the time I return, the new command will be in place.

Down Under

I had no problem going on R & R (rest and recuperation) I had coming to me. I had been in Vietnam just over a. year. Choosing Australia as my leave site was easy. I had met several Australian Special Forces who were working with our Mike Force. Their stories about home put Australia high on my list of places to visit. Your R & R had to be used within thirty days or loose it. I signed up for Sidney Australia.

"I'm Captain Mark Miles and this is Captain Sam Gordon. Sam is a member of the Australian Special Forces and I'm with 5th Group. We both are with III Corps Mike Force."

"My name is McGinley, Dan McGinley. I'm assigned to B-24 in Kontum, glad to meet you. We spent the balance of the eighteen hour flight exchanging stories. Meeting Mark and Sam, turned what I am sure would have been a boring flight into a learning experience. This was Mark's second trip to Australia and of course Sam being born just outside of Sidney, provided me with a lot of Intel on what to do and where not to go.

"When they give you a list of Hotel's to choose from, tell them you have a reservation at the Oceanic Hotel on the beach." The advice came from Sam, and turned out to be the best kept secret in Australia. The Oceanic didn't cater to all R & R (Rest & Recuperation) personnel. They only catered to Special Forces.

"Welcome to Australis." A friendly voice announced. "Please remain seated while we wait for customs." After a short briefing from customs, we were on our way to a welcoming center. The center was located in a very modern hotel. We were all given opportunities to sign up for Hotels, tours, day long boat rides and many other activities.

An adjoining Ball Room was filled with good looking gals, waiting to meet a Yank and take him under her wing. The women were gorgeous. I swear there wasn't a bad one in the bunch. However I had a couple of problems. First everyone of them was young enough to be my daughter. The age wasn't my main concern. I can't stand rejection. The second problem was I was married. The Dragon Lady, my wife frowns when I look at other women. I began having the feeling I picked the wrong place.

I decided to sign up for a days outing on a cruse ship. Because seating was limited, we were asked not to bring a companion. We were also told not to bring beverage or food, it would be provided. I could live with their request, I surely wasn't going to bring one of these young gals. I was surprise to find that Mark and Sam also signed up for the cruise. The three of us grabbed a cab and headed for the Oceanic Hotel.

My first surprise was the size and condition of my home away from home. This was a first class Hotel on the ocean. Large wide marble stairs led down to a pure white sandy beach. Matching marble stairs leading to the hotel entrance added to overall majestic look. Once inside I was sure I had entered a palace. The royal treatment from the hotel staff, I'm sure equaled that given to royalty. I was impressed.

Oceanic Hotel Sidney Australia

"May I have your passport sir?" At that moment I wished I wasn't married. I knew without hesitation I was in love with the beautiful creature making the request. I also knew that this new love would endure the test of time, and it did. It lasted until another magnificently stacked creature asked me if she could get me some refreshments. "Satin get behind me...but take your time."

My marriage was saved when my new Australian friend Sam. introduced me to the Hotel Manager and his wife. Frank Karr and his wife Betty turned out to be the icing on the royal cake. In addition of bending backwards to please their guest, they prided themselves on being match makers.

I had my work cut out for me explaining that I didn't participate in extra marital activities. Betty ended the conversation by saying she had a special friend she wanted me to meet. Apparently she wasn't listening to me.

In the back of my mind I wondered why the Oceanic only catered to Special Forces troops. There are some that don't care for Special Forces when they gather in groups. Someone down the road spread the rumor SF has a tendency to be a little wild when more than two gather at hotels, resorts and the like. They claim SF guest rappel out of their windows, and enter the resorts swimming pool from their room balconies. Some say SF have a tendency to put wild aquatic (alligators, snakes etc.) species in swimming pools. They go as far as to say they have seen SF troops jumping from high places using a beach umbrella as a parachute.

I am here to tell you Special Forces have been misjudged. Instead of classifying the repelling and entering swimming pools in unusual methods as wild-jesters, look at them as a continuation of their training. The alligators and snakes, demonstrate SF's concern for endangered species. If in fact, SF used umbrellas as parachutes, be assured there was a qualified parachute rigger on hand. It's amazing how easy it is to misjudge the Special Forces soldier.

The management of the Oceanic Hotel was proud of Australia's effort in Vietnam. Their mission was to make sure Australian Special Forces and their American counter parts, had a special time when they took a vacation from war. They more than achieved their mission. We were all tired after our 18-hour plane ride. The decision was made to get a little shut eye, then meet back in the lobby at 1900 hours.

Our rooms were on the same floor. Before retiring we decided to join Sam in his room
for a cold beer. In less than ten minutes a bellboy was at the door with three Boomerangs on a silver tray. It was a nice gesture from the Oceanic, welcoming their guest to Australia. An idea came to me like a flash of lightning. I explained my plan to my two new pals then got on the phone.

"I would like to talk to the manager." I announced in a ticked off tone.

"Mac, this is Frank, what's the matter?"

"I throw my boomerang out the window and it hasn't returned yet." I hung. up, not giving Frank time to answer. Then Mark called the desk.

"This is Captain Miles. A Boomerang just crashed through my window. What kind of a place is this?" He hung up. Of course we got a big laugh out of our on the spot prank.

About ten or fifteen minutes later another bellboy delivered a note from the management. It read in part; "I want you all to remember one thing. You guys started this." At this point we didn't know exactly what Frank meant.

I couldn't sleep a wink. I was excited being in Australia and wanted to get my new adventure started. Getting off the elevator, I saw Mark Miles talking to a very good looking Australian lass at the check out counter. I didn't want to spoil his game plan, ignoring them I headed for the lobby.

"Sergeant McGinley come over here, I would like to introduce you to a very good friend of mine.

"What's your name again?" Anna, she answered. After a very fast introduction, Mark excused us, stating we had important business to take care of. As we were leaving Mark assured the fine lass, he would see her later.

"What was all that about Mark?"

"You saved me Mac. These Australian gals are really friendly. I don't want to make my selection too early. I would rather shop around a little."

"I don't know Mark, she looked good to me. Our 5-day R & R will be over before we know it. Would be terrible ending up with no one?" He didn't have to answer, the expression on his face proved he was in agreement with me. Our next task was to get our Australian friend out of bed. We had the switchboard operator call Sam's room and tell him a Miss Stella Jordan was waiting for him in the lobby. Sam Gordon must have been a fireman in civilian life. In no time flat, Sam was in the lobby. Eager to meet his guest. Sam had her paged.

"Miss Jordan, Miss Stella Jordan, please come to the front desk."

"Stella told us she would see you later Sam. Let's go have a beer."

"Frank I'm going to kill you." Sam vowed.

"Don't blame me Sam, it was McGinley's idea." Sam forgave us and we went looking for a bar. This turned out a lot harder than you might think.

Australia drinking establishments (back in the 60's and 70's) catered to particular type of person and sometimes gender orientated. Pubs' were working men's bars and as a rule, not too fancy. They were gathering places to get a fast drink or two after work, before going home. The absence of women created an atmosphere of loud colorful conversation.

Not having a dress code, Pub's were ideal for the after work drink. Australians love to talk about politicks and religion. Add a little alcohol and the conversations get quit heated. The Australian Pubs reminder me of our old West Saloons minus the dancing girls.

Bars on the other hand allow escorted women. The only restriction is they are not allowed at the bar. They are served at tables, usually by their escorts. Unlike Pub's, Bar's have a dress code. Before five o'clock, men must wear dress slacks and shirt. After five o'clock coats or jackets and a tie must be added.

As a matter of fact, ties are required after five o'clock in all public restraints and clubs including Pub's. Come five o'clock, and you don't have a tie, no problem. The bartender will walk up and down the bar with a box full of old tie's. They may not match, but they do fulfill the requirement. At all times women are required to wear dresses as apposed to slacks or shorts.

Lounges, Night Clubs and Dance Halls, not only allow unescorted women, they encourage it. Quit often they have signs, "Ladies Free." I don't know how they prove they are ladies. Of course dress codes are strickly enforced. Ties' are required at all times.

I was all for starting at the Pub and working our way up. Sam our new Australian friend, insisted we wouldn't like the Pub and would in all probability get into trouble. Trouble, what's the big deal. We just came from a war zone. It seemed to me, trouble would be like taking a break. If I had my choice between war and trouble, trouble would win every time. Anyway we started our investigative tour at the Oceanic Lounge.

We lost our new friend at the Oceanic Lounge. Sam meet an old friend and before we knew it, Sam was gone. Next Mark meet a couple of gals at the Oceanic. They tried their best to talk me into joining them for dinner. I wasn't ready to cheat on the Dragon Lady. I declined their offer. Besides, when you go on a double date, you end up with the ugly one? Calling her, ugly might be carrying this thing too far. Lets say she had less beauty than her friend. Trouble, what's so bad about a little trouble? I headed for the Oceanic Pub.

"What will you have Mate?' The bartender yelled over the noise of the crowd.

"Give me a cold Australian beer." I yelled back.

"We have a Yank in the house." The Bartender announced. The Pub got as quiet as a church. Maybe I had better start praying.

The arguing started immediately. It was growing out of proportion. Finally the bartender hit the bar with a large walking stick. Everyone paid attention to what he had to say.

"We will start at this (he pointed to his left) end of the Bar. Anyone wanting to buy the Yank a beer will take his turn." The argument was over who was going to pay for my beer, unbelievable.

Those who started their drinking early fell by the way side. It was evident from the start, this was to be a contest to top all contests. The reputation of every Irishman the world over was on my shoulders. I was determined to prevail. They pulled every trick in the book. Getting me mellow by singing Irish songs, and saying complementary things about America and my beloved Special Forces. This devious group held nothing back. It was apparent, I had engaged the best.

I must say I put up a gallant fight, but alas, the long flight and the lack of food, was getting to me. I asked the Bar-Keep to call me a cab. It was time for me to leave.

"Call you a cab? Won't be a need for a cab Lad, your home. This is the Oceanic Hotel your room is upstairs. I'll call a bellhop to guide you to your room. Get a good night's sleep and we will see you on the marrow."

The first thing I do when in a strange city is to find a place to hide my money. I had about five hundred dollars and figured I needed every penny to finance my R & R. I took care of the task and went to sleep. The absence of exploding ordinances, small arms firing and the like, let me sleep like a baby. Of course the beer may have something to do with it.

A call from the front desk invited me to breakfast. The Oceanic Hotel management had a policy to invite all Special Forces R & R personnel to their first breakfast in Australia. It afforded them the opportunity to renew old acquaintances and make new friends. They used this time to point out things to do at the Oceanic.

Frank informed us he belonged to a Country Club and a Masonic Lodge that had a recreation facilities. We were his guests at both members only establishments. In addition the hotel had a Ballroom that had entertainment every night. The front tables were reserved for Special Forces. The cover charge was wavered for Special Forces. Then the icing on the cake. Frank announced;

"All clubs and Bars close at 01:00 hours. I don't know any parting Special Forces people that quit at that ridiculous time." Passing out keys Frank continued. "This key is to a private Bar on the third floor. Feel free to use this room as often as you like. The only thing I ask is to replace any beverage used." At this point Frank could have ran for President of the United States. "Enjoy your R & R gentlemen." We gave him a standing ovation. "Before I go, I want to congratulate Sergeant McGinley. Sergeant McGinley, you now hold the record on keeping the Oceanic Pub open. I understand the new record is now 02:30 hours." Everyone cheered.

"There must be a mistake Frank, I went to bed early." It was hard to believe I stayed that long, my aching head left no doubt We finished breakfast and boarded a Shuttle Bus that was waiting to transport us to our Cruise Ship.

You couldn't pick a worse day for an ocean cruse. There was a heavy overcast and a steady light drizzle. Hoping it might clear up we boarded the ship and headed for a greeting area on a lower deck. No wonder we were told not to bring any food or beverage. The largest display of food I have ever seen was before us. A whole-baked pig with the traditional apple in his mouth. Standing Rib Roast that made your mouth water just looking at it. Chickens, Turkey, Duck, Han, cold cuts of every kind. Salads, different types of potatoes, cooked in every way imaginable. A large ice carving of the American and Australian flags added to the artistry of this magnificent layout.

A twenty foot heavily stocked bar, answered the question why we were told not to bring beverage. Very few commercial bars have this inventory to offer their customers. And it was all included in the price of the tour ticket. All drinks were served in 12 ounce glasses.

"Say when Yank," the bartender would ask and keep pouring until you told him to stop or the glass was full. Their insistence on you having a good time was genuine. Everyplace I went, I got the feeling of sincere warm welcome. It was evident the Australians were proud of their country and honored, you came to visit them.

Standing at the far end of the room was the reason why we asked not to bring a date. The same group of very young gals were waiting to team up with an American. They were too young for this American yesterday, and one day didn't make them any older. My answer to, "Say when Yank" was, "filler up Mate."

I took my glass filled with Johnny Walker Black Label and headed for the boarding ramp. I was hoping I could get off the ship. Too late, by this time we were at mid-harbor. I could see the new Opera Convention Center being built in the distance. The thought came to mind, swim for it. I dismissed the thought and headed for the

Opera Convention Center Sidney 1968

upper sun deck. Or maybe I should say rain deck. I picked out an isolated deck chair in the bow of the ship and settled in for, I was sure, a very lonely and boring trip The deck filled up rapidly with GI's and their new friends. I started feeling sorry for myself. If only I went to Bangkok.

"Mind if I sit down Yank?" A beautiful young gal asked. Oh boy, I'm stuck on a rained out, crowed, boat ride. Now I'm asked to give up my seat. This was one of the times I wished I wasn't a gentleman.

"Not at all." (That was a lie.) I started to get up and she pushed me back down on the chair and sat on my lap.

"I won't bite you Yank, relax."

"Little gal, I'm not afraid of your bite, it's the dagger in my heart that gives me concern."

"Dagger, what dagger?" She looked at me as though I lost my mind.

"The one my wife will plant if she finds out, I'm sharing a deck chair with a beautiful Australian woman."

"Relax Sergeant McGinley." (How did she know my name?) "Frank and Betty Karr put me up to this. Frank said it was payback and you would know what he was talking about." The boomerang thing came to mind.

"I'm here as a friend, not a lover. I just want to do my part in entertaining the troops from Vietnam."

"I don't know friend, I might get weak and make a pass at you."

"Not to worry Yank, I'll see to it, you don't cheat on your life's Mate."

That was the beginning of a strong friendship that would last many years. Yvonne Bromer was one of a kind. Her husband of one year was killed in Vietnam in 1966. Betty Karr and Yvonne went to High School and later Nursing school together. They have been friends ever since. That kind of explained her involvement with the Karr's mission of making Vietnam soldiers welcome.

Yvonne turned what was sure to be a dull trip into a very pleasant experience. We talked about everything. It was surprising how much we had in common. She was a student pilot, I was a Pilot. Yvonne had made a few sport parachuting jumps, I owned a sport parachuting center. She was a Nurse, I was a Medic. Time flew by.

"Ladies and gentlemen, we will be docking in 20 minutes. Thank you for spending the day with us. Sorry about the drizzle."

Betty was waiting at the dock to pick Yvonne up. I rode back to the hotel with them. Not a word was said about the Karr's pay back As far as I was concerned it backfired on them. Or as they say in Australia, boomeranged. Yvonne invited me to a picnic to meet some of her friends.

"I'll pick you up at nine o'clock for the picnic Dan."

After a long goodby, I went to my room to take a shower and get ready for an evening at the Ballroom. Unlike the boat ride, I would be needing my wallet. My wallet was not at my hiding place. I have been robbed. I called the front desk and reported the thief. I then called Sam and Mark and informed them to go on without me, I would join them later.

The first bellboy arrived with an envelop containing $200.00 and a note. Go have a good time. Pay us back when you get back to Vietnam, Frank Karr. Shortly after the second bellboy with an envelop from Sam and Mark. It had $400.00 and a note, Pay us when we get back to Nam. I was speechless. What a wonderful jester from three complete strangers. I picked up the phone to thank them. A knock on my door interrupted, I hung up and opened the door.

"Hear is your wallet." Handing me my wallet, she continued. "All you Yank's are alike. Hiding your wallet between the mattress. Don't you know lad, tis the first place a bloody crook will look?"

"Who are you?" I asked as I opened my wallet to check it's contents.

"It's all there Mate. I'm your room-mom, I clean up after you lad." An attempt to reward her got her very angry.

"I'll not be taken money from my soldier boys. From now on leave your money at the desk. They have a safe you know." The wonderful lady departed talking to herself. Something about Yank's hiding their money. I returned the emergency money to Sam and Mark. On the way to the ballroom I stopped at Frank's office to return his money. I thanked him and insisted he give the maid my reward.

"Mac she won't take it. She looks at all Special Forces, as her boys." I made up my mind, I would buy her something or increase the amount of her tip when we departed. We headed for the Ballroom. Then the thought hit me, I should have invited Yvonne.

The Ball Room was in full swing when we arrived. Frank met us at the door and escorted us to our reserved seats. The band stopped playing and restarted, playing the "Ballet of the Green Beret." It was a little embarrassing but down deep we enjoyed our favorite tune. The audience applauded as we took our seats. Australians sure know how to make you feel at home. I was glad we wore our Class (dress uniform) A's, they fit in with the formal attire of the crowd. It also gives us another excuse to wear our Green Berets and spit shined Corcoran Jump Boots.

The music was great. The female vocalist extremely talented. This was definitely a fall in love atmosphere. I was glad I didn't invite Yvonne. It would have been very difficult just being a friend.

There was no shortage of women in Australia in the 60's. Everywhere you went, it was the same story. Maybe a lot of their men were in the Services or around the world seeking their fortune. Whatever the reason gals were plentiful. I never found anyone arguing against my estimated ratio, of two to one. Now don't hop on a plane and head for Australia. My estimate was made in 1968-70 time frame, the situation may have changed.

There were plenty of unescorted women at the dance. Finding a dance partner was no problem. I just wasn't in the partying mood. Besides I wasn't much of a dancer. I decided to hit the sack early. On my way to my room I checked out the Special Forces private bar. No surprise, a party was in progress. My mood didn't change. Parting was the furthest thing from my mind. In fact, I felt a little guilty being away from Vietnam. I tossed and turned all might. Never did fall completely to sleep.

I answered the phone on the first ring"Good morning Mac, did I wake you? I won't be able to pick you up as I promised." I started getting the feeling Yvonne changed her mind about spending any time with me. "I'm sending my brother he should be there by 09:00 hours." Apparently I was wrong. After some small talk Yvonne hung up.

David Bromer picked me up at exactly 09:00. After a short introduction from Frank Karr, we were on our way to meet Yvonne's friends at a beach just outside Sidney. Yvonne was to meet us at the beach later. The ride to the beach, in David's old VW, matched any wild automobile ride I have ever had, to include Bangkok Taxi's.

The beach was crowded. The ratio between men and women seemed to be holding. It was evident the Australians are not a shy people. As far as the eye could see the beach was saturated with beautiful, bikini clad Australian gals. I had to pinch myself. Maybe I died and I am in heaven.

"Sergeant McGinley, I would like to introduce you to Yvonne's friends." David was referring to the six gorgeous Australian gal sun bathing on an oversized beach blanket. I paid no attention to their names. In my mind I was holding a beauty contest. Picking a winner would take all my concentration. Then Yvonne showed up.

"Hi Mac sorry I'm late." Looking up I saw a beautiful creature, clad in the worlds, smallest bikini. Not that I am an authority on bikinis. War is hell.

"Hi Yvonne." Was all I could say. I knew I had to get off the beach. Temptation was getting the upper hand.

We spent the next four days together. Well not together, in each others company. Then it was time to return to Vietnam. I would see Yvonne again on my next visit to Australia. Would you believe I would be bringing her a gift from Chome (my wife). A gift thanking Yvonne for being so kind to me. You bet I told Chome about Yvonne. Better me than someone else.

On the flight back to Vietnam my thoughts were filled with the pleasant memories of my R & R. Everywhere we went, the people were extremely friendly and expressed their thanks for what we were doing in Vietnam. My final thought, "wouldn't it be great if Americans treated us the same way."

Business As Usual

I heard the explosion in town. Tren and I grabbed medical kits and jumped in a Jeep. The explosion was closer than I thought. It was fifty yards from our Gate. Bodies were flung in every direction. My first action was to sort out the more seriously, savable, injured. As I assigned the priority number, Tren and several other Montagnards applied lifesaving aid and loaded five patients on the Jeep. I headed for the Kontum Provisional Hospital just a short distance away.

I didn't want to bring them to our dispensary for a couple of reasons. First I didn't know if they were friend or foe. Second our dispensary had limited treatment areas. First glance convinced me most of the patients would need surgery.

The Provisional Hospital was locked up tighter than a drum. I asked a young nurse where the Operating Room was. She led me to it. I forced the door open and had the patients brought in. Again I sorted the patients. Placing three patients in one OR and two in another. I took the three most severe and told Tren to care of the other two.

After the bleeding was stopped, we started IV's on all the wounded. By this time more patient's arrived. We continued this process until all twenty-six patients were stable. Then we started attending to the individual wounds. Debridement, cleansing, tying off bleeders, placing drains when needed and suturing them closed.

I, Tren and six of our medics had our hands full. All this time, a Vietnamese Officer watched us. I had to ask him to move out of the way a couple of times. When Tren told me he was a doctor, I got hostile. This clown was the Provisional Hospital's director.

"Why didn't you help us Sir?" I asked in a sarcastic tone. He just stared. I had Tren ask him in Vietnamese, he walked away. I knew why. These were Montagnards, being Vietnamese he was above them.

Finally two civilian doctors arrived. Although Tren and I explained what we had done, I still wasn't convinced they would get good treatment. We loaded them on a truck and took them to Pat Smith's Hospital on the other side of town. I left four medic's to help take care of them. Reliable Pat didn't complain a bit. What a great lady.

When I got back to B-24, my dispensary was busy with activity. CSM Henge had brought two wounded to our dispensary. He and our new nurse Candy had them all cleaned up and bandaged. It wasn't the best bandaging I have ever seen but it was a great effort. Candy had no training at this point. Of course the CSM being Special Forces was crossed trained.

"Where have you been?" He asked in a ticked off tone.

"There you go Sergeant Major, using your lip for a brain. I've' been goofing off." This guy and I will never get along. When he found out what happened, he apologized and thanked me for my effort.

Pair of Giants on the Chopper Pad

I saw the two choppers circling B-24's Helo-Pad, but didn't give it much thought. We shared the landing pad with MACV (Military Assistance Command Vietnam). Since there were two choppers I assumed they were going to MACV. We seldom have more than one chopper. Our air activity was relatively limited, unless one of our A-Camps were in trouble. As I drove into the main gate of B-24, I was surprised to find that the choppers were visiting our B-Team.

I went to the mess hall to get a cup of coffee. While I was waiting to be served, one of our house girls came running to me bubbling over with information.

"Bac Si, new Colonel come, new Sergeant Major come stay B-24." It's about time, I thought to myself. I hoped it was the gentlemen I was expecting. The Army has a habit of changing their mind at the last minute.

Then I saw them coming toward me. CSM Henge and his replacement, CSM Richard Campbell.

"Good afternoon, nice seeing you again Sergeant Major Campbell."

CSM Richard Campbell

"You know each other?" SGM Henge inquired.

"Yes, SGM Campbell greeted me when I arrived in country." After a short exchange of words, CSM Henge continued showing our new CSM around the B-Team.

Then the club and dinning room became very active bringing out the ingredients for the party. To this day I don't know if it was a going away or welcome party. In Special Forces it really doesn't matter, a party is a party.

"Here's looking at you lad. May you be safe in heaven 20 minutes before the devil knows you're dead.." One hour into the party someone pulled the plug on the tape player.

"There will be a formation at the chopper pad in twenty minutes. Everyone is expected to attend. Both commanders exchanged a few words, everybody saluted everybody and one chopper took off. I wondered why the second chopper stayed behind. Then Lieutenant Cornel John Hennigan made his announcement.

"This chopper will depart tomorrow with everybody who feel they can't serve this B-team. All officers report to my office immediately after this formation. All enlisted, meet with the Command Sergeant Major, on the patio." I didn't know about the others, but I was getting second thoughts about our new command. Formations, meetings, separating officers and enlisted. I thought this was Special Forces. What's going on here?

"Gentlemen as I speak, the Colonel is telling the officers that NCO's run his B-Team. If they have any problem with that the chopper is standing by to transport them to the C-Team." Campbell must have sensed the jubilance some of us felt inside.

"That does not mean that the officers do not get the respect due them. It just means they are not to interfering with the NCO mission. The LTC puts the burden on your back. You get directly involved with the A-Team problems and help them solve them. The Officers will support you administratively and find or transfer funds to get priority problems solved." In a short speech, the new CSM just identified the problem with B-24 that I couldn't put my finger on. No wonder he is a CSM and I'm just an E-7. CSM Richard E Campbell from Jacksonville FL just was added to my list of "Giants."

"That's all I have for you, go back to the party. LTC Hennigan will interview each NCO individually. Who's on radio watch tonight?"

"I am Sergeant Major."

"OK SFC McGinley, the Colonel will see you first when you get off duty."

Radio watch is a duty all Officers and NCO's shared. Communication between the B-Team and the A-Teams they support is extremely important. Their very survival may depend on how fast we can get support to them in the event of an enemy attack. Our main concern was Camp Ben Het A-244. They have been hit several times in the past week. The Mike Force deployed to assist them was running into large NVA elements. The radio stayed busy.

Our radio operators stayed on duty, catching a few winks between decoding messages. That made my job easy. All I had to do was try and keep awake. I assumed the role of radio operator alarm clock. If a coded message came in I woke a como man for decoding. Because of the radio activity LTC Hennigan stayed in the TOC (Tactical Operations Command) Bunker with us. It was a great chance to get to know our new commander.

"Sergeant McGinley what is the one thing I could do to show the A-Teams that this B-Team is dedicated to their support?"

"Almost anything Sir, they're not used to a whole lot of support."

"That will change. What is the one thing that would show them I mean business?"

"Tell that leg (non-airborne) mess-steward to vacate the walk-in cooler just off the patio. In the past the cooler was used by the A-Teams to store their scrounged perishables while they waited for a chopper back to their camps."

"What would he use to replace it?"

"Sir MAC-V has several unused walk-in's. He's just too lazy to walk to them." I went on to explain that the A-Teams can't use MAC-V coolers to store items that may have been appropriated from MAC-V."

"Sir that would show the A-teams who's side your on."

"Sergeant McGinley you mean to tell me, it would be that simple?"

"Guaranteed it sir. Spoiled meat is no small thing to the A-Teams."

"Consider it done. I think I'll bring all my problems to you."

"Problem solving is my middle name sir. I'll take care of this cooler thing as soon as I get off radio watch."

In the past, if an A-Team member returning from a scrounging mission had meat or any other perishable item, they had to head back to their Camp. By having a cooler for storage, they could kick their heels at the B-Team a couple of days.

My plan was to close the walk-in cooler for health reasons. That would force our temporary mess-steward to move B-24's food to the MAC-V area. As soon as he had B-24's cooler cleaned, I would put a lock on the door and advise him he was evicted.

LTC John Hennigan called every B-Team NCO to his office for an interview. His priority list was short but as he put it, "in concert." We were to support the A-Teams as though our careers depended upon it. Again as he put it "they do." Then he went on to explain his three strikes and your out program. You could make minor mistake with this Colonel . They had to be minor and there were only two of them. The third strike and you were on the chopper pad waiting for transportation to your new home. Nine times out of ten, it would be to an A-Team with a reduction in rank.

Another thing the LTC would insist upon, everybody that worked on his B-Team had to have worked on an A-Team, and more specifically, an A-Team in Vietnam. The LTC felt, if you haven't served on an A-Team, there is no way you could support them properly. Another one of the ways he put it statements.

The approving authority for all A-Team request, was the A-Team making the request. The Colonel didn't care if they were authorized the item or not. If an A-Team wanted an item, we were to do everything in our power to get it for them   A-Teams didn't have 105 Howitzers on their TO&E, yet most of them had them. If the team could scrounge an unauthorized item they wanted, the Colonel would look the other way. In fact Dak Seang had unauthorized Bee-Hive (classified shells for the 105) rounds. John R. Hennigan was a great Commander. A Giant" with the rank of Lieutenant Cornel.

SFC Bobbie Joe Dunham
September 14, 1936 - January 9, 1969

By 1969 the decision had been made to transfer the CIDG forces over to the Vietnamese military, with the majority of the CIDG units being converted to Vietnamese Ranger Companies and Battalions. Those CIDG units that were situated along the border infiltration routes were renamed as Border Ranger units. Ben Het, Dak Seang and Dak Pek would be the last II Corps camps to change over. There was no way the Vietnamese could stop the NVA from taking the three camps without American Special Forces.

I was on an assistance visit to Camp Mang Buk (A-243) one of our camps that was about to be turned over. The medical mission was conspicuous by it's absence. The small Medical bunker became the living quarters for the two Vietnamese medics who were catching a few z's when I looked in. I looked no further, my recommendation to the Colonel would be to pull our SF Medic and reassign him to Dak Pek.

I was briefing the Team's medic on my intentions when four Vietnamese Strikers brought in a pregnant woman on a litter. My first thought was why didn't they bring her to the medical bunker? It turned out that is where she had been all night and apparently she was there when I poked my head into the medical bunker. The mother to be was unconscious and dehydrated. SGT Bradly the Team Medic ran to get a medical bag while I examined the lady in distress.

Her frail little body was burning up with fever and she was shaking uncontrollably.. It was apparent she had Malaria. In addition she had a troubled pregnancy. Further examination reveled the baby was crowning. This little guy was on his way. When a baby decides to enter the world, your only mission is the prevent the new comer from hurting itself. The birth was uneventful. The little guy was small but seemed healthy. I tied and cut the umbilical cord. One of the yard women that had gathered around took the new born, as I delivered the placenta, Bradly started an IV. We had to get this women to a hospital. Lleaving her with the Vietnamese, would be signing her death certificate.

"Chopper down one American hit by hostile fire." The radio operator announced as he entered the Team House. "He was blown out of the door as soon as the chopper landed."

I had just left Bobbie Dunham at B-24's chopper pad. He was loading some Mike Force troops on another Chopper. They were on their way to join a Mike Force operation just outside Camp Ben Het. I headed for the radio shack praying all the way it wasn't Bobbie. Death of a fellow American is easier to take if the deceased isn't a friend. SFC Bobbie Dunham and I were very good friends.

"God please don't let it be Bobbie." The air waves were busy trying to get a Med Evac to pick up the wounded American.

"Braker, Braker, I am a medic with chopper, near your location, over." I announced, breaking into their conversation.

"Pick him up and bring him home McGinley." A familiar voice ordered. Apparently LTC Hennigan was monitoring the radio. At that point I knew it was Bobbie Dunham. With tear filled eyes I headed for the chopper waiting on Camp Mang Buk's landing strip.

In less than ten minutes we were hovering over the contact point. A Med Evac Chopper had just taken off. The pilot confirmed they had the wounded American on board.

"Can you get a little closer." I yelled over the roar of the choppers engin. We flew alongside the Med Evac. I couldn't believe my eyes. Bobbie was sitting up. Supported by the Med Evac medic, but sitting up. We asked the Med Evac to confirm the fact his patient was sitting up.

"Roger that. Patient refuses to lay down." I was happy again. My pal from Arkansan, is going to make it.

"Call Mang Buk Captain, tell them we will pick up their patient and her new baby on the runway. We picked up the patients and flew them to Pat Smith's Montagnard Hospital in Kontum. Then headed back to B-24. CSM Campbell was waiting on the chopper pad.

"Don't look so glum Sergeant Major, I really think our man is going to make it. Can you believe that hard headed Arkansan Cowboy refused to lie down. I really believe he is going to make it."

"Mac, Bobbie Joe is dead." I had nothing to say. I headed for the dispensary. I told Tren and the other medic's to get lost. I needed to be alone.

Being alone didn't help. I felt sick inside. I had but one thought; "is all this loss of American lives worth it? After a few hours of thought, weighing the positive things we were doing against the negative. I arrived at the answer. At least the answer for me. I went to the S-1 and extended my tour in Vietnam.

SFC Charles Edward Carpenter
July 2, 1941 - February 24, 1969

It sounded like a train was about to hit the TOC. The roar was defining. First one then another. I hit the prone position, looking across the room I seen the Colonel did the same.

"What in the heck was that?"

They turned out to be two Chinese 122mm rockets aimed at our TOC. They were fired from a rubber plantation just on the other side of our chopper pad. No one could see how they missed at such a short range. That French owned Rubber Plantation was a subject of contention for some time. Dirty politics prohibited the Americans from searching for the enemy or closing it down. Another example of how we give too much authority to the people we go to help. I'm all for helping, but I'm also for Americans having one hundred percent control over that help.

Chinese 122 mm Rocket

The radio got very active again. The Mike Force (our next door neighbors) were deployed just south of Camp Ben Het. Their mission was to take pressure off the camp by hitting the NVA from the rear. They got into a vicious battle and were told to take the high ground and hold.

The Company of Mike Force had two Americans with them. Charlie Carpenter who also was just back from emergency leave and Charles Challela an American with an Australian accent. Both were very good friends.

"One American KIA." (killed in action) the radio blurted out. This was very poor radio procedure and defiantly classified information for the world to hear. Any enemy would know that half of the command structure of their opposing force was gone.

"Get off that radio fool." The Colonel ordered.

Knowing the name wouldn't have helped my sad feeling. Both were very good friends. This death stuff was getting to me, I felt beat. The next message was from a chopper inbound to our location with an American Casualty. I picked up Tren and drove my Jeep to the chopper pad.

The casualty was laying on the floor of the chipper in a little ball. Both Charlie's were small in structure, I still couldn't tell which friend I lost. I pulled my friend to the edge of the aircraft and picked him up in my arms. I felt the sobbing within, my heart was breaking. Charlie, Charlie, what have they done to you lad? As I approached the jeep, the headlights identified my friend.

Charles Edward Carpenter was from Lebanon Ohio. He began his tour of duty in Vietnam on 2 June 1968. I met him that day. Now on 24 February 1969, I am sending my dear friend home. Dam war, dam all wars. For a moment my thoughts were focused on my other friend Charlie. On a mountain top, alone, surrounded by hostile forces. Oh God, please take care of my friend Charlie.

A crowd of Montagnards were waiting at the dispensary. The Yards loved Charlie Carpenter. I laid our friend on a treatment table in the center of the dispensary. A long line of Montagnards filed by to say goodbys to their comrade in arms. I wasn't surprised to see Colonel Hennigan and CSM Campbell in line.

"Sergeant McGinley can I see you outside." The Colonel asked in a worried tone. I joined him outside.

We may have a problem McGinley. There is some talk about friendly fire. They are saying Charlie was shot by an American Door Gunner. We need that bullet."

"Yes Sir." I gave the yards another fifteen minutes, then cleared the room.

"Tren send someone to get a clean set of cloths for Charlie. Then come back and give me a hand."

"This place have new uniform for Sergeant Carpenter." Tren was pointing to bench with a neatly folded uniform. Now I was to preform the hardest task I was ever asked to do. Retrieve the bullet that killed my friend. I was hoping there wasn't a bullet. I knew that wasn't likely, there wasn't an exit wound. The projectile was lodged somewhere within the body cavity. I wasn't surprised to find Tren was gloved and had Charley's Fatigue jacket removed. I gathered some instruments. Tren helped me glove and I started my dreaded task

The bullet entered the right upper chest. Probing with my finger it seemed it headed towards the Sternum at about a thirty degree angle. I tried to reach it with a six inch prob, but failed. It became clear, I had to make an incision. It suddenly hit me, why am I being so conservative in my approach. Friend Charlie can't be hurt anymore. I made a five inch, left to right incision just below the Sternum. A little blunt bisecting and I was within the Chest Cavity. The projectile involved upper lobes of the right and left lung, with slight heart involvement. The rib-cage was the final resting place for the projectile. I was able to remove the bullet with my finger.

When I removed the surgical drapes, Charles bearded face was illuminated by the bright surgical light. I placed a razor blade in a Curved Kelly hemostat and started to remove the several day growth. My hand started to shake.

"Bac Si I can do." Tren took over. I went to see Colonel Hennigan.

"It wasn't friendly fire Sir. I'm sure the weapons people will confirm this is an AK-47 round." I handed the Colonel the retrieved round rapped in four x four gauze. At that pint CSM Campbell walked in.

"How about a drink gentlemen. It has been a terrible night for us all." I almost said no. The CSM had a bourbon and water, I ordered a vodka on the rocks. I don't know what the Colonel had, but all three drinks were very large. The CSM picked up the 4 x 4 gauze and looked at the bullet.

"AK- 47, that eliminates the door gunner theory."

All were in agreement, this was a good discovery. Nothing destroys moral more than friendly fire being the cause on a tragic event. We knew the chopper crew's in support would be relieved. Being the cause of a fellow American's death, would be a terrible thing to live with.

In a few minutes LTC Hennigan was playing his Irish records. CSM Campbell insisted he was Irish. That was fine with us. It was conceivable, Campbell could be Irish.

Building Project

Now that the new Commander and CSM were on board, with their support the dispensary went through a major transformation. The dirt catching porous cement floors were covered with polished quarry tile. The new shelving, work areas and walls were freshly painted glossy white. I subdivide the main treatment room. Each side was a mirror copy of the other. The surgical supplies and sterile instrument packs were in the exact same place. Changing from one to the other didn't slow you down a bit. Time would

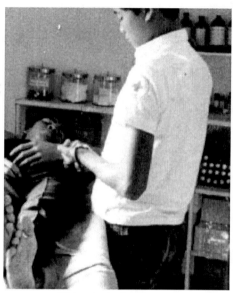

Tren, new treatment room

prove it was a very effective trauma center. A full function lab and pharmacy were across from each other at the other end of the dispensary. As the patient load reached seventy plus, it was evident we had to expand.

B-24 had a cement block manufacturing capability. We had an old Montagnard who built cement blocks day after day. The blocks were used for B-24 projects or given to the A-teams for some of their projects. We hired two more Montagnards and I went scrounging for cement. The first place that came to mind was the 4th Division. Surely they had cement. Tren and I headed for Camp Marylu, a 4th Division camp a little south of FOB-2. Then I saw it.

A flatbed semi trailer parked alongside of the road. It's cargo was sixty lbs bags of Portland cement. The Vietnamese driver looked lost.

"Tren ask that guy if we can help." That cement was to be mine.

"This man say he no can find Special Forces Camp."

"Tell him to follow us." I made a U-Turn and led the lamb to the slaughter.

"Sergeant Hollis, I need a lot of help." In no time flat half of his security guards were helping unload the cement.

The Vietnamese driver was looking for a Special Forces Camp. I showed him a Special Forces Camp. The cement was intended for Special Forces. The cement was received by Special Forces. Some say, the wrong Special Forces Camp. I say two out of three isn't bad.

We started building a twelve bed recovery ward, similar to the CIDG Hospital, with toilet and showers facilities. The hospital plan was on target. In addition to the ward, we built a dark room to develop X-Rays. I didn't have an X-Ray machine but one was on my shopping list. We were on a roll so we built a retainer wall around the patient waiting area, added a few sandbags and our waiting patients had a safe haven.

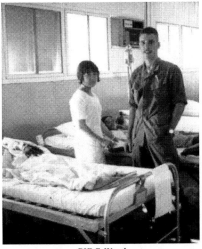

CIDG Ward

Casualties were getting heavy. Ben Het, Dak Seang and Doc Pek, were in heavy contact with the enemy. Our plan was to stabilize the patients at B-24 then move them on to hospitals in Pleiku. Good plan but we started having problems.

Vietnamese hospitals were not providing proper care for our Montagnards. Most returned with infected wounds. Ninety percent of infected wounds can be traced to poor sterile technique. I realized we were in violation of the goal of every medic; "get the patient to the highest level of medical treatment." The Vietnamese hospitals fell short of the treatment. We could provide better care at B-24. We needed more room.

I went to our Mike Force neighbors and worked out a deal to use their medical facilities for ambulatory patients. They jumped at the chance to help. I have been treating their people as though they belonged to B-24, and it was appreciated. In addition I kept medical resupply bundles ready, if needed by Mike Force troops in the field. A perfect relationship existed between the Mike Force and B-24. I ended up with an area that could house thirty patients if needed.

The B-Team had two buildings to house their security force. Johnny Hollis and his troops helped me build a treatment room at one end of a building. This enabled us to hold sick call for their people and have another expansion area of forty beds. By Stacking the beds of the second Guard building gave us another 20 beds. Without a lot of trouble we had just expanded our potential to a one hundred bed facility.

Treating patients and managing their trauma to full recovery is just the tip of the iceberg. They have to be fed and their personal hygiene has to be looked after, not to mention waste disposal. Getting a shower tent from the 4th Division was easy. I signed a hand receipt and I was on my way. I can't remember who's name I signed, oh well. The decision to use burn out toilets took care of the waste problem. The real challenge was, getting patients fed.

"Oh you sit here Sergeant." The Vietnamese cook insisted pointing to an area containing six tables. Each table having it's own table-cloth and small bouquet of flowers.

"No thank you. I'll just pick up my food and eat with the Montagnards." Tren had warned me that the CIDG at B-24 ate food that wasn't fit for pigs. The Vietnamese cook was very upset and couldn't hide it.

I could smell the serving area before I could see it. Positively I am telling the truth, our burn-out latrines smelled better. When the food came into sight. I was shocked. Large hunks of fat with a slight trace of meat on one end were floating around in dirty water. Each Striker would pick up a greasy bowl from a stack of greasy bowels. As he continued down the serving line. A large spoon of rice was thrown into the bowl. The next server would plop a hunk of fat on the rice and cover it with the dirty water. At that point the Striker would find a place to sit on the ground. The slop would be eaten by hand. No eating utensils were provided.

I haven't the slightest idea where I found the control to suppress my anger. It was apparent this problem was known to the Vietnamese Camp Commander. Attacking the situation with a burst of anger would not solve the problem. It would end up with me being relieved and the deplorable situation continuing.

About ten days later the LLDB commander from the Vietnamese C-Team held an inspection at B-24, it was now or never.

I knew the Vietnamese vender brought his garbage to B-24 at 09:30 every morning. You could almost set your clock by it. The food arrived in an old three wheeled truck, laying on the floor, covered with filthy blankets. The 09:30 delivery was for the next day's consumption. The only ice aboard the truck was reserved for food destined for the Vietnamese LLDB.

It was all in the timing. I had to make sure that when I stopped the truck for an on the spot inspection, my activity could be heard and seen by the visiting LLDB C-Team Command.

Accompanied by four Montagnard (from the Mike Force) I halted the truck as it turned into the feeding area. "Halt! get out of that truck." I hollered at the top of my voice.

That got every bodies attention. The inspection team headed in our direction. As soon as they reached the truck I pulled the blankets off the decaying meet. I didn't have to say a thing. The Major heading the inspection Team started his interrogation of the food vender. In a very few minutes he was beating the vender with his swagger stick. The vender was forced to leave B-24's compound, and ordered never to return. The LLDB inspection Team from Pleiku spent the rest of their time inspecting the Montagnard dinning area. It failed miserably. The LLDB B-Team Commander was given thirty days to correct the situation. They didn't have the foggiest idea on how to start.

LTC Hennigan and his staff held a three hour meeting with their LLDB counterparts. Surely heads had to roll because of this inspection failure. In the back of my mind, I thought mine might be one of them. After the meeting LTC Hennigan called CSM Campbell and myself to his office. I was kind of surprised to see our S4 (supply officer) Capton Romor at the meeting.

If the Colonel was going to chew me out, he didn't need a witness. LTC Hennigan opened the conversation.

"B-24 is going to loose a medic gentlemen." That saddened me I didn't want to leave.

"The LLDB Medic is being reassigned to the Kontum Regional Hospital. Effective immediately." I couldn't believe my ears. The LLDB Medic was the Camp Commanders brother-in law.

"I have decided to take over the responsibility of feeding CIDG strikers. Now the question I ask all of you, How are we going to accomplish this task.?"

Some good ideas came up for discussion. They had one thing in common. They fell short of alleviating the problem in the long run. Short term solutions are a waste of time and defiantly more costly.

"McGinley why are you so quiet? You're the one that started this."

"Sir being a shy person, I didn't want to make waves."

"That will be the day." CSM Campbell mumbled.

"Sir, I have listened to some good ideas. I am especially pleased to hear the Captain Ramor saying funds are available. Give me the task of revamping the CIDG dining facility."

"It's yours. This meeting is over." We all saluted the Colonel and went our separate ways. Sometimes the solution to problems are so simple they are overlooked. This was the a classic case.

All our A-Teams had an account with a Vietnamese vender in Nah Trang. I saw no reason why B-24 couldn't do the same. The way our CIDG security force was set up prevented the B-Team from using the Nah Trang vender. With the efforts of our S4 that was changed. Instead of paying them with our non-appropriated funds we paid them with appropriated payroll funds. A simple request and the problem was solved. The big advantage using the Nah Trang Vender was they were inspected regularly by 5th Group's Veterinarian. Transporting the food to Kontum by air was no problem. Caribou's made regular flights to Kontum.

I'll take credit for forcing attention to our CIDG food problem and the plan to improve it. But the main credit goes to B-24's S4 Officer, Captain Romor. He alone made it all come together. This giant was an expert at fighting the bureaucracy. The Major kept on them until they thought it was their idea.

"Sergeant McGinley I can get you all the paint you need to paint the old Montagnard mess hall. What color would you like?"

"That's great Captain, get me thirty gallons of white."

The old mess hall was torn down and hauled away the same day. I had no plan on painting that delapidate building. I needed the paint for future trading deals. We feed our security guards at the Mike Force for two days. In that short period of time, B-24 had a new cement block dinning facility. On one end of the dinning area, we built a cooking area with a serving line. On the far end, a screened room to wash pots, pans and serving trays. Truly a number one operation.

From day one, everywhere I traveled in Vietnam, I made a mental note of items that would make my Montagnards life a little easier. When it came time to furnish our new facility, those little bits of information came in handy.

Nah Trang Supply, had ten four-burner gas ranges stored in a warehouse. I liberated three of them. MACV had tables and padded chairs from their old club, just taking up room. I offered them four Cross-Bows and they delivered the items to my location.

My good old standby the 4th Infantry Division, came up with pots, pans and a variety of other cooking utensils. As a kind jester, they threw in 150 serving trays. I wanted hand painted china for my Yards. Oh well beggars can't be choosers.

LTC Hennigan and his Vietnamese counterpart including their staffs, were invited to attend the first meal served in the new dinning facility. Everyone was impressed. Of course the LLDB took credit for the new facility. That really didn't matter, our Montagnards knew the truth.

Lieutenant Colonel John Hennigan was the best commander I had ever worked for. LTC Hennigan was a hard nose leader. He expected, no, he demanded everyone put out their max effort. He enforced his three strike policy. It is easier to work for a hard nose Commander than a timid wimp Commander that is afraid of everyone. The hard nose CO is mission oriented. The wimp hasn't a clue.

Everyone knows that a B-Team's only mission is to support A-Teams. The C-Team's mission is to support the B-team's. John Hennigan was obsessed with that mission. He personally made an overnight visit to his (as he called them) A-Teams at least once a month. He expected his staff to do the same. After each visit you were required to brief the Colonel in detail, on the assistance you rendered. In the event assistance couldn't be given because the   B-Team didn't have the capability, LTC Hennigan would go after the C-Team. There was no love loss between the C-Team Commander and John Hennigan. He held their feet to the fire.

Camp Ben Het (A-244)

Camp Ben Het was built on Highway 512 about five miles from the Cambodian and Laos boarders. This was a tough A-Team. Their constant interruption of the enemy's mission kept the camp under constant attack from the NVA. The enemy

Ben Het A-244 Looking East 1969

spent a lot of lives trying to take camp Ben Het. If they could take Ben Het, there was nothing between them and Kontum or Pleiku.

The American forces realizing this, gave Special Forces Camp Ben Het a lot of support. A 105 mm, 155 mm, and 175mm Howitzer Battery's from the 4th Division occupied positions near the camp. Ben Het had priority if Gun Ships (C-47 with mini guns) or fast movers (fighter aircraft) were needed. This camp was loaded for bear. Being one of B-24's three most northern A-Camps, (Dak Seang and Dak Pek the other two) A-244 got a lot of attention from the B-Team.

The first two attempts to land had to be aborted. Small arms fire at our chopper caused our pilot to gain altitude and rapidly get out of the area.

"I'm going to give it one more try. As soon as I touch down, get out of the aircraft. I'm going to touch and go." His directions were clear and could be heard in spite of the aircraft noise. The next thing I knew, I was on my back looking up at a rapidly departing aircraft. Apparently the other three guys decided not to get off. I was alone. The whole perimeter started firing.

"Come on in!" An American voice directed. "We'll keep their heads down." Feet don't fail me now, I thought to myself. I ran at full throttle to Ben Het's main gate.

"You didn't pick a good day to visit us Mac. The NVA moved in on the other side of the runway last night." SSG Andy Szeliga the teams senior medic announced. I wondered why they weren't routing them out. The enemy sitting on your doorstep isn't a desired situation. I didn't make my thoughts vocal. It wasn't my mission to criticize an A-Team, it was my mission to assist them. Colonel Hennigan's statement covered it pretty well.

"Don't criticize an A-Team unless you live with them day by day, under the same circumstances. Help, suggest, but never criticize."

We went to the medical bunker. As SSG Szeliga was briefing me when SGT Glenn Ashley walked in. This was the first time I meet Ashley. He came to Ben Het directly from the C-Team to take over the Junior Medic position. Ashley was a high spirted lad with an Infantryman's complex. I truly believe he enjoyed engaging the enemy in battle more than treating the results of the engagement. Special Forces had a lot of medic's that fell in that category. The by-product of cross training. SGT Ashley's stay at Ben Het would be short lived.

"I have to head for the West Hill Mac. It was nice seeing you again."

Ben Het A-244 occupied three hills. West Hill, Central, and North Hill respectively. The Team House occupied the Central Hill. All the camp defense planning was done at their TOC located in a tunnel complex under the Team House. The West and North Hills were outposts, acting as buffers between the

Ben Het West Hill

enemy and the Camp defenders. SSG Szeliga battle position for the past six nights, has been on the West Hill. It is imperative to have an American on duty to coordinate air or artillery support in the event of an attack. SSG Andy Szeliga was an outstanding cross trained Special Forces Operative. Defiantly a Giant.

"Need some company? I plan on staying the night."

"Sure Mac, get's a little lonely out west." We crossed the no-man's land to Ben Het's West Hill.

At first sight the outpost at Ben Het's West Hill impressed me. Heavily barbed wired with a lot of tangle-foot. Fighting positions around the entire perimeter. A Tank with a large radar dug in deep. I could see at least four 30 Caliber Machine Guns. Plenty of ammo to include cases of M-79 rounds. The 4.2 mm or 81 mm Mortars were conspicuous by their absence.

"Andy, why don't we have Mortars?"

"No need for them Mac. When the NVA come, and they will, we will be too busy directing Air Strikes, Artillery and our Pal Spooky. Have you ever seen Spooky in action?" He didn't wait for my answer. "You will tonight."

I took advantage of the remaining daylight to familiarize myself with the layout of the land. Szeliga pointed out the most likely area the enemy would approach from. It was hard to visualize that the narrow path he was referring to was Highway 512. I have seen larger cow paths. All in all I was glad we had a tank equipped with Radar and fifty Montagnards on the perimeter. It just gave me a good feeling. A feeling short lived, I must quickly add. SSG Szeliga informed me the Warrant Officer running the Radar was killed three days ago. No one else knew anything about radar. Then when he told me, he wasn't sure how many Montagnards were still on duty, most of my good feeling was gone.

Our attention was diverted to Camp Ben Het's Air Strip. Two F-4's were dropping Napalm(fire) Bombs on the south side of the runway. The NVA were dug in the full length of the air strip.

After the Napalm attack, Captain Kingsley the Team Commander and several team members conducted a search and destroy mop up operation. Several charred bodies were discovered. Napalm had done its devastating job. Unfortunately Captain Kingsley was hit in the left eye with shrapnel and had to be Med-Evaced. On the bright side word got back the Captains eye was saved and he would recover with no sight loss.

SGT Glenn Ashley (without helmet)

I probably could count (on both hands) how many times I have fired an M-79. That was about to change. Using the M-79 as a mini Mortar-Tube we fired dozens of rounds down range throughout the night. Didn't have to have a target. Reconnaissance by fire they call it. We observed the surrounding area with a Starlight (night vision) Scope. If we seen anything or even thought, we saw something, a few 79 rounds were lobbed in that direction.

I saw the plane but didn't pay much attention to it. Probably another observation aircraft was my thought. Boy was I wrong. Spooky just arrived on station. Spooky a C-47 Gun Ships armed with seven .62 Caliber Mini Guns could fire over 2,000 rounds a minute. In addition to the Mini Guns the beautiful lady had 2.75 Rockets that could be fired

Spooky C -47 Gun Ship

singularly or in bursts. When the Mini Guns opened up all you could hear was a loud hum and see a contiguous stream of red tracer rounds. When you factor in the fact that every tenth round is a tracer round, you get some idea of the devastation at the receiving end. Waving like a slow moving twister, this killing machine sought out her prey.

You have to give the devil his due. The NVA must be the most dedicated and determined SOB's in the world. Continuing to press the battle against Gun Ships, Arc-Lights and the massive fire power massed against them, stood testimony to their resolve. Unlike ours, I'll bet their home front was behind them all the way. It must be nice having the people back home in support of your efforts. That's a luxury the American, Vietnam Soldier didn't have. That is not to say all Americans treated the Soldier poorly, just most.

"I was behind the American fighting man in Vietnam." We hear from the few. OK, say that is true. I have one question..

"Why didn't you demonstrate for the soldier and against the anti-war demonstrators?"

Another night passed and the determined SOB's didn't make their move against Ben Het. When SGT Ashley came to relieve us he was accompanied by Major Paul L Shetler the C-Team Surgeon.

"Nice to see you again Sir." The first explosion interrupted the Captain from answering. We all dove for cover. Then the second hit at almost the same place. This hit put a couple of us airborne. The being airborne part doesn't bother me as much as the slamming back to the ground part. I had experienced this before in Korea and wasn't looking forward to the landing.

Maj Paul L. Shetler
C-Team Surgeon

"Are you Ok Major? how about you Ashley?" The Captain was fine and SGT Ashley, thank God only had minor wounds, this time. SGT Ashley would be hit four times before this battle was over.

"How about you Mac?" After a fast inventory of body parts I reported I was OK. The minor bleeding of the head and face was probably caused by the fall. SGT Ashley was cleaning my head injury when Major Shelter announced.

"Mac, your hit in the foot.' No, impossible I thought to myself. Looking down I see the blood oozing from my torn boot. When treating any body with a foot wound I cut the tongue on the boot and with a determine motion I remove the boot. Now that's when I am treating anybody else. When it's my foot, I exercise a lot more tender care. Gently I removed my left boot. A peace of shrapnel about three inches in diameter went through my boot and lodged between my first and second toe. Major Shetler tied off a couple bleeders and was able to close the wound with butterfly tape. How many people do you know that bring their own personal surgeon to war with them?

"Now we will have to get you out of here Mac." Out of here? Oh no, I can't let that happen.

"Sir, I just have been treated by the best surgeon in Vietnam. I'm leaving here and going to the best treatment facility in Vietnam (my dispensary at B-24) including you facility at Pleiku. I don't need to be Med-Evaced. In a week or ten days my foot will be fine." I went on and on. I can't remember all the things I told the Captain. Bottom line I wasn't going to leave Vietnam.

"OK, OK, you win. Come see me at Pleiku in three days. I want to examine the foot." The Captain then re-bandaged my foot. This time placing extra gauze between the toes to keep them in line. Then he covered a makeshift arch support with a lot of four inch surgical tape. The end result I had a bandage that I could almost walk on. We got on the radio and called for transportation back to B-24. CSM Campbell picked me up at the chopper pad.

"Mac, the Colonel wants to see you. He's hot Mac, I'm sure he is going to insist you be Evacuated." I didn't answer, I needed to save all my answers for the Colonel.

"What in the hell are you trying to do. All Americans, regardless of the severity of the wound are to be evacuated to the nearest hospital. They will make the decision if you stay or shipped out of country. As a medic you should know that."

"That's not true when it comes to Special Forces Sir. I'll bet you don't have a camp that doesn't have a team members or two that have refused evacuation." I went on to tell him about a few cases I had personal knowledge of. "Bottom line sir, we can't afford the luxury of Med Evac for the slightly wounded, especially medics." That hit home. We had three camps in very heavy contact with the enemy and a critical shortage of medics.

"Are you going to be OK Mac?"

"Yes Sir, just fine." On the way out the Colonel insisted I use his jeep any time I needed it. An offer I took him up on. Then the thought hit me. Why don't I have a personal Jeep?

A couple times a week the 403rd SOD, B-24's Sneaky Pete Team drove to Pleiku with a sealed canvas mail bag filled with classified messages. Then

403rd Hdq.

263

the coded messages were sent to their headquarters in Nah Trang. They were always looking for a volunteer to ride shotgun. In case the enemy stopped the jeep the guy riding shotgun, pulled the pin on a thru-mite grenade that was tapped to the top of the bag. That white hot ordinance would burn through the bag and the floor of the jeep.

I needed a ride to have my foot looked at by Captain Shetler. I decided to volunteer to ride shotgun. I went to the 403rd 's compound and told Al Lipson I would accompany him on his next trip to Pleiku. I had one question.

"Why not take a chopper Al ? A Jeep seemed to me, you were looking for trouble."

The answer was simple. If the aircraft went down, it was possible the passengers would be killed or rendered unconscious and unable to destroy the classified material. They could also be killed in the jeep. That was true, but the people in charge decided, the destruction of the classified material was more likely by jeep.

Static Road Security

The road to Pleiku was in excellent condition. The forest on both sides of the road had been cut back about a hundred yards. Every mile or so, APC's or tanks were dug in to protect the road from attack. In just over an hour we were at our destination.

Liberated Jeep

Al delivered the bag of messages. I didn't want to see Major Shetler the C-Team surgeon, my foot was acting up. I only see doctors when I am feeling good. Before starting our journey home, Al and I stopped at the C-Team's club to get a bite to eat

Have you ever seen a shining automobile sitting on a car lot that seemed to have your name written all over it? Well that is exactly how I felt when I first saw the 1/4 ton vehicle (Jeep) and trailer.

"Al pull over to that Bar." I pointed to a Vietnamese Bar on the outskirts of Pleiku.

"Mac we had better head north it's getting late. You know they close the road to Kontum at sun down."

"Don't worry friend, this will only take a minute."

Before going into the bar I picked up a duffel bag from the Jeep's Trailer. Once inside I walked up to two GI's sitting at a small table with two Bar-Girls.

"Does this bag belong to any one of you lads?"

"It's mine." One claimed, with a startled look on his face.

"That's a good way to lose it lad. First, you shouldn't be at a Bar with a military vehicle. If you chose to violate that rule, don't leave anything of value in the vehicle. This area is full of vehicle thieves." At this point they thought they were in trouble and said they were sorry. They started to leave. This would have put an end to my vehicle procurement plan. I had to come up with something fast.

"Sit down lads, you have already violated, might as well enjoy. Bartender give these lads a couple bottles of Ba-mui-ba 33 (Vietnamese beer)."

"Thanks Sarge, you're OK." I didn't correct him on the Sarge thing.

"Give me the key's lad, I'll drive the jeep to the rear of the building. Without hesitation one of the lad's handed me the key to unlock the security chain around the Jeep's steering wheel.

I kept my promise. I drove the Jeep to the rear of the building. Then I made a right turn and headed to Kontum. Alvin followed just shaking his head. There wasn't a lot he could have said. I am sure that's how he got his Jeep.

Stealing you say? Don't even whisper the word. This Jeep was liberated. Liberated from being illegally used for bar hopping. It was my duty as a senior NCO to accomplish this mission. As I stated before, mission to Special Forces is priority one. The jeep became part of this mission. The trailer, you might say, attached to this mission.

On the way back to B-24 I formulated plans on how to convert the jeep trailer into a treatment station. I could visualize Tren and I going village to village treating Montagnards in remote areas around Kontum. This was one of the best gifts the 4th Division ever made available to me. Deep down inside I appreciated their kindness. If only I could share my thoughts with them. I didn't of course. They might have a different outlook on the situation. You know what they say, "If they can't take a joke, the heck with them."

The sputter of the engine got my attention. I was running out of gas. One would think, if you went to the trouble of stealing (excuse me), appropriating a units Jeep, the least they could do was to keep it full of gas.

"Al, did you bring any extra gas?"

"No Mac, I can make the round trip on one tank. No problem the 4th Division has a refueling point about a mile down the road. Hop in, we'll run down there and pick up a couple of cans." I didn't want to leave the jeep unattended. I heard that lowlifes had a tendency to liberate unattended vehicles. Al Lipson towed me to the 4th's refueling area.

"Ran out of gas. Fill her up please." To our surprise, both vehicles were topped off. Then the attendant went to the front of my jeep and started to copy the bumper numbers. I was in the middle of formulating a cover story when the attendant handed me his chipboard.

"Sign here, please." Why not, let's see who shall I be today?

When we got to B-24 I drove the jeep to our motor pool and gave our Montagnard mechanic instructions to paint and change the numbers on both jeep and trailer he smiled, he had done this task before. Al and I went to the patio to get something to drink. In a short while our pal SSG Glenn Watson joined us.

"Did you hear the news? Tanks hit Ben Het last night. Colonel Hennigan and the CSM went out there at first light." Glenn ordered a beer and then continued with the story.

SSG Glen Watson

On 3 March, Two Soviet-made PT-76 tanks with 76mm Guns and one BMP- 40 APC (armored personnel carrier) was detected by 1Lt Mike Linnane (A-244's Executive Officer) and his operation who were on patrol west of the Camp.　　Lt Linnane alerted the camp and took up a defensive position and directed fire to the enemy tanks.

As the NVA Tanks pulled off Hwy. 512, to launch their full attack against Ben Het they hit an antitank mine placed by A-244's demolition sergeant a few days earlier. The tank was disabled but continued to fire at the camp. Then the American superior fire power kicked in.

Bravo Company 1st Bn. 69th Armor engaged the 15-ton Soviet built tanks. This was the only tank battle of the Vietnam War. An element of 2/15 Artillery engaged the target. Their 175 mm self-propelled guns were capable of lobbing 200 pound shells 20 miles into neighboring Laos. Every 105mm and 155mm in the AO responded to this NVA Armor attack. The Special Forces A-Team through everything they had at to fool hearted attack. Even Spooky (C-47 Gun Ship) engaged the target.

Soviet made PT-76 tank
with 76mm Guns

Now of course everyone engaged in the slaughter, took credit for the complete destruction of the tank attack. Funny thing about it, no one can dispute their claim. Two 15 Ton Soviet built tanks were blown to smithereens. I for one, think the engineer from the A-Team can take a lot of credit. His planted the antitank mine, giving everyone a sitting target.

LTC Hennigan came back late in the evening and filled in all the missing bit's of information. CSM Campbell opted to stay at Ben Het overnight with the Ben Het Team. Anyone heading in that direction in a day or two was to pick him up and bring him back to B-24. I was planning a trip to Dak Seang the following day and told the LTC, I would stop and pick up the CMS. I radioed CSM Campbell at Ben Het and asked if he wanted me to pick him up on my way to, or on my back from Dak Seang.

"Mac, stay in the radio shack. I'll send you a coded message." About ten minutes or so, the message arrived. I was to pick him up exactly at 08:00. Tell the pilot, the camp will pop smoke at the west end of the runway. He was to disregard that smoke. CSM Campbell would be waiting at the opposite end of the runway. We were to come in hot, and pick him up.

The pick up went without a hitch. CSM Campbell informed us Ben Het was taking 300 to 400 rounds of motor and rockets daily. When choppers tried to come in, they were prime targets for the NVA artillery. In the last two days, three choppers were lost at Ben Het. Categorizing chopper pilts and their crews as Giants is surely justified. Their courage and disregard for danger, when called upon to assist, a besieged Special Forces A-Team is unbelievable. I have not only walked with Giants, I have flown with "Giants."

During this period 05-05-69 through 06-29-69 the NVA 28th and 66th Regt. besieged both CIDG camps at Ben Het and Dak To. This was during the heavy monsoon season which made helicopter operation's difficult. While the 42d ARVN Regt. took the brunt of the battlefield activity, the CIDG camps were continuously bombarded with rockets' and mortars throughout the period. Near the middle of June, the roads leading into Ben Het were cut off by repeated ambush and the NVA moved into dug-in positions around the airstrip in an effort to block all resupply. Aircraft were forced to run gauntlet of heavy ground fire and movement inside the camp was hindered by accurate sniper fire.

Camp Ben Het had been under constant attack for more than forty days. As high as five hundred incoming enemy artillery, mortar and rocket shells per day will raise the tension factor of even the tallest of Giants. Cornel Hennigan was fully aware of this and instructed the B-Team members to increase their visits to camps under siege.

On 16 June 1969 choppers couldn't get into Camp Ben Het. Everyone that tried was shot out of the air. That didn't stop our LTC John Hennigan. He decided to drive to Ben Het. I have to admit at this point, I questioned his

Chopper hit at Ben Het

sanity. The camp was surrounded by North Vietnamese Troops. Choppers with Gun ship escorts couldn't make it, how in the world can a jeep get in? Hopefully our believed leader will think about this a little longer and change his mind.

The next morning, before sunup the Colonel's Jeep and three, two and one-half ton trucks, loaded with ammunition and other needed supplies stood by. About ten security guards took positions between the boxes. The Colonel's driver patiently waited for the Colonel.

The plan was to drive to Dak To (an airstrip southeast of Ben Het), pick up a company of Montagnards flown in from Camp Dak Pek. Load them on three, 2 1/2's and continue to Camp Ben Het.

Three questions were on my mind that didn't have answers. First, how did the Colonel come up with a suicide plan like this? Second, how did he talk his driver into volunteering for the mission? Third, what am I doing in the back seat of the jeep?

About one mile east on Ben Het on highway 512, we started to see ARVN Rangers laying in the ditch (taking covr) on both sides of the road. Their American advisor stopped us as we got closer to Ben Het.

"You can't go any closer. The NVA are on both sides of the road. You'll have to turn around and go back." The advisor announced.

"We are going to Ben Het Sergeant. Why hasn't your Battalion of Rangers opened the road ?'

"Can't get them to move sir." By this time Lt Allen from Dak Pek got out of his truck and joined us.

"Get in the back seat with Bac Si, Lt Allen. We are going in. Everyone ready? Go for it, Frank." At that moment I felt more secure with our small group of 10 Montagnards and three Americans than I would have with that Battalion of Rangers. That poor lad is earning his money the hard way.

As we started to accelerate, I remember wishing I was a turtle. If my flack jacket were a shell, I would pull my arms and legs in out of harms way. As we came in line with a wooded area, I opened fire. Spraying the wood line and surrounding areas. Lieutenant Allen, followed suit on the other side of the road. We went through Ben Het's

30 Seconds after we got out

gate at full speed. After coming to a screeching stop, we all dove for cover. A few seconds later an NVA rocket hit the jeep we just emptied.

The third two and one-half ton truck in our convoy, didn't make it through the ambush. It took a direct hit killing two Montagnards and wounding six others.

Camp Ben Het had a 3/4 ton truck. They probably acquired it the same way I acquired my jeep. I stacked two rows of sand bags on the rear and mounted a 30-calabur machine gun. Accompanied by four of the security guards we brought with us, I headed back to the ambush site. A Lieutenant from the A-Team jumped in the truck. Wish I could remember this Giant's name. Shame on me.

"Where are you going Sir?"

"With you Bac Si, I'll ride shotgun." There was no way I could talk this dedicated soldier out of accompanying me. Giants are bull headed.

Just short of the ambush site we were blocked by an ARVN Tank. We proceeded to the ambush site on foot. Two of the wounded needed treatment immediately. The others could wait until we got back to camp. On the way back to our makeshift ambulance we picked up a NVA poisoner. He almost looked happy we took him. We had just performed a dumb act and had to get back to the relative safety of the camp. They say God watched over fools. This fool thanks him.

I started treating the captured NVA first. SGT Ashley the A-Team's Jr Medic had a problem with that. This guy was one of the enemy that had killed or wounded some of his friends. Now I was giving the enemy priority treatment over the camp defenders. Ashley had other plans for the prisoner. No doubt in my mind he wanted to send this NVA, to meet his ancestors.

After I explained the importance of getting all the intelligence from this guy, we could. Intelligence that might save some lives, Ashley calmed down. Now Ashley, like all Special Forces personnel knew fresh battlefield information of your enemy's situation is priceless. I guess in the heat of battle, we kind of forget that. Ashley a hard charging team member had been in the battle since the siege beginning. His dedication to duty was surpassed by none. The prisoner was turned over to the LLDB for interrogation.

"Sergeant McGinley, won't to spend another night on the West Hill?"

"Sure, why not." Was my answer to SSG Szeliga. We headed for the West Hill.

We were just getting settled in when Psychological Warfare Team's loud speakers started blasting away. Apparently the PHY-OPS people persuaded the NVA poisoner to get on the microphone and talk to his buddies. All night long this guy was trying to get his fellow NVA soldiers to lay down their arms and come into Camp Ben Het. The jabbering lasted most of the night.

About 03:00 hours the NVA tried another attempt to take the camp. Our friend Spooky, was busy at Dak Seang. The Camp called in another Gun-Ship. A C-130 loaded with flares and a side

firing Gatling gun. Six or eight barrels, 20mm or 40mm and a horrendous rate of fire. This craft flew low and slow, with its night vision system could put fire in close to friendly troops. It even had radios that could talk on the Infantry net. When she fired it creating a spectacular cone of fire that looks like a red tornado. Her massive fire power turned a determined enemy on attack, into a mob running for their lives. A Gun-Ship regardless of type, rains hell on its target.

The balance of the night was uneventful. Every so often we would send a few 79 mm rounds down range. We didn't want the bad guys to think we weren't thinking of them. The truth of the matter was, they were my only thoughts. I must be a coward at heart. Every time I get a chance to worry, I take advantage of the opportunity. The only thing keeping me from running, is my legs are too short.

We were all glad to see that beautiful sun ascend to its lofty position. Everything seems better in the sun light. Maybe today will be the day the persistent NVA will decide to head back north. Surely by now they must realize they are not welcome and are out matched.

"I need a Medic over here!" SFC Ray Ladner the Team Weapons Man yelled out. SSG Szeliga started to move in Ladner's direction.

"I'll go Andy. You might be needed to call in another air strike." Sure I could call in Air support, but Andy knew the area a lot better than me and could call it in a little closer. This was not the time to practice or have a dress rehearsal. This was the real thing. I decided to do what I do best, medicine.

When I got to Ray's position, he was busy trying to stop the bleeding on a wounded Montagnards leg. The pressure being applied wasn't doing the job.

"I'll take over Ray." When I removed the bandage, I could see we were dealing with a ruptured large vein. I clamped the bleeder and applied a loose dressing.

Without speaking a word SSG Ladner removed his flack jacket and through the Montagnard over his shoulder. Throwing the flack jacket over the yard, Ladner headed for the medical Bunker. This was another demonstration on how diversified and well orchestrated this Special Forces A-Team was. A-244 at Ben Het, was one heck of a gathering of tough Giants. It

SSG Ray Ladner

would take a lot more enemy, than what was encircling the camp at the present time, too win over this group. How honored I am just to be among them. "What's so special about Special Forces?".... It's people.

I was surprised to find that Colonel Hennigan had departed Ben Het by himself. That wasn't like him. When I found out, he hopped a ride with a Cessna 172 observation (Bird Dog) plane I understood. The Colonel had a private piolet license and loved flying. We engaged in a lot of talking about our flying experiences. I would bet money, the Colonel would talk the Pilot of the Bird Dog, into him flying the plane back to Kontum. The Chopper arrived to pick up Frank (the Colonel's driver) and I, for our return trip to B-24. The Chopper landed inside the camp's perimeter. On Board was CSM Campbell and a couple of cases of cold beer for Ben Het's Team.

Then everybody and his brother started loading onto the Chopper. There were News Medea personnel, VIP's from the VN Artillery Battery, Montagnard dependents trying to get to Kontum. The crowed didn't seem to bother the pilot. Overloaded was the under statement of the day. We barely lifted off when the piolet called out; "May Day May Day." This aircraft was going down.

And down we went. Fortunately the piolet managed to force land on the road leading in from the airfield. The Rotors were inches from the barbed wired perimeter on both sides of the road. The yards took off as though they caused the crash. Yes, I classify this as a crash. When your mouth is forced to close, due to a sudden stop and you chip your teeth. When your back hurts because all your vertebras seemed compressed. You find yourself in the advanced stages of shock. You definitely classify the incident as a crash.

"You people, meet me at the end of the runway. We will try this again." Like fools we followed his instructions. When the pilot seen we were all at the end of the runway, he came in and picked us up. This time he took a long running approach to his takeoff procedures.

We would fly a little, then bounce off the runway. Fly a little more than bounce again. Each time we would fly a little longer and bounce a little higher. Finally we were airborne.

"We have another problem people." Why does he keep calling us people? Why doesn't he call us by our full name, Dumb People?" Anybody getting back into an aircraft, that has crashed, has to be Dumb.

"We took small arms fire and we are leaking oil. I think we can make it to Dak To." At that moment, I promised myself, I would never ride in a chopper with CSM Campbell. This was the second time I was with him when the chopper didn't make it. I'm not superstitious but. The long and short of it we made it to Dak To (an airstrip south east of Ben Het. Changed Choppers and returned to   B-24 at Kontum.

Tie a String to the Door Knob

I could hear the yelling from the chopper pad. Someone was in extreme pain. I entered the dispensary through the side door. Pirie was working on a tooth extraction case. I walked over to see why the patient was making so much noise. Both Tren and Pirie know how to administer Novocain. Apparently this patient needed a little more. I couldn't understand why Tren hadn't intervened. It turned out Tren went to Kontum. It also turned out Pirie wasn't extracting a tooth. He was trying to put the partially extracted tooth, back into its socket. No wonder the patient was yelling.

"I'll take over Pirie."

"This man very bad patient Bac Si. He no want to give bad tooth to us."

I gave the patient more Novocain. Took a vice grip hold of the patient's head and attempted to extract the molar giving us all this trouble. Without bragging I can extract teeth. I have never come across a tooth that I couldn't uproot. I take the Charles Atlas approach to tooth extraction. This Yank can yank. However, this tooth had a mind of it's own, it wasn't budging. We didn't have X-Ray. I assumed the roots on this molar had a vice grip on the mandible (jaw bone). The tooth had to be split in two. When I released my grip and turned to pick up a chisel, the patient took off running.

It took us two hours to find him and return the reluctant patient to our field dental chair. Another injection of Novocain, chisel properly placed, quick tap with a mallet and presto, the tooth was in two parts. I removed both parts with my fingers. I sure was glad this ordeal was over. I suspect my Montagnard patient was also. We wrapped the tooth in a four by four bandage and gave it to the patient. I would give anything to hear him tell this story, of how the American Bac Si hit him in the head with a hammer.

Tren came back and told us about his trip tho Kontum. He went to look a t a 1966 Honda S90, on sale at a Vietnamese motorcycle shop.

1966 Honda S90

"Bac Si you come see, if good or no. If good, Pirie and Tren get."

The Honda looked really good for a five-year-old bike. When the owner had a hard time starting the machine, it raised some red flags. The thing that really squashed the deal was the terms. Tren and Pirie were to pay this wheeler and dealer, 5,000 ($100.00 US) Piasta a month. This was for the use of the bike. Tren and Pirie would never have ownership. The deal was off.

Bank of Mac

I managed to get to the Dispensary before Tren and Pirie. This was not an easy task. Both Tren and Pirie were early starters. I took the new Honda inside and placed it between the treatment tables. Tren and Pirie would have to walk around it when they came into the building. I turned off the lights and went to the patio for coffee. Like a bat out of the devil's hideout, Tren came running to my table.

"Bac Si, "Bac Si! You come see. Some man put Honda in hospital. Tren, Pirie not do "Bac Si. For sure not do."

"Tren, go get Pirie. We have to talk about the Honda." I am sure Tren left the patio convinced I was going to blame them for stealing a Honda. When they returned, we moved to an isolated table.

"The new Honda belongs to both of you. Each having an equal share in the Honda's ownership." That simple statement took a lot of explanation. The words equal, and ownership were words really foreign to them. They have never been treated equal nor did they ever own anything of monetary value. They were Montagnards.

Prior to this meeting CSM Campbell suggested we take up a collection at the B-team and purchase a Honda for Tren & Pirie. I convinced the CSM it was impossible to give a handout without taking part of a persons pride. And equally important, lowering the respect others have for them. Welfare doesn't build, it destroys. Haven't American welfare programs proven that?

There was no way a Montagnard would take anything as expensive as the Honda without giving something of equal value. With that in mind, I introduced the equal payment plan. The "Bank of Mac" was established.

After a lot of explanation, Tren and Pirie agreed to pay our newly established Bank 5,000 ($100.00 US) Piasta each month on their no interest loan for the purchase of their Honda. In addition they were to deposit another 2,500 Pea each, to their individual saving accounts. From that day on each and every payday, Tren and Pirie came to the Pharmacy (location of our Bank) and made the following statement;

"This for Honda (handing me 5,000 Pia). This for (2,500 Pia) for Bank." I made the entries into our bank ledger and put the money in the narcotic safe. I got a lot of pleasure watching their little nest-egg grow. A few months later when I left Vietnam, they were shocked when their savings were returned to them and their obligation to the now dissolved Bank was satisfied. Apparently they didn't understand savings as well as I thought they did. They trust like a child and perform their mission as well as the tallest Giant. God I love these little people.

Put this Show on the Road

"Gentlemen, today's class will be on building a state of the art, mobile treatment center." Tren and Pirie didn't have the slightest idea of what I was talking about. As a matter of fact I didn't have a clear picture. Quit often when I start top secret projects, I don't tell myself the whole story. We were about to turn the liberated Jeep-trailer into a mobile Dispensary.

In my mind I had a rough sketch of how I wanted the finished product to look. To put the ideas on paper and formulate a plan would make too much sense. I have never been accused of making sense in the past, why start now? Besides if you have a plan, the next thing you will need a material list before you start building. Acquiring material might cause weeks of delay. My approach, design around available material, is simpler and eliminates all the delay.

I built a 4 foot high two x four frame the exact width and length of the trailer. I added a solid roof, front, and bottom. My imagination jumped into overdrive. After adding doors to the sides and rear, the project looked good. The doors hinged from the top, allowing them to serve a duel purpose. When open, the doors became roofs over the treatment area. The left side of the project became the pharmacy. I measured 16 inches in an installed another wall. The shelves made of one x six's with drilled holes, allowed the plastic pill containers to be inserted. The caps on the pill container stopped them from falling through. Regardless how rough the road, the medication would stay in their designated place.

The right side became the treatment area. Another wall with shelves that held dressing, splints, medication needed for dressing change, and a variety of other medication. You name it, this mobile treatment trailer had it.

The rear became the examining area. After the tailgate was lowered, a stretcher mounted on wheels, rolled out. Presto an examining table. All patients would start at this point. If all they needed was medication, they were sent to the Pharmacy side. If they needed any type of treatment, to the treatment side. The space not used between the pharmacy and treatment walls was used to carry field tables, folding chairs, and other bulky items. After painting the patient areas white and two coats of OD paint on the outside, the project turned out and looked a lot better than I imagined. We started visiting Montagnard villages as soon as the paint dried.

Tren probably influenced the choice of villages we visited more than anyone. Although Pirie was from the Kontum area, Tren seemed to know more about the Montagnard villages and their health needs. I always contributed that with his association with the FULRO movement.

Pirie was quite content staying in Kontum. Leaving the city, even on short trips made him very nervous. This didn't create any problem for me. Pirie was a great worker around patients. He enjoyed teaching other Montagnard medics, medical procedures around our small hospital. For some reason I couldn't put a finger on, he never won my complete confidence. Unlike Tren, I wouldn't put my life in his hands. I would rather have Tren in the bonnies with me then Pirie.

"Tren, what do you think of Kon Monay Solam village for our first Med-Cap?" I pointed to a village just east of Kontum. The map showed it was about 5 miles from Kontum. I patiently waited for my Intel-briefing.

"Not good village "Bac Si, many, many VC live this village. We go Kon Kopat village. Many Montagnard need "Bac Si look them."

"Kon Kopat is on the other side of Kon Monay Salam Tren. Road 5B will take us through Kon Monay." I explained to Tren.

"No "Bac Si, Tren show special way we go."

We took Road 5-B past the airport and Minh Quy Hospital (Pat Smiths Hospital.) About three miles out we came to an old Bailey Bridge. It's poor condition caused me to have second thoughts about crossing it. Tren insisted it was safe. Tren was an undisputable talented Medic and loyal comrade in arms. Now is he voicing his opinion as Bridge

Old Bridge East of Kontum

Safety Engineer? Oh well what do I know. I put the jeep into gear and we crossed without any problem other than me being in the advanced stages of fright.

Just past the bridge we turned on a well-traveled winding path. The thick jungle put us in an ideal position to be ambushed. I hope my friend knows what he is doing. I started looking for a place to turn around. How would I ever explain to the Army, why I was driving a Jeep with a Trailer, down a winding jungle path? The fact I was the only American on this mission or whatever it was just compounded the problem. I guess I could plea insanity, and probably win.

"Stop Jeep "Bac Si, stop Jeep." The urgency of his request cranked my fear factor up a couple notches. Without hesitation I stopped and dove out of the jeep.

"Bac Si why you jump out of jeep? VC no come. Tren want "Bac Si, hear forest talk to us."

"Are you Dinky-Doll (nuts)? I don't want to talk to no dam forest." Tren started to laugh.

"Bac Si look funny jumping out jeep. VC no come "Bac Si."

When we reached the top of a small hill, our targeted village appeared. Kon Kopat Village occupied a large clearing in the forest. It was like stepping into yesteryear. You could truly feel the magic in the air. It was breath taking. In the center of the village was a very large structure called a Rung (activity) House. This multi purpose structure was the center of village activity.

It serves as a meeting place for the Village Elders, all celebrations including weddings are conducted in or around the Rung House. Guests are housed and fed in the Activity House.

Kon Kopat Village   Kon Kopat Village, Rung House

   Young Montagnards entering into marriage are required to attend classes on how to become good husbands or wives. All this is conducted in the Rung House.

   The Montagnard takes marriage seriously. A Montagnard marriage is forever. There is no such thing as a divorce. If for whatever reason a Montagnard marriage is not salvageable, the male is ordered out of the village. He leaves all his worldly possessors behind. They become property of the village. If the expelled husband ever tries to reenter the Village he will be shot. From that day forward his wife and children become wards of the Village. All their needs will be cared for, they will wan't for nothing. The abandoned wife will never marry again. Montagnards will not marry a woman that has been with another man.

   To the outsider the rules may seem harsh. To the Montagnard they insure children brought into the world as a result of the marriage, will have both parents to share the responsibility of their raising. We could learn a lot from the Montagnard. Their standard of morals and commitment to family is unmatched.

   I parked under a large tree in front of the Rung House. It was an ideal spot to set up our mobile treatment center. It is protocol to seek out the village Chief and exchange greetings when you enter a Montagnard settlement. That wouldn't be necessary on this visit. Before we got out of the jeep, a crowd had gathered loaded down with welcoming gifts. In a short time the Village Chief arrived in his ceremonial costume.

We must have been spotted long before we entered the village. This group was prepared for our arrival. The biggest problem before us was, how to avoid a Rice Wine ceremony before we accomplished our Medical mission.

After the formal greeting I invited the Chief to inspect our portable dispensary. As I opened each section, Tren would translate my explanation of its use. The Chief seemed impressed and asked Tren a lot of questions. By this time we were surrounded by people. I opened the rear (examining) section last. I didn't get to finish my explanation. The Chief jumped on the stretcher and opened his robe. The whole village lined up behind him. My intention was to look at villagers with medical problems. We ended up examining the whole village, including their old Witch Doctor. Later when I asked Tren why the sorcerer let me examine her, Tren replied,

"Not good sorcerer. This man, Dinky-Doll." I didn't know how to take that. Did he mean she was crazy to let me examine her?

The work load was almost more than we could handle. It became quite evident we needed another pair of hands on our Med-Caps. At the beginning both Tren and I examined the patients. We directed them to the pharmacy or treatment side of the trailer. Then Tren would work both sides. After all the people were examined, I joined my partner. I was surprised Tren had a Montagnard women helping him on the treatment side of our mobile treatment Jeep.

"This man nurse Bac Si, number one medic. Work for Vietnamese at Kontum Hospital, five years."

"Ask her if she would like to work for us Tren. We will take her to B-24 for two or three days. Then we will bring her back to run sick call in the Village."

"Oh yes Bac Si she like."

"Tren, ask her." After some conversation Tren came back with the same answer. The three of us finished our Med-Cap mission.

Nobody bothered to ask us if we were staying the night nor if we wanted to join their celebration. I haven't the foggiest idea what they were celebrating. Maybe it was because we came to their Village, or maybe because the tribe as a whole was in relatively good health. It could have been because one of their tribe was going to work in Kontum. It didn't matter, the extraordinary Montagnard calibrates everything from birth to death and everything between. Staying the night might cause a problem without

radioing B-24. I had no problem reaching B-24 with my PRC-25.

"Poker Spools, Poker Spools, traveling Buddha how copy?" I think I inherited the Buddha call sign because of my hair do.

"Traveling Buddha, copy five by, go."

"Poker Spools, mission successful, staying at target location, Go."

"Understand, staying at target. Poker Spools out." Like all Montagnard conversations, I understood about every twentieth word or so. The facial expressions and jesters were friendly. I reciprocated in kind. The end result a good time was had by all.

"Tren, is that who I think it is?" I couldn't believe my eyes. How in the world did he find us? I make a point not telling indigenous people where I am heading. In fact I don't always tell my fellow Americans.

"Good afternoon Bac Si. Good afternoon Mr. Tren. Pirie come have party with you." He just sat there on his Honda with a big grin on his face.

I guess the good time of a party, overrode Pirie's fear of leaving Kontum. About halfway into the celebration a large group of armed Montagnards joined the festivities. At first, my anxiety factor rose. After seeing Tren having what seemed to be friendly conversation with them, my anxiety was gone. This must be a FULRO thing I told myself and went back to enjoying the party. We departed Kon Kopat at first light. Our new nurse rode on the back of Pirie's Honda. I started to turn on the winding path we came on.

"No Bac Si, we stay on road to Kontum."

"What about the VC?"

"VC no stay Kon Monay now Bac Si." Another one of those FULRO things I'll bet. By this time I have learned not to push the conversation to far.

We pulled as many Med-Cap's up and down the Dak Bld (river around Kontum) as time would permit. Between NVA attacks on our A-Team's, helping at the Leper Colony, Med. Caps, training medics to staff our mini hospital and Village treatment stations, our seven-day work schedule was full. There was never enough time in Vietnam.

Koyong our new Montagnard nurse was an outstanding individual. She had taken her vows to the Catholic Church and worked as a Nurse at the Kontum Regional Hospital. As the Vietnamese took over more and more of the Highlands, the Montagnard were pushed to the side. Koyong was replaced with a Vietnamese nurse. Koyong went back to her village and continued her nursing skills.

Christian missionary tradition in the Highlands goes back to January 18, 1615, when Father Francesco Buzomi, a Neapolitan, landed in Hue, North Vietnam. Throughout the DEGA Highlands, in remote areas one can see old Catholic Churches that are monuments of the Christian effort in the area. After the French were expelled from Vietnam, Catholicism was discouraged and the beautiful old buildings stand abandoned. Many Montagnards like Koyong, quietly practice their Catholic teachings. Talk about loyalty. Old abandoned churches can be found all through the Central Highlands. They are respected not vandalized.

Many of Koyong's procedures were a little outdated. With a little correction she became an asset to our B-Team medical mission. There was no way I was going to waste this talent conducting sick call in a remote village. I asked her to stay at B-24. Koyong accepted. I trained another Montagnard to screen sick call at Kon Kopat Village. Patients that needed treatment were sent to us at B-24. If their medical problem was beyond our capability, they were sent to Doc Smith's Montagnard Hospital.

Industrialization of the Jungle

Special Forces unlike conventional forces have to generate funds for their special projects. This fund raising in Northern II Corps was accomplished by selling native artifacts:Cross Bows, Bracelets, VC Battle flags, Knifes, Baskets and the like. All were produced by our friends the Montagnards. We furnished the red, blue, and yellow material for the Battle Flags. This by far was the hottest item.

VC Flag

We offered two models. Our regular VC Flag model, top half red and bottom half blue with a yellow star in the middle was our top seller, until we offered the Combat model.

By sprinkling the flag with blood and shooting it few times, added to its popularity. The type of blood used depended on what the Montagnards were having for dinner. The donor varied from chicken blood to water buffalo. Wouldn't surprise me, if a little rat blood was used from time to time. Tell a story about the flag, and the price went up directly proportionally, to your ability to tell a story.

Another way to generate funds was to establish Service Clubs. B-24 had an officer and an enlisted club until LTC Hennigan took command. One of his first acts was to close the Officer Club. Special Forces Officers and Enlisted personnel have a close relationship. They fight together and party together. The respect they have for each other can be seen at work or play. Separating this unique fighting team just didn't work. Conventional units frown on this close relationship between Officer and enlisted.

The NCO Club at B-24 was frequent by MACV and 4th Division troops. Clubs at each of their locations had a limit on how many beverages they would sell individuals on a given day. At B-24 in addition to selling as much as they wanted, we sold the 4th Division truck loads of beer for their clubs. For whatever reason, the 4th had a problem getting beverages through their supply chain. Special Forces had special sources. Flatbed trucks leaving B-24, loaded with Black Label Beer, heading for the 4th Division compound was a common sight.

Most Special Forces Operatives are sort of loners. It's unusual to see SF Troops partying with conventional units. They get along great with other Special Operation Units, both Military and Civilian. Their missions being similar give them a common bond. For that reason, more than likely they would take their beverage to the tables out on the Patio. Fortunately all visitors to B-24 had to be out of our compound by 20:00 (eight o'clock) hours. The 4th Division had a Duce and a Half standing by to transport their troops back to Camp (4th Div. compound) Merylu. As soon as they cleared the SF compound our club would be occupied by Special Forces personnel.

Bobby Joe Dunham Club

"Everyone to the patio." Came over the intercom. "The Colonel wants to see everyone now."

It didn't take long for everyone to arrive. The B-Team only had twenty assigned to them at the time. A few troops from the 403rd SOD also showed up. Their mission made it impossible for all their people to attend. Members of the 403rd that weren't in the field, were busy monitoring high speed classified radio messages. In a few minutes LTC Hennigan arrived with a big smile on his face.

"Gentlemen, I have been asked by the 4th Division's Commander to put our club off limits to his troops under the rank of E-5." That brought a cheer from the crowd. "I have also decided to close the club at 20:00 hours after their NCO's depart the area. The group suddenly became angry, and didn't mind letting their thoughts be known. The Colonel must have lost his mind. Most of us didn't get off work until after 20:00 hours.

"That's the way it is. I don't want to hear any more moaning. This meeting is over. Join me in the club, I'm buying." The LTC didn't head for the Club entrance, he headed for the south side of the building. A few of the Officers followed him. The rest of us gathered in small groups and continued or complaining.

"What are you guys waiting for, the Colonel is buying." The CSM, reminded us. sticking his head around the side of the building, reminded us.

It was no surprise the Colonel was buying, he did that often. The surprise was the new door on the side of the building. Above the door was a freshly painted sigh. "Bobbie Joe Dunham Club."

B-24
Bobbie Joe
Dunham
Club

The door opened unto a plush well-equipped club. The Special Forces artifacts gave it additional class. The best part, it was for Special Forces only.

All of us were aware of the construction going on during the last three weeks. We were told it was additional storage space for the old club. LTC Hennigan and the CSM pulled a fast one on us, and did it in front of our face. Needless to mention the complaining stopped. After a short dedication speech from the Colonel, we all joined in singing the Colonel's favorite song, "Danny Boy." Knowing the words to Danny Boy, and being able to challenge the LTC to one arm pushups, was almost a requirement. I don't claim to be the sharpest knife in the drawer. But I knew enough not the beat (which I could) the CO in one arm pushups. I always did one or two less then his best performance for the night.

The work load in our dispensary was increasing daily. For some reason or other it wasn't tiring. I have never been a person that needed a lot of sleep. No matter how tired I get, all it takes is a couple of hours of sleep and I am ready to march on. In addition I had several Montagnard, dependents of our security force, cross trained as medics. The fact is, when a Montagnard is sick or wounded and has to go to the hospital, the whole family goes with them. You can bet your bottom dollar, I put them to work, and they loved it. The Montagnard culture is based on taking care of each other. I repeat, we could learn from them friend.

You know what they say, "all work and no play, makes Jack act funny," or something like that. I had just come off another extension leave. Like all of them, after visiting the States, I ended up in Thailand, with Chome and our son Johnny. I also had another R & R earned. I never get off a winning horse, so it was back to Australia.

I had told Chome all about Yvonne. This great lady insisted I take my Australian friend a gift. It was Chome's way of showing her thanks for the friendly treatment extended to me. I knew the pure Thai

Silk scarf would please the gal from down under. I can't help wondering, how many wives would even think about a pleasant jester like that. Chome, my wife, my life is one of a kind.

Like my first trip, I had a great five days in my second favorite country, Australia. And like my first trip I was eager to return to Vietnam. I must have a screw loose or something. A person looking forward returning to a war zone, is kind of stupid. I know it wasn't true, but I had the feeling they couldn't do without me. On the other hand maybe it is true. When I finally left Vietnam the whole place fell apart. I not bragging here, check your history.

Our Medical facility at B-24 was organized to expand its operation on a moment's notice. By utilizing the Security Force buildings, we had room for sixty beds. The MIKE Force which adjoined our compound to the east, had a dispensary that would hold another twenty or more patients.

We had a major flaw in our overall evacuation plan. Where do we send seriously wounded patients? American or Vietnamese patients no problem. We are talking about Montagnard patients. They are not welcome at all medical facilities. Pat Smith's hospital, in the event of an attack, would be loaded with civilian patients. Kontum had a Provencale Hospital that was a good place to take a patient, if you wanted them to die. I kid you not, I wouldn't take a dog to that bone-yard. The civilian hospital in Pleiku was a little better, but not much. That left the CIDG Hospital in Pleiku. Problem was it was filled to capacity.

"Colonel Hennigan, how about me going to Pleiku, TDY (temporary duty) and see what I can do about expanding their treatment facility?" Owen Wright and I had talked about the expansion on several occasions.

"Who can we call in to run our operation while you are gone?"

"No one sir, Tren can handle the job just fine. If he runs into any problem, I'm just a short distance down the road." The Colonel had the highest regard for Tren, but he wanted an American to oversee the operation. SFC Linguist from the CIDG Hospital volunteered. I strongly suspect, with a little help from Owen Wright. Linguist was a good medic, but not much of a builder.

Chapter Five

CIDG Hospital Pleiku

I took off for the CIDG Hospital. Since they were not letting Tren take charge of the B-Team Dispensary, I took him with me. I had a special plan for Tren.

The CIDG Hospital in Pleiku was the right arm to all Special Forces, A-Teams, B-Teams, and Special Projects. They were equipped to handle the most serious cases. Vivax and Falciparum Malaria, Tuberculosis, Bubonic Plague, and Typhoid Fever. The hospital had an up to date Operating Room, capable of handling almost any type operation. Limited only by the talent of assigned personnel. Surgical repair to the skeletal structure, Amputations, Debridement of forgone material and devitalized tissue, Skin Grafting and of course Child Birth was well within the Special Forces Medics' capability.

American Surgeons and Surgical Nurses from the 71st Field Hospital in Pleiku, loved to come and work at the CIDG Hospital. Their visit gave them an opportunity to work on extreme cases. Extreme American casualties were all Air Evacuated to Japan or the States.

I remember one such person from the 71st Field Hospital that came to the CIDG Hospital quit frequently. He was a full Colonel and his speciality was Orthopedic Surgery. He took Owen Wright under his wing and taught Owen advanced surgical procedures. Bone grafting and radical repair to

Owen Wright and Tren

shattered bone. I scrubbed into a few cases and was amassed to see what my friend was capable of.

On one particular coffee break I witnessed the Colonel offering Owen, a full tuition paid medical school, if Owen would specialize in Orthopedic Surgery. The only payback, Owen had to work for him at his Hawaii practice, for two years after graduation. Owen turned the offer down. He didn't want to leave Special Forces. You can be sure of one thing, I throw that in Owens face every time I see him.

A case I will never forget, was a stump repair on a double amputee Montagnard. We called the lad Speedy. This guy could maneuver a wheeled chair faster than anyone. Speedy lost both his legs saving a wounded American.

More times than not the first operation done on an amputated arm or leg is performed for Debridement of the wound, saving as much of the tissue as possible. The closure used is called a Purse String Closure. This procedure is tough to all Special Forces Medics. Remember the marble bag, with its string closure when you were a kid? That's the closest thing to describe the surgical closure.

Later when the wound heals, they will go back and shorten the bone, construct a muscle flap and fit the patient for a prosthesis. Well that never happened to Speedy. He was left to struggle through life with the painful Purse String closure. Speedy would never be able to wear a prosthesis unless corrective surgery was performed.

These two Giants, before my eyes, started to demonstrate their talent. Owen on the right leg and the Colonel on the left. After both stumps were surgically opened exposing the bone, the bones were shortened. Pulling the long muscle from behind the thigh forward, a pad was formed that would enable Speedy to use a prosthesis.

Speedy with his Prosthesis

The Colonel was demonstrating the skill of his craft. Working alongside him was a SFC Special Forces Trained Medic, who demonstrated crafts can be learned to accomplish the mission. When I left Vietnam, Speedy was walking. I have been asked many tines, sometime sarcastically. "What's so special about Special Forces?" The answer (I say again) is relatively simple, "it's people."

Equipment Liberation

As I mentioned before, in my travels I was always looking for items that could help any mission I was involved in. On one of my trips to the 71st Field Hospital I noticed a portable field X-Ray machine, just sitting in their hall, not being used. It was soon to change ownership. But first I needed an X-Ray Technician.

WW II Portable X-Ray

The CIDG Hospital had a very good x-ray set up, and a trained X-Ray Technician. Everybody raved about Billy Bune and the films he turned out. I didn't share their enthusiasm about Billy. Maybe it was because I had training in X-Ray, and that made me a little more critical. Whatever the reason I wanted Tren to be trained by an American X-Ray Technician.

I had no problem convincing the 71st Sergeant Major to give Tren a job in their X-Ray Section. Since there was no pay involved, the 71st Field jumped at the chance to get a volunteer worker. In no time they were praising how hard Tren worked and how fast he learned. They were simply amazed. They were truly happy with my dear friend's capabilities. For some reason Tren was not happy at all. That bothered me.

"Tren what's the problem? Why are you so sad? Don't you like working at the 71st?"

"Yes Bac Si, I like 71, 71 no like Tren, I think."

"You got them wrong Tren. They talk very well about you."

"They like Tren, why they no feed Tren." I couldn't believe what I was hearing. Tren walks about three miles a day from the CIDG Hospital. Works in their X-Ray section about ten hours a day, and they don't feed him? I headed for the 71st.

"SGM sit down, we have to talk." He leaned against his desk. "What's the matter with you people, do you have brain damage?" He sat down. "Why aren't you feeding Tren in your mess hall?"

"We're not allowed to feed indigenous personnel in our dinning facility. Tren's a Montagnard, it's just against regulations."

"Tren is not a Montagnard, he's from the Phillippines. Tren's a civilian Filipino worker, on contract to the Americans." (Remember a few chapters back, I stated; "if a person can't handle the truth, don't burden them with it?") This is a classic example.

"I thought he was a Montagnard, Mac, honest I thought Tren was a Montagnard."

"No, No, how did you ever make SGM? Can't you tell the difference between a Filipino and Montagnard?"

"I thought he looked a little different. Here, give Tren this Dinning Facility Card."

"Thank you SGM. Wait until I tell Tren you thought he was a Montagnard."

"Do you have to tell him?"

"No, not really, we'll keep it our secret." I left the SGM's office bubbling over. Couldn't wait to tell Tren he is a Filipino.

I was on a roll. Might as well negotiate on the X-Ray Machine collecting dust in the 71st hallway, but first I had better put on civilian clothes. Isn't it odd, if most of the people are in civilian clothes, the uniform intimidates them. On the other hand, if most are wearing uniforms, the civilian attire does the intimidation. The people I will be negotiating with, will be in uniform.

"Where did you get this X-Ray Machine Captain?"

"I don't know, you'll have to see the property-book officer."

"No, the property book officer will have to see me. This machine is not getting out of my sight. Tell him to get over here ASAP. I'll be waiting for hin."

The young Captain almost took off on a run. I am sure he thought I was from the CID (Criminal Investigation Division.) I am also sure, like myself, he knew the 71st Evac Hospital does not have a Field X-Ray Machine on their TO&E (Table of Organization and Equipment).

"Can I help you sir?" A clean-cut Staff Sergeant asked.

"I'm waiting for the Property-Book Officer."

"That's me Sir. I got stuck with the job when the P.B. Officer rotated back to the states."

"Is this Field X-Ray on your books?" I asked in a firm voice.

"No Sir, it's not authorized. I don't know where it came from." I expected the answer, from here on it would be a cake walk.

"Sergeant, you can't have expensive unaccounted for items laying around. That just leads to trouble. I know it's not your fault. You probably inherited this problem. Let me see how can I help you."

"I sure appreciate your help Sir. Anything you can do will be appreciated." That was the green light. He was not only happy I was taking his unauthorized machine, he had some of his troops load it on a hospital pick-up truck.

"Follow me to the Pleiku Airport young man." We took off for the airport, but more specifically, the Caribou Ramp. Supplies designated for the B-Teams are held in a designated area until they are put on a manifest, then flown to the designated Special Forces Team.

"When is the next flight to Kontum? " I inquired.

"Tomorrow afternoon. What do you have for them?"

"An X-Ray machine and a crate of parts." I forgot to mention my PB-Officer at the 71st volunteered to crate of parts that belonged to the Field X-Ray. It was as simple as that. My X-Ray mission was accomplished. I went back to the CIDG Hospital hoping no scum-bag would steal my new toy.

"Watch your thoughts now, I didn't steal the machine, I liberated it."

Bigger Is Better

After a short meeting with Owen Wright and the other NCO's at the CIDG Hospital, we were in agreement that my main job was to expand the Hospital. I would use whatever equipment and material I could get my hands on. There was no project material or budget available. No problem. I am used to under funded projects. I didn't expect nor get much in the way of a helping hand. This group was busy taking care of the ever increasing patient load. As a matter of fact, I had to pitch in occasionally and help them with patients.

At a minimum we needed to build a 30-bed ward and expand their patient dinning facility. This tasking would require a lot of manpower. To complicate the problem, it had to be free manpower.

Getting anything free from the Vietnamese would be impossible. I decided to try my luck at the Pleiku POW (prisoner of war) Camp, run by the Vietnamese Army.

POW Camp Pleiku RVN

Knowing anything run by the Vietnamese is corrupt, I brought a case of corruption hid under a GI blanket in the back seat of my jeep. American booze was a high ticket item in Vietnam. They love our liquor. I did it one step better. Underneath the blanket was a case of Johnny Walker Black Label scotch.

"Good afternoon Captain, I'm SFC McGinley from the CIDG Hospital. We shook hands. I need a few workers to build an additional Medical Ward at our Hospital."

"How many people, how many day you need?"

"I'll need six good workers for about seven, maybe ten days. I'll pick them up every morning and bring them back each night."

"Maybe I give you three."

"I need six, but I will take whatever you give me." At the same time I uncovered the case of scotch, and handed him three bottles." I purposely left the blanket off the remaining bottles.

"I give you five man, you give me two more bottle?

"You give me six, and I'll give you three more bottles of scotch." The deal was made.

In about twenty minutes six very small Vietnamese were standing before me.

"Sorry, they're to small Sir. (beside they were Vietnamese. We will be working with cement. I need strong people. Let me pick the workers." The Captain agreed. I picked six Montagnards.

"Tren, tell the prisoners, that if they run, they will be shot. I'm to old to chase them." We put all six in the Jeep Trailer. Tren sat in the back seat with my Car-15 at the ready.

On the way back to the Hospital I stopped at a Montagnard Village. Using Tren as interrupter, I told the chief I was going to give them a building. They had to take it down and carry it off the Hospital compound before sun down. They agreed and followed us to the CIDG Hospital. Within five hours after their arrival, the old patient dinning building was taken down and piece by piece carried off.

"Bac Si, this man work for you, they work you no give pay." Then pointed to four Montagnards standing near the POW's. Sometimes I don't know if Tren works for me or I work for him. I got the feeling, Tren knew the gentlemen in question. I also had the feeling the gentlemen in question, knew the prisoners. But then, all Montagnards are friendly to each other.

"OK Tren, maybe they can help us keep tabs on the prisoners. We would be in trouble if they ran on us."

"Bac Si, this man not prisoner from NVA, this man work for Montagnard Army. They no run away, they work for Montagnard Army in camp." I didn't want to hear any more. I put them to work building a frame for the new mess hall cement floor. I left Tren in charge. I went to look for a few bags of cement. Of course I headed for the 4th Division compound.

"Why do you want to mix your own cement Mac? The Engineers have Ready Mix and will deliver it to your location. Just put your request in. I hate paperwork, I decided to go to the Engineers and have an eyeball to eyeball.

"How are you Mac?" Was the friendly greeting from SFC Richard A Walker. SFC Walker was no stranger to SF. He and his crew drilled many wells at our A-Teams throughout Northen II Corps. This was one talented individual, always willing to give a helping hand. When I told my friend what I needed and what it was for, I didn't have to look any further for material to expand the CIDG Hospital. Richard loved the Montagnards. SFC Walker followed me back to the Hospital area. He took out his clip board and started an ever expanding equipment list.

SFC Walker and Drilling Team

"You don't have to build forms for the floor's Mac. I'll send metal forms over and a man to show your people how to put them together." By seven thirty that evening we had two thirty by seventy cement floors, poured and finished. Walker never did send anybody over to help lay the forms or run equipment we borrowed from time to time. He, personally stayed with our project until it was finished.

The construction project pressed on, only to be interrupted by heavy casualties arriving without notice. Fortunately I was able to talk the POW Camp commander to give me the same prisoners every day. I ended up with a work gang of ten prisoners, each one possessing a needed building skill. The best part, they didn't need any supervision. The were happy to get out of the stockade and work.

Falling Short of Giant Status

Major Shelter was about to leave Vietnam. Cpt Henry Thornton was to be his replacement and had arrived. I was to have problems with Capt. Thornton. It was not that he wasn't a good guy. Captain Thornton was a great guy. The problem was he was mal assigned. He wasn't Airborne nor SF qualified. In fact he quit the SF Qualification Course. This guy didn't have the foggiest idea what the SF mission was, nor seemed to care. How this guy went to the SF "Q" course without being Airborne qualified was a mystery to me. Again that doesn't make him a bad guy. Everyone is not cut out to be Special Forces. I am sorry to say, my opinion of Thornton was shared by many.

One major fault Cpt Thornton had was not having faith in the NCO's he worked with. He strongly felt he should be consulted before any operation was done to any patient. Now here is a guy fresh out of Medical School. With an experience level of zero, he wanted to make all surgical decisions. Everyone assigned to the CIDG Hospital could out perform the lad, in surgical or any other medical task. Yes he had a Diploma stating he was a Doctor, but the ink wasn't dry.

As I turned in the gate of the CIDG Hospital, I was shocked to see Speedy sitting on the ground without his prosthesis nor his Wheel Chair.

"What are you doing Speedy?"

"Bac Si Thornton say I no can stay at CIDG Hospital. American finished with me." I hung my arm outside the Jeep. Speedy hung on while I swung him into the back of the Jeep. Hot under the collar, I went looking for that poor excuse of a Bac Si.

I looked everywhere. The wards, lab, x-ray, and his office. Usually we tripped over him. He was always in the way. Now that I really wanted to give him a peace of my mind, he was not to be found. My last attempt was the emergency room. I didn't expect to find him there. I never did see him work on Montagnard patients. Our illustrious doctor confined his activities to the American personnel sick call. As I was entering the ER, my target was exiting, heading for his quarters.

"Captain, I have to talk to you. now!" I hollered as I pounded on his door. Knowing I would not go away the sorry bast--- opened the door.

"Are you looking for me, SGT McGinley?"

"Who gives you the right to evict a legless Montagnard to fend for himself? Montagnards with both legs have a hard time making it. This Montagnard lost both legs saving an American. You're a sorry SOB Thornton." I was hot, but that didn't make me right. Talking to an officer in this manner was not acceptable. I had better cool it.

"Why don't you like me SGT McGinley?", the Captain asked as he slowly sat down.

"It's not a question of like or dislike Captain. It's the way you treat Montagnards that tick's me off."

"I don't know them as well as the rest of you. I admit they upset me. They're an ignorant dirty group. I just can't get used to them. What am I to do?"

"Teach them something. In the process you will learn from them. Give them some soap, emphasize the importance of its use. If you're not willing to do that, request a transfer to the 71st Field. I am positive that one day you will be a fine doctor." With that I started to leave.

"I had hoped I would have learned something being assigned to a Special Forces unit."

"We hopped we would have learned something from you Sir."

The Captain was on target when he said there was nothing more American could do for Speedy medically. What about finding something for Speedy to do, that would improve his ability to be self sufficient, a productive member, of his limited world?

I opened a small canteen by converting a closet to a storage area. Donations from other team members kept it stocked with candy, cigarets, gum and soft drinks. Speedy in turn would sell the merchandise to the patients. I set the sale price on each item. Price control was a must to keep the items affordable for patients with limited funds. Speedy was to keep the funds collected.

It worked for a while, then the Vietnamese got involved. Like everything they touch it became corrupt. What was intended to be a service to the patients and a small income for Speedy, turned into a small black-market. I closed it down without blinking an eye.

We put Speedy to work in the Lab in addition to giving him a small salary. Part of the deal was he could keep his cot on Ward Two. Speedy was on cloud nine. After his shift in the Lab, the lad worked helping the patients on the ward.

The only problem we had with Speedy was to get him to use his new prostheses. I took care of that by posting a schedule on the Bulletin Board. Giving Speedy strict instructions, that if I ever saw him without his new legs, during scheduled times, I would fire him and send him home. What home? Speedy's village was destroyed by the VC two years ago.

I was summoned to Ward Two. I found Speedy laying in his cot, crying his eyes out. It was obvious my little friend was in pain.

"What's' the problem Speedy?" Tren answered for him.

"This man no can use new leg Bac Si. New leg no like him." I pulled back the bed sheets exposing Speedy's modified stumps. They were raw and bloody. It was no wonder this little guy was in pain. I had Tren clean them while another medic went for a surgical pack.

While I was waiting, I examined the prostheses that apparently was causing this trauma. Early on, during the healing process, both modified stumps had a predictable amount of swelling. Our little friend removed most of the padding to make more room. I don't know how he walked on the artificial legs at all. With the padding gone, the cups of the prostheses were sharp hard plastic.

"Speedy, why did you use the legs in this condition?"

"Bac Si speak, Speedy walk every day, Speedy walk." I had the modified prostheses sent to the 71st Brace Shop for repairs. There was no rush. It would be awhile before any weight could be put on the very raw stumps.

Another example of how you have to be careful on what, you tell and how you tell a Montagnard anything. They will do whatever you ask, without question.

Dr. David Pratt replaced Thornton Doc Pratt had a positive attitude, and although not Special Forces Qualified, he agreed to go to Jump School in Vietnam and take SF training as soon as he returned to Fort Bragg.

Of course when he returned from Jump School, he gave him a Prop-Blast party. We threw every alcohol beverage we could get our hands, to include Vietnamese whisky and Rice Wine, on into an Army Steel Pot. By the time the Helmet made its third or forth pass, the new Doc was talking to himself. The best thing that could be said about Doc Pratt, was he didn't try to run the CIDG Hospital.

Activity was picking up at Camp Ben Het. It was time for me to return to B-24 in Kontum. I explained to Tren, that when he finished X-Ray School I would come and pick him up. He didn't like staying behind. It was what I wanted and that was all that mattered to Tren. I knew he would be in good hands, everyone liked this extraordinary, Montagnard. of the Jai Tribe.

Just before I left for B-24, Martha Raye paid a visit to the CIDG Hospital. The world suddenly gets brighter when Maggie shows up. This talented lady has been visiting and entertaining troops since 1940. Maggie known for her comedy, has a surprisingly good singing voice. A talented actress tops off this multi talented lady's accomplishments.

LTC Martha Raye (Maggie)

While getting acquainted at our CIDG Mini Club, six patients arrived by chopper. Without hesitation Maggie followed us to the Emergency Room and helped treat the patients. Martha Raye was a Registered Nurse with the rank of LTC in the Army Reserve. Add that to her talent list.

When all patients were stable, we returned to our Mini Club. Martha and I engaged in a Vodka (Maggies favorite) on the Rocks contest. I am not going to tell you who won, you don't have a need to know. Of course Maggie left her mark on our wall, "God Bless, Maggie."

This was the second time I had the pleasure of meeting this great lady. While I was at Dak Seang, Maggie paid the team a visit. The team took a group picture holding a black flag with skull and crossbones. The wording on the flag suggested what should be done with communism. "My sentiments exactly." Martha was quick to point out.

I would see her again when I stopped at her Team House in California while on one of my extension leaves. All Special Forces had a standing invitation to visit her Team House. This great lady loved and was loved, by the Special Forces community.

Maggie Team House

Back To B-24

On my flight back to Kontum, I thought over the things improved or accomplished at the CIDG Hospital. They cooked over open wood fulled fire. Now they have a new dinning hall and six new, gas fired cook stoves. The new dinning facility gave the patients a fly free area to eat. Tables and chairs, scrounged from the club system, added class to the eating area. Their patient capacity was upgraded by a new fifty bed ward. To include showers and toilets. New septic tanks cured the continuous damp ground problem. All the credit had to go to my Engineer friend SFC Walker's crew and the borrowed POW's. The only credit due me was, I ram-rodded the project. Any project I get involved in, has to make a difference, or I'm not happy . . . I was happy.

I think SFC Linguist was glad I was back so he could return to Pleiku. I know the Montagnards were. Linguist changed a few things that upset the Yards. He limited the amount of time dependents were allowed to visit patients. When a Montagnard goes to the hospital, the whole family goes. This may even include the grand parents. It's their tradition. I went back to the anytime visiting schedule. The little people were happy again.

In about one week, someone coming back from Pleiku, (I think it was Glen Watson) brought me a letter from Tren. I decided to print it here, word for word. Keep in mind this is from an unschooled Montagnard. Indigenous people pick up GI slang, without knowing what it means. Like children they mimic, and like small children they mean no harm by the use.

Dear SSGT McGinley
Stay B-24 Kontum
Despense

dear SSGT McGinley Good afternoon Bac Si" Right now I am have time to speaks with I want to tell you about me before I am tell come get me 25 February But Right now I not get pay days I Till SSG Thompson call with Telephone SSG McGinley you don't come 25 Feb I am not very get pay days maybe day 26 feb. May Be get pay or not But I m don't know. I tell you about when I call you from here and you come get me oKay Ba0 Ssi

hay SSGT How Kontum now, preaty good or not Im know Kontum Batter and Pleiku right SSG Im take live and CIDG Hosp Pleiku May Be 26 Feb You know what I tell some Body in Here I go and live Kontum All SSG in Here get pist off me, all Body Say Know want me go and live Kontum Working, Body SSGT Say Wont me stay work and CIDG Hosp- But I am no like to stay here. I Wont to Be With You again, Im like you very much But I think you Know like me Right SSGT McGinley think very much good Bye SSGT see you 26 Feb

Thanks From CIDG Hosp
TREN-BREN

(This scribbled note is safely kept with my most treasured possessions).

It was obvious my Montagnard Friend was home sick. I dropped everything I was doing and headed back to Pleiku and picked him up.

"Mac I need a favor."

"Name it Owen, and it's done."

"We have a patient from CCC in Kontum. He's dying Mac. He wonts' to go home."

The patient was a member of a MACVSOG Recon Team working out of CCC. He was hospitalized with a Compression Fracture of the Cervical Spine. Treating the fracture called for two holes to be drilled into the skull and a clamp attached. A Tension rope was attached from the clamp, through a pulley and attached to weights. The constant weight was important for proper healing.

Like all Montagnards, his family come to the hospital every day. With all the good intentions in the world, they would remove the clamp to make him more comfortable. The constant handling, probably with dirty hands, caused the patient to get Tetanus. The dreaded infection was in it's advanced stage. Sammy would not be with us long.

"Owen send your driver to pick up Tren at the 71st. I'm taking him home. In the mean time I'll get the jeep ready to transport Sammy." The lad was in a lot of pain. I decided to take his mattress and pillows to make his ride to Kontum as comfortable as possible.

"It's time to go home Tren. Put your things under Sammy's mattress. We are going to take Sammy with us." Tren was all smiles.

While Tren was packing, I went to the C-Team and had them radio CCC that I was bringing Sammy home. They appreciated the help and said they would have people on the way to escort us. CCC lost five Americans on the Pleiku Road recently.

I have always known it wasn't the smartest thing to do, traveling between Kontum and Pleiku without an armed escort. My only defense was, the 403rd SOD, taught me bad habits. They always travel without an escort. The logic behind their action was the didn't want to bring attention to their classified trips. The nature of the 403rd business keeps them abreast of the daily activity of the enemy. My excuse was, I had Tren and his friends looking after me. At least I like to think that . . . OK, OK, I didn't have any logic for my activity.

When I got back to the Jeep Tren and Sammy were ready to go, but they weren't alone. Somehow we picked up a Lab Technician. Speedy was in the front seat, with a sheepish look, as though he knew something I didn't.

"Bac Si, this man work B-24, OK? Tren pay him, OK?" I just shook my head and smiled. Again I wondered, who's in charge, the Montagnards or me.

We headed North to Kontum. About halfway to our destination, a 3/4 Ton Truck with about eight armed Montagnards, pulled out of the woods and followed us to the CCC Compound just

South of Kontum City. Sammy had a lot of friends, I'll bet everyone of them showed up to greet us. No big surprise, Special Project people are very close. Can you guess what happened next? Correct, they broke out the Rice Wine.

Speedy attracted everyone's attention when he started to put on his artificial legs. They were amazed. A man without legs can walk. In a few minutes, Speedy was letting a one legged Striker try his leg. Of course it didn't fit. If it had, one will get you ten, Speedy would have given the leg to him. Montagnards are that way, they take care of each other.

Strong Believer's Everyone

You can maximize positive results when working with third world countries, if you don't try to change their traditional beliefs. If they are superstitious, so be it. We are not going to change hundreds of years of belief. To try only takes away from your main mission.

I recall an incident that happened at the Kontum Mike Force. One of their Strikers was killed in action. The team removed his shirt to treat his wounds. All attempts to save his life failed. The body was wrapped in a poncho liner and returned to his village just outside Kontum for burial. Every night after that, the guards on the Mike Force front gate, opened fire on the lad's ghost. The ghost that came looking for his missing shirt. This happened nightly for three nights and always about 01:30.

A Mike Force team member came up with a great solution. One night just before dark, a team member hung a new fatigue shirt on a tree across the road from their main gate. After dark, and before 01:30, they clandestinely, removed the shirt. There was no doubt in any Montagnards mind, the deceased Striker took the fatigue shirt.

50 Cal Machine Gun

Another incident occurred at B-24, we started having trouble with someone sabotaging our 50 cal. Machine guns. Every night without fail, the barrels of our 50 Cal's were being screwed all the way down, rendering all three 50 Cal's on our perimeter useless.

In order for the Machine Gun to fire properly, the barrel has to be screwed all the way down, then backed off a turn and a half. We kept it quiet for a while, hoping to catch the villain in the act. We were confident it was one of our Vietnamese counterparts.

Then one night, I was called to a bunker on the perimeter to treat a Montagnard who had been shot. I jumped into the bunker to render whatever medical aid needed. I didn't have to open my medical bag. The size of the exit wound in the back of the lad's head was the size of a grapefruit. The little guy put the barrel of an M-16, set on full automatic in his mouth. Tied the weapon to his leg with Ace-Bandages, and pulled the trigger with his toe.

The Montagnard believes, if you lie to a friend, the punishment should be death. Earlier in the evening, when asked if he knew anything about the sabotaged 50-Cal's, his answer was negative. Further investigation showed he was given one canteen cup of rice every time he rendered the weapons useless. Further investigation also showed one of our Vietnamese counterparts, furnished the rice.

An old saying but unfortunately it wasn't true in Vietnam. It got worse but it didn't get better. By May 1969 the enemy buildup west of Ben Het was unbelievable. Every day new elements were being detected. The NVA 28th Infantry Regiment Augmented by artillery, the NVA 1st Artillery with mortars and recoilless rifles, the 40th NVA Artillery armed with RPG 7 Rockets, 122 and 140 mm Rockets. The list kept growing. NVA 26th Infantry Regiment and 60th Regiment. All were being controlled by the NVA B-5 Front Senior Command Headquarters located in North Vietnam near Highway 1. When the NVA, K-80 Sapper Battalion moved in the area, we knew that an attack was not to far in the future. The only question was which camp will be hit. The force was large enough to take all three of our boarder Teams, Ben Het, Dak Seang and Dak Peak.

By February 1970, B-24's medical facility's role as a screening station expanded daily. We were handling up to thirty-five casualties a day from the action around Ben Het. The Kontum 4th Mike Force, who went to assist Ben Het, received more than its share of the wounded.. This was in addition to our regular, increasing sick call.

Siege of Dak Seang

On 1 April 1970 at 06:45, the largest enemy force that ever hit any of our A-Teams, hit   A-245 Dak Seang. Enemy forces consisted of the 28th and 33rd North Vietnamese Army Regiment, the 101D, NVA Regiment, the 40th North Vietnamese Artillery, and elements of the 66th North Vietnamese Army Regiment and all their support elements, including a Sapper Company

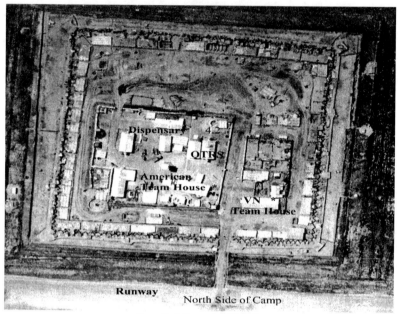

Camp Dak Seang A-245 1970

The 101D NAV Regiment took advantage of the darkness and bad weather to attempt a quick victory. At 0330 hours they shelled the compound with mortars and B-40 rockets followed by a three company assault on the western perimeter while a reinforced company hit the eastern wire. After 20 minutes these assaults were broken up. At 0425 hours another assault breached the wire. Air support was hindered by the weather. The enemy assault was beaten back with artillery and defensive fires. The battle of Dak Seang was a splendid example of the ability of a fortified CIDG camp to defeat a determined enemy with a minimum of outside assistance.

Sergeant Gary Beikirich Dak Seang's Senior Medic was severely wounded on the first day of the siege. The following sequence of events, were taken from an article written by Gary "For His Honor."

While treating a Montagnard, Gary states he heard the 122-mm rocket coming. Without hesitation Gary throw himself on top of the wounded yard. The blast threw Gary about 25 feet against a sandbagged mortar pit. Alive but unable to move, this dedicated soldier could see his Montagnard friend was blown to pieces.

Two Montagnards came to help. They wanted to take Gary to the Medical Bunker. Gary told them "No" and had them carry him around on a stretcher to treat other wounded. For hours they carried their wounded friend around treating the wounded, distributing ammo, directing fire, and as Gary puts it, "fighting for our lives. " By this time Gary was wounded two more times. Finally he lost consciousness. When he awoke, he realized they had taken him to the underground medical bunker and were in the process of calling a Med-Evac.

"Med. Evac! No way." He screamed to his beloved Montagnards, "Get me out of here. If I am going to die, I am not going to die down here." As the battle raged on, Gary's two Yard friends carried him for hours. Taking him where he directed them and helping him care for the wounded. The dedicated Montagnards held him up as they continued to fight. A loud explosion throw them to the ground. Another rocket coming in, Gary's friends covered him with their bodies. The explosion shook the earth, engulfed them in a cloud of smoke, sending shrapnel and other debris raining down on them.

"Let's go!" Gary yelled, but only one yard moved. Gary rolled the still lifeless body of his friend off of him and began to check for wounds. His back had been ripped open from the shards of exploding metal.

"Bac Si." The other yard said. "He's dead." As Gary puts it, in a battle there is little time for grief. It becomes anger and hate, and you use it for strength. From somewhere another Yard came picked him up and they continued to fight.

From that point on Gary states his memories are a swirling stream of sporadic events. Unending, deafening, explosions, firing a 30-Calabar machine-gun into clouds of smoke and shadows. Looking at bodies crumpled in the barbed wire perimeter. Lying in a ditch watching a helicopter exploding in mid air. Another one trying to come in for a Med-Evac then, strong arms reaching down and pulling him into the "warm belly" of a chopper. The face of a young medic shocked at seeing him still alive, but telling him he was going to be OK.

For Gary's action and sacrifice, under extreme hazardous conditions, Gary B Beikirich was awarded our nation's highest award given to a soldier in battle.

"The Medal Of Honor"

DEPARTMENT OF THE ARMY

Washington, D.C., 5 November 1973

AWARD OF THE MEDAL OF HONOR

By direction of the President, under the Joint Resolution of Congress approved 12 July 1802 (amended by act of 3 March 1863, act of July 1918 and act of 25 July 1963), the Medal of Honor for Conspicuous gallantry and intrepidity at the risk of life above and beyond the call of duty is awarded by the Department of the Army in the name of Congress to:

SERGEANT GARY B. BEIKIRCH

Sergeant Gary Beikirch, 069-40-9496, United States Army Medical Aidman, Detachment B-24, Company B, 5th Special Forces Group (Airborne), 1st Special Forces, who, while serving in Kontum Province, Republic of Vietnam, distinguished himself during the defense of Camp Dak Seang, on 1 April 1970. On that date, the allied defenders suffered a number of casualties as a result of an intense, devastating attack launched by the enemy from well-concealed positions surrounding the camp. Sergeant Beikirch, with complete disregard for his personal safety, moved unhesitatingly through the withering enemy fire to his fallen comrades, applied first aid to their wounds and assisted them to the medical aid station. When informed that a seriously injured American officer was lying in an exposed position, Sergeant Beikirch ran immediately through the hail of fire. Although he was wounded seriously by fragments from an exploding enemy mortar shell, Sergeant Beikirch carried the officer to a medical aid station. Ignoring his own serious injuries, Sergeant Beikirch left the relative safety of the medical bunker to search for and evacuate other men who had been injured. He was again wounded as he dragged a critically injured Vietnamese soldier to the medical bunker while simultaneously applying mouth-to-mouth resuscitation to sustain his life. Sergeant Beikirch again refused treatment and continued his search for other casualties until he collapsed. Only then did he permit himself to be treated. Sergeant Beikirch's conspicuous gallantry in action, his complete devotion to the welfare of his comrades, and his intrepidity at the risk of his life are in keeping with the highest traditions of the military service and reflect great credit on him, his unit, and the United States Army.

The White House   **Richard Nixon**

Gary's Giant characteristics were evident from the first day I meet this magnificent soldier. It was no accident Gary was assigned to Dak Seang. A-245 was my first assignment in Vietnam and held a special place in my heart. By assigning Gary Beikirich to Dak Seang, I knew they were getting the best.

My Montagnards loved him (and he them) from day one. Many people would live because of Garry's medical talent and dedication to mission. 1LT Ed Christensen the officer mentioned in the Citation was just one of many. 1Lt Christensen, the team's XO took a direct hit in the shoulder from a rocket. Under heavy fire, Gary carried the LT to the Medical Bunker.

I feel a little guilty for his injures, I am the one who assigned Gary to Dak Seang. If I had to do it all over again, I would have given him the same assignment. Gary B Beikirich, was the best man for the medical mission at Camp A-245.

The NVA, hoping to prevent Dak Seang from getting needed supplies, set up antiaircraft fire coverage, of the likely air supply routes. Special Forces old reliable friend, the C7 Caribou came to the surrounded camp's aid. Three C-7 airdrops were made on the afternoon of 1 April, with one aircraft taking minor hits.

When it became clear that the enemy was making a determined attempt to destroy the camp, reinforcements were sent in. Two Mobile Strike Force Companies, a Company of CIDG from Plateau Gi, and Vietnamese Ranger battalions came to the aid of the camp and helped to inflict heavy casualties on the enemy.

On the morning of 2 Apr, two C-7s of the 537th Tactical Airlift Squadron at Pleiku went in again. The first aircraft made a successful drop but reported ground fire. The second C-7 (tail number 61-2406) made its drop but was hit while climbing through

400 feet. The pilot took a southerly heading, possibly for   Dak To, but

the aircraft burst into flames and crashed about five miles south of Dak Seang, killing all three crewmen. 1st Lt Steve W. Train, pilot, 1st Lt Charles E. Suprenant, copilot, and MSG Dale E. Christensen, load-master, and six more unidentified C-7A Caribou crewmen, were with great sadness added to the list of Giants, who gave their all.

The airdrops continued despite the intense antiaircraft fire. Two more C-7s were shot down, another from the 537th TAS on the 4th of April and one from the 457th TAS on 6 April with the loss of six more aircrewmen. Their efforts permitted the defenders to withstand the overwhelming attack.

Shoot straight and communicate is the name of the game. To the man, the A Team at Dak Seang, distinguish themselves throughout the battle. They shot straight. A-245's small como-team, consisting of SGT John Liner and SGT Patrick Dizzine kept the communication lines open between the camp and all the supporting elements. The ability to communicate is an absolute must in every battle.

Badly beaten, the NVA withdrew after a twelve-day siege. Once again, this little Special Forces camps on the Tri-Border, held it's own against a superior force. Dak Seang and its defenders earned the "Valores Unit Award" for their superior performance against a determined enemy. With great pride, I list their names and salute this magnificent Team of Giants.

Original Team

CPT Paul **Landers**, Team Leader (WIA) 1LT Ed **Christensen**, Team XO (WIA), MSG Tom **Drake**, Team Sergeant (WIA), SGT Jack **Colligan**, Heavy WPNS man, SGT Gary **Beikirch**, Medic (WIA), SGT Pat **Noonan**, Medic, SGT John **Liner**, Radio Operator (WIA), SGT Patrick **Dizzine** Radio Operator, SSG Gordon **Wiley**, Demo man, SSG Eric **Pekkaia**, Demo man.

Replaced the WIA (wounded in action)

CPT Udo **Walters**, Team Lesder , 1LT Steve **Hatch**, Team XO, MSG Ralph **Loff** , Team Sergeant, SGT Larry **Woodlock**, Medic

The Siege of Dak Pek

A-242 Dak Pek

On 12 April 1970, twelve days after the beginning of the attack on Dak Seang, the enemy turned his siege tactics on Camp Dak Peck. The NVA struck with extreme force, putting their main effort on the hill occupied by the American Special Forces Team. While the camp was almost completely destroyed, enemy losses were extremely high. Like Dak Seang, the enemy miscalculated the resolve of the Special Forces Team defending the large camp. Dak Peck, 17 miles North of Dak Seang, on the Laotian boarder, occupying seven hills, each a fortress to be reckoned with.

The attack started on 12 April 1970 at 02:00 hours. The NVA hit Dak Peck at several spots, with the main force hitting the American hill. The entire hill was engulfed in flame. The following eye witnesses accounts (from a book, Assault on Dak Pek by Leigh Wade) unveil the devastating sequence of events which took place during the attack;

The Communications bunker was completely destroyed. Unbelievably the senior radio operator was knocked unconscious but not killed. As Sergeant First Class Leigh Wade put it; when he came to, he thought he was in hell. Although he had been hit in several places, Wade remained in the bunker waiting for the ground attack that would surely follow. Fortunately Sgt. Hull the Jr Radio man was in the team house at the time. The NVA were all over the place. Several Team members gathered together at the 81mm mortar pit and fought for their lives. Coming out of the team house on his way to the mortar pit, SFC Tom Weeks (A-246 Team Sergeant) zapped two enemy soldiers trying to rase the NVA flag.

"This is Lima Sierra, they're in the open coming across the runway!" One of the guys from the SOG unit was yelling through the radio hand set. (SOG had a launch site just outside Camp Dak Pek.)

"Stinger do you copy Lima Sierra? Enemy on the runway!" Lt. Alexander, the Team XO said talking to the Gun Ship overhead. (The Team Leader Captain Walters was off site with a company of Strikers, helping the besieged camp Dak Seang.)

Stinger Gun Ship Firing

The Stinger Gun Ship was one of the old C-119 cargo planes that had been converted for ground support. Shortly before this particular gun ship had been on station over Dak Seang. When the attack on Dak Peck started it was immediately diverted and flew up the Valley to aid the camp. Stingers' 40 mm cannon repeated firing. Flying the long axis of the runway, cutting the NVA's assault to pieces. There were wild cheers and congratulations on the radio. The SOG position called in the results.

"You creamed them good. They've pulled back to the eastern edge of the runway. Make your next pass just off the asphalt."

The next stupid mistake the NVA made, was to form a long line and remove items from the team's supply building. Observing this Ton Weeks fired the 81nn from a straight up position, with zero charges. (Because of the closeness) Tom managed to put seven HE rounds with delay fuses, right through the tin roof. The rounds exploded inside with excellent effect. What little remained of the supply building, caught on fire and burned to the ground, incinerating all the NVA who had took cover inside.

"Camp this is Ambush." It was SSG Wolf, the Team's Sr Medic with only ten Montagnards for company. In the confusion, everyone had forgotten about him being outside the camp. Wolf reported there were NVA wondering all around his position, but so far they didn't know he was there. He asked what he should do.

"Just lay low until it gets light." He was advised. "If we don't all get wiped out, try to come back in after sunup. If you stop hearing American voices from camp on the radio, contact the aircraft and ask for a chopper ex-filtration." This was excellent advice. If SSG Wolf and his Yards triad the move at night they wouldn't have made it. If the NVA didn't get them, the camp defenders would have. In a situation like this, everything that moves, will get shot. Remember Murphy's law, "Friendly Fire Isn't."

Jim Erickson the Jr Medic at Dak Pek spent the entire night in the Medical Bunker where he'd been sleeping when the attack started. The bunkers firing port covered the area around the front gate and supply building, where there had been so much enemy activity. The clickers (firing device) for the claymores covering that side of the hill were in the medical bunker. Jim fired them first, killing ten or fifteen NVA

A Montagnard nurse that worked for the team lived with her mother and father in a hutch on the other side if the hill. When the shooting started this gallant little gal, picked up an M-16 and made her way to the medical bunker. Approaching the bunker she noticed an NVA soldier on top of the bunker. Without hesitation, she sent him to meet his ancestors. How's that for dedication to duty?

Without much notice the Dak Peck Team was sent a radio message, reinforcements were on the way. The First Mike Force Reconnaissance Company, augmented by members of the Strike Force from Camp Plei Mrong (A-241) would be making an air assault,  but for security reasons, the message didn't tell where the LZ exact location. The team went to the trench lines to watch.

The flight of HU-1Bs was accompanied by Gun ships and Sky Raiders approached the besieged camp. The Sky Raiders entered the valley first, flying aggressively low and shooting up targets of opportunity. The slicks came in next, surrounded by gun ships, and without hesitation the slicks landed, all at once in formation on the runway. The choppers were only on the ground for a few seconds, then immediately took off as soon as the troops had unloaded. By the time the enemy gunners were able to react, the well trained Special Forces Mike Force, were moving through the camps wire and into the trenches. After a short briefing, it was agreed, the main priority was to retake the enemy-held portion of the camp.

By noon of April 14 the enemy was driven from the camp, but not without cost. Staff Sergeant Frier took an AK round through the pelvis. Sergeant Charlie Young was also wounded retaking Hill 203. Both Frier and Young were awarded the Silver Star for valor that day.

Slowly the NVA, unable to take Camp Dak Pek, withdrew across the border to Laos. However, they kept up sending a sporadic rocket or two to keep the camp alert. The remaining team members with replacements started to rebuild the camp.

Good By Dear Friend

I tried everything to get another extension and stay in Vietnam. My medical mission was far from being over. There was a lot more I wanted to accomplish. Unfortunately, all extension's requests were being disapproved The antiwar protest was in full swing back in the states. Our gutless leaders gave into the protesters and made the decision to back away from the not too popular war.

That's the past you say, and best be forgotten. I'll go along with that. But remember one thing; the Vietnam war could have been won. We beat the North Vietnamese every time we engaged them. The United States Military did not lose the war in Vietnam, we were denied victory. The gutless politicians, influence by the antiwar demonstrators, lost the war in Vietnam. Every time we had the enemy on the run, some lame brain in Washington gave the order to stop the bombing in the North or stop the pursuit of a fleeing enemy. Sending your Armed Forces to battle and then tying their hands, is in fact signing their death warrant.

Jim Erickson drove me to the airfield in Pleiku. Tren, my right arm accompanied us. The most difficult task I had leaving Vietnam was convincing Tren I wasn't coming back. Tren had seen me off at the airfield many times. When I went on extension, ordinary or emergency leaves, Tren Bren was there to say goodby. Each time I returned to Vietnam, Tren Bren was there to welcome me home.

"For sure Tren, I am not coming back to Vietnam."

"Bac Si always come back to Montagnard."

"Not this time my dear, dear, friend. Not this time. I went on and explained that soon all United States troops would be leaving Vietnam. The Vietnamese and Montagnards would have to go it alone.

"Bac Si, why American ask DEGA People to help fight North Vietnamese, now go home?" I had no answer for my friend. Nor did I have any answers for questions of my own; Why did we sacrifice so many American Lives, when as a nation we had no desire to win? Why did we leave so many MIA's and POW's without accountability? Why did we treat returning Vietnam Vets so poorly? There are many why's and so few answers . . .Why?

As my plane gained altitude I thought my heart would break. The big "WHY" filled my thoughts. If I claimed to love Tren like a son, why didn't I try to bring him back to the states with me? Am I as phoney as the politicians?

Although my extension was disapproved, I did manage to get an ITT (Inter Theater Transfer) to the Ryukyu Islands (Okinawa). I had twenty three days to report in my new assignment. I decided to hop on Flight 101 and head for the States to see my family and some old friends.

Chapter Six

Ryukyu Islands

I was looking forward to my assignment to Okinawa. While on leave I went to the local library and did an Area Study. I have done many Area Studies for the Army, this one was to be for me. My study revealed;

Okinawa is the largest and most important island of the Ryukyu Islands. The Ryukyu's are a chain of islands in the North Pacific Ocean that belong to Japan. Naha, the capital and largest city of the Ryukyu's, is on Okinawa.

Okinawa has a subtropical climate. The average daily temperature in Naha is 72 °F the year around. Rainfall averages about 83 inches yearly, most of it falling in the typhoon season, from April to October.

The people of Okinawa look much like the Japanese, but are shorter and have darker skin. Their language belongs to the Japanese language family, and most Okinawans also speak Japanese. Many Okinawans' live in small villages of red tile-roofed houses. Their main food is rice, but they also eat much pork. Most village people farm or fish for a living. Many wear traditional Japanese clothing--kimonos or cotton pants and jackets. Naha and other cities in Okinawa have modern buildings and traffic-choked streets. In the cities, many people wear Western-style clothing.

Okinawa was under Japanese control before World War II (1939-1945). Before then the Chinese also lay claim to the Ryukyu Islands, but China recognized Japan's rule in 1874. The United States captured Okinawa during the war and administered the island until 1972, when it was returned to Japanese control.

One of the bloodiest campaigns of World War II was fought on Okinawa between U.S. and Japanese troops. The Americans landed on the island on April 1, 1945, and conquered it in late June. During the fighting, more than 90 percent of the island's buildings were destroyed.

The United States built military bases on Okinawa after the Chinese Communists gained control of China in 1949 and the Korean War broke out in 1950.

Okinawa has had great military importance for the United States because it is located within easy flying distance of China, Japan, the Philippines, Taiwan, and Vietnam. The United States built air bases and other installations on the island and continued to maintain them even after having given up control of Okinawa to Japan.

During the 1950's to present time, many Okinawans demanded that the island be returned to Japanese rule. The United States returned the island to Japan in 1972. Under an agreement between the two nations, U.S. military bases remained on Okinawa.

Dover Air force Base has always been a good place to catch a military flight to the Far East. They had C-5A Jumbo Cargo Planes and KC-97 Refueling planes leaving daily. I rented a car and headed for Dover Delaware.

Talk about, luck of the Irish. There was an aircraft leaving one hour after I checked in. I headed for a phone booth to call Hertz Auto to cancel my rental. My rental contract allowed me to leave the rental at any airport I departed from.

"SFC McGinley." I turned to see who was addressing me. "I'm CSM John Lockart. I'm the CSM of Company C of the 1st Special Forces on Okinawa. You will be assigned to Charlie Company."

"Nice to meet you Sergeant Major. Are you booked on this flight?"

"No, it was full. I hope there is another one soon. I have to get back to Okie."

"Take my seat. I'm not in any hurry. I'll catch the next flight I insist, take my flight." CSM Lockart thanked me and departed for Okinawa.

"I got out of Dover the next day on a KC-97 Tanker (Refueling Plane). One hour into the flight I received an invitation to come to the cockpit.

"Do you remember me, Sergeant McGinley?" The pilot inquired.

"No Sir I don't think I do." He took off his sun glasses and turned so I could get a better look at his face.

"Lieutenant. Mimes, excuse me, I see its Captain. Mimes now. What are you doing flying a big bird like this?" The last time I saw the Captain was when he ran out of fuel and made a forced landing at Dak Seang. He was flying a Helicopter then. CPT. Mimes went on to tell his copilot the whole story. He emphasized the part about our team, radioing his headquarters in Pleiku that he was OK. And that we also told them the weather had the crew socked in. We explained to his higher headquarters, it would be a couple of days before the LT now CPT. Mimes could get back to his home base. Mimes's Co-Pilot enjoyed the story. Some might call the Team's radio message, "lying to higher Headquarters" But first they would have to interpret the term "socked in." It could have been a simple misunderstanding, maybe my glasses were dirty.

The truth is, helicopter pilots and crews were worked to their maximum in Vietnam. LT. Mimes and his crew, looked very tired after their forced landing. Nobody asked for my input but that didn't stop me. It was my medical opinion they needed a rest. There was no enemy activity in our area at the time. This made it an ideal spot for a little R & R (Rest and Recuperation).

We continued our chat for a few minutes. Then CPT Mimes told his Crew-Chief to show me around the aircraft. It's nice to have friends in high places. We were at 28.000 feet. The crew chief informed me the KC-97 was an Air Mobility Command advanced tanker and cargo aircraft designed to provide increased global mobility for U.S. armed forces. Although the KC-97 primary mission, is aerial refueling, it could transport up to 75 people and nearly one hundred seventy-thousand pounds (76,560 kilograms) of cargo for a distance of about 4,400 miles. I was surprised to find the aircraft receiving fuel from the Tanker, just maintained a given altitude. Then the KC-97 Boom-Man, actually flew the fueling boom to the waiting aircraft. I was given some hands on demonstration and enjoyed every minute.

We made a refueling stop in Alaska and then a non stop flight to Kadina Airport Okinawa. I seemed odd to me, a tanker stopping for gas. Maybe they were collecting green stamps or something.

A short, high speed taxi ride and I was at, 1st Special Forces Group (Abn) USARPAC Okinawa at, Samsong. The Staff Duty NCO informed me the Command Sergeant Major was on leave. He was headed back to Okie when his aircraft experienced mechanical problems. He added it might be a few days before he gets back.

"Who is your SGM?"

"Lockart. SGM John Lockart. Do you know him?"

"Yes, we have meet." I didn't bother telling him about me giving the CSM my seat on the now grounded aircraft. I always say, if they can't take a joke, the heck with them.

"I'm sitting in for the CSM. My name is Danny West, Command Sergeant Major type. We have been waiting for you McGinley (CSM's can get away with not using your rank when they address you) You're going to be assigned to C Company at Yamitan, then Detachment 110. That's my Detachment, welcome aboard." After an in-depth briefing we were joined by SFC Olney Knudtson.

Every time a Soldier is sent to a new unit they are assigned a sponsor of equivalent rank or higher to assist processing in the unit. SFC. Olney Knudtson was to be mine. I didn't have to ask where Olney was from. Ever notice how all those guys from Minnesota talk alike. Olney was from Mankato Minnesota. In spite of the fact SFC Knudtson was a career soldier with assignments all over the world to include two wars. Olney hung onto his Minnesota accent. SFC Olney Knudtson distinguished himself in Korea, by earning two Silver Stars. This Giant was a soldier's soldier.

"Give me your records Mac." I did. On our way out of the Headquarters Building, Olney handed my records to a clerk. "Take care of this processing Private."

"Sure thing SFC Knudtson. I'll be finished by Friday morning."

"Make it Tuesday next week. I have to show SFC McGinley Okinawa."

"I'm glad we got the extra time Olney. That should give me time to find a place to live."

"You'll get extra time to find a place after you're fully processed Mac. 1st Group is lenient on processing in or out. But don't let that fool you. There will be times we get so busy, you're lucky to get a day off for three months or more." I think I'm going to like Okie. 1st Group policy fits in with my life style. I like to play hard and work hard, never mixing one with the other.

"Mac do you mind if I make a stop."

"Not at all Olney, like you said we have plenty of time." We drove to the North end of the island. It didn't take long, Okinawa is only about 35 miles long by 20 miles wide. First Group is about mid-island on the East side of Okinawa.

Our destination was a bakery on the outskirts of Naha. We doubled parked. Olney darted into the Bakery and was back in the blink of an eye carrying a large cloth bag of what appeared to be coins. Maybe this guy is not from Minnesota. He is acting more like that Capone guy from Chicago. Is this what Olney meant by getting more time? My mind was eased when he explained the Bakery belonged to his wife's parents. Olney was a coin collector and purchased all American coins collected by the Bakery from American customers.

About halfway back to our starting point (1st Group Headquarters), we turned into a quaint Okinawa housing area. We stopped in the middle of the narrow street. We got out of the car and Olney handed his car keys to a young Okinawa boy.

"It's impossible to find a parking place in this neighborhood Mac. I pay that guy a few bucks a week. Not only does he find a parking place, my car is washed every day." We started our journey down a narrow path.

The path took us in and around beautiful oriental landscaped houses. It was hard to determine where one property started and the other ended. Land is at a premium in Okinawa. Houses are close together and built on small parcels of land. This will take a lot of getting used to, living this close to your neighbor.

Our journey ended when the narrow path disappeared at the edge of a large field with an ocean frontage. Setting in the middle of the field was a beautiful oriental house facing the North China Sea.

"This is my home Mac. How do you like it?"

"Like it! When are you moving?" Olney didn't get a chance to answer. We were greeted by an Okinawan lady in a beautiful Kimono. She was accompanied by her 14-month-old Daughter dressed in a matching little Kimono.

"Macson, this is my wife Niriko. Niriko, my friend Macson."

Then the greeting ceremony started. A lot of bowing intermixed with short Japanese phrases wishing everybody (including their ancestors) a long life and happiness. Then Olney's wife Niriko, pointing to large pillows on the floor, gave the command, Dozo (please). A couple more bows and we all sat down. Niriko's little daughter Rosanna, acting very grown up followed suit. Then the bamboo framed, rice paper-covered doors slid open. Kneeling with bowed head was another Kimono clad lady with a large tray of refreshments.

"Don't tell me you have maids Olney." I whispered.

"No, we don't. I think my wife is trying to fix you up with her friend."

First we were given a near frozen cloth to cool our face. Next a cup of hot green tea. Olney and I were then given a large glass of Japanese Beer. At that point the women left the room to prepare the food.

Most husbands wouldn't appreciate this formal greeting. Here the guy is coming home from work and had to go through all this ceremony. How about and old fashion lip-lock and a big hug followed by "I missed you honey. Of course I know better than that. Okinawans like most Orientalis, consider it poor taste, demonstrating their affection in public. I had to ask the question.

"Olney does this happen every day?"

"Heck no Mac. This is for your entertainment. I consider myself lucky when she throws me cold rice and a raw fish."

"Yea, that will be the day. I think I will tell Niriko what you said."

"Go ahead. I'll see to it you're called to report for duty at 06:00 tomorrow morning." I decided to keep my mouth shut.

The balance of the evening and the week end was extraordinary. My sponsor his family, and I became good friends, a friendship that would last a lifetime. Later I was honored when I was asked to be Rosanna's God Father.

Dan, Rosanna, Niriko

Time flew by, it was time to check in the unit I signed in 1st Special Forces Group, 8 June 1970. My first in-processing stop was to meet the Commander of Charlie Company. LTC Robert E. Furman was one of a kind, thank God. Apparently he came from a well to do family. He was one of those one dollar a year people you hear about. Since he had never been married, I suppose he could live on just one dollar a year. I love my country, but I charge more than one dollar a year for my talent. All in all he wasn't a bad commander, just a little excitable and had a tendency to exaggerate. Unfortunately I am unable to classify the LTC a Giant.

When I left the LTC's office, I was stopped by the company clerk who was putting a jump manifest together.

"Sargent McGinley, do you want a night jump, day jump or a ruff terrain jump. The choice is yours. We have open slots on all three.

"What's a Ruff Terrain jump?"

"We have a Ruff Terrain DZ at Camp Hardy. You know, large rocks, trees and all that good stuff."

"Put me down for a day jump. I have no problem hitting trees. I don't need to purposely jump into them." I was surprised to learn I had only an hour to make it to the airstrip, draw equipment and get on the manifest. No problem I thought, another hurry up and wait project the Army is famous for. Not this time, we were given a final briefing from the pilot on the tailgate of the waiting C-130.

"If you land on the runway, hurry and get off. I don't have a lot of gas. I'll need to land fast." Is this guy joking? Maybe I should have taken the Ruff Terrain jump.

We no sooner got airborne and we were over the ocean. Where in the heck is the DZ, I thought to myself. We were given the commands to stand up, check our equipment, stand in the door and before I knew it, GO!

After checking my canopy, I looked around for Yometon DZ. I was over water and could tell I was drifting toward shore. Still, didn't see the DZ. I saw the runway we took off from, a lot of towers with radio antennas, but no Drop Zone. It didn't matter, by this time I was slamming into the runway. No other word to describe my landing, I slammed into the runway. A brisk wind drug me across the runway into a drainage ditch. When I took my helmet off, blood was everywhere. A snap on the helmet liner came loose and gouged my scalp.

"We have enough gas for one more jump." The pilot announced. Sometime jumps are hard to come by. We welcomed the chance of a second jump. Who knows maybe this time I'll do it right.

"Are you hurt Sergeant? The piolet asked.

"No Sir, cut myself shaving."

Like the first jump we were in and out of the aircraft in no time flat. Unlike the first jump, there was no way I was going to get anywhere near the DZ (which I learned paralleled the runway). I was heading for the Radio Antenna field. I pulled on the right control line that took me to the north side of the antennas. This area had several rows' of small doghouse looking structures. I lined myself up with one of the rows and went in for the landing.

"Don't move, don't move!" A dog handler yelled, at the same time trying to control his assigned K-9. The buildings that looked like doghouse, were. My chosen landing area was a Guard Dog training site. I was highly ticked off at myself for messing up two jumps. The barking dogs didn't worry me. I was meaner than any chained K-9.

"Hold him back buster or I'll ram my fist down his mouth, grab his tail and pull him inside-out." Buster (the name I assigned to the handler) shortened the chain hold. I rigger rolled my parachute. I knew there would be a lot of harassment when I turned in my equipment.

Quite often the Okinawa Communist Workers Party would demonstrate against the American Occupation of their island. On more than one occasion LTC Furman called Charlie Company to alert, claiming gun shots were fired. He ordered us to wear flack jackets and steel pots. Wearing a flack jacket and replacing our Green Beret with a steel pot ticked off most Special Forces Operatives. Gun shots were never fired at any of their demonstrations.

Many times, large groups of demonstrators tried to break into our compound using long poles and chanting anti-American phrases. Always without success. The process of relieving the mob of their long poles, unfortunately caused a few injuries. After the ambulances removed the injured protesters, usually the demonstration broke up.

All Special Forces Groups are assigned areas of responsibility throughout the world. Each Group's training schedule reflects special training to meet the challenges of an assigned area. The 1st Group on Okinawa had mountainous area's with heavy snow in their area of responsibility. To meet this challenge, advance ski training was scheduled annually, climaxing with a Ski Trip to Aporoi Japan.

In addition to their speciality qualifications many SF Operatives are certified Army Sky Instructors. The 1ˢᵗ Group was fortunate they had MSG (soon to be SGM) Perkins as their Chief Sky Instructor. In addition to being a great instructor, MSG Perkins was a great story teller. Most of MSG Perkins students looked forward to his classroom instruction. They were guaranteed a wild story that Perkins swore was true.

One morning at formation MSG Perkins announced that he had made Sergeant Major. That in itself was not surprising, he deserved the promotion. What was surprising he had set up a celebration party in the mess hall with all the food and liquid of choice, you could consume. Why the surprise you might ask?; our new SGM was a tea toddler. No one had ever seen him have a drink that contained alcohol.

Our second surprise was when he held a mandatory Ski Class in preparation for the annual Sky Trip to Apori Japan. The class was conducted on a straw-covered sloop, in the hot Okinawa sun. Top that one if you can. SGM Perkins a veteran of the Korean War and the Vietnam war, was a credit to the US Army and Special Forces. This Giant was one of a kind.

Detachment 110 was located on a high hill, a short distance from SF Headquarters. That hill turned out to be a mountain, especially during our morning runs. Without exception we would leave the compound gate at 06:00 hours and run down the hill. We continued our run around a small village than back up the hill. By some magical process the hill turned into a mountain. I not only didn't like running, I wasn't very good at it. Something had to be done.

My solution was ingenious, if I have to say so myself. I hired a taxi cab to meet me in the village every morning. When no one was looking, I jumped into the taxi. Keeping a low profile as we passed the other runners. Near the gate, at the top of the hill (by the same magical process the mountain turned back into a hill) I would get out of the taxi and continue the run. That worked for a while, until one day a voice called my name.

"McGinley! How did you get in front of the team?" The voice belonged to SGM Dan West. Trying to come up with an answer, I came up with a question.

"SGM, how did you get so far in front of the team? SGM West was not the fastest runner in our team. He was faster than I, but no one else. It turned out the SGM would turn around as soon as the team entered the village. We had an undeclared gentleman agreement to keep our secrets to ourselves. My assignment to Detachment 110 was short lived.

Noho Shima

Special Force had several offshore missions going on at the same time. One was a Civic Action Mission on the island of Noho Shima. Noho Shima was a small island about twenty miles from Okinawa. The island was only accessible by chopper or boat. The small village on the island relied on the ocean for its main source of income and food. Small farming plots seemed to supply enough vegetables for its population. All other items had to be purchased at the village run store.

Each family had an account established at the store. Their account was settled each month when a resupply ship would visit to purchase their fish and resupply the store. Any money left over was divided evenly among the villagers. Surprisingly, the island had a modern brick building school, staffed with teachers from Japan.

All this and no water supply. The island relied on stored rain water and water shipped from Okinawa. Every house or building had a large baked clay container to capture the precious commodity.

The communal type living seemed to work for this small group. The villagers were a happy outgoing people ready to help each other with life's chores.

The team medic assigned to the Noho Shima Project received orders for Vietnam. I was to be his replacement. Sometimes I can't figure the Army out. I wanted to stay in Vietnam but couldn't, now less than a month later they are short medics' and pulling them off other assignments. Could it be, higher Army Headquarters, can't chew gum and walk at the same time?

I reported to the Hamby Boat Basin, where Special Forces kept their LCM (Landing Craft Medium). The LCM would be my transportation to Noho Shima.

"Hi Mac, I heard you were on island." Turning around I saw my old pal from Kontum, Al Lipson.

"Small world Al, how are you? Aren't you a little out of uniform pal?" I was referring to his black shorts, T-shirt and baseball cap.

"This is my duty uniform Mac. I'm the engineer on this LCM. Come aboard and I will show you around."

Al's tour was very enlightening. LCM's (Landing Craft Medium) were built during World War II for use in the Pacific Theater of Operation to retake islands lost to the Japanese and in Europe for the invasion of Normandy. I was impressed they were still operational today.

LCM (Landing Craft Mediem)

The 74 foot craft had a top speed of 12 knots with an unbelievable cargo load. The twin Screw, each one powered by two GMC 6-71 engines, made this water craft ideal for supporting Special Forces offshore projects. It also served for a recovery boat for water Parachute jumps and a platform for Scuba Diving operations.

"Come aboard Mac, we will be shoving off in about ten minutes." Didn't have to tell me twice, I was looking forward to the ride on the LCM. Down deep I have always had a little Navy in my soul. The LCM looked very large tied up at the pier. The further we got from shore, the smaller this Special Forces luxury liner looked.

The almost flat bottom design troubled me a little. The little I knew about water craft, reminded me that flat bottom boats tipped over easier than V-shaped craft. The sea was relatively calm so the thought didn't linger long.

Okinawa disappeared from the horizon. There was nothing but ocean in every direction. I asked to and was given permission to take the wheel. I was having a great time and rejected offers of relief from my duty as helmsman. Steering the LCM over the massive Pacific ocean gave me a great feeling of control. Far off in the distance, I thought I spotted land.

"Al! Is that Noho Shima?"

"No Mac, that's Goat Island. There's a story about that Island, want to hear it?"

"Sure."

Al went on to explain the most difficult problem early (15th thru 18th century) maritime trading expeditions had, was the limited quantities of fresh meat and potable water they could carry to feed their crews. The problem had a relatively simple salution. Someone came up with the idea of placing live animals on islands that had fresh water. The animal had to be a fast breeder and sturdy enough to be self sufficient. The mountain goat filled the requirements without question. The story about Goat Island amazed me. What a clever ides I thought to myself. Apparently, goats have a lot in common with rabbits.

As we got closer, we could see the hills were saturated with white mountain goats. Al also informed me that the Okinawa government has open season on goat hunting once a year. Surrounding islanders can shoot as many goats they need. Cruel you say? No, population control. About an hour past Goat Island our destination Noho Shima appeared on the horizon.

As we approached the island, I was relieved of my Helmsman duties. SFC Mike Modd (Not his real name) took over. Our first landing was at a concrete ramp the SF Team built for the island. After a cement mixer was unloaded, we backed off the ramp, made a circle and docked at a well-built pier, also built by the SF Team. Let me rename the procedure "docked." We rammed the pier.

Why we changed Helmsman, I don't know. I could have rammed the pier as well. I was soon to find out SFC Mike Modd had a reputation of ramming piers. A representative from the Noho Shima SF Team greeted me as I debarked the LCM.

"I'm Staff Sergeant Cooley. I'm the guy you are going to replace.

Jimmy C. Cooley was an outgoing and friendly person. He didn't hesitate to explain the excitement he felt about his next assignment in Vietnam. Knowing I had spent almost three years in Vietnam, there was no let up to Jim's questions about a SF Medic's duties in a combat environment. The quiz ended abruptly with;

"This is your new home Mac? We were standing in front of a tiled roofed Okinawan house. The three room house was in excellent condition. The roof was extended on one end to cover an open cooking area. It was obvious, the tenants were military, GI stuff all over the place.

Team House Noho Shima

"You can bunk here Mac." Jim pointed to an air mattress in the back room. It will be a couple of hours before the Team returns from the work site. Would you like to take a look at our village?"

"Sure." The village was less than a city block from the SF Team house. It was obvious, something was wrong. Most of the villagers had gathered in front of the largest thatch-roofed structure, I suspected was the village meeting hut. As we got closer, we could see the reason. Laying on a blanket was the lifeless body of a young girl. Habit compelled me to kneel and check the child's pulse. I found none.

"What happened here?" I asked. A silence fell over the gathering. Then an Oriental looking lad made his way over to where I was kneeling.

"I'm Sergeant First Class Bobroski, the Team Interpreter. This little girl was found on the beach this morning. Are you the new medic?

"Yes, I'm Sergeant McGinley. Who found the girl?

"This man." Bobroski answered, putting his hand on an old fisherman's shoulder.

"Did he try to revive her, give her CPR? A conversation started between our interpreter and the fishermen and then the whole crowed.

"Sergeant McGinley, they don't know what CPR is. I tried to explain, they just don't know what I'm talking about. Unbelievable I thought to myself. A group of people surrounded by water, making their living off the sea, and they don't know how to treat a drowning victim.

I walked over to the village meeting building. Looking through the door I saw a large room with a wall to wall grass woven mat covering the floor. Good I thought to myself, good place to hold a CPR class.

"Sergeant Bobroski, ask the Village Chief or whoever is in charge, if I can use this building to give CPR classes to the whole village." Bobroski relayed my request to the village elders. Their response almost knocked me off my feet.

"Sergeant Mac, they're pleased with your offer, but first they must get permission from the head Japanese School Master." The islanders did nothing without permission from Japan. The school staff was the eyes and ears of the Japanese government. I learned later they didn't like input from outsiders, especial Americans.

Speaking of the devil, coming down the dirt path leading to the school, was the school master. The Bamboo-Intel net is up and running. Nothing is done in the Orient without everybody knowing about it. I didn't understand Japanese at the time, but I could tell from the volume of the talk and the angry facial expressions, this little weasel was very upset. First he directed his anger to the Village Elders, then to Sergeant Bobroski. When he turned to me, I decided to cut him off at the pass.

I adjusted the volume of my voice, to his. I knew I could match or surpass his facial expressions. I had an advantage, I'm ugly to start with. I didn't let him get a word in, I went on the attack.

Instructing Sergeant Bobroski to interpret every word; I emphasized how shocked I was finding out the islanders didn't know CPR. I told him I didn't blame the villagers, I blamed him and his teaching staff. My final statement was there would be a CPR class in one hour. He and his staff were invited to attend, but with then or without, the class would take place. I ended my declaration by removing the tarpaulin covering the young victim, and announcing;

"This will never happen again."

I headed for the meeting area. I wasn't surprised when the room filled with villagers. I was surprised how eager they were to learn. The enthusiasm they demonstrated on the hands on portion of the class, was on par with the best. The biggest surprise of all was when a school teacher observer, shook my hand and thanked me after the class.

On the walk back to the Team House I learned a lot about our Team Interrupter. Sergeant First Class Mizubo Bobroski was the son of a Special Forces Operative and his mother was from Okinawa. Mizubo Bobroski was a career soldier with a splendid war record from Vietnam. His command of the Japanese language was an unparallel factor contributing to the success of the Special Forces mission on Noho Shima.

As we waited for the SF Team to return from the project sight, Sergeants Cooley and Bobroski brought me up to speed on the Teams mission. I learned the Team was given a Civic Action project for the island of Noho Shima The Special Forces team was to establish a fresh water storage tank on top of a steep hill, then pipe the water to the school and village below. When completed, the dependance on expensive bottled water and rain water storage, would be a thing of the past. Sergeant Cooley excused himself and went to the cooking area.

The team members took turns cooking the evening meal. They were in for a surprise when it became my turn. I truly think my cooking abilities could be classifies as Un-American.

The first to arrive from the work site was the Team Leader, 2ⁿᵈ LT Mallard (Mallard is not his real name). His opening statement started us off on the wrong foot.

"I understand you started quite a disturbance in the village this afternoon. That's a poor way to start a new assignment. I will make decisions on your activities from this point on." I interrupted this young Lieutenant with the Napoleon complex.

"Talking about poor, we are getting off to a poor start LT. I have problems with people who engage their mouth before their brain. The medical mission of this Team or any other Team I'm assigned to is my responsibility. I assume that responsibility without hesitation. My mission will not be diluted by any who think they know it all. Lieutenant. If you have a problem with that, I suggest you take this matter to the Group Commander."

The surprised and sad look on the LT's face, it almost made me feel sorry for him. The loud mouth Lieutenant walked away without muttering a word.

Next to arrive was the Team Sergeant MSG Charles L. Harper and the team Engineer, SFC Frederick W Henry. I knew MSG Harper. Our paths crossed in Vietnam. I think he was with one of the projects, probably FOB-2. Harper introduced me to SFC Henry. He continued his introduction when SFC's Harold E. Hillard, Dudley L. Nutter, and Billie Mckeithe arrived at the Team House. All had different MOS's (job titles) and were borrowed from other Teams. They were TDY (Temporary Duty Assignment) for this project, and would return to their assigned Team's at project end. It didn't matter what their Primary MOS was, for this assignment, all were filling the role of assistant engineers. Cross training makes this, out of MOS assignments possible and is used quite often throughout Special Forces.

The team got along very well with each other. To the man, they had the same opinion as I, about the Lieutenant. The LT had a thing going with one of the Japanese School Teachers. This widened the gap between the head School Master and the American Team. The fraternization caused a lot of problems with the Islanders. To start with the Islanders didn't like the tight hold Japan had on their island. An American playing Footsie with a teacher, had them thinking we were favoring the Japanese over them. This could put the project in jeopardy, at least the public relation portion of the project.

Apparently feeling pressure from the Team, our young Lieutenant left the Island. He hired a small fishing boat to take him back to Okinawa. Rumor had it the Lieutenant quit Special Forces and went back to a conventional unit. I honestly hope he got a unit that thought 2nd LT's were God. Of course, if our 2nd Lieutenants was God, he wouldn't have needed a fishing boat for transportation, he could have walked on water. Fortunately most Lieutenant are not know it all's. Most realize they have a lot to learn. Learning is accomplished by listening. This process develops great Officers.

With the opposition off the island, things really soothed out. Most of my time was spent on preventive medicine. I showed the villagers how to build, burn out sumps to manage household and fish cleaning wasteand a Septic Systems to manage human waste. I initiated a rat control program that had positive results from the start.

We attached (via a copper tube)a five-gallon container filled with pesticide to the exhaust manifold of an old WWII jeep. Once a week we drove the jeep around the village. The dense fog produced when the pesticide hit the Jeep's hot manifold, kept the mosquito and fly problem under control. Another Septic Systems and a long, ceramic tiled, hand washing sink was also built at the school.

Hand Washing Area

At our team house I had an Okanagan carpenter build bamboo racks to raise our sleeping bags off the floor. The sleeping racks also had a shelf to store our personal items. The floor space we gained made our hut look twice the size. We no longer had to trip over duffel-bags and other junk. To add finishing touches, I ordered mosquito nets and racks from our supply depot on Okinawa. With money from our team fund I hired a house keeper who also cooked our evening meal. That was probably the most important PM measure I did. My cooking could make a person very ill.

I spent about half of my time helping the Team on the project. As our relationship improved, the village involvement in our water storage project increased. At times we had too many workers. We utilized the workforce by adding to the overall project. An example, we graded the narrow path leading to the project. When we finished, it was close to being a road. Day by day the workforce became closer together. The language barrier was no problem. Smiles and laughter are understood world wide.

The LCM crew made frequent trips to Noho Shima, bringing cement, gravel and other material needed to complete the project. On one trip they brought a Dump Truck to move the cement mixer and supplies, from the beach to the work sight. The LCM couldn't get close to shore. They off loaded the dump truck in about knee deep water. Normally that wouldn't have been a problem. This time the truck stalled and all efforts to restate the vehicle failed.

Compounding the problem, it was getting close to the time the tide would be coming in. Then like the Lone Ranger, Sergeant Bobroski showed up with about 30 school kids and a long rope. I don't know if they were getting a kick out of our dilemma or just glade to be out of school. Whatever, they were laughing and having one heck of a time. Would you believe it, when the

truck was on shore, it started as though nothing was ever wrong. The truck kicked the project into high gear. The cement, gravel and sand was moved to the project site with ease. Before its arrival, the team was forced to use an old horse and dilapidated wagon for this monumental task.

With the reinforcement rods in place, the forms readied, it was cement mixing time. Anyone that has ever worked with cement, will agree that calling any work involving cement, "back breaking." is right on target. We were fortunate having a cement mixer. Unfortunately, the mixed product had to be carried up a ladder, then poured into the form, bucket by bucket. Once you start pouring cement, it's important to keep pouring. This enables the cement to bind together as a single unit. To pour section by section, opens the door to possible leaking. With that in mind we started our back breaking work at 05:00 hours. At 22:30 (10:30) the last bucket of cement was powered. Hot, dirty, and extremely tired, we let go with a half-hearted cheer.

To celebrate the end of the project, the villagers had a feast set up at the bottom on the reservoir. We chow-downed like there was no tomorrow. Of course there was also Japanese Sake and beer, consumed with the same enthusiasm. The get together lasted until 03:00, then we headed back to our quarters.

Green Beret II

Several members of the LCM crew were due to rotate back to the States. Because of my injury, I was assigned to the LCM (with help of my friend Lipson) as medic / navigator. The only navigation experience I had was associated with flying. That bothered me for a while. Then I learned there was not much difference navigating a boat or airplane, if the distance you were traveling was less than seven hundred miles. Any mistake made could be corrected visually.

Roof Top

Front Garden

My apartment was close to Hamby Boat Basin, the mooring location of the LCM. I could see the Boat Basin from the roof of my second story apartment. Talk about living high on the hog. I was fortunate finding a large second floor apartment. The four room apartment was one of a kind. It had a covered porch on three sides. The flat roof with its walled sides was designed for outside activities. I built a weather-proof bar and hung Japanese lanterns around the perimeter. When tables and chair were added, it looked like a night club. The Chief of Police owned the building and lived on the first floor. When I was off island, I didn't have to worry about anybody stealing my property. My landlord would have shot them.

When I threw a party, and I threw several, I always invited the Chief. That took care of anybody calling the police if the parties got a little wild, and they did. All my parties were held on the flat roof of my building, over looking the North China Sea. The colorful Japanese lanterns, sound of the ocean crashing against the coral rocks and the oriental music, must have excited the minds of the Special Forces attendees. Without fail, the parties ended with repelling down the two story wall, to the rocks below, then diving into the ocean for a midnight swim. Just thinking about those foolhardy activities today, gives me a slight chill.

Unlike most assignments on Okie, we didn't get much time off. When we were not on a support mission, the Group Commander keep us busy helping with his public relations projects. All our week ends were spent entertaining different groups.

We took the Boy Scouts out on all day fishing trips. When they got bored with fishing, we put them on paint chipping details. Paint chipping and painting are chores' without end. That salt water plays havoc on a metal boat. For their help we let them take turns at the wheel. They seemed to enjoy being on the LCM.

Special forces also had a V-bottom boat ("Green Beret II') in dry dock at Naha Port. For some reason SFC Modd didn't want to bring it back in service. The 65 foot craft had a 24-ton cargo area that could was convertible to a 18-bunk sleeping area. The T-type craft was powered with a Catapillor 300 HP Engine, equipped with Radar, two generators, and 100 Gal (Gas) Day tank that would last three hours. In addition it had a six-bunk crew's quarters with galley, and large cabin behind the wheel house. Two heads, one on Port side and the other on Starboard. The Starboard Head was converted to a radio room. This craft was ideal for Special Forces operations.

Green Beret III

Enter SFC Alvin Lipson. Al kept pressuring Group Headquarters to bring the Green Beret II back into service. Al had an Electrical Engineering Degree and was more than qualified to keep this craft running. My pal Lipson finally convinced Group.

Over Mood's objection the Green Beret II was ordered back into service. Al spent more than three weeks working with the Nautical Engineers at Naha Port preparing the craft for launch. Operating this craft called for a Coast Guard Boat Licence. Both Al and I took their course and earned a Coast Guard Licence for an ocean going craft, 65 Ton or less.

The Green Beret II expanded our mission capabilities. We now could reach more distant areas and rough seas became less important. The nautical engineers at Naha Port made a statement about the Green Beret II that impressed me;

"If the Green Beret ever sunk, it wouldn't be because of rough seas, it would be crew failure." The statement, would not only remain in the back of my mind, it would influence decisions that would save seven lives.

We could transport two A-Teams and their equipment. Unlike the LCM we were armed and could do battle if need be. Our arms-room contained a 50, and two 30 caliber machine guns. We had an 81-mm mortar, six M16 rifles, and one 30-caliber sniper rifle with scope. We were loaded for bear. To train the crew and put the GB-II through her shake down check we visited all the Islands around Okie.

Al Lipson had a Honda Trail 50 he took on all trips. While most of the crew spent their time fishing, Al explored the islands by bike. I don't know how he did it, but Al talked me into buying a Trail 50. On all our trips we took the two Hondas with us.

Hnda Trail 70's ready to load

Taking a motorcycle aboard ship to explore islands is no great story in its self. Factor in the fact that I have never been on a motorcycle, never mind riding one, you just might have a story that will raise the hair on the back of your neck. Assuming of course, you have hair.

I didn't bother learning to ride the Honda on Okie. I decided to wait until we were on some deserted island. Ishigaki island filled the bill. We off loaded the Hondas and Al took off like a bolt of lightning, headed up a very steep hill.

"What are you waiting for Mac? Come on up." My pal yelled down.

I'll show him, I thought to myself. I put the bike in first gear with my left foot and turned the handle-grip throttle, away I went. I didn't go up the hill, I went up in the air. That little Trail 70 had a lot of power.

On the way down, I got ahead of the bike. I landed hard and the Honda landed on top of me. There I was laying on my back, holding on to both handle grips. The Honda still running, with its wheels pointing to the sky. What do I do now was my only thought? Didn't have many options. I threw the bike as far as I could. That worked, the machine wasn't on top of me anymore, but I wasn't out of harms way. The handle grip that was also the throttle, imbedded into the mud. The bike spun around and the hot manifold burned my left leg. All this time my pal Al almost split a gut laughing. My, "I'll show him" thought, was still with me.

I got back on the Honda and started up the steep incline. A little wobbly, but I didn't do to badly. As I got closer to Al, I saw a strange look on his face. In fact the look, in addition to being strange was a look of fear. For some reason, (I didn't put on the brakes) my motor died and I came to an abrupt stop. Looking down I saw the ocean crashing against the rocks at the bottom of the three hundred foot cliff, I almost went over. I am sure my facial expressions matched Al's. After a few tries' I became more efficient and started enjoying, off trail riding.

Of course the Commanders' public relation program not only continues, it expanded. Everyone and his brother wanted a ride on our new toy. Now all this took place on week ends, making any time off an impossibility.

Unfortunately, not all weekend outings were enjoyable. One in particular comes to mind. We had to take eleven school teachers out for a weekend voyage. There were five of us and eleven beautiful bikini clad gals. Like they say, rough job, but somebody had to do it. The thing's Special Forces are called on to do, are above and beyond

the call of duty. Being
professional soldiers, we
performed this most difficult
mission with enthusiasm and most
important, without grumbling.

Above and Beyond the call of duty

The second teachers'
outing was put on hold. We
received orders to pick up an A-
Team on Miyako Island. Miyako
was a good six hundred-plus
miles from Okinawa the furthest
mission to date. The mission was classified. To conceal our true
destination, we were to head for Ishigaki, Island. Spend the night on
Ishigaki, then head for our true destination at first light. Simple enough
plan we all thought. Little did we know the disaster that would unfold.

We left Hamby Boat Basin at 06:30 and headed straight to
Ishigaki Island a trip we made several times. As soon as we cleared
port, SFC's Dudly Nutter and Harold Hillard attached their fishing lines
to the ship's outrigger. A routine they followed on every trip. I'll bet
they dream about fishing. Of course everyone on the boat took a turn
at deep sea fishing. That is everybody except me. I got no pleasure
out of fishing. Drowning worms is not my idea of a good time.
However after the fish were cleaned, seasoned and slightly sprinkled
with lemon juice, wrapped in foil and placed on a waiting charcoal fire;
I would be the first in line.

Most of our meals aboard the
Green Beret II consisted of raw (Sushi or
Sashimi) fish. Don't turn up your nose. If
you have never tasted, Magurd (Red
Tuna), Taco (Octopus), or Wahoo
Sawada (white fish), you are in for a treat
of your life. Any of the fish mentioned,
placed on top of a ball of white rice held
together with a seaweed rapper is very
appetizing,. Dipping these bundles of
nourishment in a small bowel containing,
Soy Sauce seasoned with Chinese Green
(hot) Mastered, will excite your taste buds
and give you a dining experience of your

Al with Wao Fish

life. The trick here is to forget the words "raw fish," they would turn anybody off. I'm getting hungry just thinking about it.

We left Ishigaki Island before sunup and headed for Miyako. Looking up I saw SFC Mood on top of the wheel house. At first I thought he was doing some sort of exercise. First he would point at the rising sun. Then he would point to the wide-open sea. He did this a couple of times before it dawned on me. This guy doesn't have the slightest idea where he is going.

"Mike come on down here, we need to talk."

"I'll be down in a minute, I'm plotting our course." My suspicion was confirmed.

"I need to talk to you now Mike, and I mean right now. Mike must have detected the urgency of my request in the tone of my voice. He joined me at the ship's bow.

"Did I understand you to say you were plotting our course?" He answered in the affirmative. From that point on, I didn't let him get a word in. I emphasized the fact you can't plot a course by drawing an imaginary line on the ocean surface. I pointed out that we had a complete set of nautical charts in the wheel house. In addition to the charts, we had a gyroscope compass and a functional radar. I interrupted my lecture with a question;

"Who taught you how to navigate Mood?"

"My daddy." He answered in his strong Louisiana accent. All of us have heard about his daddy and his shrimp boats. And we heard it over and over again. I continued my lecture by telling Mood, I didn't want to embarrass him in front of the crew. This conversation was between him and me. But from this point on, he was no longer the Green Beret's navigator, I was taking the job. After all on paper, I was listed as the Green Beret's medic / navigator.

I had a meeting with Al Lipson in our multipurpose cabin. Using triangulation we located our position on the chart. From that point we plotted our course to Miyako Island. As I stated before, if the distance you plan to cover is less than seven hundred miles, the procedures used to plot a course for an aircraft, will work on plotting a course for a ship. I was counting on that theory, as I applied my piloting navigation skills to our mission. If we miscalculated and missed Miyako, we would enter the hostile waters of China.

"Mac, take a look in the cargo area. I have a surprise for the crew." Now what is Mood up to, I thought as I opened the forward cargo hatch.

I switched on the light and started down the ladder. Halfway down I saw our surprise. Sitting on a top bunk was a thirteen to fifteen-year-old Okinawan girl. The little respect I had left for Mood, ended with my discovery. Don't get me wrong. I am not, and do not claim to be a puritan. In addition I don't dictate morals or tell a person how to live. But if a person is married, with or without children, and I know their family, I don't want to hear about their extra marital activities. Mood was married to a great lady and had two beautiful children. To make matters worse, his family was on Okinawa.

I was furious and almost ran up the ladder. I had Al Lipson gather the crew. Standing on the cargo hatch, I started my lecture. This time I didn't care if I embarrassed Mood in front of the crew. I told the crew what I had found. I also told them that transporting women on international waters for immoral purposes is against International Law. I informed them that my first thought was to return the girl to Ishigaki. That would put the mission behind schedule. I informed them we will continue on to Miyako. The girl will be returned to her island on the way back. I ended our meeting with;

"Being the ranking NCO of this crew, I put you all on notice. Any person that I see fraternizing with our under age guest will be recommended for court martial." This was a difficult thing to say. Most of the crew were good soldiers. I made an entry in the ships log; "Stowaway found on board. Will return said person to Ishigaki on our return trip."

The balance of our voyage was uneventful. The navigation theory was working. When we spotted Miyako on the horizon, we had to make a slight correction in our heading.

It was at this point things started to fall apart. The Team we were to pick up, was picked up by the Navy. They left one team member and their gear on Miyako, to meet us. The weather was deteriorating rapidly. It was Typhoon Season and a large one was beginning to form. We refueled, picked up our passenger and his equipment, then headed back to Okinawa, via Ishigaki Island.

Our new passenger wasn't very talkative which came as no surprise. It was none of our businesses to know what he and his team were up to. As the military call it, "Need to Know," we didn't have a Need to Know. Special Forces live by that simple phrase. He didn't volunteer any information and we knew better than to ask. But that didn't stop me from wondering. The equipment our passenger brought aboard told part of the story. The three RB 17's (rubber assault boats) and more than the usual radio equipment the average A-Team would carry, set the stage for clandestine thinking. The only land mass near Miyako Island was China. That really got my devious mind working. I put my thinking on hold. I didn't have "Need to Know"

Typhoon

By the time we got to Ishigaki, the sea was very rough. After we unloaded our stowaway, we entertained the thought of waiting out the storm at Ishigaki. Although the harbor was protected by a sea wall, we were not certain the Green Beret could be protected from the approaching storm. We had no other choice, we headed for Okinawa. Halfway to Okie we radioed for a storm update. We were particularly interested in the exact time the Typhoon was to hit the main island.

The answer was not the one we wonted. There was no way we could beat the Typhoon. When Al asked to talk to the head engineer, the one that he worked with getting the Green Beret ready for launch, he was surprised to find that he was in the radio shack. He had been waiting for us and one other ship to report in. Al relayed the engineer's message to us.

"Rig the ship for extreme weather, take the Typhoon head on."

Al Lipson checked the engin and made sure the day tank was full. Mood, Nutter and Hillard made sure all hatches were tied down. The three rigged a lifeline the length of the boat. If anyone had to be on deck for whatever reason, the lifeline was there to give them something to grab, preventing them from being washed overboard. Our passenger was given a life jackets and assigned a bunk in the crew's cabin. I never did explain our stowaway story to our new guest. Didn't figure he had a "Need to Know."

The best qualified to be on the wheel, storm or no storm was SFC Al Lipson. That was not to be. Al was needed to keep the engin running and maintaining radio contact with Naha Port Authority. That left the helmsman job to me. The rest of the crew went to the crew's quarters at the bow of the ship. All wearing a life jacket and carrying a second one for additional buoyancy, if needed. And in the crew's quarters they stayed the rest of the long, long night. The only time we saw them was when they were forced to come topside to barf. To the man, they were seasick. I saved Mood's life on one of his many trips to the barfing rail. I controlled my thought of reaching down from the wheelhouse, and kicking him overboard.

"If the Green Beret ever sunk, it wouldn't be because of rough seas, it would be crew failure." The Marine Engineers's statement was on my mind as I spun the wheel to the left, heading into the Typhoon.

The swells were large, but not as hard to manage as I imagined. It was like riding a roller coaster. Up one side and down the other. For the most part, they were coming from the same direction. On occasion, I had to spin the wheel to catch a wave dead center. I never lost the feeling of being in control. I was not only getting the hang of maneuvering the craft in rough water, I was beginning to enjoy it.

Then without warning, there it was. A mountain of water, heading straight for us. I didn't have time to be afraid. There would be plenty of time later for fear, at least I hoped there would be.

"Oh Lord!"
Didn't have time for the rest of the prayer. By
this time he knew, that when I call upon him, I'm in trouble.

We headed up at what seemed to be a forty-five-degree angle. Nearing the top, the wave broke and we had thirty-five feet of white water over the wheel house. In spite of the ocean's loud noise, we could hear the propeller spinning in the air, as we went over the top. Then down the other side of this out of control roller coaster. When we hit bottom, the screw dug into the rough water, restoring maximum control. Our 300 horse power engin. was up and ready for the fight. By the third mountainous wave, I was no longer a new-be, storm helmsman. I was up to the challenge and in fact looked forward to the next wave. I found myself talking to the storm;

"Is that all you got to offer?" My conversation with the storm, was not generated by lack of fear. It was generated because of fear. I don't know if that makes sense or not. It's one of those, you have to be there to fully understand.

The main surge of the storm lasted about three hours. After that, although very rough, the treacherous ocean was manageable. Al and I had just brought this magnificent craft through weather, that some people, who make their living on the sea, never experience.

We were a great team Al and I, each one depending on the other. While I navigated the craft trough the storm, Al kept the engin working at its maximum potential. Maintaining the craft's balance by switching, back and forth, from the right fuel tank then the left. Without that balanced buoyancy we wouldn't have made through the Typhoon.

We could see a burning ship far on the horizon. The law of the sea is to go to the aid of any ship in distress. We were already heading in the direction of the troubled ship. I had doubts about what assistance we could render. We were having one heck of a time keeping our craft afloat. We maintained our heading.

Al got on the radio to notify Naha Port of the situation. He was told us to stand by. In a very short time they came back, notifying us the Coast Guard was on their way to assist the troubled ship. Again Naha asked us to maintain our heading and stand by for further transmission. Within an hour, Naha radioed, back. We were thanked for our assistance and told the Typhoon was past Okie and it was safe for us to head home. I was relieved. I really don't know what we could have done to help the troubled ship. I knew we would have come up with something, but what? With a 180-degree turn we headed back to Okinawa.

What a beautiful sunrise. The sun's golden ways reflected on the calm water. It was hard to visualize, that just a few hours ago, the calm water was a raging, life threatening, fury. Now its surface was as smooth as glass. I know I only call on God when I'm in trouble. But one thing I never forget to do is thank him. You can be assured, I thanked him for his performance last night.

Al and I just looked at each other. We didn't need any words of praise to be spoken. We knew, each of us had performed well during the perilous night. To this day, when we reflect on this adventure, a sense of pride is shared by both of us.

Heads started to pop up from the Crew's quarter's hatch. It reminded me of gophers peeping out of their holes to see if it was safe to come out. They seemed to have a sense of guilt about it. If that was true, they shouldn't have. There was nothing they could have done to help us through the storm. None of them could have done Al Lipson's job. The probability of me giving the helmsman job to anyone, was nonexistent. The only guilt they should have had, was not offering to help. Maybe they didn't think we would have refused their help. The only thing I knew for sure, I wouldn't serve with any of them again.

I was packing my personal gear in my car when the disturbance broke out. I ran into the boat house to see what the trouble was all about. Al was giving Mood a piece of his mind. The fact that Mood was twice Al's size didn't matter. Al Lipson was hot, he was ready for battle, ready to climb Mood's frame. I got between them, and was successful in keeping them apart. I didn't have to ask what the problem was. Mood's actions and lack of action on this mission more than justified Lipson's anger. Like myself this would be Al's last trip on the Green Beret II. In fact it would be the last trip for the Green Beret. She stayed tied to the pier for a few weeks, then sometime in December put back in Dry-Dock.

Our passenger needed a ride to Naha Port. All our Crew Members were married and wanted to get back to their families. There was no rush for me to get home, my family was in Thailand. I volunteered l my services and drove our guest to Naha Port. This Guy seemed to know the Port area well. He directed me straight to the Sea King's mooring.

The Sea King was one of the two submarines used to support 1st Special Forces. Most Special Forces operatives assigned to Okinawa, spent many hours training on this unique vessel. Wet Launch and Dry Launch were the focus of the training. A Wet Launch is when the craft is submerged

Wet Launch Training

and the SF Team is in a Lock-out Chamber. The Sub, submerges and the chamber is filled with water. The Team would leave the chamber through an opened hatch.

A Dry Launch is when a Team is on a Rubber Raft on the deck of the Sub. As the craft submerges slowly, the Team paddles away to start their mission.

The amount of activity around the Sub indicated, the Sub wasn't in Port very long. I got the impression, this might have been the second missing craft Naha was referring to we radioed them during the storm. The size of the Sub answered the question, why we picked up the Team's Equipment. I didn't ask any questions. I didn't have a "Need to Know"

Rumors and More Rumors

About this time a lot of activity in the Far East was taking place. When you have activity, you are sure to have rumors, and we had plenty to go around. Some were saying we were about to invade North Vietnam. As the rumors spread they grew in scope. We were not only going to invade North Vietnam, we were going to gather our forces in Thailand. From Thailand, they were to hit North Vietnam through Laos. At the same time, the Navy would put troops ashore by sea. It sounded like a great plan to me. I had always been in favor of hitting the North. But alas, it was just a rumor.

In late November, the State Department had a news release stating in fact, Special Forces conducted a POW rescue attempt in North Vietnam. To this day I wonder if our rumors were associated with that event. I sure hope not, that would suggest a possible security leak. The Raid on Son Tay Prison Camp came as no surprise to me. It was the kind of mission Special Forces is trained for. I was pleased to find out ten of the participants were Giants" that I had served within Vietnam. It made me feel a little guilty. Here I was, fat-caten it on Okinawa.

Operation Red Hat

Chemical weapons have been stored on Okinawa since World War II. The problem was the Okinawans didn't know about it. When they found out, they were very upset. The anti-American protest was put into high gear. "Americans Go Home" was their battle cry

Sometimes I don't understand our decision makers. We spend billions of dollers pacifying and winning the hearts and minds of people. Then with one dumb act, destroy any good we might have created. Are they really that dumb? Or is it, they just don't give a dam? It's time for you and me, to watch and scrutinize the records of people we vote for. Time to forget political party affiliation. The only question we need ask, "Is this person good for America?" This is not a political statement folks. This is a statement of concern.

The balance of my assignment on Okinawa was spent on the Nerve Gas Project. Special Forces was given the task of securing the removal of all chemical weapons. At the time there were many people in this world, hoping America would have a problem removing this hazardous material. For that reason, extreme measures had to be taken.

A new road had to be built, extending from the storage site, directly to Military Shipping Port at the most southern portion of the island. The road had a ten-foot high, chain-link fence on both sides. The warning was posted and order was given, "Shoot on Sight." Anyone venturing on that road, would not get a warning. They would have been "Shot on Site."

Armed, Special Forces troops were stationed along the rout, on every truck, on the pier, and on the ships that would transport the hazardous material. They stood at the ready, round in chamber, ready to fire. Our Scuba Teams were constantly monitoring the waters under and around the ships. We knew the seriousness of our mission and would have reacted to any threat.

The USNS Sealift and USNS Comet, were assigned the mission to transport the hazardous material. The Army leased 41 acres on Johnston Atoll in 1971 to store 1,000 Ton Nerve Gas chemical weapons. The operation was called Red Hat.

My assignment to Okinawa was almost over. I tried everything I could think of to be assigned to Thailand. Because of Vietnam shutting down there was, for the first time, an overage of Special Forces Medic's in the Far East. There was no way I was going to be assigned to Thailand. It would have been great, to be stationed near my family.

I left Okinawa on 14 December 1971for my new assignment with the 10th Special Forces Group (Airborne), 1st Special Forces Fort Devens Massachusetts. I had a twenty day delay in route and decided to spend it in Thailand. I knew it would be a long time before I would get a chance to see my family again.

I have been asked many times, why I didn't bring my family to the United States. The answer was simple, but dumb. My government didn't recognize our marriage.

Chome and I were married in a Buddhist Temple. The Government like most people, don't understand, that Buddhism is more of a philosophy than a religion. Chome was raised as a Catholic. Although she doesn't go to the Catholic Church, Chome believes in God and the teachings of the bible. A few years ago my sister gave Chome, a Kings version of the bible, translated into Thai. My wife reads that precious gift daily. It would be hard to find a person who lives the life they profess, any better than this great lady, my wife, Chome. I rate the legitimacy of my marriage with any.

Leaving Bangkok this time was more difficult than any of our previous goodby's. Unlike the 5th and 1st Special Forces, who's area of responsibility was the Far East. The 10th SF's area was Europe. This ensured my next visit to Thailand would be far in the future.

I had mixed emotions leaving Thailand. I was the saddest guy on the planet, when I boarded the aircraft for the US. At the same time, I was looking forward to my assignment at Devens. Many of my friends from Vietnam and Okinawa were assigned to the 10th. It was like going home.

Chapter Seven

10th Special Forces Group

Ft Devens Massachusetts

Before I start my experience with the 10th Special Forces Group, it is only fitting, I start with a brief History of this Giant packed organization.

10th Special Forces History

During August 1956, six Special Forces Operational "A" Detachments of the 10th Special Forces Group (Airborne) stationed at Flint Kaserne in Bad Toelz, West Germany, were relocated to West Berlin under the **7761 Army Unit** (also known subsequently as **39th SFOD**) and embedded within Headquarters and Headquarters Company, 6th Infantry Regiment, Regimental Headquarters. Their mission was "stay behind" Unconventional Warfare.

Each team at that time consisted of one Master Sergeant and five team members. Overall Officer in charge of the group was a major, assisted by a Captain. On 1 September 1956, the group moved officially to the top floor of building 1000B at McNair Barracks, West Berlin, under the name of **Security Platoon**, Regimental Headquarters, 6th Infantry Regiment.

In April 1958, the unit found its final home in Building 904, Section 2, at Andrews Barracks, West Berlin, and was assigned to HDQ Company, US Army Garrison Berlin with a new name **Detachment "A"** (Det A). In April 1962, Detachment "A" was separated from the Garrison and became **Detachment "A,"** **Berlin Brigade,** US ARMY Europe (USAREUR), which it remained until its deactivation on 30 December 1984.

As the 10th Group became established in Germany, a new item of headgear, the green beret, appeared in rapidly increasing numbers. The Group Commander, Colonel Eckman, authorized the wear of the beret and it became Group policy in 1954. By 1955, every Special Forces soldier in Germany was wearing the Green Beret as a permanent part of his uniform. Department of the Army did not, however, recognize the headgear.

Captain Roger Pezzelle designed the silver Trojan Horse badge for wear on the beret. It remained the unofficial badge until 1962, when the Department of the Army authorized the official Distinguished Unit Insignia and green cloth "flash" which is worn today.

Differences in mission, organization, manning, and modus operandi set the 10th Special Forces apart from conventional Army units. Notable differences in other external symbols began to appear. The 10th Group soldiers carried the mountain rucksack rather than the standard field pack. Likewise, the men soon did away with spit-shined jump boots, opting instead for mountain boots, which was a more practical field boot for the European climate. Mountain boots became a trademark of the 10th Special Forces Group.

The original "A" Detachment was called a **FA Team** and consisted of 15 men. Each FA Team was designed to advise and support a regiment of up to 1,500 partisans. A **FB Team** (equivalent to the current ODB or Company Headquarters) commanded two or more FA Teams. An **FC Team** or **ODC** (Battalion Headquarters) was designed to command and control FA and FB teams including Guerrilla Warfare (GW) area commands operating in a single country. The Group Headquarters, called the **FD Team**, was designed to command and control the entire Group when employed in two or more countries. The fact that this original organization has changed very little over the many years is indeed a tribute to those who devised the first Tables of Organization and Equipment (TO&E), which were largely taken from the OSS-OG structure.

As time passed, "A" Detachments trained routinely with Western European and Middle Eastern armies. Men of the 10th Special Forces Group trained with airborne, commando, ranger, raider, militia and clandestine organizations in England, France, Norway, Germany, Greece, Spain, Italy, Turkey, Pakistan, Iran, Jordan, and Saudi Arabia. "A" Detachments worked across cultural and linguistic borders, learning how to subsist on native food and establishing and maintaining rapport with the host nation forces. Today this program is an extensive and key part of the Group's training and spans countries from Turkey to Estonia. In Africa, the 10th Special Forces served without fanfare, often wearing no identification patches, berets or other insignia, sometimes even operating in civilian clothes. This deliberate low profile should not obscure the story of those missions. In the summer of 1960, the Commanding Officer of the 10th Special Forces Group, Colonel "Iron" Mike Paulick, received orders to support evacuation efforts in the Congo. A wave of violence against the remaining whites in the former Belgian colony developed following its independence on July 1, 1960. There was no hint in the news media that the 10th would be involved.

US Ambassador Timberlake ordered a small unit to Leopoldville in the Congo to help save American and European lives. This team consisted of three helicopters, three light single engine airplanes, an Air Force radio expert, and the SF element from Bad Toelz. A meeting with Ambassador Timberlake and Belgian paratroopers took place and the mission was defined. At the larger airfields, Belgian paratroopers would be in charge. The SF team would control operations on the smaller airfields. The mission was to evacuate as many Europeans and Americans as possible and move them to Leopoldville for large scale evacuation.

As the 1960s continued, counter-insurgency, rather than unconventional warfare, became the primary mission for SF. Although the 10th SFG(A) was not directly involved in Southeast Asia, most of the Group's soldiers, by normal rotation, served with SF units in SE Asia.

In addition to Europe, it's area of responsibility grew to include North Africa, the Middle East and Southwest Asia, as far east as Pakistan. Two battalions, or C Detachments as they were called at the time, remained responsible for the East European GW role. The third C Detachment trained for foreign internal defense and counterinsurgency missions. Besides the normal SF training, this C Detachment gathered intelligence and started language training in Arabic, Urdu, Farsi, Greek, Turkish and Pushto. In Jordan, MAJ. Joe Callahan and his B Detachment established and ran Jordan's first airborne school. The mission was a complete success. An enthusiastic King Hussein attended the graduation parachute drop.

One B Detachment and three A Detachments later traveled to Iran and trained with the Iranian Special Forces (ISF). The ISF was at that time actually only an airborne battalion. An A Detachment also trained Kurdish tribesman in the mountains of Iran.

CPT Mike Boos and his detachment went to the hills and deserts of Pakistan to train with the Baluch Regiment of Special Warfare Warriors. CPT Steve Snowden and his A Team trained the nucleus of the Turkish Special Forces, including airborne qualification, SF tradecraft and SCUBA operations for selected officers. They constructed a training apparatus for the airborne course, conducted classroom instruction for 350 officers and NCOs and presented training on operations for land, operations in water and operations in the air.

Special Forces, as with all armed forces, was severely affected by the end of the Vietnam conflict, including force cuts and reduction in overseas deployments and basing. In September 1968, the 10th Special Forces Group, minus the **1st Battalion**, was re-stationed to Fort Devens, Massachusetts. The Group survived the lean years and was not dropped from the rolls, as were the 1st, 3rd, 6th, and 8th SFGs, but Fort Devens was a far cry from Flint Kaserne in the Alps of Bavaria.

The Bad Tolz area of southern Germany is still one of the best SF training environments in the world with ideal terrain as well as a staunchly supportive local population. The 10th SFG(A) continues to maintain the relationship which was developed over the years with its Bavarian friends.

The "lean years" of the 1970's saw an absolute decrease in the number/frequency of operational deployments for 10th SFG(A) - in fact they all but ceased completely. During this time, however, the 10th SFG(A) maintained its training edge through continuous deployments into the European theater to train with NATO allies, and to do unilateral training on environmental skills. These deployments and the annual FLINTLOCK Exercise became the central points of every ODA's training program. Of course, those events were complimented by language training, as well as environmental training that was possible in and around our home at Fort Devens. In addition to our Bavarian friends maintained by 1st Battalion, 10th Group was able to build an "underground" of sorts in the New England area which would reap benefits for the duration of our time in Massachusetts.

Giant Country

Arriving at a new assignment on a Sunday, is not the smartest thing to do. Most headquarters are closed. If you had to sign in, you could if you didn't mind signing in with the CQ (charge of quarters). Personally I like to sign in at the headquarters of the unit I am assigned to, preferably with the CMS. After freshening up at my motel, I started my clandestine tour of Ft Devens. Surprising to me the Fort was relatively small. In spite of the size, Fort Devens housed several high speed units. The Army Security Agency (ASA) sharing an area with Special Operations Detachment (SOD) Headquarters and it's school, seemed to be the largest tenant. They were housed in very impressive new brick buildings.

Finding the Special Forces area was not difficult. They were housed in old World War II buildings. That was true all over. Back in the 70's, if Special Forces was a tenant, they were assigned to the oldest buildings on the installation. That has now changed.

Trojan Patch

I went to the Trojan Sport Parachuting Club. They were glad to see me, I was their second costumer. I took a seat about mid-bar and ordered a Vodka on the rocks with a lemon twist. Our female, good-looking Bar Tender started mixing my drink. Immediately the guy from the far end of the bar, brought his drink, and stood at my left side.

"I'm John Riley, and this is my drink." At that point, he reached up and removed his left glass eye, and put it in his drink. Then he walked to the washroom.

I was a little surprised, but not shocked. I was in Special Forced land, and Special Forced has been known to do strange things on occasion. This was the first eye trick I had ever seen. Usually, partial plates or whole sets of dentures are used to establish ownership of a drink or food.

I remember one occasion; After making a night jump at Fort Carson Colorado, we went to the NCO Club to have a beer party after the jump. As I recall, beer was only sold by the pitcher. To establish ownership, of your pitcher, in went your dentures. When the club closed and resupply stopped, the contents of half empty pitchers, were pored into other pitchers. A great way to share with your friends. The fun part was when all beer was gone, denture ownership had to be established. No doubt, it must have looked a little odd watching individuals, trying on one set of dentures then another. Disgusting you say, not at all, you had to be there.

There seems to be many SF toppers with partial dentures. The reason I really don't know. Probably rough training, resulting in mouth injury is the main reason. One thing is certain, if dental problems cannot be fixed, out it comes. A severe tooth problem could compromise a mission. I didn't wait for Riley to return. I moved to the far end of the bar. Sure enough, when Riley returned to the bar, he picked up his drink and joined me.

"What do I owe you young lady?" I wanted to get out of this place before something happened, that would affect both our careers. Didn't see Riley much after our first meeting. I learned Riley lost his eye in Vietnam. I also learned he had several artificial eyes. One had the CBS logo imbedded in the eye. Others had a variation of colors and pictures. All in all John Riley was not a bad guy sober. But drunk he was a pain in the south end of a horse heading north. In spite of his short comings, John had an overall, Giant rating.

My next stop was at the Special Forces Association club house. This turned out to be the true hangout for Special Forces, on their off time. This was more like it. I meet many old friends that I haven't seem in a few years. David Lanning, Al Lipson, Joel Shenkelberger,

John Burdish, and Roger Smith just to name a few. An old friend from Kontum Vietnam, SFC Glenn Watson made a call to his landlord and got me an apartment in Shirley MA, a small village next to Fort Devens. Glenn had a key to every apartment in his building. I guess he was the owner's part time superintendent. We jumped in his Corvette and checked the apartment out.

The one bedroom, 1st floor apartment was like it was made to order. The large great room and dinning area off the well-equipped kitchen, had great potential. It's close proximity to Fort Devens added to its worth. I gave Glenn a check to cover the first months rent.

Although I didn't have to sign in for a couple of day's, I decided to stop by headquarters and let them know I was in town. While I waiting to see the CSM, I couldn't help overhearing the conversation taking place in his office. Apparently an aircraft was available to make a jump, but they couldn't find a medic. A cardinal rule is to have a Medic and ambulance on the DZ or no jump. I popped my head in the door and made the announcement;

"My name is McGinley, I'm a medic how, can I help?" I thought they were talking about jumping tomorrow or even the next day. The jump was in one hour. Me and my big mouth.

I'm just arrived from Okinawa. I was dressed for temperatures in the 70's and low 80's. This was Massachusetts, in December, the temperature was 10 degrees above zero. Couldn't change cloths, my whole baggage was still in storage. I haven't signed in the unit yet, so I had no field gear issued. I'm here to tell you, "it was cold outside."

"I'm Harry Pope, the unit's CSM, I won't forget this McGinley." With that the CSM grabbed the phone and called the Commander, LTC Vaughn, "The jump's on Sir, we got a Medic. SFC Dillon, take your people to Turner DZ. Sergeant Hudelson, take McGinley to the Motor Pool and sign out an Ambulance. Someone find McGinley some warm clothes." This guy was giving out more orders than Napoleon gave at the Battle of Waterloo.

The Motor Sergeant wouldn't let me sign for an Ambulance because of my civilian cloths. Minor problem, SFC Pat Hudelson signed for and drove the ambulance to Turner DZ across Highway 2. The chopper was on station and the first load was chuted up. As soon as they saw us, the chopper was airborne. Everything was working like clockwork with one exception. That somebody, didn't find me any warm cloths. Sorry I have to repeat myself; "baby it's cold outside."

The first to go were my feet. The loafers were not much help in the deep snow. My nose started to drip. I couldn't wipe it, my nose was too cold. Then nature took over, the dripping froze. I might have looked funny with an icicle on the end of my nose. But at least it wasn't dripping. You only can get so cold. Then it seems not to make any difference. By the time someone throw me a hooded poncho and a large pair of boots, I am sure my core temperature was dangerously low. I learned one big lesson. I should have been listening instead of talking. I think I have just told you a lie. I haven't learned to listen before talking.

Wax Your Ski's

I signed in Co. D, 10th Special Forces on 15 December 1971. By this time my whole baggage had arrived and I was dresses in winter uniform. Command Sergeant Major Pope thanked me again. We were off to a great start. I would have a hard time rating CSM Richard Campbell against CSM Harry Pope. Both where the greatest CSM's I had ever worked with.

"Mac, take all the time you need getting settled in. We are going on a ski trip to Sundown Valley in New Hampshire Won't be much going on until we get back. Of course, if you want to go with us, we will make a max effort to get you equipped in time." I had the feeling as though I had just been tricked.

I was issued a white camouflage outer garment to include a white cover for my rucksack. At that time Special Forces didn't have ski-boots. We wore Chippawa Climbing Boots. The boots had to be notched on each side of the toe to accommodate the White Star Ski binders. I was looking forward to learning how to ski. The little training I had was on Okinawa. Surely this will beat going down a straw-covered hill in the hot sun.

I started to get concerned when we went to Selker Army Airfield and chuted up. We hung our rucksacks in front of us and were issued a pair of White Star Ski's. White Star Ski's dates back to WWII. The wide ski's were secured to our left side and we boarded the waiting aircraft. Surely they knew by looking at my records, I was not a qualified skier. They probably just wanted us to get used to jumping with skis'. When we got over the jump area, the ceiling was to low. The jump was called off. Another big thank you to the man upstairs.

We were bused to Sundown Valley Ski Resort. The resort was in the White Mountain Range near Gorham New Hampshire The 10th leases the whole Resort twice a year for ski practice. The rest of the Ski Season, the Lodge offers reduced Ski Lift tickets to the 10th. These guys at the 10th are hard core skiers.

Being a little behind in schedule, we were rushed to a waiting Ski Lift. The instructions were to get off at the first cable-booster wheel house, make a sharp turn to the right to the Skiing area. Getting on the chair lift was simple. Just stand in front of it. The moving chair would force you to sit.

Up, up, and away. The view was great. As we got close to the wheel house my ski's started dragging on the packed snow. The only effort needed was to stand up. The packed tracks made by the skier's ahead of you forced you to make the proper turn. Around the cable-wheel house I went. Then the horrible site. A straight down snow packed steep slop. In no time I was flat on my back, speeding down the slope about 200 hundred miles an hour. Well maybe not quite that fast. The good part, God decided to grow a small clump of trees to stop me. I took my ski's off and walked to the bottom of the hill.

I was meet at the base of the hill by a group that witnessed my activity. Their laughter was almost uncontrollable. They truly thought that because of my age, I must have been to ski training, at one point in my career. The correction was put into action. I was directed to the bunny slope. Bunny slop is a nickname given to an area set aside to train beginners.

By the end of the first week after learning how to fall uphill, snowplow, and a few other basic monomers, I was back on the main slop. I found it incredible, they could turn me into a fairly competent skier in less than a week. Like all good things this great outing had to come to an end. We were bussed back to Fort Devens.

In my spare time, I designed and built a portable Dispensary. Unlike the Jeep treatment unit I built on a trailer in Vietnam, this one would have to be smaller. Small enough to jump with, or at the very least, small enough to kick out of an aircraft or chopper. I started the project by assembling every medical item I might need on a two-week operation, Then I built containers to fit the assembled items. Like the jeep in Vietnam, I had three sections, an Examination, Treatment, and Pharmacy section. Each had its own container.

Each container was two by two and one half feet, by eight inches deep. They were piano hinged on the back and locked on the front. The carrying handles were recessed to allow them to be stacked, one on another. I used camouflage paint on the outside and white paint on the inside.

The examination section had all the necessary tools to make a thorough examination including an ophthalmoscope for eye examination. It also contained a mini microscope, slides, and stains. Test strips and sterile specimen collecting containers were also kept in this section.

The well-stocked treatment section could take care of any injury that might occur. From a simple band-aid, dressing change, to burn packs, we could cover it. Sterile minor surgical packs, cut down packs, and the addition of a shock-tray, made it more efficient.

The pharmacy section, put class to this field treatment center. Each shelf had 1 and ½ half inch holes drilled in them to hold clear plastic pill containers. The wide caps on the containers prevented them from falling through. During travel a spring loaded doll-rod held everything in place. There was room for fifty types of medication. The type of medication carried was influenced by the area we were going to and any particular medication a team member might need. And of course, epinephrine was at the ready in case of a reaction to medication. Now it was time to test this portable unit in the field. I know it was strong, I saw no problem jumping out of an aircraft with it. The only concern I had was carrying it for any long distance. I would have to work that out.

The balance of the winter was quit severe. On a couple of occasions we had to use skis' to get to work. Work might be the wrong word. All our activities were geared to the 10th's annual FTX (field training exercise) in Gorham New Hampshire. Of course we had to maintain our community relations mission. Parties are good relation builders. We partied a lot.

Gorham FTX

The "lean years" of the 1970's saw an absolute decrease in the number and frequency of operational deployments for 10th SFG, in fact they all but ceased completely. During this time, however the 10th SFG maintained its training edge through continuous deployments into the European theater to train with NATO Allies and to do unilateral training on individual skills. These deployments and the annual FLINTLOCK Exercise became the central points of every ODA's training program. Of course those events were complimented by language training, as well as environmental training that was possible in and around our home at Fort Devens. In addition to our Bavarian friends maintained by 1st Battalion in Bad Tolz, 10th Group was able to build an "underground" of sorts in the New England area which would reap benefits for the duration of our time in Massachusetts.

Shakespear stated, "the world is a stage, you and I but players." Or something like that. There is a lot of truth in that statement. The daily interaction between groups of people is the plot of life's great play. The laughter, sadness, love or hate, adds to the drama. Surely achievements or the lack of, contributes to life's mystery. The thing to remember is the play can be manipulated by outside forces. Sometimes without the knowledge or consent of all the players. I believe I have just explained a Special Forces exercise. Let's see how it fits in an actual Special Forces exercise.

The 10th Special Forces annual FTX in the town of Gorham New Hampshire, involved the whole town. Everyone was involved in some way, or to some extent. Some played the roll of an unwanted occupying Army. Others assumed the role of a Guerilla force in opposition. This was an annual event for the 10th. The citizens of Gorham looked forward to being involved in the training.

I was in Delta Co. of the 10th for the summer of 72 exorcize. We were to play the role of the Occupying Army. Charlie and Bravo Co.'s sent A-Teams to play the Guerrilla Roles in opposition. Long before the FTX starting date, participants sent advance parties to Gorham to set up and prepare for the exercise. Sergeant Major Donald Brown and I were the advance party for the Occupying Army.

Our mission was to find a building suitable for a headquarters. The building had to be large enough to house about thirty people, situated in an area that could be defended, and fall within operation budget restraints. It was wheeling and dealing time. My favorite part of any operation.

Our first stop was at the Court House. We were greeted by a very enthusiastic Mayor. I don't think he knew what the word "No" was. Everything we asked for we got. We asked for a fifty-person occupying force. They had a list of one hundred twenty-five individuals who had already signed up. We needed a jail cell to hold our prisoners. They gave us two, and the use of their office to process our POW's. When we asked for a building for our Headquarters, there was a slight hesitation. Then the Mayor spoke out.

"My brother-in-law just closed his service station. I'll bet my bottom dollar he'll let you use it." This turned out to be an ideal location. One mile out of town on a very large fenced in lot. The four car repair area took care of our housing needs. To this point we had not spent a cent. Then our enthusiastic friend asked;

"Who was going to be President of our make believe Nation?"

"You are sir! You are President El Supreme of Gorham Kingdom. Was our political correct response.

We had the main part of our mission completed in one day of an allotted three day tasking. The difficult decision of renting an upscale Resort Chalet on the East side of town. This had to be discussed in depth. The Army frowns on spending TDY money on the most expensive lodging in town, especially when an adequate less expensive one is available.

This difficult decision took a lot of time before we reached the answer. We had to measure the pros and cons. We were fully aware of the possibility of we two Pros, could be two Cons, if we couldn't justify our decision. The clock was  running, second by second time was passing. Finally the decision was made. We rented the expensive lodging. This decision process took the better part of two minutes. Our cover story would be; We didn't want to take the risk of being detected by A-Team members that also might be in town on a similar mission.

First class, top shelf, high on the hog. There wasn't a phrase that could describe this wonderland; Swiss Alp style cottagers, separated by beautiful landscaping. The beauty almost took my breath away. (Or was that my asthma acting up again?) Our Chalet was ten feet from an Olympic size, heated pool. The only negative part was, we had to walk another five feet to a state of the art workout-room. We spent most of our days pool side, ordering refreshments with a press of a button.

As soon as it got dark, we went to Gorham and started our reconnaissance. We were looking for signs of any of the A-Teams setting up their guerrilla sites. Most people are creatures of habit. Special Forces go out of the way trying not to follow that trend. Creatures of habit are predictable. Being predictable makes one vulnerable. Because of this, the rules for the Runford Main FTX had to be changed.

Starting with the first Runford FTX, SF A-Teams stayed at small inexpensive motels. Arriving several days before the start of the exercise, afforded them time to fix-up their host motel. They cleaned, painted, repaired and planted. When they left the slightly run-down motels looked like little gems. Appreciating their work, owners invite them back for the next exercise.

Due to the fact, the opposing force knew where they bedded down, a "no hitting them at base camp" had to be added to the FTX engagement rules. This took a little excitement out of the war game. All agreed it was worth the trade off. It built good relations with the towns people and the A-Teams received free lodging. I think that is called a win, win situation. SGM Brown slammed on the brakes.

"Mac the guy by the motel, do you know him? I think he belongs to Charily Company." I wasn't sure, I might have seen him around 10th Group. I just wasn't sure. We needed gas and pulled into a full service station on main street. The outside attendants had 10th Group written all over them. The one coming to serve us looked very familiar. When he got closer, I made a positive identification.

"Sergeant Major Boggs, I didn't know you lived in Gorham, how are you. It's tap-dance time.

"Ya Mac, I retired last month. Took this job until I figure what I want to do. What are you doing up here? SGM Billy Boggs could tell you a lie, staring you in the eye, and make you believe it.

"Been doing a little fishing with my cousin Don. Don, meet CSM Boggs. We're on the way home." I could tell a pretty good lie myself. But I don't think Billy was buying it. We had our tank filled and headed back to our warm pool.

Time Out

We had a slight delay getting the exercise started. There were a lot of Hippy's camping out in the hill's around Runford. As a matter of fact, throughout the New England States. The low life, subculture, drifters, didn't work. If they needed a little pocket money, they broke into autos and stole valuables, or raided campsites of people trying to enjoy the beautiful outdoors of New Hampshire This wasn't just a local problem, it was wide spread.

The small Police Department of Gorham had little control over this lawless group. Occasionally they ran them out of the area with the aide of the State Police. Without fail the scumbag drifters would come back. We decided to give the local law enforcement a helping hand, policing the area of scum bags. With the assurance of the local law enforcement, they would turn their head, a group of us raided their main camp. The sun was almost ready to make its daily run and brighten the world with its golden rays when we hit.

A stern warning convinced about ten of the group, still in their sleeping bags, to remain where they were. We proceeded to knock down the tent's on top of their occupants. Then at random, we punched every bulge that was frantically trying to escape. At the end of the twenty minute engagement, we had thirty-two, very sorry hippies. Sorry they ever came to New England to practice their subculture, perverted lifestyle.

We marched the scum out of the woods, wearing only what they had on at the time of the engagement. Gave then a very matter of fact briefing, about ever coming back to this area. By this time the Chief of Police and his Deputy arrived. They followed the group as the headed south, out of this now restricted area. The Police method of getting ride of the Hippy's didn't work, because of one reason. They are forbidden by law of hurting them. Our method worked because of one reason also. If you come to this area, to practice your perverted life style, you will be hurt. We violated their Human Rights, some may say. Wrong, they were not acting like humans, therefor they had no rights.

Captured

Training exercise at Gorham were meaningful largely because there was no predetermined winner. The winner of this war game, would be determined by who out foxed who. Consequently the main goal for both the Occupying Army and the Guerilla Forces was to capture or destroy the command structure of their opponent. I was in the chain of command of the Occupying Army, making me a target.

One day while on a reconnaissance mission I stopped at a Burger King for lunch. I finished my lunch and was plotting out my afternoon surveillance area. My attention was on a map, I didn't notice a gentleman approaching my table. When he sat down, I looked up.

"Hi Mac, fancy meeting you hear way out in the bonnies. We have some great things planned for you McGinley." It was CSM Billie Boggs, one of the Guerrilla Chief's.

Being captured in bad enough. Being captured by a friend is devastating. Friends have a tendency of being a little harder on you than a stranger would be. CSM Billie Boggs and I were very good friends. I had to come up with something, quick. Brain don't fail me now.

"Boggs you got me. Now before we get to far into this capture, answer this question. Who would you rather have had captured, than me?" I was a good capture since I was in the command chain. But there were bigger fish in the kettle. "How would you like to capture Captain Thomas?"

Captain Thomas was not SF qualified. He was a supply officer attached to SF for this training mission. The assignment was to give him first hand experience on how important supply was to troops in the field. In addition to that, Captain Thomas was a wimp. Nobody liked his, "I am better than anybody attitude."

"That's almost impossible Mac. Thompson never leaves the Headquarters Compound."

"I can deliver the Captain, to this table, tomorrow at noon." I knew that would take a lot of doing, the S-4 Captain and I were not friends, nor would we ever be. Billy hesitated, he was deep in thought.

"How do I know I can trust you to deliver Thomas, Mac?

"You have my word on it Boggs." We shook hands and I departed before he changed his mind.

I relied on the fact that Captain Thomas was among other things, a Cheep Charlie. You could buy this guy coffee and doughnuts all day. He never figured it was his turn to pay. In fact his dog ate as many doughnuts as he did. I almost forgot to tell you about his little, high strung, mut. The Captain took him every place he went. Yes even to this training exercise. He treated the mut as though it was a child. If you heard the conversation, but couldn't see them, you would swear he was baby talking to a small child. "Does poopsy want daddy to give him a biscuit?" You got to be kidding me.

"Captain Thomas, I want to buy lunch today. We have many broken fences between us that need to be fixed. Let's go to Burger King." He jumped at the offer of free lunch.

As we drove into the parking lot, I saw Boggs and his Team sitting at the wood line. Although crowded, the designated capture table was empty. There was no doubt in my mind, the customers were briefed on the event that was about to unfold. We took our seats and ordered. Would you believe, the Captain ordered a hamburger to go, for his mut? Of course, it was added to my bill.

Then they struck. In the blink of an eye, I was declared dead. and the Captain taken prisoner. The customers were enjoying every minute. Some were taking pictures. This by far was the biggest event of the year. I wasn't surprised when a lad working behind the counter, joined Boggs and his Guerrilla force when they departed with their reluctant prisoner. He was assigned to Billie's team.

"McGinley, are you part of this?" The Captain screamed.

"How can you ask that Captain? Didn't I just give my life for you? That got a chuckle out of the crowed.

For safety reasons, the rules of engagement state, any person that is taken prisoner, has to be released in twenty-four hours, at the same place captured or other agreed upon location. It's a good rule. When captured the individual probably doesn't have their survival gear with them. In New England even in the spring, survival gear is important. The allotted twenty-four hours is ample time to interrogate a captive. When I went back to Burger King to pick up Captain Thomas, my Guerrilla Chief friend, and three of his team were waiting. Captain Thomas was not in sight.

"Mac we almost have Thomas ready to spill his guts. We need just a little more time."

"You actually have about three more hours Billy. I can come back later to pick the Captain up."

"No, that won't do it. Now if this guy was Special Forces, we could get a little tougher with him." Getting too rough with non-S F people, is not good policy. It has a tendency to start unwanted rumors, which may lead to outsider involvement or poking around. I suddenly got an idea, let's involve the Captains mut.

"Billy, I can get him to talk. But it will involve me going to your camp site." Normally this would have been unsatisfactory. But they were about to change locations. Not good to stay in one place too long. It increases the chances of detection.

After exchanging assurances, me not revealing their location and them not pulling a switch, me for the Captain. I was allowed to go to their site. SGM Boggs told one of his men to show me where their camp was. We headed for their camp in my vehicle. Less than one half mile down the road, I was told to turn at the next dirt driveway. In about two hundred feet we arrived at a very old barn.

Entering the rear door, there it was, paradise in the ruff. SGM Boggs had his self-contained camper set up in the barn. The balance of the Guerrilla force had camping tents' scattered around. Their communications tent was on the second level. We have been looking for this Group since the first day of the operation. They have been under our noses all the time.

I was taken to a stream two hundred yards behind the barn. Standing in ice cold water, wearing only his birthday suit, was our very cold, Captain Thomson. They were right, our young Captain was ready to spill his guts.

"I have some bad news for you Captain Thomas, your dog got out of his cage. Well you know how busy the highway in front of Headquarters is." He turned white as a ghost and started to cry. The thought occurred to me, that maybe we were taking this to far. "Tell them what they want to know Captain and we will get out of here ." I went outside. In a short time, Captain Thomas joined me and we headed back to our location.

"Your mut is OK Captain. This was a trick to get you to talk."

"Are you sure Sergeant McGinley?" This guy was more concerned about his dog than about his reputation of being an Officer.

"Yes Captain I am sure." The balance of the trip was made in silence.

This guy was definitely not Special Forces material. If this had been done to a Special Forces person they would have asked, how we cooked the road kill and if it was served with potatoes or on a mound of rice. The following day, Captain Thomas was gone, bag and baggage.

The only place in town off limits to all FTX participants, was the American Legion on the outskirts of Gorham The building was used by the FTX Controllers. The Controllers, all 10th Group personnel, had the responsibility of keeping the exercise moving. If there were no problems, they would create some. Learning is increased when there are problems to be solved. The larger the problem, the more learned.

The only exception to the usage rule, members of the Headquarters Staff of the Occupying Army were able to come and go as needed. Most of the time to coordinate close Air-Support. Sergeant Major Brown and I took advantage of this. It was a good place to get a cold beer and relax a few minutes. Unlike the A-Teams, whose mission kept them busy all night, our assignment kept us busy day and night.

Anyone that has ever been deployed on a Special Forces mission knows that a percentage of the people you are attempting to help, belong to the other side. They say, "if you shoot, the top one percent of the high achievers, of a class, regardless of the subject matter, you have probably shot the enemy." That's not to far from the truth. Our enemy's are dedicated SOB's. For this operation, 10th Group imbedded informants to aid the opposing forces. It wasn't difficult, assigning a spy in the Occupying Army. This group was put together, just for this operation and would disband at it's close. They didn't have to work with each other at home station. Quit different with the A-Teams. They were tight-nit, they would rather die then-rat on each other. Yes, even during a game. This comradery lasts a lifetime.

SGM Brown and I were having a cool one at the American Legion one afternoon. I was in a relaxed mood listening to the CSM's great Golden Knight stories. His assignment to the Army's Parachute Team and my background in Sport Parachuting, gave us a lot in common. This was probably the main factor that sparked a friendship that would last.

I was facing SGM Brown, fascinated by the story he was telling, when someone sat next to me. I paid no attention, and Brown kept telling the story. I didn't say anything when the guy next to me bumped my bar-stool the first time, nor the second. The third bump got my Irish up and I turned to tell the clown to back off.

Sitting next to me was the last person in the world I wanted to see. Sergeant Major Billy Boggs. Sitting there, with an ear to ear grin on his face. I don't clam to be a Rocket Scientist, but I figured immediately, I had been set up.

I threw my beer in Boggs face and headed for the rear room and the back door. After pushing the door opened, I made a hard right and instead of going out the door, I headed for the latrine area. His or Hers, I chose Hers. I lucked out, the young lady washing her hands was an employee and up to date on the operation. I darted in one of the stalls, shut the door, and stood on the seat so my feet couldn't be seen from the outside. I hoped this gal would take my side.

"Anybody come in here?" One of Boggs team members asked.

"No, what are you doing in here, this is the ladies room." My new pal answered with a sharp tongue. The embarrassed, Boggs Team member departed.

"Stay put, I'll get some of my brothers cloths. I'll be back in a minute." I was wearing the uniform of the Occupying Army. I wouldn't have gotten ten feet dressed like this. Strange place to meet a new friend, I thought to myself. I think I'm in love again.

Before I was able to get a plan together, my asset was back with a shirt and some pants. A quick change and I was out the back door. The bright sun made me decide to hide in the near by foliage until dark. Another reason for my decision, the cloths I was wearing were not tailor made. Her brother must have been a big guy. I stood out like a sore thumb.

I got well into the bushes, pulled branches and grass around me and began my long wait. As I stated, we were on the go day and night. I was tired and fell asleep. I slept like a baby until people leaving the Bar at closing time, woke me with their loud goodnights.

I had no difficulty getting back to our headquarters building. I went to the police station and told them I was a POW, and had just escaped and I need a ride. I couldn't tell them the truth. The officer on duty might have been on the other side. The town used Auxiliary Police to man the jailhouse during our operation. Some were on our side and some on the other.

Sergeant Major Brown was the first to greet me. He was almost bent over laughing. He honestly thought, I had been captured. I didn't tell him different. I spent a couple of hours telling the group things I had to endure as a captive. Brown almost split a gut. I had a plan to get even with my humorous friend.. Exactly how, I didn't know, but even I would get.

Resupply

The second week of the FTX, was devoted to resupply. The A-team's mission was to request resupply by radio, set up a drop zone, and recover the supplies. All this had to be done without detection.. This was a very critical task. Some where hidden within the resupply were the marching orders for the balance of the exercise. The critical item of the marching order was the exact time and place the FTX would end. More importantly was how the Teams were going to be extracted. The mission of the Occupying Army, was to prevent the A-Teams from being re supplied.

There were only three clear areas that were suitable to set up a drop-zone. We could cover them without too much difficulty. Of the four Teams that had to be supplied, we figured we could stop three of them. How wrong we were.

The FTX came to a screeching halt. The State Police radioed for help to evacuate several injured occupants of a multi vehicle wreck north of town. We sent everybody we could find. A radio message went out to the A-Teams, to drop everything they were doing and lend us a hand.

The Fire Department and three ambulances were on station when our first group arrived. I hate to complain about volunteer Firemen and Paramedics but they didn't seem to have a sense of urgency. Myself and two other Medic's started to remove the injured from the wreckage.

Immediately, we realized, the people we were trying to assist were not real casualties. This accident was staged. About the same time we heard the Helicopters overhead, heading for their resupply mission. We felt the sick feeling of "being had." At the same time I was proud of the resourcefulness of the A-Teams. It took a lot to put this stunt together. End result, all four A-Teams were supplied.

Lesson learned. "Don't take you mind off of the Mission." We were justified attending to the accident, some might say. They are wrong. We were practicing how to deal with, real world problems. How well we learned to solve the problems would affect the lives of thousands. All Special Forces Training is serious business and in harmony with a changing world. If the accident was real, us helping, would not have changed the outcome. Accomplishment of mission is paramount to everything.

I made a trip back to Fort Devens on three different occasions. The reasons were varied. Pick up mail, pick up home cooked food, the wives were sending out and pick up official correspondence for our Commander LTC Vaughn.

On one of my trips, Sergeant Major Brown asked me to bring his son out to the field. Don Jr was a good kid, but like a lot of seventeen year-old's, didn't have the foggiest idea of what he wanted to do in life. Lackadaisical kids will sometimes force parents to do extraordinary things. Donald Brown Junior would be, SGM Boggs next prisoner.

Turning Don Jr. over to the guerillas was easy. I drove to the old barn and honked my horn. Three members of Billy's Team, took my reluctant passenger. On the way to the ambush I had warned SGM Brown's son of the possibility of anybody driving this particular road, might be taken prisoner. His reply;

"That's cool." Little did he know how cool it would be. The SGM's son was returned, excited about his experience. In fact Don Jr asked his father if he could stay. Of course SGM Brown was pleased and agreed.

When exercisers get near the end, they seem to have a built in slowdown. This one would be no different. Items of equipment that were not going to be used, were loaded onto a Duce and a Half Truck and scheduled to leave early Saturday morning. The main body would leave for Fort Devens on Sunday.

On Saturday a Block Party was held for all the participants. There were ton's of food and beverage. The local country band got your foot tapping with the music and of course an awards ceremony. Everyone got a Letter of Appreciation and or Plaque from 10th Group. Old Granny, the oldest lady in Gorham was present with her scrap book. The grand old Gal kept a record of every FTX the 10th had in Gorham. The book was full of pictures and signatures of hundreds of Special Forces Operatives. If you weren't in Granny's scrapbook, you didn't belong.

This was a big event for the town. A chance for Gorham citizens to brag about their role in the exercise. An opportunity for the young ladies of Gorham to parade around in their finest gowns. Who knows maybe on of those Green Berets will fall head over heals in love with them.

Please do not misunderstand me. I am not knocking New Hampshire women. The fact is New Hampshire women are not small. They claim there is a reason to their size. It is to keep their men warm in the winter and shaded in the summer. I didn't say that, they did.

I wasn't surprised when SGM Brown and SFC Pat Hudelson got on the makeshift stage and started to play their instruments. Both were first class guitar and banjo players and could sing country and western songs with the best. This earned them an instant fan following. Every single gal in town fell in love with them. As a matter of fact I wouldn't be surprised if a few old gals followed suit. Don and Pat didn't discourage their attention.

Tragedy Strikes

"Sergeant McGinley, there's been an accident come with me." LTC Hoffman had a very strange look on his face. I grabbed my M5-Medical bag and followed him to a waiting chopper. All the way to the crash site, I was hoping this would be another set up, like the accident staged by the A-Teams. Then the reality, we could see the burning wreck on the horizon.

Our pilot landed the helicopter on a clearing very close to the wreck. The State Policeman that greeted us pointed to a tarpaulin, as he explained what he knew to LTC Hoffman. I lifted the tarpaulin to identify the victims. The two bodies were burnt so bad, it was hard to believe they were human beings. The black charred remains made it impossible to make an identification. A sudden sadness fell over me, I felt compelled to say a prayer.

"Sergeant McGinley, Meadows and Henry are in the hospital, badly burned but alive." Then who are the other two victims? I thought. My prayer was for Meadows and Henry. Then the State Trooper explained what he knew, about the horrible crash.

Witnesses told the State Police, two women, in a sports car, pulled out of their lane to pass slower autos in front of them. Apparently they seen our Duce and a Half Truck, coming down the steep hill. Their attempt to get back into their lane failed. On impact both vehicles exploded. Meadows was seen pulling Henry out of the wreckage. The two women perished in the resulting fire. It was learned that the two women were wives of service members. Both their husbands were in the U S Navy. Before going shopping, the ladies dropped their two children off at a baby sitter. This doesn't make the tragedy any easier on the families. However they can rejoice, their children were spared. Several things about the wreck were puzzling and generated a lot of "why's."

Why was the Duce and a Half Truck on top of the convertible? Both were facing the same direction. The convertible heading uphill, and the Army truck heading uphill. Logic would dictate, if the vehicles hit head on, the larger Army vehicle would have knocked the convertible, way off the road. Why was the contents of the truck thrown down hill? Every item in the truck was thrown downhill and landed in a straight line, alongside the road. Why was there such a humongous fire? The only item that was combustible on the Army truck was it's fuel. None believed the fuel could generate the heat it would take to literally melt the truck. The total wreckage height, truck on top of the auto, did not exceed four and one half feet. A lot of "why's" but at this point, no answers.

I stayed at the wreck site to secure the equipment scattered down the road. I had a couple of hours before dark. With the help of some onlooker, I gathered the equipment in one location. I figured it would be a lot easier to guard. Surprisingly, all the equipment was in good shape. Darkness set in, this would be a long night. I couldn't sleep, the "why's" kept me awake.

Back at Fort Devens it still bothered me. By this time rumors about the State Police investigation hinted, our lads might have been drinking. They found empty beer cans at the site of the accident. This infuriated me. You can find empty beer cans along any highway in America. Many Americans are chronic litterer's. When I found out no one has paid our guy's a hospital visit, I blew a gasket. This wasn't like Special Forces. I went to see the Sergeant Major.

"Calm down McGinley. There is a reason nobody has visited the hospital. They are talking about a law suit. The Army wants us to keep a low profile on this case." The Sergeant Major continued and told me that the beer cans were very damaging to the case.

"Bull, Sergeant Major, Meadows doesn't drink. Henry would never drink on duty. I think the Army is looking for an escape goat. I'm putting in for a ten-day leave. I'll get to the bottom of this."

"You won't need a leave Mac. Take as long as you need, we will cover for you." Then Command Sergeant Major Pope did a strange thing. He stood up and saluted me and said;

"I'm glad we have NCO's like you." This was strange coming from a hard-core Sergeant Major like Harry Pope. I returned his salute. A salute is the highest gesture of respect, one soldier can give another.

I didn't have to pack a bag. I kept a five-day change of cloths on the ready. I gassed up my 1965 Corvette and headed north. I felt great. I was on a mission that would have a positive impact on the careers of two young solders.

Heading straight to the Hospital, I asked to see Meadows and Henry. I had a lot of questions to be answered. Hopefully, the answers would give my investigation a direction or at least a starting point. As of this minute I don't have a plan, not even a poor one. I felt that was good. My mind was open for facts. I wouldn't have to weigh one theory with another.

"Are you a relative?" The young receptionist asked. If I answered in the negative, chances where I would be denied visiting rights. I decided to use my "if they're not geared to accept the truth, don't burden them with it." Plan.

"Yes I am. Specialist Meadows is my son and Specialist Henry is my nephew. That sure is a good looking neckless young lady." I wasn't lying about that. The beautiful neckless was hanging on a beautiful neck, attached to a gorgeous face. I think I'm in love again.

"Thank you. Both your relatives are on Ward 3-B. Have a wonderful day.

Meadows and Henry, were happy to see me. I was their first visitor. If I accomplished nothing more, their burst of happiness, made this trip worthwhile. Meadow's parents from Iowa, were on the way to see him . Henry's father would be coming in a few days.

My care package took care of small items like shaving supplies, snacks, cigarettes and a few magazines. A quick trip to a local store for a couple changes of underwear, shirts, and socks, took care of their immediate needs. I had another plan to visit them with cloths and personal items from Fort Devens.

I asked the lads to explain the accident from their point of view. I told them to take their time and be as explicit as possible. It was obvious, they were under a lot of strain. The deaths of the two women tore them apart. These were two fine young men, proud of serving their country. Finding themselves in this dilemma, was difficult for them to handle. Their explanation was very much in line with the State Police investigation.

They had just refueled and started down a steep hill. They saw the convertible pull out in their lane. A dumb move they thought, but they had plenty of time to stop. Specialist Henry, the driver applied his brakes, they didn't work. Repeated tries produced the same results. His only hope of stopping was the emergency brake and gearing down. This seemed to work for a short time. Then something snapped and the truck catapulted forward, landing on top of the oncoming auto. The next thing Specialist Henry remembered, was an explosion and Meadows pulling him out of the wreck.

The truck catapulting, explained why the contents of the truck were thrown downhill in the same direction, the vehicle was heading. It also explained why the truck was heading uphill, the opposite direction, it was going. The humongous extremely hot fire, was probably caused by, both vehicle fuel tanks exploding at the same time. The remaining question, what caused the truck to catapult? I decided to visit the crash site.

I parked my Corvette at the service station where the truck was refueled and walked down hill with camera in hand. As I approached the charred crash area, I noticed deep scrapes in the pavement. As the scrapes got closer to the crash area, they became deep gouges. The gouges ended abruptly. I visualized the truck's drive shaft causing the scraps and gouges. I could also visualize the drive shaft digging in the cement, causing the catapulting.

I took a lot of pictures, from many angles. I placed my wristwatch next to the gouge so I would have a comparison in size. The only thing that bothered me, I didn't think the drive shaft of a Duce and a Half, could support the loaded weight. I had to see the wreckage. But first I better get a place to bed down, it was getting late.

I didn't bother with breakfast, I had no appetite. I was still a little sick about the two ladies that perished in the fire. I couldn't help them, but maybe I can help the other two victims of this tragedy. I went to the salvage yard, where the wreckage was being held.

"Good morning, I'm Sergeant First Class McGinley. I'm looking into the Army Truck accident. I would like to see the wreckage."

"Its out back. What are they going to do with those two guys?" He asked in a sarcastic tone.

"Those two guys, are members of our Armed Forces. We are going to see that they get a fair trial. Is that OK with you? Or should we hang them without a trial?" I answered, trying my best, to match his sarcasm.

The truck wreckage stood out like a sore thumb. At first I didn't see the convertible. With a little closer observation, there it was, still under the Army Truck. I suddenly felt a little spooky. I honestly could feel a chill, running up and down my back. I had to finish my work and get out of there.

The whole undercarriage was exposed. Sticking up was a short stubby portion of the vehicle's drive shaft. It was plane to see where the universal joint had broken and the shaft worn where it apparently drug against something. In my mind, that something was cement. I took a lot of pictures and headed back to Fort Devens. I was happy, I could make a case for my two comrades.

I took my exposed film to the Army Photo Lab, before I went to see CMS Pope and the CO. My pictures were on 35MM film. If I took them to a civilian processor, it would take days. In less than two hours they were mounted and ready for showing. I borrowed a slide projector and went to see CSM Pope.

I made my slide presentation to Sergeant Major Pope and LTC Voughn. Slide by slide, I went through my theory on what happened the day of the accident. They both agreed, what I was pointing out made a lot of sense.

The LTC promised he would brief Group Headquarters. My suggestion that Specialist Meadows be put in for the Soldiers Medal, for saving Specialist Henry's life, fell on deaf ears. There was no way the Army was going to award a medal when the death of two women occurred in the same incident.

Meadows and Henry returned to the unit without any charges being lodged against them. In the long run, the Army lost, neither Meadows nor Henry reenlisted, both went back to civilian life. I often wonder what happened to them. The Army lost two great soldiers.

Uninvited Guest

Thank God, Fort Devens was a closed post. Visitors were unable to get past the Main Gate without the person being visited signing them in. Most of the time, civilian or military, know when a visit is planned by friend or family. On rare occasions, surprise visits show up. Nine times out of ten, it would be an old sweetheart or somebody that thinks they are your sweetheart. Without stretching the imagination, most will agree, this could be embarrassing or downright dangerous. While at a Special Forces Decade Association meeting one Saturday, the announcement came over the loud speaker.

"Sergeant Major Brown, you have visitors at the Main Gate." I know from experience, this brought terror to SGM Brown.

"Mac, do me a favor, go see who it is. Tell them I'm not on post, anything, just get rid of them." SGM Brown had a good reason to be nerves. He lived on Post with his wife Peggy and his three children. Even though Don had never gone any further than flirting, I don't think Peggy would have understood. I had no problem doing Don a favor. I had a slight problem coming up with a plan to discourage the visitors and make them head for home.

Bat Tolz Germany

I could come up with a story that would put my friend out of the picture permanently. Like he was struck with lightning, or his parachute failed. No that's to morbid. If Peggy found out about his visitors, she would kill him, making my story a reality. I decided to give Don an emergency reassignment. The 10th had a Battalion (1st BN.) in Bat Toltz Germany and a classified Detachment in Berlin. I decided on Bat Toltz.

"Hi Mary, Janette, what are you gal's doing so far south?"

"Hi Doc, Janette got a crush on Donald, he doesn't know it yet, the gal can't sleep at night. She has plans for that boy." When Mary talks, it's hard to get a word in.

"Slow down a little Mary. Apparently you haven't heard about Don Brown. He was assigned to Bat Tolz, he left yesterday." I thought that would cool the fire a little, but no such luck.

"What are you doing tonight Doc?"

"I've got a hot date tonight. Wish I knew you gal's were coming. I'm going to try to break the date If I can, I'll meet you at Paul's. Paul's was a hangout for SF, just outside the Gate in Shirley MA. Both Mary and Janette have been there many times. I knew after a couple of beers, they would forget all about me. We said our good-by's and I went back to the Decade to tell Brown of his new assignment.

The visitors from up north were not gullible. They have been around SF Troops for a long time. They knew it was quite possible, you could be having breakfast with a SF guy in the morning, then not see him for a couple of years. Sometimes you would be on what you thought was a routine jump, and end up in a foreign country. These little excursions are affectionately called, "Fly Away's."

Another way to move people around without too much fan-far, is to put them in civilian cloths and travel with a civilian passport. This doesn't mean that they are on highly secret or classified missions. It may be as simple as keeping a low profile.

For whatever reason, it is good policy not to recognize other SF Operatives at Airports, Train, Bus Stations or other public place. You don't want to blow their cover. The rule is, contact is made by the person or persons, that don't belong at that location. Let me explain;

Let's say, you are assigned to Bangkok Thailand, and you have been assigned there for quit some time. Your mission is not classified.

Everyone knows of your assignment, the good guys, the bad guy's, everybody. While at Don Maung International Airport, you see an old friend in civilian cloths. Say this is your best friend and you haven't seen him for years. Your first impulse is to run up to him and give him a warm welcome. That's a no, no, you might blow his cover. Now on the other hand, if your friend initiates the warm greeting. That's OK, his action indicates he is not on a classified mission, he has no cover to blow. Of course, he had better make sure he doesn't blow your cover.

I remember one time I was at an airport in the Philippines. I spotted an old friend, Johnny Hollis. I wasn't sure if he saw me or not. Not wanting to blow his cover to bring attention to myself, I looked in the opposite direction and hollered;

"George Derby, George, it's me McGinley." There was no George. I just wanted Hollis to notice me.

He didn't bat an eye. Johnny continued on as though I didn't exist. I wasn't surprised. SFC Hollis went on many classified trips. His ignoring me, started the old brain working overtime. What kind of trip was he on? How many people are involved? Why didn't I know about it? The answer was very simple, "I didn't have a need to know."

FLINTLOCK "72"

The annual "FLINTLOCK Exercise" to train NATO allies became the central points of every ODA's training program. Of course, this event was complimented by environmental skills and language training, The 10th was assigned to Denmark for the 72 Flintlock exercise.

Like all the exercises I went on at Fort Devens, I was on the advance party with SGM Don Brown, SFC Pat Hudelson and MSG Ernest Tabata. We flew from Massachusetts to Greenham an RAF airbase in England. This would be the staging area for our jump into Denmark, at the start of Flintlock 72.

I knew MSG Tabata before this exercise, but we have never worked together. Ernie was assigned to Special

Greenham RAF Base England

Forces for most of his career and had an outstanding combat record in Korea and Vietnam.. For this operation, MSG Tabata was the S3 (plans & operations) NCOIC. Because of his experiences and attention to detail, Flintlock 72 would be an outstanding success.

Each of us went about our assigned tasks in preparation for deployment. I checked the medical supplies and the portable dispensary we brought with us. After our area study briefing, I decided to add a few more splints. The terrain we were going to jump into would be a little rough. It was a little early to check out the Med-Evac routs. We were going to use Danish Hospitals. Of course I screened all medical records of everyone going on the operation. I don't like surprises after deployment.

Everything went smoothly giving us a lot of time to kill before the main body arrived from the states. SGM Don Brown, Pat Hudelson and myself, decided to take a tour of the local area. MSG Tabata declined our invitation to join us. He knew of our mischievous ways and decided to pass. Besides it's nice to have a friend at base station to bail you out, if by chance the world doesn't understand your activities.

If a tour is to be enjoyable, it must be planned and have some sort of schedule. I'm sure you would agree, it is important to do You're planning at a comfortable location. We headed for a local bar in a near by village. We had trouble from the get go, couldn't find a bar. We had to settle for an English Pub.

You experience a culture shock when you enter an English Pub for the first time. Unlike bars in America, the English Pub's are extremely quiet. It was almost like entering a library. Without exception, all eyes were on us. The ones you couldn't see, you could feel. It was evident the English patrons were not used to noisy people entering their establishment. I am sure there are people noisier than Don, Pat, on myself. I am equally sure that we could hold our own in a noise contest. We ordered a beer at the bar. The bar tender, a very sad looking guy, served the beer as though he was being forced. This guy didn't show an ounce of friendship. I couldn't help myself, I had to ask; "You still mad about Bunker Hill?" I don't think he got it.

We moved our drinks to a table and ordered another beer from a waitress. Her attitude was as bad or worse than the bartender's. We used our best lines on this gal. All our lines attempting to generate a little friendship or maybe a date. All our clever lines, flattered her as a beautiful creature. She shunned them all. We dropped the beautiful in our classification.

Early in our planning, we decided we needed to rent an automobile. Since I was the only one with an International Drivers License, I was assigned the task to rent one. They say, that when I left the British Pub, half of the noise left with me. What are they trying to tell me?

I hailed a cab and told the driver to take me to the nearest car renting office. Driving on the wrong side of the road didn't bother me, I have been in many countries that have similar driving patterns. However the speed this clown was averaging did. I had intended on making a mental note of the direction we were going and turns we made, so I could find my way back the Pub. But this guy's driving kept me in the advance stages of fear, I was almost lost. When we entered a traffic circle and missed our turn off twice. The almost lost, became complete. Finally we arrived at the Hertz Rental Agency, I wasted no time paying speedy and considered myself lucky to be alive.

When Irish Eyes Are Smiling

"I need a little help, can you tell me how to get to Greenham Airbase?" I asked a gentleman walking his dog.

"You can't get there from here. You'll have to go back to the turnaround." I have always heard the term; you can't get there from here, thought it was a joke. He was wright, I couldn't get there from here, but what is a turnaround? I think he meant Traffic Circle. I thanked him and started my search.

The trip to the Car Rental office only took thirty minutes. It took me two hours to find the Traffic Circle. I had a slight problem entering the Circle. I cut a Double Decker Bus off. He in turn hit a truck. I would have stopped, but the traffic was extremely heavy. I was locked in bumper to bumper traffic for over an hour. I passed the accident site three times. Each time slumping down in my seat, keeping a low profile. Finally, I lucked out and found the road to Greenham RAF Airbase. The Pub was closed. My pals hung in there, Don and Pat were waiting for me at a Bus Stop bench.

"Where in the hell have you been?"

"I don't want to talk about it. Besides you wouldn't believe I found that mystical place, where you can't get there from. They didn't have the foggiest clue to what I was talking about. Nor did I. We drove back to the Airfield. However we had to park the car in a Government parking lot off Base, I didn't have a Base Sticker for the rented car.

On our walk back to Base we heard music coming from an apparently closed Club. Closer investigation revealed, the music was Irish. Now an Irishman cannot ignore Irish sounds. Without hesitation and against the advice of my two pals, (they had enough to drink) I knocked on the Pub's locked door. Apparently the music was too loud, no one answered. I gave it another try with a little more effort. I accomplished my task. A very angry gentleman opened the door.

"Are yea daft, man. You're not seeing we are closed. Be off with yea, or you'll be feeling the back of my hand." I wasn't sure if he was a Brit or Irish. What I was sure of, he was very upset. We turned to go, but not without the last word.

"The Queen wears combat boots." I haven't the slightest idea what I meant, nor why I said it.

"Would you lads' join a body, in a pint or two?" He motioned for us to enter, the now very quit Pub.

"Would you be repeating what you were saying out side lad?" I didn't know what he was talking about. I think the puzzled look on my face, prompted him to coach me. "Tell them lad, what the Queen, God bless her sole, be wearing on her feet."

"Oh, the Queen wears Combat Boots." I don't know what they read into that stupid phrase. I didn't intend any insult to the Queen. In fact I like the pageantry, that is associated with a monarchy. I am sure they took it as an insult. The end result, everyone gave out a cheer and the party continued. I'll bet we shook hands with about a hundred people. When we revealed our military status, all wished us a long life and inviting us to join their cause. It became clear, this was an IRA gathering.

We were given a large mug of a dark colored liquid. I don't to this day know what it was. I do know it would give drinking a bad name. This stuff was terrible. All three of us, dumped the foul tasting stuff in the trash, a little at a time. When our mugs were refilled, the dumping continued. The experience proved, you don't have to drink to have a good time. We had a great time. Singing Irish songs, dancing the Irish Jig, and a whole lot of tomfoolery.

When Don picked up a band member's guitar and Pat started playing the piano, they brought the house down. I was a little shocked, I didn't know Pat could play the piano. The lads were talented, and that's a fact. I love an audience and don't hesitate to play the fool. There are some that say, I play the part well. I am not too sure that is a compliment. It matters not, I enjoy my corny act, and don't mind patting myself on the back a time or two. I can guarantee you there is no conceit in my family, I have it all.

The time just flew by. The sun was about to make its entrance. It was time to go back to the airbase. Before we left, our host with the heavy Irish brogue, assured us if we joined their cause, we would all be promoted to whatever rank we desired.

The main body arrived from Fort Devens and we had our final briefing before we departed for Denmark. Maj. Larry P. McIntosh our CO at the time, asked for input from the group. He assured everyone that all ideas would be discussed and the pro and cons given serious consideration. This request puzzled most of us. We were scheduled to make a simulated combat jump into Denmark and link up with the Danish Special (Jaeger Corps) Forces, then march on with the training mission. The Drop Zone had been selected by higher Headquarters and as far as we knew, it was a go. We questioned the CO on just what he meant.

"Gentlemen, I would like to spice this operation up a little. Make it a little more exciting. Make it an operation that would be remembered." The Major went on explaining a couple of his ideas. The first was the granddaddy of all plans. He proposed we jump into the North Sea and rendezvous with a submarine. Then have the sub drop us off in Denmark. I don't remember who jumped up in opposition to this plan first. We all took our turn.

The opposition ranged from safety, to cost, to compromising the mission. The north Sea is extremely cold and turbulent year round. Special Forces was struggling for training dollars this idea would take a lot of money. All those parachutes in the sky, jumping into the North Sea would draw too much attention. The success of all Special Forces missions, training or real, is secrecy. They have to be conducted in a clandestine manor.

Finally MSG Tabata made the point, that our original plan was approved by higher Headquarter, aircraft and support elements having been laid on. The vocal response from the meeting attendees, convinced the Major to back off his North Sea plan. But that didn't stop him. The Major had another great plan.

"How about jumping in with bicycles? Most people in the area use bicycles for transportation. We would blend in." The response to this plan was meet with equal opposition. If I were asked, and I wasn't, I would have advised the Major to take two aspirins and go to bed. He would feel better in the morning. A final check of the operation plan, loading equipment on the aircraft and we were off to Denmark and the start of Flintlock 72.

It was a great day for a jump. Cloudless sky's, marginal winds, and a DZ as flat and unobstructed as could be. Our link up with the Jaeger Korpset (Jaeger Corps) was a little disappointing. Their lackadaisical approach to a serious training exercise was the worst I have ever seen. My first impressions of the Danish Jaeger Corps, was low, and kept getting lower as the mission progressed.

In every country Special Forces conduct training exercises, we are invited to visit their Airborne Training Center and make a jump with their cadre. It's kind of a protocol thing. At the end of the jump we are awarded that country's jump wings. We reciprocate when they come to the United States.

The jump at the Danish school was from an old C-46. It brought back memories to the older jumpers and an opportunity for our younger troops. It's surprising this vintage aircraft from World War II is still flying. The C-46 cargo plane has proven to be a dependable work horse. I  don't think it will ever lose its utility.

Part of our exercise involved the Danish HALO Team. The plan was, our HALO Team would join them in a night jump. The operation plot was to clandestinely reinforce an existing guerilla movement. A relatively simple manoeuver. Under the cover of darkness, move the Guerrilla Force close to the drop-zone. Dig pot holes and mix diesel fuel with lose dirt. When you hear the sound of the aircraft, light the pot holes. This will guide the aircraft to the drop zone. When the Pilot radios the jumpers are in the air, fill the pot holes, then link up with the jumpers and head for cover. What could go wrong? The answer, add Danish Officers.

They insisted we were not to dig holes. We were to carry one gallon metal containers filled with sand. In addition we had to carry a five-gallon can of diesel fuel. The fuel and sand had to be mixed on the DZ. We were hopeful the Major would put his foot down. Apparently he didn't want to make waves.

Keep in mind this was a clandestine mission and here we are tramping through the countryside with a gunnysack full of clanking tin cans. Hang on it gets worse.

We had to remove the sod from a three-foot square area for each can and place the can in the middle of the square. After the jump we had to replace the sod, water it, and then move out. This operation was compromised from the beginning. The whole town came to watch the dog and pony show.

Most training of foreign troops have a built in evaluation. As they accomplish a given task, more difficult tasks and standards are added. It's a good approach to avoid embarrassing the host nation. It's a great feeling when you take a group of people to a higher level of performance. A great pride building experience for both, the trainer and trainee. This was not possible with the Danish troops in 1972. Their level of training was unbelievably low.

We gave up on Unconventional Warfare training. Part of UW training contains sensitive subject matter. Care has to be exercised on who you give it to. In addition it would have been a waste of time and money. They were just not up to it. We devoted most of our time on weapon firing and parachute jumping. This seemed to please them the most. These guys were fun jumpers at heart, not Special Forces.

SGM Billy Boggs, made a left turn into the target. His turn was to close to the ground and his Para-Commander parachute slammed him into the ground. I think Billy was grandstanding. SGM Don Brown just made a dead center and Billy wanted to match him. A difficult task, SGM Brown a former Army Golden Knight Parachute Team member, hit dead center on most of his jumps.

"I think I broke my wrist Mac."

"Yes Billy you have."

The ninety degree bend in his wrist and radios bone protruding through a gaping hole, made that a fairly accurate diagnosis. We had an ambulance on the DZ for medical support. However, both Danish Medics were sleeping. Literally, stretched out on the stretchers. I drove SGM Boggs to the hospital in my rented vehicle. While Boggs was sitting, a young well-proportioned Danish nurse, squatted and began to unlace his jump boots. Being a gentleman, I attempted to help her.

"McGinley, I'm going to kill you. She's doing fine. She doesn't need your help." It doesn't take a ton of bricks to fall on me. Looking down, Boggs had an excellent view of this well endowed gal and wanted it to last as long as possible. I sat alongside of him and enjoyed the scenery and/or floorshow. They took Billy into surgery, leaving me with some time to kill.

Entering a beer garden close to the hospital, I remember being surprised it was so crowded. It was mid afternoon and the joint was full. Don't these people work? As customary in most European bars and restaurants, you can occupy any available seat, without the other occupants permission. The only table off limits is the one belonging to the owner and his family. You sit at that table by invitation only.

I ordered a beer. As a friendly gesture, asked if anybody else wanted a drink. They declined and one by one left the table. I saw this happen before when Don and Pat were with me. That puzzled me. When the waitress came back with my half empty beer, I popped the question.

"Why did they get up and leave? Do I have a bad breath or something?"

"Some Danish people don't like to drink with Americans sir. Aren't you going to complain about you half glass of beer?"

"No sweetheart, you drink it. The only Great Dane I have ever seen, was a dog." I was highly ticked off. From that day on, I kept my visiting Danish restaurants and bars to a minimum. I went back to the hospital to check on Boggs.

The balance of the operation was equally nonproductive. I haven't the slightest idea what the cost of this operation was to the American Tax payer. Whatever the cost, it was too much. Why can't we tell the truth when a host nation preforms poorly? Tell them the way it is and suggest additional training for their improvement.

These clowns couldn't fight their way out of a paper bag. Maybe it is not their intention to fight if the balloon goes up. They didn't fight in World War II. Denmark was attacked by Germany on the morning of April 9, 1939 and surrendered before noon of the same day. Now they would probably surrender by phone. Shame on me for thinking they might fight today.

One must give credit where credit is due. In WWII Denmark warned the Danish Jew's the Germans were going to put them in prison camps. Because of that warning, most Danish Jews escaped to Sweden. Over the course of the war a resistance movement steadily grew but when Germany invaded Russia some Danes volunteered to fight for Germany.

In about 95 percent of training missions at home or abroad, leave you with a sense of accomplishment. Denmark fall's in the other 5 percent. We didn't do a thing that amounted to a hill of beans. The Danish people I met seemed to have an attitude problem. They say a people represent the pulse of their nation.

Denmark is a welfare state. Welfare has a tendency to break the spirt and pride in a man (No gender intended). Spirt and pride are the main ingredients of a positive attitude. Another trat you will find in a welfare Nation or people on welfare, they make a lot of demands for more of the same.

They not only demand more, they demand how it is to be distributed or given. The one thing you can depend on when you are the giver of welfare, the receiver will end up disliking you. The giver is always blamed for the recipients loss of pride.

Take a look at our so-called allies. Every one of them were brought from the rubbles of a devastating war, to a productive nation status. All on American (Marshall Plan) welfare. Take a closer look at their attitude toward the United States today. That should prove my point.

ORTT Rocky Rival

The first thing I did when I got back to Fort Devens, was go to see Mrs. Billy Alexander at the Special Forces Assignment Branch in Alexander VA. Like always Billy promised to do whatever she could to get me assigned to Special Forces Thailand. When Mrs. Billy Alexander states, she will do whatever, you can pack your bags. She will make it happen. My desire to leave the 10th was a hard one to make. I liked the unit, the people and their training area in the states. What I didn't like, was their area of assignment, Europe and the Middle East. If I never saw a Great Dane, a French Frog, or Alibaba and The Forty Thieves again, it would be to soon.

Mrs "A"

The same day I got back from Virginia, Delta Co. 3rd SFBN 10th SF took off for a hilly area north of Syracuse New York for their annual communications evaluation. The area was selected because of the high level of iron-ore. Iron-ore-made radio communication difficult. Back in the 70s, we didn't have satellite communications. Some of you old radio guys' will remember bouncing an ANGR-9 Radio signal off the ionosphere to reach a receiver far beyond the normal range. You had to be good. I guess you could call the technique, radio-billiards. Well, D Company had one of the best radio-billiard guys around, SFC Lanning

David Lanning was a lay back guy. Dave didn't spend much time at clubs. All his off time was spent with his family, hunting, fishing and a lot of camping. He definitely wasn't antisocial, he just had family oriented commitments.

As I recall, we had to attempt communications with Fort Devens every ten hours. To receive a passing grade, sixty percent of your como attempts had to be successful. David received a one hundred present grade for Company D. Needless to say, we bragged about this for a while. Like they say, communicate and shoot straight.

I knew I would be going back to the Orient. I also knew Orientals have an above average, ear, nose and throat medical problems. I requested OJT (on the job training) at the Fort Devens Army Hospital, ENT Clinic. My request was approved two hours after I submitted it. CSM Pope saw to that.

I liked Major Gaynor the first time I meet him. He came in the Army as a Major and was immediately put on the LTC promotion list. This was one talented surgeon. He was impressed with the reason I wanted to work in the EMT Clinic. He took me under his wing from the very start. To this day, I haven't been in a more productive learning situation.

"Sergeant McGinley, how do I look. The Hospital Commander wants to see me. This is the first time I have worn my class A uniform. How do I look?"

"Not to bad Sir." I said as I straightened his Cap. "But those orange tennis shoes have to go. Orange shoes with a Class A Uniform is a no,no." It took all the composure I could muster, to keep from laughing.

We exchanged shoes. Let me fine tune that. I exchanged my jump boots for his orange tennis shoes. He was still out of uniform, he should have been wearing low quarters. But his trousers would help conceal his boot wearing. I had many memorable times working with Major Gaynor, some bring a chuckle when I think about them and a few, very few, bring a tear.

I not only accompanied the Major on all of his surgical procedures, I scrubbed in on every case. Without exception, I was given a task to assist in the completion of a given surgical procedure. This by far was a rare happening. Non doctors and especially enlisted personnel are never allowed this latitude.

Nobody questioned my presence in the OR. They assumed because of my involvement in the procedure, I was a medical officer. The fact that I was much older then Major Gaynor, reinforced their assumption. Then it happened;

"Gaynor, who is that scrubbing next to you? I don't think we have been introduced." The question came from the OR's Chief Nurse, Colonel Wallen.

Colonel Wallen ruled the OR with an iron hand. In spite of her rough mannerism and sometimes loud tone to her voice, the Colonel was highly respected. She knew her job. For some reason Major Gaynor was scared to death of the Colonel. I could feel the tension building up inside him. Then like a bolt of lightning it hit. I knew this Colonel.

"Colonel Wallen, we have meet. You were a Lieutenant then, and one of my favorite instructors at the Academy." I was referring to the Academy of Health Sciences at Brook Medical Center, San Antonio Texas. The Colonel walked closer.

"I don't recall." Then she changed direction and asked; "Were you a sergeant, a Special Forces Sergeant?" I acknowledged in the affirmative. "Yes I remember. How could I forget the things' you Special Forces people did? My what a small world. I apologize, but I forgot your name."

"McGinley Colonel, Daniel T. McGinley."

"Yes, yes, McGinley. I didn't know you went to Medical School."

"You would be surprised how many schools I have been to since we last met Colonel."

After a little more chatting, this talented Colonel left the scrub room. There I just did it, I described a truly great American, without playing the Race Card....Yes she was.

By this time Major Gaynor was walking on air. He was amazed, I knew his most feared person in the Hospital. He acted as though I had just slain a dragon.

This next incident falls somewhere between a chuckle and a tear. We were conducting routine ENT clinic examinations. One of our patients arrived in handcuffs and was accompanied by two MP's. This was the first time I saw Major Gaynor get upset.

"Take those handcuffs off and both of you can wait outside while we examine the patient." When the MP's emphasized that the patient might be dangerous, the Major replied; "Sergeant McGinley can handle anything that might happen." I think the Major has been reading too many books about SF. I'm a lover not a fighter. The cuffs came off and I didn't relax until they were put back on and the MP's removed the patient.

Another one of our patients was a seven-year-old girl. A sweet little tot in need of a Tonsillectomy. The operation went well and the little girl was sent to recovery room and then the pediatric ward.

I have always thought, Tonsillectomy was a routine procedure. Positively not true. In addition to risks incurred, putting anybody under general anesthesia, hemorrhaging is a constant threat. Sometime during the night, this precious little girl started to hemorrhage and aspirated her own fluid. Major Gaynor was devastated over the loss of this precious young life. He wrongfully blamed himself.

I spent more than three hours convincing the Major this was a nursing care inefficiency. If any blame was to be given, and I was not sure there was, it had to lay at the door of nursing care, or the lack of.

Quite often, the nursing stations on wards, turn into social gathering places. I have personally observed this, as a health care provider and/or a patient. It is true, in both military and civilian hospitals. This transformation is especially apparent after 20:00 hours when most of the hospital is closed and visiting hours are over.

The late evening and early morning hours are critical times for patients. Patients should be personally observed more often, not less. I think if we were looking for the reason why we wouldn't have to look far. The more experienced staff members and health care providers usually have their choice of what shift they work. The less experienced and new workers are left with, the appropriately named, graveyard shift.

Another predicable thing that happens on the late shift more than on the early shifts, is social gathering at the nurses station. This nonproductive activity lasts most of the night. This activity is only interrupted by a patient ringing for attention. I emphasized this theory to Major Gaynor.

Neglect is not a word, you could associate with this Giant of a surgeon, Major Gaynor. His dedication to his patients was above and beyond. He conducted ENT Clinic walk in care, five days a week, from 08:00 to 13:00 (catching lunch on the fly). From 13:00 to 16:00 and beyond (depending on the procedure) he spent in the operating room. He would pause just long enough to vocally record his notes for the patients charts   Then off to the surgical ward to visit and monitor every patient's progress. It was not usual for the Major to be on the ward late into the night. Most doctors will tell their patients every Friday, "I'll see you on Monday" Not Gaynor, he visited his patents, Saturday's Sunday"s and holiday"s.

My schedule duplicated his. If Gaynor was in the Hospital, McGinley was in the Hospital. But I had an alternative motive. I did it for personal gain. You couldn't be with this great man without learning something new. And I had a lot to learn. The more time I spent with Maj. Gaynor, the more he would let me do in the OR.

On Deviated Septum procedures, we took turns on who would be the mallet man and who would hold the chisel. The procedure involved correcting the alignment of a previously broken or malformed nose bone. This was done by actually re-breaking the bone and realigning it. A properly placed surgical chisel and a sharp blow with a metal surgical mallet, and presto a broken nose. The realignment was done by hand, at the discretion of the surgeon.

"How does that look Mac?" Gaynor would ask.

"Not bad Sir. Well maybe a little to the left, that's better." I swear to you, that's how it went. If you saw the chisel and mallet, you would have thought they came from a body and fender man's tool box.

The main procedure Major Gaynor was known for was Tympanoplasty (replacement of ruptured ear drums.) First he prepared an extremely thin skin graft. After he made a circular incision around the entrance to the Auditory Canal, holding the shin graft in

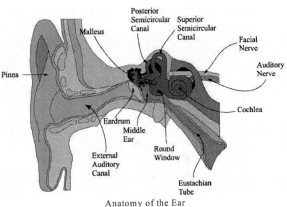

Anatomy of the Ear

place with a suction probe, he then tucked the skin graft in the incision. All this was done with a two-prism microscope, allowing two people to observe the procedure. It surely was a sight to behold.

I received my reassignment orders to Thailand late December, with a reporting date of 14 January 1973.

Chapter Eight

Lopburi Thailand

I decided to depart for Thailand from Travis Air Force Base in California. It was a long cross country drive but it afforded me the opportunity to visit friends and relatives along the way. My restored 1966

Corvette was in excellent condition and looked like a million dollars, and I felt like a million dollars driving it. Well you don't actually drive a Corvette, you aim it. I aimed this beauty west.

My first major stop was in Chicago to visit some old friends. I surprised myself, I didn't have any desire to visit the Sky Diving Center at Hebron Airport. Like an old girl friend, our relationship was over. Then off to Denver Colorado to visit with my Sister Sara and her family. I continued my trip to Colorado Springs to see my Brother Jack and his family. Then a nonstop trip to California.

During the whole trip I pondered with the idea of selling my Corvette or putting it in storage. The first dealer I stopped at offered me more money then I have ever hoped for, and I could use the Corvette until my departing day. After the dealer dropped me off at Travis, my heart broke as the Metallic Brown, love of my life drove off.

That Green Beret stands out in a crowd. I spotted one lad sprawled out on a bench and approached him.

"My name is McGinley, where are you heading?" I announced reaching out my hand.

"Lester Jackson, I'm headed for Thailand." Then he went on to tell me he has been waiting two days for an aircraft. What was worse, he was told, he might be at Travis for another two days. There was only one flight a day scheduled, and priority assignments were getting to the head of the line.

"No problem Sergeant Jackson. Come with me and keep your mouth shut. It's important, you go along with whatever I say. Can you handle that?" He agreed. We went to the head of the line.

"Excuse me Sir, I have a prisoner." The Captain we got in front of, almost jumped back.

"I need two seats with priority loading." That meant we could board the aircraft without delay. The guy issuing boarding passes, started to process us with a special urgency.

"Do you have a weapon Sergeant? Will you need any type of restraint?" I answered both questions with a negative.

"I could handle this runt with one arm. If he tries to run, I'll break both his legs." I added to reinforce my negative answers. In five minutes we were headed for Gate Four. Flashed our boarding passes, and boarded the 707. I wish I had a camera. The look on Jackson's face was something to see. He was playing the part well, he looked like a prisoner.

We had a two-hour wait before departure. No problem. We were in a warm aircraft, sipping on cocktails served by good-looking flight attendants. It took a little manipulating to be served while the plane was still on the ground. Again, no problem. After all, isn't life just one big manipulation? All in all, this beat the heck out of that crowed airport waiting room.

Lester Jackson was a young radio operator relatively new in Special Forces. This was his first overseas assignment.

We had a one day lay over at Clark Airbase in the Philippines. Because the country was under Martial Law, leaving the airport was limited to Officers and Senior NCO's. It was time for Lester to return to prisoner status. We hailed a cab and headed for the main gate.

"I'm sorry Sergeant, only top three grades and officers are allowed off Base."

"This guy is my prisoner, where I go, he goes. The Gate Guard saluted, and we were on our way.

I started to get a little funny feeling. The further we drove the funny feeling turned into a deep concern. There wasn't a sole on the streets. An occasional colorful Jeepney but that was it. It was amazing what the resourceful Filipino did to the left behind Army Jeep. They transformed them into people carrying, works of art.

Jeepney (World War II Jeep)

I directed the taxi driver to stop at the Police station. Registering with the Police, was a requirement it you chose to live off Base. They had to know where all Americans were in case of trouble. If you decided to change hotels or go to a restaurant or club, they had to be notified by phone.

I chose a Hotel directly across the street from the Police station. I figured it would be safer near the fire power. I wasn't choosing sides, I was initiating a CYA (cover your back side) plan. A habit I acquired living in the Far East. Nations are known to have changed governments in the middle of the night.

I was ready to compliment the hotel manager on the excellent service we received. We had four bellboys greeting us. Then I realized, we were the only guests in the lobby. If there is anything worse than poor service, it's too much service. This would be true every place we went. People were tripping over each other, trying to get to us first.

This was Lester's first trip outside the United States. I felt compelled to give him a survival, don't trust anybody, briefing. I started with securing his valuables, especially his wallet. I told him I usually hid my wallet in the commode's flush tank. I also told him not to take his jewelry off. Keep his watch rings, gold chines or whatever on. If anybody stole my jewelry while I was wearing them, it wouldn't matter. Death would take care of the problem, theirs or mine. The more I told Jackson, the more concerned he became. I ended the briefing.

After we freshened up, we decided to take a look at the town. With the recommendations, from the Desk Clerk we headed for a local club. Like the greeting at the Hotel, we received a welcome fit for a king. And like the Hotel we were the only customers in the club.

"Are you redecorating?' I asked the bartender. I was referring to the pile of rubble in one corner of the club.

"No, No we had boom, one week tomorrow." He replied is broken English. What in the heck is a boom? I thought to myself. Then came the dawn, he was talking about a bomb.

Lester Jackson didn't pay any attention to our conversation, he was to busy checking out the thirty plus beautiful hostesses, setting around waiting for suckers, I mean clients, customers, dates, ...well you know what I mean. I didn't pass on my newest revelation to my new pal. I used the intelligence, "need to know" rule. In fact, I am going to start using the, "need to know" rule on you, the reader. There are some things, that if I tell you, I'll have to kill you. Or more correctly, if I tell you, my wife Chome will kill me.

"Mac I have never seen so many beautiful women in one place."

"You haven't been to Thailand yet son. Thai women would make these gal's look like guy's." I don't think Jackson believed me, but he would soon find out.

We did a lot of dancing and chitchatting. Some would say conducting interviews for possible classified missions. We finally narrowed the large group down to a few of the best lookers. Then I initiated my master plan.

I told the group that Special Forces were coming back to the Philippines and that we needed a place to live. I told them that the place I would rent must have a swimming pool, exercise room and at least four bedrooms. And above all I needed someone to be my main housekeeper. Her duties would be supervising all other household staff to include the chauffeur. This was not an unbelievable story. In the Philippines like most Far East Countries domestic help is cheap.

Then like in the animal world, the dominating female emerged. All the gals left the table taking Jackson with them. Setting at my side was the gal with all the power. A beautiful creature with the mannerism of a queen. I felt like King Daniel. From this point on you don't have, the need to know."

The next morning, Lester knocked on my door and to my surprise he was holding a fist full of very wet money. His wallet fell in the flush tank water. We hung money everywhere. My room looked like a hand laundry, Is this what they mean by "money laundering?

Back to Clark, we were running a little late and almost missed our flight. We spent the rest of the flight talking about what we have been through the past few days. Lester Jackson was impressed with what could be accomplished with a little imagination and a lot of guts. I classified it as, training your subordinates. Like they say, it's a rough job but somebody has to do it.

Bangkok

Lester went on to Lopburi, home of Special Forces 46 Company. I stayed in Bangkok a few days with my family. Although we had a modest home in a Bangkok suburb, I decided we should live it up a little in one of Bangkok's many modern hotels. I rented a suite at the Siam Hotel. The hotel's restaurant was great. The Olympic size pool and

River Taxi

recreation area was especially liked by our son Johnny. I started to feel like and act like a tourist. We visited many places of interest including a ride on Bangkok's famous river taxi's.

The Siam Hotel would not allow taxi cabs anywhere near their property. Instead, they had drivers with their privately owned automobiles waiting at an assigned parking area. It was possible to hire one of their drivers for twenty dollars a day. In addition to driving, your private Chauffeur would recommend merchants, places of interest, establishments that wouldn't rip you off and advise you on Thai customs. Having your personal driver in Thailand is the way to go.

We were lucky. A lad named Lek who once worked for Chome's family was our driver. Lek was a well dressed, well-mannered Thai gentleman. Above all, Lek could handle the supersaturated Thai traffic. They say, if you can drive in Bangkok Thailand, you can drive anywhere. I know they say that about many cities. Tokio Japan, Sole Korea, Frankfort Germany, yes even our own Boston MA. I have to go along with them, I have driven in them all. I can tell you without reservation, Bangkok Thailand wins, hands down.

When I ran out of leave time, I had Lek take me to my new assignment. This way my wife Chome could accompany me and have transportation back to Bangkok.

We arrived in Lopburi Thailand on a Sunday afternoon. My reluctance of checking in a new unit, on a week end still held. I rented a room at the Lopburi Hotel, the only hotel in Lopburi at the time. Chome and I had lunch at the hotel's restaurant.

"Lek, join us for lunch." I was sincere about the invitation. The short time I have known Lek, I considered him a friend.

"No thank you Mr. Mac. I will eat at a noddle stand. Thank you for your kind offer."

"Lek, you will have lunch with us, or you will never drive for me again." Lek's appreciation was apparent, he joined us. I had no input as to what was to be on our menu. In fact I had no say on what I would be eating the balance of my stay at the hotel. Chome preordered all my meals.

Thai cuisine is pungent and spicy, seasoned with heaps of garlic and chillies and a characteristic mix of lime juice, lemon grass and fresh coriander. Galanga root, basil, ground peanuts, tamarind juice, ginger and coconut milk are other common additions. Fish sauce or shrimp paste are mainstays of Thai dishes, and of course rice is eaten with most meals.

Main dishes include, hot and sour fish ragout, green and red curries, various soups and noodle dishes. Thai food is served with a variety of condiments and dipping sauces. Snacks and appetizers include fried peanuts, chicken, chopped ginger, peppers and slices of lime. We ended up with a great Thai meal.

The traditional greeting is a wai. This is a prayer-like gesture, with the palms pressed together and the tips of your fingers level with your nose - the neutral position. The higher the wai, the more respect is being shown. It is used when you are arriving or leaving. In the wai position, I bid my farewell.

"Sa-wai-dee Krahp." I bid Chome good-by.

"Sa-wai-dee Ka." Chome replied. There was no hug or kiss. Demonstrating affection in public, is frowned upon in Thailand.

Chome and Lek headed back to Bangkok. I was alone in the mysterious city of Lopburi.

They sure didn't spend a lot of money on decorating my room. Bed, chair and small night stand, was the extent of the furnishings. It was a good thing I didn't have anybody to call, the phone was down the hall. The ceiling was a good ten feet high. As I lay on my bed looking up, the movie Casablanca came to mind. There was a hotel-room in that Humphry Bogart movie, exactly like this one. I couldn't sleep. I got up to check out the city.

The first neon sign I saw was Bell's Bar. I expected to see a lot of Ding Dongs (that's a joke pal) when I opened the door. I was mistaken. There were only three other people at the far end of the bar. I took a seat about mid-bar and ordered a vodka on the rocks with a lemon twist. The continuous movie on a large screen behind the bar showed a lot of parachute pictures. This was probably a SF hangout.

This place was as boring as the hotel room. It was my intention to finish my drink and go back to the hotel. Then a gentleman from the far side of the bar, came over and sat beside me.

"Who are you?" He asked in with a not so friendly tone.

"Who in the hell is asking?" I fired back in a tone that reflected my anger. When confronted with a consultation, I am the kind of person (because of my size) that will jump in, deliver whatever it is I have to deliver, win or lose, just get it over with. I ordered another drink. This was not the ideal moment to leave. When the drink arrived, I took a sip and then turned, facing the possible threat.

There would be no consultation. Beside me, with one pant leg rolled halfway to his knee, exposing his prostheses, sat mortar mouth. Staring at his empty glass left no doubt in my mind he was drunk. I poured my drink into his glass and headed for the door. It was now the ideal moment to leave. I would see this one legged drunk again.

Before I dozed off, I read a short history of Special Forces 46 Company from a pamphlet I brought with me. For your information. it read;

United States Army Special Forces Thailand
History In brief

United States Army Special Forces Thailand, was originally organized as The Reactivated Company D (Augmented), 1st Special Forces Group (Airborne), 1st Special Forces, in 1966. In October of that year, after intensive pre-mission training, the unit deployed to Thailand. An SFOB was initially established at camp Pawal, Lopburi, Thailand. At this time, major training camps were established at Nom Mung Dam, Nong Takoo, and Ban Kachong.

On 15 April 1967 the unit was redesignated 46 Special Forces Company (Airborne) 1st Special Forces. The organization no longer possessed the Lineage of its previous designation but shared the linage and honors of the parent regiment, The First Special Forces. In December, 1967, the headhunters moved from Camp Pawai to the home of the Royal Thai Army Special Warfare Center at Fort Narai in Lopburi.

On 1 April 1970, the 46th Special Forces Company (Airborne) 1st Special Forces was inactivated, the unit was reactivated as United States Army Special Forces Thailand. Many diversified missions have been levied upon United Stated Army Special Forced Thailand, with the emphasis placed on counterinsurgency training. Initially, the unit was tasked with training selected infantry units of the Royal Thai Army prior to their deployment to northern and southern Thailand.

Close coordination with Thai Armed Forces in formulating Training Programs, to include counterinsurgency and staff training for the Royal Thai Army. Specialized coursed for the royal Thai Army Special Forces and Airborne Battalion personnel, Ranger training, and Boarder Police courses were as effective.

During 1967, selected personnel of the 46th Special Forces Company (Airborne), 1st Special Forces, provided the Royal Thai Army volunteer Regiment (Queen's Cobra) with training in preparation for deployment to the Republic of Vietnam.

As time passed, additional programs were added to original missions to encompass the training of paramilitary and police organizations, such as the Volunteer Defense Corps/Mobile Reserve Platoons, National Police and Police Aerial Reenforcement Units (PARU), to mention a few.

Accomplishment of the units many diversified missions and enjoyment of the admirable history the unit has been possible only through the efforts of the Officers and men of the United Stated Army Spacial Forces, Thailand. They are proud, they are pleased, they are;   "The Professionals"

Traveling Monkeys

I hired a Baht Bus to take me to 46 Company Headquarters. Baht Buses are similar to the Philippine Jeepney. The major difference is they are built around small pick up trucks instead of jeeps. The driver was all over the place. It seemed he was looking for potholes to hit. This by far was not a good driver. Then all of a sudden, the ride got as smooth as silk. I could have walked faster than this guy was driving.

Baht Bus

Without notice a large monkey jumped in the doodles rear end of the bus. It scared the heck out of me, since the apple carrying monster almost landed on my lap. The event didn't bother the other passengers. They told me it happens all the time. Looking outside I could see hundreds of the beasts walking around the downtown area as though they owned it. As a matter of fact, they did. These critters were protected by law. Anyone hurting or mistreating them would be put in jail. It was no wonder the driver slowed down. You might say this was the safest street in Thailand. My curiosity compelled me to get off the bus. I took a seat at a sidewalk café. I not only received excellent service, my english-speaking waiter filled me in on the legend of the monkey.

Lopburi was formerly Ayutthaya, a city founded by King U-Thong or King Ramathibodi I in 1350 and Thailand's (Siam) first capital. The Ayutthaya period lasted for 417 years during which 33 Kings of five dynasties reigned over the country. Ayutthaya was the ancient capital of the Khmer empire which later fell to the Thai army. It boasts a number of interesting monuments. Saan Phra Kaan (Phra Kaan Shrine) or the High Shrine is an ancient Khmer shrine. At present, it is still the place for worshiping and it is believed that the herds of monkeys living around the area of the shrine are former disciples. The macaques of Lopburi are very fortunate monkeys, indeed. They are fed by the city residents, and tourists. People believe they make merit by feeding the monkeys.

Once a year, in late November a passenger train is provided to transport the monkeys to Chiengmai Thailand for a religious celebration. The train is loaded with fruits and vegetables to lure the monkeys aboard. They stay about three days, then the same train brings them back to Lopburi. They will often on their own, hop rides on the train to Chiengmai and back and beg for food at train stations.

The monkeys are everywhere in Lopburi and some people say they are being trained to rob tourists. I do not believe that. But they are not shy at all, so you have to take care of your belongings. Time was flying by. I hired another Baht Bus to take me to 46th Company.

46th Special Forces Company

I had a long walk from the main gate to 46th Company Headquarters. Baht Buses were not allowed on post. I couldn't believe how hot it was for January. My duffel bag got heavier with every step I took.

"McGinley." The voice sounded familiar. Turning around I was happy to see SGM Harry Pope. Early into our conversation. SGM Pope pocked up the phone and told whoever was on the other end, that I was assigned to his company.

SGM Harry Pope

My assignment to the 46th Company was getting off to a great start. I looked forward to, working with Harry Pope again.

"Sergeant Sutter." SGM Pope summoned his administrative NCO, "Take the Jeep and help McGinley find a place to hang his hat. There are a couple vacancies in my compound. Show him around." As we were leaving the SGM added, "I don't expect to see you until morning." SSG Ronald Suter was an outgoing type guy. Easy to make friends with, and friends we became.

All Special Forces Operatives working in Thailand, lived on the local economy. There were several housing compounds with upgrade houses, built by the Thai's to meet the American market needs. Each compound had two or more houses and an elaborate security fence. Security is a major concern when living abroad.

With Ron's help, I found a two story, three bedroom home with servant quarters. The compound had two other houses. A smaller one in front occupied by a HALO Team Radio Operator, SFC James Whitley and his wife Kim. The other behind me, the home of SSG John Burdish and his wife Noi. John was the HALO Team's Medic. Great home, great neighbors, that were soon to be great friends. It doesn't get any better than that.

While I was settling in, SGM Pope made an appointment for me to see the Commander of 46 Company LTC William P. Radtke and CSM Marshall C. Lynch. The interview went extremely well. Both gentlemen were going to be easy to work with. This was going to be a great assignment. As I was about to leave, LTC William L. Shelton, 46 Companies Deputy Commander, asked to see me.

" I understand you ran a Sport Parachuting Center in civilian life." He stated enthusiastically."

"Yes Sir, Land of Lincoln Sky Divers." I was proud to announce.

"We need your help. How would you like to run our Sport Parachuting Club?" LTC Shelton went on to explain the former manager of the Sport Parachuting Club, CSM Carlos Leal was killed on a Sport Parachuting Jump. The club has been closed ever since the accident. It would remain closed until they can find someone with the proper credentials to run it. He figured with my background, he could convince higher headquarters, to let them reopen the parachute club.

CSM Carlos Leal

The LTC went on to explain, the club was in poor administrative condition and needed restructuring from the ground up. He added he wanted the club to follow USSPA (US Sport Parachute Association) rules and would try to find an FAA (Federal Aviation Agency) licenced rigger to pack the Club's reserve parachutes. By law all reserve parachutes have to be packed by a licenced rigger. At present, they were being packed by a military rigger.

"I'm a FAA Licenced Rigger Sir." The LTC perked up.

"Sergeant McGinley, we really need your help. Take a few days and think it over. I realize I'm offering you a difficult job, maybe an impossible one. Think it over, I'll understand if you turn it down." Difficult, impossible, right up my ally. Turn it down, never.

"Sir I don't need to think it over. I'll take the job with one condition, I am in full charge, nobody will be over me or tell me how to run the club."

"Agreed, the job is yours," At that point the LTC handed me a ring of keys, stating he didn't know what they belonged to.

"By the way Sir, where is the Parachute Club?"

"I'll have my driver take you there tomorrow."

"Tomorrow. What's wrong with today?" In fifteen minutes I was on my way to my Thai. American Sport Parachute Club assignment. I haven't felt this good since I first opened Land of Lincoln Sky Divers.

The overall appearance of the club was quit impressive. It had a rigger section equipped with sewing machines and parachute packing tables. An adjoining larger room was apparently used for meetings and social gathering. Outside of some deferred maintenance, the overall condition showed a lot of potential. I was looking forward to my new assignment as custodian to the U.S. Special Forces Sport (Carlos Leal) Parachuting Club Thailand . All I needed now was transportation.

Most Team Members solved this problem by purchasing a bicycle. I tried that solution at first. However the first big rain storm soon had me looking for an automobile

It was old, rusty, needed a paint job and had two flat tires. I'm sure it also had some negative points, but I just had to have it.

"How much do you want for that old Baht Bus?" With the help of a passerby we negotiated a sales price. Part of the negotiation was the two flats had to be fixed and the old relic had to be

Bath Bus

running. In a remarkable short period of time I was the new owner of an old Thai Bath Bus.

From the beginning it was my intention to remove the bus portion and use the Toyota Truck as my private transportation. But that would have to wait a couple of weeks. I was having too much fun driving the Baht Bus around town. People would flag me down for a ride. They had a big laugh when they seem an American driving the bus. One of the great characteristics of the Thai people, they laugh easily. Thailand is known as the Land of Many Smiles

I was assigned to the HALO Team, SFT 44, my duty station was at the Thai American Sport Parachuting Club. This didn't create any problem. All of the HALO Team members were very active in the Parachute Club. Although they called it the Thai American Parachute Club, I didn't see many Thais in the beginning. I would have to work on that.

I asked LTC Shelton to hold off announcing the Parachute Club was reopening. I wanted to take a look at the books, take inventory and just get a feel of the place. Well it almost worked. I had about a day and a half before people started coming back to the club.

First to arrive was MSG Joel Schenkelberger, the HALO Team Sergeant and SSG John Burdish the team medic. I knew Joel and John from Fort Devens. Both were good jumpers and dedicated to the HALO mission.

It wasn't long before SFC Roger Smith, SFC Sammy Hernandez and SSG Al Drapeau joined us. You can bet the conversation was about how soon the club could start jumping again. We didn't have long to wait before Cpt Michael Grady, SSG Fran Quet, SGT Robert Shank and SGT Dennis Carter made their appearance. The only HALO Team member conspicuous by his absence was SSG John Tippy.

American HALO Team

During my limited inspection I found a large field safe but couldn't find the combination. I looked all through the files and asked the S-2 if they had it on file. Now that everybody was together, I figured it was a good time to ask the sixty-four-dollar question.

"Does anybody know the combination of the safe?" Nobody did. No problem I would ask the S-2 to send a locksmith and change the combination. A few days later when the safe was opened, I discovered a little more than four hundred dollars in an unmarked envelope. I asked everybody who it belonged to. Again nobody knew.

"That's a lot of money guy's. Whoever it belongs to, just clam it. Give me a receipt for the money, and I'll turn it over to the owner." Nobody came forward.

No problem, the Army has a solution for overages or property not on the books. A simple entry in the ledger, Found On Post. With the stroke of the pen, the club had cash on hand. I had the feeling nobody wanted to admit the money was part of a slush fund. A fund used for parties or whatever. Well they still had a slush fund, but now it was legal. As time went on I would see to it, the fund would grow.

Another slight problem area. They had about three hundred plus, T-10 parachutes not on the books. When Vietnam shut down, thousands of military parachutes were sent out of country. This pile found its way to Thailand. That would have been great if they were properly stored and put to use. But some clown piled them in a poorly ventilated wooden shack. The rotting process probably started immediately. This had all the ingredients of a plan to make illegal money off of Uncle Sam, gone sour.

I inspected about fifty of the poorly stored parachutes and came to the conclusion it wasn't worth the effort. There wasn't one that I would certify airworthy. I hired a few local villagers and supervised cutting the shroud lines from the canopies rendering them useless. The final distribution, the canopies and the lines would be a gift to the locals. Turned out to be a great Public Relation tool.

One of the lads I hired was an exceptionally hard worker. Most of the workers picked up one parachute at a time, Kuk picked up two or three. While his fellow workers took a break, Kuk kept on working. An amazing lad, bubbling over with enthusiasm, smiling all the time.

When the workers got near the bottom of the pile, panic broke out. They ran out of the building as though it were on fire. The only person that didn't leave the building was Kuk. He emerged a few minutes later with a dead King Cobra. I needed a full time worker and hired him on the spot. Among his other duties, Kuk would be in charge of all snakes in or around the Parachute Club. Now don't think for one moment that snakes bother me. Don't think it, be assured of it. I have been around and handled a lot of snakes during my Special Forces career. I can truthfully say, I have never enjoyed one minute of it. Just thinking about it sends a chill up my spine.

Kuk was an exceptionally bright lad, always looking for new challenges. Add that characteristic to his enthusiasm for work, I almost had a cabin copy of my Montagnard medic in Vietnam, Tren. Show both of these lads something one time and they could do it. I wasn't long before Kuk could pack a parachute as good as any. When there were no parachutes to pack, and I didn't assign him a new task, Kuk would find something to do that would improve our operation. I literally had to force Kuk to take a break.

In order to carry out its primary intelligence mission, the Thai Border Police worked to establish rapport with remote area villagers and hill tribes. They engaged in civic action projects to gain the confidence and loyalty of rural peoples, building and operating more than 200 schools in remote areas and helping the army to construct offices for civilian administration. In addition, they established rural medical aid stations, gave farmers agricultural assistance, and built small airstrips for communication and transportation purposes.

Both Thai. and American HALO teams were heavily involved in this MITRAPAB. Program. MITRAPAB became a highly politicized program that attracted civilian jumpers. I often wondered who those people were. I didn't have the need to know, so I never asked. In all

Thai HALO Team

probability, big brother was keeping an eye on things. That simple explanation satisfied my curiosity. I never went on any of the MITRAPAB jumps. I was busy running the drop zone at an abandoned airstrip just outside of Lopburi.

I structured the Thai American club after my civilian club, Land of Lincoln Sky Divers. It was too strict for some, but just right for command, due to the recent loss of CSM Leal. Sport Parachuting is safe if you don't violate a few simple rules. These rules have to be imbedded in the student's mind during training.

Special Forces Thailand did not have their own Parachute Riggers. All rigging support comes from the Quartermaster Corps. One of the new Riggers attached to SF, claimed to be free fall qualified. His log book indicated he had ten sport jumps. Two of them were ten second delays. None of the jumps were signed by a licenced jumper which compelled me to put him back on a static line status, with a dummy rip cord pull requirement. After observing his performance, I would make a determination if he would be allowed to free fall or be required to make additional static line jumps. It was obvious this upset him.

"Young man, there is no way, we will let you jump without a checkout jump."

He went to his jeep and came back with a packed parachute and reserve. He became upset once more when I insisted he use our parachutes. Again no way, I would let him use equipment that I hadn't inspected. I fully understood why a rigger might be upset by someone questioning their packing ability. Riggers take pride in their work. But packing a military parachute and packing a Sport Parachute is as different as day and night. Reluctantly SP4 Melvin Wright put on a club chute and one of our Jump Masters took him up for his check out jump.

I meet Melvin on the drop zone, he landed way off target. I was surprised to see that the dummy ripcord was still in its pocket. I didn't say a word. We walked back to the loading area and waited for the jump master to give his critique. SP4 Wright received poor marks. Poor exit and body position, no attempt on a dummy pull. And very little attempt to steer his canopy to the target.

"Melvin. What would you do, if you were in my shoes?"

"Keep me on static line, I suppose." This kid is smarter than I thought.

I not only kept the lad on static line, I required him to attend canopy classes. As far as his equipment was concerned, I found it not airworthy. The modification was cut too high, increasing the parachute's downward descent.

His reserve, although packed properly, still had a pilot-chute attached. In military jumping because of the close proximity to the ground, the jumper needs a fast opening, second chute. In Sport Jumping because of the jumpers speed, a slower opening is advisable. There was nothing wrong with his equipment that couldn't be remedied. I offered to help him fix the problem. Wright rejected my offer and made the repairs himself. I would have to give him good marks on his workmanship.

I had no idea on how long I would keep Melvin on Static Line. Like many Military Jump Qualified, Wright's transition to Sport Jumping was difficult. Military Jumpers are trained to bend at the waist when they exit the aircraft. That bend at the waist is pounded into the student military jumper. Sport Jumpers arch their backs. Breaking the bend at the waist habit is sometimes difficult.

Wright was not a bad guy. He just had a problem accepting criticism. He had a "I know everything" attitude that hindered his learning new techniques. SP4 Melvin Wright, no matter what you told him, came back with why he couldn't do it his way. This slight flaw in his character would cost him his life.

It was getting time for me to reenlist. I knew that because of my age, I would be given a Bar To Enlistment. I had to go through this routine every time enlistment time came around. I needed someone with good administrative skills to be standing by. No one filled that bill better than SGM John J. Self. A former SF operative and Team Sergeant at Dak Pek (A-242), SGM Self was the Administrative SGM at US Army Thailand. His duty station was in southern Thailand.

I picked a time to visit SGM Self, when the HALO Team was not on MITRAPAB. That would insure the club had enough Jump Masters and most important, the club's other Safety Officer, Joel Schenkelberger, was on the Drop Zone. USSPA and Army regulations both required one of us on the DZ. Knowing the Club was in good hands, I went to see SGM Self.

My first stop when I got back from down south, was to check out the parachute Club. To my surprise, a new padlock was on the front door. What clown put the wrong lock on the door? I knew the S-2 would have a duplicate key, I went to Headquarters to retrieve it.

"Sergeant McGinley, we had another death at the club. SP-4 Wright drowned at a near by pond." LTC Shelton announced in a sad tone.

"What pond Sir? We don't have any hazardous water near our DZ." We were well within any safety regulations of the Army and USSPA. I was concerned, knowing how the Armies, knee jerk solutions to unusual situations can explode out of control. I was right on target. LTC Shelton handed me a list of possible corrections to our jumping procedures.

I couldn't believe what I was reading; Place a rubber boat with two men in every pond within one mile of the Drop Zone. All jumpers must wear flotation gear. Add water safety classes to our training program, and all jumpers must be able to swim fifty yards. A perfect example of knee jerking. Most ponds anywhere near the DZ are less than two feet deep. Most are too small to handle a two-man raft. There were about fifty small ponds near our DZ. That means we would need at least, one hundred people to man the boats.

"Who came up with this list Sir?"

"Myself and COL Radtke from JUSMAG." Col Radtke (not related to our Commander) was also a Sport Jumper and one of those civilian clothes individuals I mentioned earlier. It was obvious both officers were trying to come up with a list that would satisfy higher headquarters. No one wanted the club to shut down again.

"Sir hold off on that list for a while. Army and USSPA Regulations require the Club's Safety Officer to conduct an investigation on any Sport Parachuting jump resulting in death. I'll start my investigation right after lunch."

Accompanied by two Thai. soldiers that helped recover the body, I drove to the accident site. The body of water in question, was a man-made water source for some near by homes. The size of the water storage pond was remarkable in its self. It would be hard to hit, if you were trying to. It raised the question, was SP-4 Wright was conscious when he hit the water? That theory vanished when my helpers told me Wright was sitting up when he was driven to the dispensary.

At first light the next day, I took the Colonel's Chopper and took pictures of the area in question. The pictures reinforced my belief. The pond would have been hard to or impossible to hit. Although the water was downwind, it was too far from the Drop Zone, if in fact the jumper left the aircraft at 2800 feet. The next phase of the investigation would be interviewing jumpers present on that fatale

day. After several interviews, there was no doubt in my mind, SP4 Melvin Wright had a full canopy much higher than 2500 feet. (The opening altitude for a student on a Static Line jump) It was also evident that Melvin, made no attempt to steer his parachute away from the pond. I have to point out, a slight turn to the left or right, Melvin would have missed the pond by several yards.

This lack of performance was inconsistent with deceased training record. Melvin went to Military Jump School and logged 26 jumps. He had 12 Sport Jumps logged. Being a certified Military Parachute Rigger, he surly understood the workings of a steerable parachute. As a matter of fact he modified the parachute he used on the tragic jump. Could it be, Wright was rendered unconscious at opening and remained in an unconscious state until impact?

SP4 Melvin Wright was sent home to his native country Canada. MSG Harry Brown from 46 Company Lop Buri Thailand, escorted Melvin back home. Lt. James E. Collier from Ft Devens also attended..

SFC Alvin Lipson Fort Devens, Massachusetts. was in the 10th Special Forces Group and assigned as Communications Chief, of "A" Company, 3rd Battalion, was the Non Commissioned Officer In Charge of the funeral detail for Melvin. The Honor Guard consisted of; SGT Gary Ballard, SGT Richard Patrick, SGT John Radosevich, SGT Edward Desimone, PFC Gerald Jacobs, and PFC Henry Spaulding

Their professional performance ended with the presentation of the Flag of the United States of America to the family,

Command was satisfied with my report and the Sport Club stayed open. I can't take full credit. The Club had a lot of help from 46 Companies XO, LTC Shelton. The LTC was working on his Military Master Jump  Wings and his Sport Parachuting, C Licence. Every time you saw jumpers in the air, you could bet, one of them was the LTC. You would be hard pressed to find anyone that enjoyed jumping like LTC Shelton. The icing on the cake was he was a great guy to work for.

As time went by more and more Thai jumpers started jumping with our club. Jumping competition between the Thais and the Americans, strengthened the relationship between the groups. It finally became a Thai / American club. In a short time the Sport Parachuting Club doubled in size.

Time to Move Again

Special Forces had a small detachment in Bangkok. Part of their mission was to monitor specialized equipment and on occasion house individuals and teams being deployed on missions that were somewhat classified. Although not top secret, some times it is desirable to move people around without too much fanfare. The detachment was located in an industrial area of Bangkok, ideal to conceal its safe house mission.

Another mission the detachment took seriously was the monitoring of their radios. They had radio communications with all the Special Forces Teams and Special Operations in that part of the world. When their Team Medic went back to the states, I jumped at the chance to move to Bangkok.

Although Chome and I had a small house on the outskirts of the City, it was too far from my duty station. The search for a new home resulted in us finding a large villa in the center of Bangkok. The two story home had it all. Oriental hard wood, highly polished floors and a winding marble staircase to the bedrooms on the upper floor. The large dinning room was ideal for entertaining. The fourteen-foot high ceiling in the great room, sculptured with exotic figures, promoted the feeling of being in a palace. This would be what my southern pals call, living high on the hog.

Our favorite place in the villa, was the columned veranda. Chome and I spent many hours sprawled out on its plush furniture. Overlooking a well cared for oriental garden added to its enchantment. It was at this special place, Chome announced we were to have our second  child. She insisted it was going to be a girl child and her name would be Dow. Dow, a Thai name translated means; "coming from heaven." Time would prove the name fit the child to a "T," she was from heaven.

At the rear of the property was a small house, used to house the domestic workers. To my surprise it was occupied. A middle-aged Thai lady and her fifteen-year-old daughter had been working on this property for more than ten years. They took care of the whole place, inside and out. My first thought was I couldn't afford full time domestic help. My plan was to hire part time workers to help Chome. I didn't have time for a second thought. Before I knew it, Chome was doing a walk through with the Thai lady and her daughter, explaining how she wanted things done. They talked for about three hours. The end result, I had two domestic workers and their dog. Chome must have done some wheeling and dealing. The cost for this domestic staff was thirty dollars a month and the use of the small house.

It didn't end there. I came home one evening and was greeted by an armed guard at our front gate. A very polite Thai gentleman with a shotgun slung over his shoulder asked me to prove who I was. When I satisfied him, he opened the locked iron gate and let me pass. What is this going to cost was the only thought in my mind?

I was greeted by an unfamiliar face. The Thai lady standing in front of me kept bowing and reciting the customary "Sa-wa-dee Ka." I was about to return the greeting when Chome introduced the lady as an addition to our household staff. She was a sister to our housekeeper and the armed guard was her husband. What is this going to cost, kept running through my mind? It turned out that it didn't cost a nickel more. Our housekeeper's sister and her husband were new arrivals in Bangkok. They needed a place to live. In exchange for a roof over their head the new couple took over some of our housekeeper's duties.

I thought that maybe we should have been notified before any new staff was added. When I confronted Chome about my concern, she told me that it was none of our business. We had hired the housekeeper to be in charge of maintaining our property. How she does it and how many people she has help her, was up to her. Property may change ownership, but quite often the domestic staff stay put. The exception to this rule is, when the domestics move on with the old owner to their new property. The owner of our property moved to India. The Realtor handling their property paid the domestic help until we rented the property.

We lucked out and had a great household staff. Outgoing, friendly, always in a pleasant mood. Very typical of the Thai People in general. The only exception to this relationship was their dog. That K9 and I didn't sing off the same sheet of music. Without fail, that bugger would wait until I was about to fall asleep, then beneath my window, he would start his midnight serenade. I tried everything to shut him up. Cursed at him, yelled (hoping the owners would take a hint.) I even tried barking back. This dummy couldn't understand dog talk. Finally I decided to have a face to face with this batty-barking-machine.

As I stepped off the veranda, skunk breath took a lunge at me. Fortunately for him he was chained. (I would have bitten him back.) I grabbed a push-broom that was leaning against the wall and swung it with all the force I could muster. The at hand weapon, struck the dummy square on the head. Come to think of it, there was more than one dummy at this consultation. The blow didn't faze him. He lunged forward again, breaking his restraining chain. There I stood, broken broom handle in hand and a very angry K9 about to have me for dinner.

It was at this point that I relied on my bayonet training. I lunged forward as thought the broken broom handle was a bayonet. My weapon landed mid chest. With an upward push the enemy went flying through the air with a broom stick implanted in his chest. There was no time for further evaluation. It was time for a strategic withdraw.

I was awakened by a lot of chatter below my window. Looking out I saw our two housekeepers and my wife Chome standing around the casualty of last night's battle. This was going to take aa little explaining, its tap dance time. As I approached the mourners, Chome shouted out,

"Mac look what someone do last night." Someone, that means they don't know who. Looking down I could see my vicious foe of yesterday was still alive, in fact very much alive.

"Mac, you're a doctor can you help him?" I wasn't a doctor, but I liked being called one. They say some things are lost through translation . . . true. But some things are gained.

I immobilized the animal's muzzle with a cloth belt. I didn't want any payback. I then anaesthetized the area before attempting to remove the broom handle. It was at this point I started to have a little respect for this downed victim. Although he was tied and held down, he growled at my every move. That's what I call spirit. I have a fast rule, I never treat anybody I wound. Why wound them if you turn around a treat them? This will be the exception to the rule.

When the broom handle was removed and surprisingly, the damage inside the chest cavity was unremarkable. To facilitate healing by keeping them in line, I sutured some slightly damaged neck muscle with catgut (dissolving sutures.) After irrigating the cavity throughly, I closed the wound. From that date forward, this K9 avoided me. However, it didn't change his late night serenade. In desperation Chome had the housekeeper chain him as far from the house as possible.

Things were going great. The only flaw in my utopia life style was not having an automobile standing by. Of course we had Lek with a minimum notice, but my working hours caused a scheduling problem. I really needed an automobile standing by.

"Lek, I need your help in finding me an automobile to lease.' My statement put him off balance at first.

"Mr. Mac, not safe for you to drive in Bangkok. I will reduce my charge to you. I don't wont you to drive in this wild city." We went back and forth, finally Lek said he would find a good deal for me. The final outcome was a very good deal. I leased a one year old Toyota for $250.00 per month.

Wild City, understatement of the year. Bangkok would be a challenge to any driver. Yes even Demolition Derby Drivers. Driving in Bangkok was one big game of chicken. "Man on the right has the right away." Wrong! "First man to the intersection wins." is the rule. Without going into stories about driving in Thailand, you can take this as fact; "Drive like the Thai or don't drive at all. "

For some reason or other, long periods of time spent in the warehouse type safe-house caused me to have breathing problems. I went to the Army hospital in Bangkok and was admitted for further evaluation. It was coincidental, my Bar to Enlist arrived the same day.

Several tests were preformed with negative results. Finally the hospital staff decided to Med Evac me to the states for further evaluation. My doctor informed me on their decision one day while making his rounds.

"No way Sir!" I informed him that I would go AWAL from the hospital before I would let that happen."

"Sergeant McGinley, you'll go wherever we decide you will go." This was no time to enter into an argument. It was time to formulate a plan. The doctor was still on the ward when I called Chome and gave hers a list of things to accomplish, before her visit this evening.

She was to have Lek drive her to the hospital. Bring a full change of cloths and stop at the bank and draw out $2,000.00 in Thai money. The money was needed incase I had to bribe anybody to facilitate my leaving the hospital without discharge papers. A little money up front can influence almost anything in the Orient. When the visiting hours ended Chome left my ward and waited for me in Lek's auto. Around twelve, I decided to execute my portion of the escape plan. I changed clothes and was about to leave the ward when my doctor appeared.

"I had the feeling you were serious about leaving the hospital. You Special Forces guys are hard to understand. Most people would look forward to going back to the states." The doctor's tone surprised me. He wasn't mad, in fact he sounded friendly.

I explain that it was not possible for me to leave Thailand now. My government didn't recognize a Buddhist marriage to a Thai-national. It would be impossible for my wife to go with me if I left for the States. I needed time to change my marital status. I told him about my large and expensive home that had to be disposed of before I left. There was no way I would or could leave Thailand at this time. He asked how this would affect my Army Career. When I told him about my Bar to Enlistment because of age, he reached for my records. He scribbled in large letters Discharged, and signed them. Handing me the records;

"Give the records to your Dispensary and good luck. I saluted the man who just a few minutes ago I was ready to punch. I had no time to lose. I put in for and received an In Country Leave.

My wife Chome and I have never thought about getting married American style. Our Buddhist Marriage was as holy to us, as any other marriage. Our ccommitment and devotion to each other and family would match the best of them. For those who would say differently, are fools and are insulting my family.

My first stop was the Chaplains' office at Army Headquarters Thailand. Regulations required me to get permission to get married. Keep in mind that I didn't have a chip on my shoulder, I had a 2" x 4" piece of lumber. As we sat in front of this over feed, poor excuse for a soldier, I was not prepared for what we were about to hear.

"I assume you are sexually active, since you have been living together." You assumed what? I thought to myself.

"Major, sign that paper next to "visit to Chaplin." I don't need any thing else from you. You can take your assumptions and shove them where the sun doesn't shine." I was hot and he knew it. Without saying a word he signed off on our paperwork. As we were leaving, he suggested that I could have shown more military courtesy.

"You know I could turn you in to command."

"Major, look in the mirror. Surly you wouldn't appear in front of the Commander looking like that?" I didn't bother to salute. My salutes are reserved for soldiers I respect. Our next stop was at the US Embassy. A quick hand on the bible and a Thai national muttering a few words and it was official. We were legally married. I just don't get how that dog and pony show made our marriage holy. We had pledged our troth, in front of our creator many years before. Back to the S1 to change my marriage status, pick up Choms' military ID and Pass Port.

Thinking I just slew the bureaucracy giant, I took Chome out for a celebration dinner. Then the slain giant started to come back to life. Our son John was born in Thailand and the US Government didn't consider him a legitimate son nor an American. To get this straightened out would take months. Then a Thai lawyer came to the rescue. We drew up adoption papers and I adopted my own son.

Things were happening fast. We had never talked about our family going back to the states. This was a big move for Chome and even a bigger one for Johnny. It was time for an in-depth family meeting at our favorite place, the veranda.

I explained how things would be a little different living in the states. If I lost the battle to reenlist, I would have to find a civilian job or maybe open a business. I have never been highly successful in business, but that has never stopped me from trying.

"Not worry Mac, you very good soldier. Army crazy not keep you. Mopinli Ka (never mind) Army not keep you, you smart, you can do anything." Boy have I got this gal fooled.

Unlike Thailand, domestic help is very expensive in America, more likely than not we wouldn't have housekeepers. At this point Chome interrupted with another.

"Mopinli-Kralip (doesn't matter). Housekeeper not important, we need family together." She was right on target. My Army career has kept out family separated most of the time. However it didn't change the fact there would be a lot of adjustment on her part. To this point Chome has never had the responsibility of house keeping or even changing a diaper. Her adopted aunt did all the household and child care chores.

You will find very few orphans in Thailand compared to other countries. When a child becomes parentless, some other family will assume the responsibility of raising the child. The unofficially adopted child will be cared for as though it were their own. Like their children, the adopted child will be given household duties at a very young age. As they grow older, more and more chores are added. By the age of ten or eleven, most Thai children are self sufficient, to include cooking and taking care of the younger brothers and sisters. The remarkable thing is they never complain. They take pride in the amount of chores they are give responsibility for.

Chomes' aunt was no different. She has taken care of all the children in Chomes' family, her brothers, sisters and of course Johnny. This was one great little lady, loaded with talent. She could measure a person for a suit in the morning. By noon they had their first fitting. That evening the garment could be worn. The was all hand stitched. Truly a remarkable lady.

When I suggested we bring her to the states with us, Chome and Johnny were thrilled. It was at this point we decided that Johnny finish this semester in school and then he and the aunt come to the states. That brought more smiles. Johnny didn't seem to thrilled on coming to America. The aunt coming with us subdued most of the apprehension.

I don't think Johnny understood why we had to adopt him. The adoption put him in the same category as the adopted aunt. I took him aside and explained that he was our oldest, making him my number one son and he would have the responsibility that came with that position. I emphasized that I was counting on him to take care of his yet unborn sister, Dow. How did we know it was going to be a sister you might ask? Chome told us, and Chome never lies.

Chome's family held a fair well dinner for us, at a well known Thai outdoor Restaurant. It was a beautiful setting, if you didn't know better, you would swear you were in a forest, winding streams and all. Many of Chome's lifelong friends joined us. A very good friend of ours, Glenn Watson SFC type, was in Bangkok for the week end . Glen was a close enough friend, he didn't need an invitation.

Throughout the years Glen and I played jokes on each other, some were quit elaborate. This would probably be my last time to catch Glenn in a prank. Why not I thought to myself.

Now Glenn know several of Chome's friends were very good lookers. It wasn't difficult getting my pal to agree to a blind date. He bombarded me with questions about how his date looked and what she liked. This guy fell hook, line and sinker. I responded with, the gal I picked for him made Chome look ugly. I emphasized the fact, the selected gal loved flowers. When I told him I thought this Thai Lady was a nymphomaniac, the boy was almost uncontrollable.

Chome and I arrived at the restaurant early. Shortly after Glenn drove up in a taxi.

"Is she here yet? Was she here yet? Were the first words out of his mouth.

"Not yet pal. Slow down you might blow a gasket." Then I asked a waiter to put the very large, beautiful bouquet of flowers in a cool place.

"Glenn that gal is going to tear you apart when she sees that bundle of weeds. Isn't this overdoing it a little?"

Before he could answer, five of Chome's friends arrived. As they were going through the lengthy Thai, greetings' Glenn kept asking me.

"Which one is she Mac?"

"No one in this group, I told you she was beautiful. The one I picked for you Glenn would make this group look like boys'." That really excited him. All these girls were good lookers. Shortly after Chome's, mother, aunt, and Johnny arrived. I didn't have to introduce Glen to Johnny or the aunt, Glenn knew them well. In fact when I wasn't in Thailand, Glenn would take Johnny on many outings. Johnny was close to my pal, he called Glenn, uncle.

"Glenn, this is Chomes' mother, your date for the afternoon." I truly believe, at this point, Watson wanted to kill me. Mrs. Kemtong was about eighty years old.

"Sa-wa-dee Krahp." Glenn said with a deep bow. At this point I had the waiter bring out the flowers and present them to mother Kentome.

"Sa-wa-dee Kra." Mother Kemtong replied. She was delighted with the flowers.

L to R Chom's Mother, Aunt and Johnny

Chome's mother was a tall majestic looking woman. When she entered a room, you could feel her presence. Similar to Chome everyone that meet her, liked her. Similar to Chome she didn't have a mean bone in her body. As they walked to the waiting table, it was evident that Glen in fact, was with a beautiful Thai lady.

A table paralleling our table was loaded with every exotic dish imaginable. When I tried to compliment Chome's friend that planned this, she informed me that she had nothing to do with the menu. In fact she told me that it would not be polite to suggest a type of food to be served. She went on to explain, that it was the restaurant staff's job to please us. They take great pride in that responsibility. Any suggestion on what to be served would be insulting.

She also informed me, since Chomeyong and I were the honored guest, and I being the head of household, it was my duty to order the food first. The restaurant was known for their baked fish dinners. Like they say,

"When in Rome, do what the Romans do," I ordered baked fish. In a short time, a very large Baked Fish, still sizzling, was placed on the table before me. I didn't have the slightest idea of how to serve this monster of

the sea. I asked Chome to do the honors. Then the big shock. The fish wasn't for the table, it belonged to me. I couldn't believe it. This monster of the sea had to be at least, 20 inches long. I am sure there was enough for everybody. I have a habit of amazing the Thai people with my ignorance. Everyone laughed.

Unknowingly, I kept the show going. I loaded the fish with an especially prepared souce I had the feeling everyone was watching me in amazement. When I took my first bite, I gave out a yell that made our table the focal point of the restaurant. This was by far the hottest thing I have ever put in my mouth. Of course, gobbling all that water down to cool my throat, generated another laugh. A laughing waiter place another fish in front of me.

Thai meals last a long time. In addition to pleasing the pallet, like going to market, they are used as socializing and information gathering sessions. Most of the talk was in Thai. It didn't take long before Glen and I got a little bored Using the excuse that I had to get Glenn back to the Opera Hotel, (a hotel SF frequent often.)we left a little early. Of course like greetings, Thai departures are formal and take a little time.

Opera Hotel Bangkok Thailand

"Free, free at last! Now what are we going to do Glenn?"

"Let's go to Patpong. I know a gal that owns a nightclub, she's nuts about me." I wanted to tell my war buddy it was his money she was nuts about, instead I surprised myself. I kept my big mouth shut.

Patpong earned its notoriety during the Vietnam War when GI's made it their base for R&R (rest and recreation). The nightlife strip runs along two short lanes, Patpong one and two, with a couple of short interconnecting sois (streets). Bars share street-space with restaurants, massage parlors, a couple of hotels. Although touts and overzealous salesmen will pester the tourist for their dollars, Patpong is one of the safest and least expensive nightlife areas in the world and should remain on the itineraries of every visitor to Bangkok.

The first night club we entered must have been celebrating something that required everyone to wear formal dress. That should have been a warning, a warning we chose to ignore. I could feel the stares as we took a seat at the bar. A bartender dressed in a formal gown, tried to tell us something, I ignored that also.

"Give us a couple of beers, and make it quick." Glenn yelled out. This surprised me, Glenn Watson was a polite guy most of the time.

"What's your problem Glenn?"

"Didn't you hear what she said? She told us to leave, this was a private party" I think it was the way she asked was what bothered Glenn. Glenn got up and went over to a table loaded with food. When he came back to the bar, he was steaming mad.

Let's get out of here Mac. They won't feed us, this is a private party. I'm starved, lets get out of here." I wondered how he could have been starved, we just ate an hour ago. I have a problem being rejected. Oh yes we would have to leave, but it will be at our pace.

"Take this Glenn, it will curb your appetite." I handed Glenn a long stemmed rose, I took from one of many large bouquets on the bar. Of course I took one for myself. Sprinkling the blood red rose with salt, I started to eat it. Glenn cracked up. He put salt on his rose and followed suit. After about four roses, a large gentleman asked us to leave. No problem, we didn't want to stay anyway. By the way, roses taste terrible. The no problem turned into a big problem. Our escort to the door, decided to grab Glenn by the arm. One thing you don't want to do in this life, is to grab Glenn Watson by the arm in an unfriendly manner. Glenn is an advanced student of Marshal Arts.

Our escort became airborne, then landed on the food-covered table. At this time three other gentlemen came to his assistance. We must have performed well. Everyone backed off. It was now time to leave the club without delay, at our pace.

Halfway out the door someone pushed me. I went flying into a noodle stand parked by the door. Plates, bowls and cups went flying in every direction. The guy that pushed me, and the noodle

Noodle Stand

man, both showing sings of hostility, were coming straight at me.

Glenn had his hand's full, so I lunged at the approaching target. The noodle man fell over his noodle-stand, my punch intended for the jaw, landed on the other guy's chest. He went head over heels back through the Club's door. I didn't know I could throw a body punch that hard. Well I can't. Glenn informed me later the clown stepped on a plate and his feet went one way and his body went in the other direction. It was over almost as fast as it was started. The night was young, there was plenty time to find a new adventure. We started to walk away.

"Mac, Dan." A voice called. Odd, very few people call me Dan. Turning around I saw an MP friend.

"Mac you have to come with me. This noodle guy is going to press charges. Don't worry, we'll straighten this out at the station." Watson was standing on the side line smiling.

The noodle guy was in the front seat of the MP Car, and I was in the back seat. I knew that no ticket would be issued. Eugene (the MP) was a friend. There was just one slight problem. Most of the time, when I'm in a foreign country, I carry. I had to get rid of the 38mm Walters tucked in my belt. As we made a right turn, heading to the MP Station, out the window went my 38. I payed attention to where it landed. My plan was to come back and retrieve it.

During the ride to the station the Thai Noodle man was as quiet as a mouse. As soon as we entered the building, he wouldn't shut up. An interpreter informed my MP friend, that all he wanted was payment for his noodle stand.

"What kind of money are we talking about." I asked, knowing it would be a lot more than I wanted to pay. When they came back with a price of $100.00, I jumped at the chance to be the new owner of a slightly bent Noodle Stand.

"Want a ride back to Patpong, Mac." My MP friend asked. I declined, needed to retrieve my weapon. I remembered that there was a ditch filled with water near the place my Walters landed. I searched for about an hour with no success. More likely than not, the weapon went into the water. The water-filled ditch was more waste water than drainage liquid. The smell made me make up my mind to write it off as a loss. Then a young Thai kid happened by.

"Sa-wa-dee Krahp, want to earn 20 Baht?" The kid jumped at the chance. To be more explicit, he jumped into the water. His thorough search failed agin, to produce the elusive weapon. I started to feel sorry for the lad in that scummy water.

"Mopinli-Kralip (never mind). The simple phrase ended the search. I didn't bother looking for Glenn, I went home.

After bringing Chome up to speed on the evening happenings, I took a very hot shower and sat down to a superbly prepared meal. Many people are surprised that I tell Chome about everything that happens in my life. Many more don't believe I tell her everything. Well it's true and there is a good reason for it.

Very early in our relationship, while waiting for Chome to get off work, I went to a local club to get a refreshing cold drink.

"Excuse me, may I seat next to you?" The request came from a very good looking oriental gal.

"By all means, be my guest." I felt it was my duty. Being a visitor of a foreign country and sort of an ambassador, I might add. I had the duty, not to offend the host country's citizens. I further expressed my ambassador qualities by ordering a cool refreshment for the gorgeous creature next to me.

After some small talk, I found out she wasn't from Thailand, she was from Malaysia. She claimed to be a student working her way through college. I doubted it but then what do I know. Maybe she was studding "Basket Weaving 101." Looking up I saw a gentleman sitting where the base of the "L" shaped bar meet the wall. His face was familiar. Then it dawned on me;

"Lek, what are you doing here?" It was my driver. I gave him the day off, what in the world is going on? "Bartender, give my friend a drink."

I have very poor vision in my left eye. I tell people it is an old war wound. Actually I think I injured the eye when I was learning to eat with Chop Sticks. (That's a joke son) I didn't see the person sitting on my left, a couple stools away. As I turned back to the Malaysian gal, someone tapped me on the shoulder.

"We go home now Mac." It was another very, very good looking gal, my wife Chome.

It was tap dance time, Fred Astaire, stand aside. I knew this would have to be a great performance. I started by introducing the Malaysian gal to Chome. The Malaysian gal walked away. I called the barkeep over to order a cold drink for Chome. She came over, had a short Thai conversation with Chome, then walked away. A short while ago, I was the center of attraction. Now nobody would talk to me.

"Yes Chome, we go home now." Later, after another great meal Chome had something to say.

"Mac, I don't want to know if you go with other Puyeng (girl). Don't tell me, don't break my heart. Please don't tell me story. You never have to lie to me. You lie, you break my heart. I ask you "Chin Chin" (for sure), you speak "Chin Chin."

Chome's little statement hit me hard. It was at that moment I knew, I had found my life's mate. From that day forward I have never looked for greener pastures. I tell her everything, not because I have to, it is because I want to, "Chin Chin."

The Special Forces mission in Thailand was winding down. There was a lot of political pressure to move the 46 Company and all other uniformed Americans out of Thailand. Par for the course I would say. We have a history of getting involved helping foreign countries. Just when we get a handle on the situation, political bickering generates unrest in the citizenry, and we pull out. They call it saving the tax payers money. As if the politician worries about taking our money. Of course when things start deteriorating, we go back in. The cost to reenter is tripled, wiping out any taxpayer money thought saved. We have done this time and time again. Proving one thing, "you don't have to be smart to be a politician."

To move American troops out of Thailand at this point in time was, in my opinion a mistake. The search for POW and MIA's was in full swing. JCRC (Joint Casualty Resolution Center) was running very successful missions launching out of Thailand. Searching for MIA and POW's in Laos Cambodia and Vietnam from distant launch site would be counter productive. We had a lot of Special Forces medics assigned to JCRC. Every one of them a Giant.

A civilian company I.I.I. (International Investigators Incorporated) was working on a similar project. They were looking for SF medics for their Recovery Teams. With the help of some friends in the US Embassy, I went to their location in Vientiane Laos for an interview.

These guys live good. A fancy Villa with plenty of domestic help. Each two-man team had their own civilian Jeeps. The pay was above average with a food and clothing allowance. Their field duty was conducted in casual dress. I liked what I saw. The interview went

well, I told them I needed a little
time to make up my mind. I felt
good, I had a backup job in the
event I was unable to stay in the
Army. Life is like jumping from
a plane, you need a reserve.

Laos (white area

    We flew first class back
to the States. I wanted my very
special Thai lady to enjoy her
first adventure away from
Thailand. We had the choice of
entering The United States
through Honolulu Hawaii or San
Francisco CA, both were Ports of Entry, I chose Hawaii. I had been to
Hawaii in 1951 on my way back from Korea. My visit was confined to
Tripler Army Hospital in Honolulu. Didn't have a chance to do much
site seeing. This time it will be different. The Dragon Lady and I will
discover this enchanted land together.

    We didn't get off to a good start. My first mistake was renting
a room at the Army R&R Center. The delapidate buildings dated back
to WWII. The furnishings were not much better. This wouldn't do.
My Thai lady deserved much better than this, I have to find other living
accommodations. But first a good meal at Honolulu's famous
Fishermen Wharf.

    The welcome was lukewarm at the best. The half-hearted
receptionist ushered us to a table far back in the restaurant, next to the
kitchen door. Being a gentleman, I took the chair facing the very busy
entrance to the kitchen. I summoned the Manager.

    "This table won't do Sir. I have been in hamburger joints with
better seating arrangements than this. Get us a table with a better
view."

    'We are very crowded tonight Sir, we do our best. Everyone
can't have a prime table." Normally I would have understood. But we
had passed several acceptable tables on the way to this poorly placed,
extremely small accommodation. We got up and I ushered Chome to a
very nice table overlooking a beautifully lit garden.

    "This will do fine." I announced." The manager with a frown
on his face, instructed a waiter to bring us a menu.

I ordered a drink. While we were waiting for our lobster dinner to arrive, I noticed, Chome was the only Oriental in the dinning room. Could it be Orientalis are not welcome? No not in this day and age. Hawaii is full of Orientalis, it's their major ethnic group. This really bothered me. I called the manager again and didn't give him a chance to speak.

"Were we given that crummy table because my wife is an oriental?"

"We don't discriminate Sir." It was obvious the question startled him.

"Why is it, my wife is the only Asian patron in this garbage bucket?" I am polite most of the time. But when I am mad, I can give new meaning to the word rudeness. The clown didn't get a chance to answer. Our food had arrived.

"Unacceptable, take it back. I don't eat lobsters before I inspect them, alive." They knew what I meant. All the time we were waiting, I observed all the waiters bringing live lobsters to the ordering table for approval.

The manager accompanied the lobsters to the kitchen. In no time flat they were back with two, very large, live lobsters.

"They will do fine, Thank you." Please note I wouldn't know a good lobster from a bad one. In fact I hate lobsters. The lobsters headed for their hot swim. Almost immediately, a waiter was asking me to taste a sampling of a wine he had brought with him. Now I know as much about wine as I do lobsters. But I went along with the gag. I swirled it around in the glass, smelled it, put it to my lips for a taste, then announced,

"Excellent."

"This is from the staff Sir. You have made many friends tonight." The waiter announced as he fille our glasses. What a pleasant surprise I thought to my self. On the way out came the second surprise. The Manager marked our bill, No Charge. By the way the waiter was an Oriental.

I booked the first flight out of Hawaii. I knew I had a fight on my hands trying to reenlist. I was eager to engage the wizards of Washington or anybody else who wanted to jump in.

Fighting the Bureaucracy

I was not a happy camper on my flight back to the United States. I really thought I served my county well in three wars. Now because of my age, I'm being kicked out of the Army. Isn't there a law against Age Discrimination? The answer is yes. The Army get's around that by using the term, "convenience of the government." I knew if I signed in at Travis Air Port, I would be transferred to an Out Processing Center and discharged from the service. Not being a stranger to fighting the bureaucracy, I didn't sign in. I headed straight to Washington, D.C.

I wanted Chome to enjoy the beauty of America so the mode of transportation was a prime consideration. Flying was out. The fastest mode, but the view is boring. Travel by train is a great way to see everybodies' backyard. America by Bus, wasn't even considered. I rented a car. This would maximize my control over what to see, and how much time we spent seeing it. Besides I love to drive, regardless of the weather, I love to drive. This trip would modify the "regardless of weather" statement.

It was a clear February day when we departed California. If the weather remained this way, I had planned to make my periodic pilgrimage to see my Brother and Sister in Colorado. As soon as we hit the Rockies, Mother Nature had a change of mind. The blinding snow storm accompanied with high winds, created perilous driving conditions.

Large Tractor and Trailer rigs were tossed around like toys. Ever few miles we passed turned over rigs. I had no choice, we tailgated a large truck and hoped he could see where he was heading. Fortunately for us, the driver pulled into a Truck Stop. I parked as close to the snack shop as I could. This would be a long cold night. I really did it this time. Trapped in a major snow storm with a wife that is six and one half months into her pregnancy. The only smart thing I did was to purchase winter cloths in California. Chome saw a blanket set she liked and fortunately we purchased them also. It would take all we could find to keep warm this night.

"This is beautiful, I love this snow." Chome stated as I pilled the winter cloths and blankets on her. Typical attitude on my Thai lady. She can find something good in everything. Then I remembered this is the first snow, she has ever seen.

I mentioned my wife was pregnant on one of my trips to get hot coffee from the café. From then on hot beverage and food was delivered. Every few minutes, a trucker would knock on our window to see if we were OK. We rejected their pleas to come inside. We were as warm as toast under the mountain of cloths. Besides I enjoyed snuggling up to my lady and unborn child. The words to a popular song came to mind, "The weather outside is frightful . . . let it snow, let it snow" or something like that.

We were awakened by truckers digging us out. The snow was up to our windows. About a dozen of these magnificent knights of the road, dug a path to the now, snow plowed interstate. We thanked them and continued our journey to Washington, D.C.

With the help of some contacts at the Pentagon, an appointment was made for me to appear before the Board to Correct Military Records in Arlington VA. In three days the Bar to Reenlist was removed. and we were on my way to Fort Bragg North Carolina.

Back in friendly country, Special Forces reenlisted me and assigned me to Company B, 1st BN, ODA 521. ODA 521 was a newly formed HALO Team. About half of the team were HALO qualified and the other half scheduled to go to the next HALO class.

At first the reception was lukewarm. This was unusual in Special Forces. MSG Lonnie R. Willhite, the Team Sergeant put me through a mini question and answer drill.

"Every member of this Team is, or will soon be HALO Qualified. Are you willing to go through HALO training Sergeant McGinley?"

"No, I am not." Wallet's eyes glared. My lukewarm reception was cooling rapidly. I immediately informed him that I was already HALO Qualified. The glare remained, apparently this guy can't take a joke.

Willhite went on to inform me that everyone on the team scored high enough on their MOS Test, to receive Proficiency Pay. He seemed proud of that, and rightfully so. It represents excellence on you assigned job knowledge

"You're scheduled for a MOS Teat on Monday, how do you think you will do?" What a dumb question. Like all SF operatives, I'll do my best.

Back in the 60's and 70's, Special Forces Medics took the same MOS Test as Conventional Force medics. That was a problem. You had to be sure to answer the multiple choice question, with the answer the Conventional Forces wanted. If a Special Forces Medic answered questions by what they would actually do, the score would not be high enough for Proficiency Pay. One example question;

If a patients IV was accidently pulled out, what would you do?

A. Call a Doctor
B. Call the Nurse
C. Restart it
D. Nothing, just make an entry on the patient's chart

The answer they are looking for is B, call the Nurse on duty. In reality, the Special Forces Medic would chose C, restart it. More likely than not, it was he who started the IV in the first place. To make a long story short, I answered all the questions, the way they wanted them answered, and received Proficiency Pay. My cooling, lukewarm reception, became warm. I was accepted by the Team.

The mini quiz by the Team Sergeant, was wrong. A "welcome to the Team interview," yes, but not a quiz. If you are not HALO qualified and you refuse to get qualified, you will be reassigned to another Team. It is defiantly not a requirement to receive Proficiency Pay.

When it came time for the non-HALO qualified Team members to be qualified, all went, with the exception of the Team Sergeant. He went to another team. When the HALO class started, the downsized team became inoperable. I was sent TDY to the Special Forces Medical Lab (school) as an instructor. I felt honored by the assignment and was determined to make the Temporary Duty Assignment, permanent.

Special Forces Medical Lab

Couldn't believe my eyes. Laying on the ground in a puddle of very dirty water was a soldier with his arm in a sewer pipe, clean up to his armpit. As I got closer, I discovered the water was not only dirty, it had a horrible smell. The guy looked familiar, I just wasn't sure. Then it dawned on me; It was MSG Mike Hollingsworth. I hadn't seen Mike for a long time. I think it was in Bangkok Thailand, at the Opera Hotel sometime in 1969.

Mike Hollingsworth

"Mike Hollingsworth, what in the hell are you doing? What is that horrible smell?"

""Hi Mac! We have been waiting for you. It's been a long time buddy. I'm pleased to announce this is goat shit, you'll get used to it." I suddenly realized my assignment at the Special Forces Medical Lab, would not be all sterile, surgical procedure. I think it was at this point, I started to hate goats.

Mike got up and reached his hand out to shake mine. He had second thoughts, thank God. There are two things you don't do when your working in Goat crap. One is to shake hands with a friend. The other, is to pick your nose. We continue are small talk as Mike walked over to an outside shower. The lad got in the shower, cloths and all.

"Go on inside and have a cup of coffee Mac. I'll be in few minutes and show you around."

No one was in the Team room. Not being a shy person, I helped myself to a cup of coffee and a stale donut. My studying of the Team's Picture album was interrupted when Bob McGriffert and Jimmy Jackson walked in. MSG McGriffert introduced himself as NCOIC of the Medical Lab and then MSG Jackson as the Medical Lab's Administrative NCO. (MSG Jackson was the last Special Forces POW released by the North Vietnam) Just when I was thinking there was a lot of rank on this team, Specialist 4 Dan Lyman joined us. MSG Jackson introduced us and added;

"Next to MSG Hollingsworth, Lyman is the hardest worker on the Team." For now that may be true. I was going to do my best to change that. By this time Mike joined us. He was accompanied by a Buck Sergeant. Mike started introducing him when I interrupted him

"SGT Wilson (not his real name) and I know each other Mike."
"Hi Mac." Wilson, looking at the floor, muttered. I didn't
return the greeting. The last time I saw Wilson was when, SGM
Campbell and I drove him to prison.

SGT Wilson, then SFC Wilson, reported into B-24 for
assignment. He was two days' late and to top it off under the
influence. He started complaining from the start. Because this was his
second tour in Vietnam and he was a new E-7, and he figured he
should be stationed at B-24 as the NCOIC

"You can take that up with the Sergeant Major, Wilson. But I
highly recommend you wait until morning, after you sober up." He left
the dispensary and headed for our Transient Barracks. I finished what I
was doing and went to the patio. We were to have a movie, a John
Wayne picture as I remember. In addition to the patio being full, a
group of young Montagnard, (Security Guards) were huddled behind
the screen. The were looking at the movie backwards. They didn't
care, they loved John Wayne.

About a half hour into the movie, a shot rung out. Someone
had fired a 45 pistol into the huddled group of Yards. I ran in the
direction of the shot. I saw SFC Wilson bending over a Montagnard
who was apparently the victim. At first I thought Wilson was giving the
young lad aid. Then I noticed, the bastard was trying to hide a 45,
under the victim. I wrestled Wilson to the ground and took the 45
away from him. By this time Cpt Ramirez arrived and held Wilson
while I examen the victim. The MP's from the MACV unit adjoining B-
24, took Wilson for interrogation.

The little guy was dead. He took a shot in the chest. The end
came fast. I instructed Tren, my main Montagnard medic, to take the
body to the dispensary. I needed to write a report and have the young
man cleaned up for his shipment back to his Village. I was called by
the MP's to check Wilson out. The MACV Medical Officer was off
sight, I was the nearest Medic.

"He's a Chummiest, all of them are Chummiest. I'll kill them
all!" Wilson completely out of control, was yelling over and over.

A quick examination confirmed my previous suspicions, Wilson
was under the influence, but not of alcohol. The bastard was under the
influence of narcotics. A short interrogation and he admitted, he as
taking Morphine. The use of controlled substance is a rare occurrence
in Special Forces. The caliber of people that qualifies for Special

A Walk With Giants 1958 - 1974

Forces are not prone to the use of drugs. On rare occasions, a low life like Wilson is found. I can assure you, they are dealt with severely. First they are kicked out of Special Forces. Sent for detoxification, then recommended for separation from the Service.

In a calm voice Wilson told me the story. He knew they were all Chummiest and gave each of them a cigarette. He went into his quarters and retrieved his 45. He walked up to the happy group and at point blank shot the young Montagnard in the chest. His plan was to kill all of them. I pray to God, it was my intervention that prevented the slaughter.

Two days later CSM Campbell and I drove Wilson to Pleiku and turned him over to the MP's, to be held for Court Martial. I was shocked to learn later, all he received was, reduced to the rank of Private. Fined two months pay and reassigned to the 101st Division. They call that justice. This clown murdered a human being. Of course, everyone knows that Montagnards aren't truly human. They have no rights.

Goat Lab was originally created as a clandestine laboratory to provide surgical training for Special Forces Medics. Most of the soldiers who live and work within Fort Bragg don't even know of its existence. Those

Old WWII Hospital Bldg.

military personnel not in the loop, assume that the rickety clapboard hospital buildings dating from the second world war, are derelict. In fact, they are filled with one hundred de-bleated goats.

To leave out some unnecessary details, essentially the trainee was then given the goat which was put into an operating theater, and anaesthetized. During this more conventional phase of the goats' lives, each one was taken through a soundproofed door into an above ground bunker, they were put on a hanging rig and shot in the upper thigh, using a bolt action, 30 caliber rifle. Then the Special Forces trainees would rush the goat back to surgery for debridement of the wound, insuring all Necrotic Tissue is removed. The goat was then nursed back to "health" by the Special Forces trainee. Students went to extreme measures to bring their post-op patient back to an acceptable and gradable recovery state.

On one occasion, a goat-patient developed a cold. Worrying the cold might turn into pneumonia, the student checked into a local motel with his goat. Over a long weekend he nursed the animal back to health. I know people have checked into motels' with a bow-wow on occasion, but never a goat. The SF student will take unbelievable extreme measures to protect their patient. They are motivated by the fact, their patient must survive all surgical procedures to graduate.

One of my students had a goat that didn't make it. His plan was to purchase another goat to replace the issued one. Unable to find a black and white (the color of his patient) Goat, he purchased a white goat and sprayed the animal with black paint. The black and white pattern was almost identical to the issued goat. His plan almost worked. It had one critical flaw, the paint he used was automotive paint and didn't dry fast.

The anaesthetized animal was put into the shooting gallery to receive the properly placed gun shoot wound needed for the surgical procedure. We were running slightly behind schedule. To save time, I told the class to go to the operating room and I would deliver the patient after I wounded him. Hesitantly they followed my instruction. This should have tipped their hand. Normally, when I give a class instructions, they hop to it.

I bore sited the Springfield 03. Put a round in the chamber and fired the weapon. I slapped a surgical dressing on the wound. As I was picking the goat up, it was at this point I realized the animals spots were coming off. I had black paint all over my hands. A very large smile started to develop deep within me. I was amazed at the resourcefulness of this student and the class covering for him. Who am I to burst their bubble? I didn't say a word to anyone about the black paint. I flipped the patient on the OR table and departed to remove the paint off my hands. The student graduated with honors.

Worth noting. Some 30 years later I received a phone call from Papa New Guinea. The caller stated he had seen my name on the internet, and wondered if I were the same Dan McGinley that instructed in Special Forces Medical Lab. I answered in the affirmative. It was my goat spraying friend. He was now a Physician

Assistant working for Chevron Oil Company. He was surprised I knew about the black paint. For the life of me I can't remember his name. I will have to leave a space open on my Giant list.

After a passing post-op physical the animal is anaesthetized again. During this stage amputations are performed, using the purse-sting closing procedure. In the real world, human patients would then be sent to an Orthopedic Surgeon for stump reconstruction. Time allowing, other surgical procedures are accomplished. C-Section, chest tube insertion, cut-downs for plastic tube insertion and any other procedure that time will allow. The animal is not suffering during any of these procedures, and is terminated at this point.

Goat Lab used to be called Dog Lab, but it turned out that nobody wanted to do all that to dogs, so they switched to goats. It was apparently determined within Special Forces that it was just about impossible to form an emotional bond with a goat. Animal rights people are very vocal about this training. They have even suggested we work on each other in-place of goats'. Because of this Special Forces Medical training, many of their sons and daughters are alive today.

The most difficult decision I have ever made, was to leave Special Forces. After a lot of sole searching I came up with two reasons. My promotion to E8, not many slots for E8 Medics in Special Forces at the time. Another, my age. To keep up your share of the workload in Special Forces, you have to be young and in great shape. I was Forty-eight, although I was in very good shape for my age, I knew I was nearing the end of my usefulness to the mission of a Special Forces Operative.

The wearer of a Green Beret draws a lot of attention. It represents accomplishment and the doer of difficult tasks. I felt that a 48-year-old might dilute that reputation in the public eye. I had too much respect for the "Green Beret" to embarrass it. My decision to terminate didn't mean I would no longer wear the Green Beret.  I just didn't wear the Beret on my head. I wear it in my heart, where it remains today.

"DE OPPRESSO LIBER"

A Walk With Giants

by T. Daniel McGinley

Because of it's size, A Walk With Giants had to be published in three Volumes. Copies of all three Volumes and other books by this author can be obtained through our Web-Site
www.searchour.net Then click on Book Shelf

Volume One 1927 - 1956

Starts with light-hearted stories about a family living through the Great Depression. Then a few stories about a people, dealing with the horrors of a world war that was ready to strike America. Stories about a nation that gathered all it's human resources and stood up to be counted.

Continues with McGinley s' involvement with the Illinois Reserve Militia until he was drafted. A few basic training stories that should bring back a memoire or two. America has never looked better, then she did in World War II.

After a few between war stories, this volume covers the Korean War, sometimes called "The Forgotten War." The Korean War was very difficult to write about, it brought back many sad memories. Even though the Korean War Veteran, was treated like second class citizens, the after war stories, was easer to write.

Volume Two 1956 -1974

Starts with assignment with the 302nd SF Reserve. The story continues with the early years of Sport Parachuting. And the development of Land of Lincoln Sky Diving Center. While others were burning their Draft Cards and going to Canada to avoid service, it took the author two years and out of pocket expenditure of over $5,000.00 to serve in Vietnam. From 5th SF to 1st SF in Okinawa, to 10th SF Ft Devens., to 46 Co Thailand The Volume ends with McGinley's assignment to SF Medical Lab, Ft Bragg North Carolina

Volume Three 1974 - 1985

Cover's all McGinley's Non-SF assignments, Ft Sam Houston TX, Reediness Region One MA, Reserve Medical Units upstate NY, 8th Med BN. Germany, 1st Med. BN. Ft Riley KA, 11th Combat Support Hospital also at Ft Riley KA. Throughout this Volume you will find, flashback stories not covered in the other two Volumes, and Special Forces Association stories.

A Walk With Giants 1958 - 1974